Fate of the Jedi

BACKLASH

STAR WARS

Fate of the Jedi

BACKLASH

AARON ALLSTON

Ballantine Books • New York

Published in the United States by Del Rey,
an imprint of The Random House Publishing Group,
a division of Random House, Inc., New York.

DEL REY is a registered trademark and the Del Rey colophon
is a trademark of Random House, Inc.

This book contains an excerpt from
Star Wars: Fate of the Jedi: Allies by Christie Golden.
This excerpt has been set for this edition only and may not
reflect the final content of the forthcoming editon.

ISBN 978-0-345-50908-6

Printed in the United States of America on acid-free paper

www.starwars.com
www.fateofthejedi.com
www.delreybooks.com

2 4 6 8 9 7 5 3 1

First Edition

Book design by Elizabeth A. D. Eno

To everyone in 2009 who helped me get through a very hard time

Acknowledgments

On March 27, 2009, while on a book tour promoting *Outcast* (the first book in this series), I suffered a heart attack. Six days later, I underwent quadruple bypass surgery. I'd like to offer thanks to the doctors and nurses of the Baylor Medical Center, Grapevine, Texas, without whom I would not have survived to write *Backlash.*

Thanks also go to Troy Denning, Christie Golden, Shelly Shapiro of Del Rey, and Sue Rostoni of Lucas Licensing, not only for doing their usual fine job, but also for offering endless patience with me during the trials and tribulations of my recovery;

My agent, Russell Galen;

and all the fans who have embraced this series and offered their support.

THE STAR WARS NOVELS TIMELINE

OLD REPUBLIC
5000–33 YEARS BEFORE
STAR WARS: A New Hope

Lost Tribe of the Sith*
Precipice
Skyborn
Paragon
Savior

3650 *YEARS BEFORE STAR WARS: A New Hope*

The Old Republic
Fatal Alliance

1020 *YEARS BEFORE STAR WARS: A New Hope*

Darth Bane: Path of Destruction
Darth Bane: Rule of Two
Darth Bane: Dynasty of Evil

RISE OF THE EMPIRE
33–0 YEARS BEFORE
STAR WARS: A New Hope

Darth Maul: Saboteur*
Cloak of Deception
Darth Maul: Shadow Hunter

32 *YEARS BEFORE STAR WARS: A New Hope*

STAR WARS: EPISODE I
THE PHANTOM MENACE

Rogue Planet
Outbound Flight
The Approaching Storm

22 *YEARS BEFORE STAR WARS: A New Hope*

STAR WARS: EPISODE II
ATTACK OF THE CLONES

22–19 *YEARS BEFORE STAR WARS: A New Hope*

The Clone Wars
The Clone Wars: Wild Space
The Clone Wars: No Prisoners

Clone Wars Gambit
 Stealth
 Siege

Republic Commando
 Hard Contact
 Triple Zero
 True Colors
 Order 66

Shatterpoint
The Cestus Deception
The Hive*
MedStar I: Battle Surgeons
MedStar II: Jedi Healer
Jedi Trial

Yoda: Dark Rendezvous
Labyrinth of Evil

19 *YEARS BEFORE STAR WARS: A New Hope*

STAR WARS: EPISODE III
REVENGE OF THE SITH

Dark Lord: The Rise of Darth
 Vader

Coruscant Nights
 Jedi Twilight
 Street of Shadows
 Patterns of Force

Imperial Commando
 501st

The Han Solo Trilogy
 The Paradise Snare
 The Hutt Gambit
 Rebel Dawn

The Adventures of Lando Calrissian
The Han Solo Adventures
The Force Unleashed
Death Troopers

REBELLION
0–5 YEARS AFTER
STAR WARS: A New Hope

Death Star

0

STAR WARS: EPISODE IV
A NEW HOPE

Tales from the Mos Eisley Cantina
Allegiance
Galaxies: The Ruins of Dantooine
Splinter of the Mind's Eye

3 *YEARS AFTER STAR WARS: A New Hope*

STAR WARS: EPISODE V
THE EMPIRE STRIKES BACK

Tales of the Bounty Hunters
Shadows of the Empire

4 *YEARS AFTER STAR WARS: A New Hope*

STAR WARS: EPISODE VI
RETURN OF THE JEDI

Tales from Jabba's Palace
Tales from the Empire
Tales from the New Republic

The Bounty Hunter Wars
 The Mandalorian Armor
 Slave Ship
 Hard Merchandise

The Truce at Bakura
Luke Skywalker and the Shadows of
 Mindor

Dramatis Personae

Allana Solo; child (human female)
Ben Skywalker; Jedi Knight (human male)
C-3PO; protocol droid
Drikl Lecersen; Moff (human male)
Dyon Stadd; former Jedi candidate (human male)
Han Solo; captain, *Millennium Falcon* (human male)
Haydnat Treen; Senator (Kuati female)
Jagged Fel; Head of State, Galactic Empire (human male)
Jaina Solo; Jedi Knight (human female)
Kaminne Sihn; chief, Raining Leaves Clan (Dathomiri female)
Leia Organa Solo; Jedi Knight (human female)
Luke Skywalker; Jedi Grand Master (human male)
Natasi Daala; Galactic Alliance Chief of State (human female)
R2-D2; astromech droid
Vestara Khai; Sith apprentice (human female)

A long time ago in a galaxy far, far away. . . .

Fate of the Jedi

BACKLASH

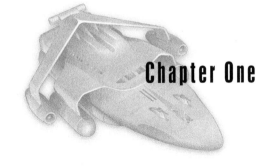

Chapter One

IT WAS DARKNESS SURROUNDED BY STARS—ONE OF THEM, THE UN-lovely sun of Kessel, closer than the rest, but barely close enough to be a ball of illumination rather than a dot—and then it was occupied, suddenly inhabited by a space yacht of flowing, graceful lines and peeling paint. That was how it would have looked, a vessel dropping out of hyperspace, to those in the arrival zone, had there been any witnesses: nothing there, then something, an instantaneous transition.

In the bridge sat the ancient yacht's sole occupant, a teenage girl wearing a battered combat vac suit. She looked from sensor to sensor, uncertain and slow because of her unfamiliarity with this model of spacecraft. Too, there was something like shock in her eyes.

Finally satisfied that no other ship had dropped out of hyperspace nearby, or was likely to creep up on her in this remote location, she sat back in her pilot's seat and tried to get her thoughts in order.

Her name was Vestara Khai, and she was a Sith of the Lost Tribe.

She was a proud Sith, not one to hide under false identities and concealing robes until some decades-long grandiose plan neared completion, and now she had even more reason than usual to swell with pride. Mere hours before, she and her Sith Master, Lady Rhea, had confronted Jedi Grand Master Luke Skywalker. Lady Rhea and Vestara had fought the galaxy's most experienced, most famous Jedi to a standstill. Vestara had even *cut* him, a graze to the cheek and chin that had spattered her with blood—blood she had later tasted, blood she wished she could take a sample of and keep forever as a souvenir.

But then Skywalker had shown why he carried that reputation. A moment's distraction, and suddenly Lady Rhea was in four pieces, each drifting in a separate direction, and Vestara was hopelessly outmatched. She had saluted and fled.

Now, having taken a space yacht that had doubtless been old when her great-great-great-grandsires were newborn, but which, to her everlasting gratitude, held in its still-functional computer the navigational secrets of the mass of black holes that was the Maw, she was free. And the impossible weights of her reality and her responsibility were settling upon her.

Lady Rhea was dead. Vestara was alone, and her pride at Lady Rhea's accomplishment, at her own near success in the duel with the Jedi, was not enough to wash away the sense of loss.

Then there was the question of what to do next, of where to go. She needed to be able to communicate with her people, to report on the incidents in the Maw. But this creaking, slowly deteriorating Soro-Suub StarTracker space yacht did not carry a hypercomm unit. She'd have to put in to some civilized planet to make contact. That meant arriving unseen, or arriving and departing so swiftly that the Jedi could not detect her in time to catch her. It also meant acquiring sufficient credits to fund a secret, no-way-to-trace-it hypercomm message. All of these plans would take time to bring to reality.

Vestara knew, deep in her heart, and within the warning currents of the Force, that Luke Skywalker intended to track her to her homeworld of Kesh. How he planned to do it, she didn't know, but her sense of paranoia, trained at the hands of Lady Rhea, burned within her as though her blood itself were acid. She had to find some way to outwit a Force-user several times her age, renowned for his skills.

She needed to go someplace where Force-users were relatively commonplace. Otherwise, any Force use on her part would stand out like signal beacons to experienced Jedi in the vicinity. There weren't many such places. Coruscant was the logical answer. But if her trail began to lead toward the government seat of the Galactic Alliance, Skywalker could warn the Jedi there, and Vestara would face a nearly impossible-to-bypass network of Force-users between her and her destination.

The current location of the Jedi school was not known. Hapes was ruled by an ex-Jedi and was rumored to harbor more Force-sensitives, but it was such a security-conscious civilization that Vestara doubted she could accomplish her mission there in secrecy.

Then the answer came to her, so obvious and so perfect that she laughed out loud.

She doubted the destination she'd thought of would be on a galactic map as old as the one in the antique yacht she commanded. She'd have to go somewhere and get a map update. She nodded, her pride, sense of loss, and paranoia all fading as she focused on her new task.

TRANSITORY MISTS

Jedi Knight Leia Organa Solo sat at the *Millennium Falcon*'s communications console. She frowned, her lips pursed, as though she were solving an elaborate mathematical equation, while she read and re-read the text message the *Falcon* had just received via hypercomm.

The silence that had settled around her eventually drew her husband, Han Solo, to her side; his boyish, often insensitive persona was in part a fabrication, and he well knew and could sense his wife's moods. The chill and silence of her complete concentration usually meant trouble. He waved a hand between her eyes and the console monitor. "Hey."

She barely reacted to his presence. "Hm."

"New message?"

"From Ben."

"Another letter filled with teenage talk, I assume. Girls, speeders, allowance woes—"

Leia ignored his joking. "Sith," she said.

"And Sith, of course." Han sat in the chair next to hers but did not assume his customary slouch; the news kept his spine rigid. "They found a new Sith Lord?"

"Worse, I think." Finally some animation returned to Leia's voice. "They've found an ancient installation at the Maw and were attacked by a gang of Sith. A whole strike team. With the possibility of more out there."

"I thought Sith ran in packs of two. Vape both of 'em and their menace is ended for all time, at least for a few years, until two more show up." Han tried to keep his voice calm, but the last Sith to bring trouble to the galaxy had been Jacen Solo, his and Leia's eldest son. Though Jacen had been dead for close to three years, the ripples of the evil he had done were still causing damage and heartache throughout the settled galaxy. And both his acts and his death had torn a hole in Han's heart that felt like it would last forever.

"Yes, well, no. Apparently not anymore. Ben also says—and we're not to let Luke know that he did—that Luke is exhausted. Really exhausted, like he's had the life squeezed out of him. Ben would like us to sort of drift near and lend Luke some support."

"Of course." But then Han grimaced. "Back to the Maw. The only place gloomy enough to make its next door neighbor, Kessel, seem like a garden spot."

Leia shook her head. "They're tracking a Sith girl who's on the run. So it probably won't be the Maw."

"Ah, good." Han rubbed his hands together as if anticipating a fine meal or a fight. "Why not? After taking off with all those barvy Jedi that Daala wanted to deep-freeze, we probably have an arrest warrant waiting back on Coruscant anyway."

Finally Leia smiled and looked at Han. "One good thing about the Solos and Skywalkers. We never run out of things to do."

JEDI TEMPLE, CORUSCANT

Master Cilghal, Mon Calamari and most proficient medical doctor among the current generation of Jedi, paused before hitting the console button that would erase the message she had just spent some time decrypting. It had been a video transmission from Ben Skywalker, a message carefully rerouted through several hypercomm nodes and carefully staged so as not to mention that it was for Cilghal's tympanic membranes or, in fact, for anyone on Coruscant.

But its main content was meant for the Jedi, and Cilghal repeated it as a one-word summation, making the word sound like a vicious curse: *"Sith."*

The message had to be communicated throughout the Jedi Order. And on review, there was nothing in it that suggested she couldn't preserve the recording, couldn't claim that it had been forwarded to her by a civilian friend of the Skywalkers. Luke Skywalker was not supposed to be in contact with the Jedi Temple, but this recording was manifestly free of any proof that the exiled Grand Master exerted any influence over the Order. She could distribute it.

And she would do so, right now.

DEEP SPACE NEAR KESSEL

Jade Shadow, onetime vehicle of Mara Jade Skywalker, now full-time transport and home to her widower and son, dropped from hyperspace into the empty blackness well outside the Kessel system. She hung suspended there for several minutes, long enough for one of her occupants to gather from the Force a sense of his own life's blood that had been in the vicinity; then she turned on a course toward Kessel and vanished again into hyperspace.

JADE SHADOW, IN ORBIT ABOVE KESSEL

Ben Skywalker shouldered his way through the narrow hatch that gave access to his father's cabin. The auburn-haired teen was a little shorter than average height, but he was well muscled in a way that his anonymous tunic and pants could not conceal.

On the cabin's bed, under a brown blanket, lay Luke Skywalker. Similar in build to his son, he wore the evidence of many more years of hard living, including old, faded scars on his face and the exposed portions of his arms. Not obvious was the fact that his right hand, so ordinary in appearance, was a prosthetic.

Luke's eyes were closed, but he stirred. "What did you find out?"

"I reached Nien Nunb." Nunb, the Sullustan co-owner and manager of one of Kessel's most prominent mineworks, had been a friend of the Solos and Skywalkers for decades. "That yacht did make planetfall. The pilot gave her name as Captain Khai. She somehow scammed a port worker into thinking she'd paid for a complete refueling when she hadn't—"

Luke smiled. " 'The Force can have a—' "

"Yeah, so can a good-looking girl. Anyway, what's interesting is that she got a galactic map update. Nunb looked at the transmission time and determined that the download was pretty comprehensive. In other words, she didn't concentrate on any one specific area or route. No help there."

"But it suggests that she did need some of the newer information. New hyperspace routes or planetary listings."

"Right."

"And she's gone?" Luke asked.

"Headed out as soon as her yacht was refueled. By the way, its name is *She's a Chancer.*"

"Somehow appropriate." Finally, Luke did open his eyes, and Ben was once again struck by how tired his father looked, tired to the bone and to the spirit. "I can still feel her path. I'll be up in a minute to lay in a course."

"Right. Don't push yourself." Ben backed out of the cabin, and its door slid shut.

SEVERAL DAYS LATER
JADE SHADOW, IN HIGH DATHOMIRI ORBIT

Luke stared at the mottled, multicolored world of Dathomir through the forward viewport. He nodded, feeling slightly abashed. Of *course* it was Dathomir.

Ben, seated to Luke's left in the pilot's seat, peered at him. "What is it, Dad?"

"I'm just feeling a little stupid. There's no world better suited to be the home of this new Sith Order than Dathomir. I should have realized it long before we were on our final leg here."

"How so?"

"There are a lot of Force-sensitives in the population, most of whom are trained in the so-called Witchcraft of Dathomir. There's not a lot of government oversight. It's the perfect place for a Force-user to hide. And eventually, if she figures out that I'm following my own blood straight to her, she may get rid of it and elude us entirely." Luke paused to consider. "There are mentions in ancient records that there was a Sith academy here long, long ago. I wonder if she's looking for it."

Ben nodded. "Well, I'll prep Mom's Headhunter and get down there. I'll be your eyes and ears on the ground."

Luke gave his son a confused look. "I'm not going down with you? I'm feeling much better. Much more rested."

"Yeah, but there's a Jedi school down there. The terms of your exile say that you can't—"

Luke grinned and held up a hand, cutting off his son's words. "You're a little bit behind the times, Ben. Maybe you need your own galactic map updated. More than two years ago, when the Jedi turned against Jacen at Kuat?"

"Yeah, and we set up shop on Endor for a while. What about it?"

"We pulled everyone off Dathomir when Jacen's government shut the school down. The Jedi have yet to reopen it."

Comprehension dawned on Ben's face. "So there's no school, and it's legal for you to visit."

"Yes."

"That's kind of getting by on a technicality, isn't it?"

"All law is technicality, Ben. Get authorization for landing."

DATHOMIR

Half an hour later, Luke had to admit that he was wrong. *Most* law was technicality. The rest was special cases, and he, apparently, was a special case.

He stood on the parking field of the Dathomiri spaceport. Perhaps *spaceport* was too generous a term. It was a broad, sunny field, grassy in some spots, muddy in others, with thruster scorch marks here and there. Dull gray permacrete domes, most of them clearly prefabricated, dotted the field; the largest was some sort of administrative building, the smaller ones hangars for vehicles no larger than shuttles and starfighters. A tall mesh durasteel fence surrounded the complex, elevated watchtowers dotting its length, and Luke could see the wiring leading to one of the permacrete domes that marked it as electrified.

The spaceport facilities offered little shade, so the Skywalkers stood in the darkness cast by *Jade Shadow,* but even without the heat of direct sunlight, the moist, windless air was still as oppressive as a blanket.

Luke poured thoughts of helpfulness and reasonability into the Force, but it was no use. The man before him, nearly two skinny meters of redheaded obstructiveness, would not yield a centimeter.

The man, who had given his name as Tarth Vames, again waved his datapad beneath Luke's nose. "It's simple. That vehicle—" His wave indicated *Jade Shadow.* "Neither it, nor anything with an enclosed or enclosable interior, can be inland under your control or your kid's." He turned his attention to Ben, who stood, arms folded across his chest, beside his father. Ben glared but did not reply.

Luke sighed. "Is any other visitor to Dathomir operating under that restriction?"

"Don't think so, no."

"Then why us?"

Vames thumbed the datapad keyboard so that the message scrolled downward several screens. "Here, right here. An enclosed vehicle, according to these precedents—there's about eight screens of legal precedents—can be interpreted as a mobile school, especially if *you're* in it, especially if its presence constitutes a continuation of a school that's been here in the past."

"This is harassment." Ben's words were quiet, but loud enough for Vames to hear.

The tall man glowered at Ben. "Of course it's not harassment. The order came specifically from Chief of State Daala's office. Public officials at that level don't harass."

Ben rolled his eyes. "Whatever."

"Ben." Luke added a chiding tone to his voice. "No point in argu-ing. Vames, are you also prohibited from answering a few questions?"

"Always happy to help. So long as it's within latitudes permitted by the regulations."

"Within the last couple of days, have you seen any sign of a dilapi-dated yacht called *She's a Chancer*?" Luke knew the yacht had to be here; he had run his blood trail to ground on Dathomir, and the girl had not departed this world. But anything this man could add to his meager store of knowledge might help.

Vames entered the ship name in his datapad, then shook his head. "No vehicle under that name made legal planetfall."

"Ah."

"Dilapidated, you say? A yacht?"

"That's right."

Vames keyed in some more information. "Last night, shortly after dusk, local time, a vehicle with the operational characteristics of a SoroSuub yacht made a sudden descent from orbit, overflew the spaceport here, and headed north. There was some comm chatter from the pilot about engines on runaway, that she couldn't cut them or bring her repulsors online for landing."

Ben frowned at that. "Last night? And you didn't send out a rescue party?"

"Of course we did. As per regulations. Couldn't find the crash site. No further communication from the vehicle. We still have searchers up there. But no luck."

"Actually, that *is* helpful." Luke turned to his son. "Ben, no en-closed vehicles."

"Yeah?"

"Get us a couple of speeder bikes, would you? Beg, borrow . . ." Luke glanced at the spaceport official and decided that the man wouldn't grasp that *steal* would have been a joke. "Or rent them."

Ben grinned. "Yes, sir."

Fifteen minutes later they were on their way, equipped with two rented speeder bikes and one piece of useful information that they had not possessed before, courtesy of questions asked and credcoins dropped by Luke.

The model of SoroSuub yacht the Sith girl had taken from Sinkhole Station was not one that normally came equipped with a hypercomm system. From the time it had left the Maw Cluster to its arrival on Dathomir, it had not lingered at any star system long enough for its pilot to make any substantial contact with locals. And in the time since its arrival on Dathomir, the planet's sole hypercomm system, based out of this spaceport, had not been utilized to send any message packet large enough to include the complex navigational data required to instruct someone how to enter the Maw and find Sinkhole Station.

What that meant, ultimately, was that the Sith girl had likely not been able to communicate instructions to her Sith masters on how to reach the station or the powerful dark-side Force mystery it held. Luke probably did not have to fear that the Sith would find that power— until and unless they retrieved the Sith girl.

For once, if only temporarily, time was on Luke's side.

Chapter Two

DATHOMIR RAIN FOREST

THE RAIN FOREST AIR WAS SO DENSE, SO MOIST, THAT EVEN ROARING through it at speeder bike velocity didn't bring Luke Skywalker any physical relief. His speed just caused the air to move across him faster, like a greasy scrub-rag wielded by an overzealous nanny droid, drenching all the exposed surfaces of his body.

Not that he cared. He couldn't see her, but he could sense his quarry, not far ahead: the individual he'd crossed so many light-years to find.

He could sense much more than that. The forest teemed with life, life that poured its energy into the Force, too much to catalog as he roared past. He could feel ancient trees and new vines, creeping predators and alert prey. He could feel his son, Ben, as the teenager drew up abreast of him on his own speeder bike, eyes shadowed under his helmet but a competitive grin on his lips, and then Ben was a few meters ahead of him, dodging leftward to avoid hitting a split-forked tree, the recklessness of youth giving him a momentary speed advantage over Luke's superior piloting ability.

Then there was more life, *big* life, close ahead, with malicious intent—

From a thick nest of magenta-flowered underbrush twice the height of a human male, just to the right of Luke's path ahead, emerged an arm, striking with great speed and accuracy. It was human-like, gnarly, gigantic, long enough to reach from the flowers to swat the forward tip of Luke's speeder bike as he passed.

Disaster takes only a fraction of a second to bring about. One instant Luke was racing along, intent on his distant prey and enjoying moments of competition; the next, he was headed straight for a tree whose trunk, four meters across, would bring a sudden stop to his travels and his life.

He came free of the speeder bike as it rotated beneath him from the giant creature's blow. He was still headed for the tree trunk. He gave himself an adrenaline-boosted shove in the Force and drifted another couple of meters to the left, allowing him to flash past the trunk instead of into it; he could feel its bark rip at the right shoulder of his tunic. A centimeter closer, and the contact would have given him a serious friction burn.

He rolled into a ball and let senses other than sight guide him. A Force shove to the right kept him from smacking into a much thinner tree, one barely sturdy enough to break his spine and any bones that hit it. He needed no Force effort to shoot between the forks of a third tree. Contact with a veil of vines slowed him; they tore beneath the impact of his body but dropped his rate of speed painlessly. He went crashing into a mass of tendrils ending in big-petaled yellow flowers, some of which reflexively snapped at him as he plowed through them.

Then he was bouncing across the ground, a dense layer of decaying leaves and other materials he really didn't want to speculate about.

Finally, he rolled to a halt. He stretched out, momentarily stunned but unbroken, and stared up through the trees. He could see a single shaft of sunlight penetrating the forest canopy, but not far behind him it illuminated a swirl of pollen from the stand of yellow flowers he'd just crashed through. In the distance, he could hear the roar of Ben's speeder bike, hear its engine whine as the boy put it in a hard maneuver, trying to get back to Luke.

Closer, there were footsteps. Heavy, ponderous footsteps.

A moment later, the owner of that huge arm loomed over Luke. It was a rancor, standing upright but bent forward.

The rancors of this world had evolved to be smarter than those elsewhere. This one had clearly been trained as a guard and taught to tolerate protective gear. It wore a helmet, a rust-streaked cup of metal large enough to serve as a backwoods bathtub, with leather straps meeting under its chin. Strapped to its left forearm was a thick, round durasteel shield that looked ridiculously tiny compared with the creature's enormous proportions but was probably thick enough to stop one or two salvos from a military laser battery.

The creature stared down at Luke. Its mouth opened, and it offered a challenging growl.

Luke glared at it. "Do you really want to take me on right now? I don't recommend it."

It reached for him.

The rancor's extraordinary musculature gave it speed not usually found in creatures so large. Luke kicked downward, propelling himself into a backward somersault, and rose to his feet as the rancor's fingers plowed into the soft, mossy ground where he had just been lying. He put an edge of anger and fearsomeness into both his voice and the Force. "It's time for you to leave before you get hurt. Badly hurt."

But the rancor merely bellowed at him again, apparently unfazed by the Jedi mental touch. It did not bother trying to grab Luke a second time; with its other arm, it swung its ponderous shield down at him, the object's circumference making it a huge weapon, difficult to avoid.

Difficult for an ordinary man to avoid. Luke leapt over it as it swung at him. He landed directly in front of the rancor.

He could feel the giant beast's resistance to his Force nudge, and that resistance was not natural. Something nearby was feeding the rancor thoughts and motivation, also through the Force. And that individual would be the more dangerous of the two, but Luke could scarcely turn his back on the rancor to go looking for the Force-user.

In the distance, he heard Ben's speeder bike end its tight turn and settle into something closer to straight-line flight as it hurtled back toward Luke's position. Through the Force, Luke sent a feeling of caution, warning Ben to be mindful of other possible hazards. At the same time, he unclipped and ignited his lightsaber, then lunged at the rancor's extended shield hand, still sweeping away from him.

His energy blade caught the rancor's wrist and cut a bloody trench from that point deep into the forearm, severing the shield's laces, leather or sinew cables as thick as those used on ancient seafaring ships. Lightsaber attacks normally cauterized the flesh they contacted, but the rancor's limb was too thick, the wound too deep for that. Dark rancor blood gouted up, and the shield dropped away from the arm.

The rancor howled and straightened. It glanced at the injury— Luke knew it not to be a life-threatening cut by rancor standards, for all that his strike would have severed a tauntaun leg or wampa arm— and glowered at Luke. Then it took a step back, looked left and right, and saw what it wanted, a fallen tree trunk some eight meters long. It sidestepped to the trunk and, using both hands, unimpaired by Luke's attack, lifted it by one end, clearly intending to use it as a club.

In his peripheral vision, Luke saw movement, the bob-and-weave of Ben's speeder bike.

At almost the same moment Luke felt a pulse in the Force from the opposite direction. He spun around, dropping into a ready crouch.

Ten meters away, standing in front of a thornbush, stood a human woman. Luke saw a mane of black hair, strands of white animal teeth hanging from it to frame her face, and abbreviated garments and ac-coutrements fashioned from ruddy tanned hide.

Then it was as though Luke, the rancor, everything within sight was enveloped in a ball of lightning. Arcs of electricity a few centime-ters thick and several meters long snapped and crackled between ground and sky, incinerating vines, igniting leaves, causing the rancor to howl as though it were witnessing the end of the galaxy. As the bar-rage began, Luke let the Force flow through him, let it direct his in-stincts, and leaped where it guided him, bounding forward–left–right in a seemingly random pattern that kept all but a few errant lightning strikes from hitting him. The woman vanished from his sight and other perceptions as he moved.

The lightning strikes that hit Luke did not seem too dangerous, though he felt the hair all over his body stand on end. Suddenly his lightsaber switched off.

The engine howl of Ben's speeder bike turned into a series of coughs, then cut out entirely.

And then the lightning storm was over. Luke saw the oncoming speeder bike dip, nose-down, toward a rock outcropping. Ben leapt free, clearing the jagged black stones by less than a meter, and somersaulted toward a trio of tree trunks.

Luke raised a hand, extending control through the Force, and directed his ballistic son to one side of the trees, slowing Ben's velocity as he did so. By the time Ben came to ground, he was hurtling at a pace his gymnastic skills could handle. The boy shoulder-rolled through a shallow patch of algae and came to his feet, slick green slime adhering to his back and right arm, poised and ready to fight.

But their visible opponent was no longer interested. The rancor looked around, an almost human expression of fear on its face, then glanced again at its forearm injury. It turned away from the two Jedi and plunged into the forest, heading directly away from them.

Ben frowned and prepared to give chase, but Luke gestured for him to stand down. "That's not our real enemy. Look for a Force-user."

"That woman? Who was she?"

Luke shrugged. "A Dathomiri Witch, I expect."

They cast about in the Force, but the woman was not to be found. They could feel teeming rain-forest life in the Force, could detect the lumbering rancor moving away from them at high speed, and Luke could still feel, distantly, his own blood the Sith girl was carrying, but there was no pulse to suggest that anyone was using the Force.

Ben sighed. "What was that all about?"

"Somebody did not want us to proceed." Luke reignited his lightsaber. It came on, but its *snap-hiss* of ignition was more faltering, more unsteady than usual, and the weapon remained lit only a few seconds. Its energy blade retracted from view. "Try yours."

Ben did so. The blade did not ignite. "Stang." He scowled, then checked his comlink and datapad in turn. "Fried, Dad."

"Mine, too."

"How is it that your hand's still working?"

Luke looked at his right hand—the prosthetic one. He had lost the original when he was only a few years older than Ben. "The artificial skin offers a fair amount of insulation." He balled his hand into a fist, felt no indication that it was damaged. "Come on, let's get out of the immediate vicinity—in case our enemies return—and then see if we can get any of these electronics working again. A Jedi without a lightsaber—"

"Is a lot less dashing to the girls."

"Not what I was going to say, but probably true."

JEDI TEMPLE, CORUSCANT

Master Cilghal—who, like all the Mon Calamari, possessed a stocky, powerful body and bulbous head, with protruding eyes that routinely moved independently in their sockets—left Master Hamner's quarters at a fast walk, this unaccustomed speed causing her Jedi robes to swirl around her.

Jaina Solo, Jedi Knight and daughter of Han and Leia, dressed in ordinary robes like a scaled-down version of Cilghal's, saw her emerge. Jaina hurried to catch up and walked beside the Master Jedi. A tiny woman and a delicate beauty, had Jaina not been famous because of her parents and her own exploits, she might have been mistaken for the sort of athlete who won fame for some sports victory, then spent the rest of her professional career fulfilling lucrative product endorsement contracts. In truth, she cared little about her looks or money; her continued service to the Jedi was proof enough of the latter. She waved to catch Cilghal's attention. "I take it that something's up."

Cilghal nodded. "Something is very, very up. I just had a message from your cousin." Cilghal's voice was the sort of resonant, gravelly rumble common to the Mon Calamari. Hers was usually a trifle softer, as befit a healer, but now it was as hard as that of any member of her species.

"From Ben? Is Luke all right?"

"He is hurt and tired, but he will recover."

"Well?" Not as diplomatically adept as her mother, Jaina did not bother keeping impatience out of her voice.

"Jedi Skywalker has informed us—and I point out that, because it comes from young Ben, it is no violation of the Grand Master's terms of exile—"

"You're splitting hairs."

"I have no hairs to split. Young Ben informs us that the dark side of the Force is powerfully represented in the Maw cluster, and the Sith are at large again in the galaxy."

"What?"

"Sith. Your uncle and cousin fought them. But these do not follow the Sith Rule of Two. They apparently follow a Sith rule of However Many They Need. The Grand Master is pursuing one to try to find her planet of origin."

Jaina was silent until the two of them reached the end of the marbled corridor and the turbolift. It opened before them, and they stepped in. "What's Master Hamner's response? To assume that Ben is wrong and ignore the problem?"

"The Master is no fool. Medcenter, please." The turbolift doors closed and the lift plummeted. Unmoved by the lift's heart-stopping speed, Cilghal continued, "He knows no Jedi Knight would lie about such a thing—or even report it when not absolutely sure. Master Hamner will be calling for the Masters to convene and strategize." The lift shuddered to a halt and its doors opened, allowing the two Jedi to exit on the level where most of the medical offices were located. "But we can be sure that whatever we decide, whatever we do, it will have to be without the knowledge or approval of the Galactic Alliance government."

Jaina nodded. That was a given. The GA Chief of State, Natasi Daala, was no fan of the Jedi and would oppose any military action unilaterally initiated by the Jedi Order. But the Sith were a menace recognized chiefly by the Jedi; to the population at large, they were either fairy-tale monsters or just another philosophical Order, little different from the Jedi themselves. In fact, Jaina's brother Jacen had, at different times, been both Jedi and Sith, and had blurred the distinction between them in the public eye.

"Make sure I get invited to the meeting," Jaina said. "If the Sith are under discussion, the Sword of the Jedi needs to be there." She had a distaste for referring to the title that had been conveyed upon her during the Yuuzhan Vong War, but at times like this it needed to be invoked.

Cilghal nodded again. "The Sword of the Jedi needs to be lit and swinging at the enemy."

MILLENNIUM FALCON, ABOVE DATHOMIR
SPACEPORT

Han looked down through his viewport at the unpromising spectacle of the grassy field and prefabricated domes that constituted Dathomir's preeminent spaceport. He sighed and shook his head. He was going to need to call some backup, because if Luke and Ben were down there somewhere hunting Sith, the last thing he was going to do was let Leia go looking for them alone, and Dathomir was the last place you'd want to leave a little girl to her own devices—especially a Force-sensitive girl who just happened to be the Chume'da of the Hapan Consortium, the supposedly deceased daughter of Jacen Solo and former Jedi Knight, Queen Tenel Ka.

That last, of course, was a well-kept secret, necessary to protect young Allana's life. To everyone but close family, the little girl now seated in Leia's lap in the copilot's seat to his right was "Amelia," a child Han and Leia had adopted to help heal their grief over the loss of their two sons. Almost from toddlerhood, Allana had learned to cultivate the deception in public, even if she didn't understand the reasons for it.

Now she squirmed around and looked at Han. "What's wrong, Grandpa? Is it a bad place to land?"

"No, sweetie. I can land the *Falcon* during a groundquake and keep your cup of milk steady. It's just a bad *place*."

Leia snickered. "Believe it or not, your grandpa used to *own* this planet. For a few weeks, and not entirely legally. He had some bad times here. With Witches, and monsters, and an Imperial admiral who just wouldn't go away, and a rich, handsome prince who wanted to marry me."

"You're making all that up."

Leia shook her head. "The prince was your other grandfather, Isolder."

Allana's eyes got round. "Isolder was going to marry *you?*"

Leia nodded. "He wanted to. But I was in love with Han, despite his—"

Han cleared his throat. He looked uncomfortable. "Forget that part."

Allana blinked and looked thoughtful. "So, no matter what, you were going to be my grandmother."

Leia's features blanked. Han knew the little girl's words had caught Leia by surprise and made her really think, something Allana did far more often than most adults of Leia's acquaintance.

Finally, she smiled down at the girl. "You know, the Jedi say that the future is always in motion. Meaning, even when we think that things are supposed to happen, sometimes they don't. But I think you're right. No matter what, I think I was always destined to be your grandmother."

"Good."

Han allowed the two to share a tender moment, then suggested, "Allana, go check on Anji. You know how nervous she gets when we come in for a landing."

"Yeah." Allana looked up at her grandmother. "You should have seen all the nexu barf when we landed on Shedu Maad!"

"I *did* see it," Leia reminded her. "I was the one who cleaned out Anji's traveling crate, remember?"

"Oh . . . yeah." Allana hopped down from Leia's lap. "I'll go make sure you don't have to do it again."

Leia smiled. "Thanks." She waited until Allana had disappeared down the access corridor, then turned to Han. "All right, now tell me what *that* was about. You know Anji is going to be ill whether or not Allana is with her."

"Sure, but you need to call Zekk and Taryn."

Zekk had been their daughter's mission partner—and Jagged Fel's rival for her affections—until a couple of years earlier, when he went missing in action during the Battle of Uroro Station. After a weeks-long search, the Solos and the entire Jedi Order had finally given up and declared him dead . . . only to have him show up six months later, fully recovered and romantically involved with an agent of the Hapan throne, Taryn Zel. Neither Zekk nor Taryn would discuss what had passed during those six months—or why Taryn had neglected to inform the Jedi of his survival—but Leia thought it likely they had been on a mission for Allana's mother, Queen Mother Tenel Ka.

Given that Taryn was under orders to render the Solos assistance whenever requested, Leia could see why Han wanted to send for the pair, but she did not understand why Han had wanted her to do it out of Allana's presence. "Is there a reason you don't want Allana to know we're calling in a security team?"

Han nodded. "First, I don't want her to worry about us while we're gone. And, second, she needs to learn independence."

"*Independence*, Han?" Leia asked. "At *eight*?"

"Hey, she's already behind the curve," Han said. "At eight, I was stealing my first starship."

Leia shook her head in exasperation, then leaned forward to activate the holonet transceiver. "Why don't I doubt that?"

Han smiled with pride, then continued the approach toward Dathomir. It was vaguely possible, of course, that they would find Luke and Ben hanging out at the spaceport cantina and never have to leave Allana behind at all—but he wasn't betting on it, not when they had come hunting a female Sith on a jungle planet full of Force-witches.

"I'm not stupid." And while the man was a touch belligerent, there was indeed no sign he was stupid.

Han, standing near the man in the shade between the *Falcon* and *Jade Shadow*, folded his arms and grinned. "Whatever you say, Darth."

"It's *Tarth*. Tarth Vames. And I don't care if your transponder says you're the *Naboo Duckling*, that's the *Millennium Falcon* and you're the Solos. And there's a Report Location Request on you from Coruscant."

Han pursed his lips and turned to look at his wife, an expression that meant, *You take this.*

Leia frowned. "So you know who we are."

Tarth nodded, his motion brisk enough to stir his red hair. "You haven't gone to any effort to hide it."

"Of course we haven't. It clearly wouldn't have fooled you. So I can take it that you know something of our histories?"

Apparently a bit mollified, Tarth nodded again. "Who doesn't?"

"So, historically, when the government has disagreed with us on some minor matter, how has it turned out?"

"Well, um, they're mostly out of office now. Or dead. The ones who disagreed with you. And you're still here. Right here."

Han caught Tarth's eye. "It's because the politicians are in it to save their jobs, while we're in it to save some little guy."

"Or a lot of little guys," Leia offered.

"Or a family member. Or a bunch of family members," Han added.

Clearly uncomfortable with the direction the conversation was taking, Tarth grimaced. "I'm the deputy director of operations here. The fact that you have, eh, a history of success in your confrontations with the government doesn't mean I can just abandon my duty. Neither does the fact that your husband has a blaster on his belt. Oh, I'm certainly not going to take a swing at him. But—"

"We're not asking you to abandon your duty." Leia shook her head. "We're asking you to *do* it. Just in a different way."

"Uh . . . what way?"

Han grinned. Tarth was doomed. He'd taken Leia's bait, and the hook would be set long before the man realized it was there.

"Come with us." Leia put on her brightest, welcome-to-the-company smile. "Since they're not answering our comm, we're going to look for my brother and my nephew. We need local guides and a local coordinator. That's you. You make sure that all local ordinances are obeyed—"

Han suppressed a snicker.

"—and you can testify to that effect when it's time to deal with the authorities."

"And you'll have a great story to tell . . . or sell." Han mimed typing on an imaginary datapad. "How I Saved Luke Skywalker. By Darth Vames."

"*Tarth* Vames." Tarth's grimace continued unabated. "I don't know . . ."

Leia pointed up toward the *Falcon*'s cockpit. Allana was visible there, in the canopy, with her nexu beside her, staring down at her grandparents. "See that little girl? My adopted daughter. She's already grief-stricken at the thought that something might have happened to her uncle Luke."

From behind Tarth, Han looked up at Allana, made a sad face, and stroked both his cheeks as if tears were running down them. Obligingly, Allana put on a child's expression of tragedy and rubbed at one eye with a knuckle.

Tarth's expression turned to one of defeat. "Oh . . . forget it."

Leia's tone became brisk. "We'll need a couple of airspeeders, camping supplies, preserved food, and guides with experience with the local terrain and clans. We'll pay the going rate, but if you show me the public rate sheets of everyone and everything you hire, and you've negotiated them down below those numbers, you get half the difference in addition to your own fees."

"Good man." Han nodded approvingly. "Well done, Tarth."

When Tarth was gone, Han glanced at his wife and shook his head. "I can't believe that you, of all people, pulled out the sad-little-girl card."

"I know, I know. My husband is a bad influence on me."

Allana's eyes went wide. *"Alone?"* she gasped, looking up from the cockpit captain's seat. "Have you guys gone barvy? I'm *eight*!"

"So?" Han shrugged. "When I was your age—"

"Han!" Leia shook her head. "You don't need to give her any ideas."

Han scowled. "Come on, she'd never—"

"She *might*," Leia insisted. "Just tell her when we'll be back."

Han sighed. He looked back to Allana. "We don't know when we'll be back. It could be awhile."

A disbelieving expression came to Allana's eyes. "Like an *hour*?"

"Longer," Leia said.

"A *day*?"

"Longer," Han said.

Allana's jaw dropped. "A *week*?"

"Yeah," Han said. "More like a week."

"Maybe even longer," Leia said. "It's hard to be sure. So don't be worried if we're not back, all right?"

Allana looked back and forth between them, then began to giggle. "Good one! You guys really fooled me."

Leia dropped to her haunches and took Allana's hands. "Sweetheart, your grandfather and I have to go find Luke and Ben. They need our help, and their lives may be in danger. So we're counting on you to stay aboard the *Falcon* and keep yourself and the ship safe. Can you do that?"

Allana's face grew serious. "You're not kidding, are you?"

Han shook his head. "Not in the slightest, kid. Think you can handle this?"

Allana scowled at him. "Of course I can. What do you think I *am*, a kid?"

"Yeah, but a pretty darn tough one," Han answered. He glanced out the cockpit canopy, at a small Batag Needle Ship resting on its struts about fifty meters away. Standing beneath it, pretending to work on a stuck cargo hatch, was a tall, dark-haired man in an expensive eletrotex jumpsuit: a Jedi Knight named, simply, Zekk. "Still, you and Anji are going to be on your own here, so stay aboard the *Falcon*, keep everything locked up tight, and don't let any strangers aboard. Got it?"

Allana gave him a crisp salute. "Got it, Captain."

"All right, then." Han continued to look out the canopy, this time at a pair of airspeeders that were crossing toward the *Falcon*. "It looks like Tarth finally has everything ready. Time for us to go."

He leaned down to give Allana, who was seated in the captain's seat, a kiss, then waited as Leia did the same.

"Do as Threepio says," Leia instructed. "And call us on the comlink if you have any problems."

"Grandma, I've *got* it," Allana said, waving them toward the back of the flight deck. "Now go save Uncle Luke and Ben!"

Han took Leia's hand and led her down the corridor. "Come on, Grandma. Can't you tell when we're not needed?"

* * *

Outside, they found Tarth waiting with two airspeeders—one a lumbering yellow hauler with a large flatbed cargo area in back, and one that must have been a sporty red model when it had been first manufactured, about the time Han was being born, both open-topped—and four men and women.

Ignoring Zekk and his Batag Needle Ship, Han and Leia stepped away from the *Falcon* to greet them. Seeing an almost familiar face, Han approached the man, who was young, clean-shaven, brown-haired, dressed in dark shorts and a vest of hard-wearing green cloth. The vest had many pockets and attachment points and was festooned with tools, knives, and items of electronic gear; his knee-high boots were a hardy brown leather, and he wore matching belt and wrist braces.

Han gave him a curious look. "I know you, don't I?"

The man extended a hand. "You have a good memory for faces. I was only a kid then." His accent was Coruscanti. "Dyon Stadd. We met during the Yuuzhan Vong War. I was a Jedi candidate."

Han glanced over the man's gear but saw no lightsaber. "Candidate?"

Dyon offered a grin with some self-deprecation in it. "I didn't quite have what it took to be a Jedi. More a Force-sensitive than a Force-user. But I took firsts in xenopology and language studies on Coruscant. Here, I help with trade negotiations between merchants and the Dathomiri clans."

Leia shook his hand. "And you know how to dress for the climate."

Dyon flexed a bare arm, showing well-defined biceps. "That, and the Dathomiri ladies like to see skin. Helps with negotiations."

Han snorted. "Introduce us around, will you?"

The smallest member of the assembly, smaller even than Leia, was a Dathomiri woman named Sha'natrac Tsu, nicknamed Tribeless Sha. Dark-haired and unsmiling, built lean as if she were artificially constructed of cables and bone under skin, she had on interestingly vented trousers and a tunic of imported rust-colored ironcloth; in addition to an authentic Dathomiri knife with a hilt made of carved tusk, she wore a blaster pistol at her hip and went barefoot.

The second male, introduced as Carrack, was huge, two meters or more in height, muscled as if an exercise regimen were his sole intellectual pursuit. He was fair-skinned and fair-haired, but his face was all Han or Leia could see of him; he wore a full set of what looked like re-purposed Imperial stormtrooper armor, painted in a green-and-black camouflage pattern, as were his oversized blaster rifle and the blaster pistols he carried on a baldric across his chest. His armor gave off the quiet but distinctive whine of a built-in cooling system.

"I take it you're the valet," Han said.

Carrack grinned. When he answered, he was soft-spoken. "The Witches respect shows of strength." He shrugged. "Mostly, I blow stuff up."

The last of Tarth's finds was another woman. Her beauty and the distinctive delicacy of her features proclaimed her a Hapan, and she wore garments that only a Hapan might have considered appropriate for Dathomir: a red mini dress, gold sandals and accessories nearly matching the color of her hair, and a holstered blaster pistol plated in reflective metal so shiny that it dazzled. Her accent, though, was pure backcountry Corellian: "Yliri Consta. I'm your lead driver."

Han snorted. "*I'm* my lead driver." Then he frowned. "You look a lot like . . ." He struggled for a moment for the name, then he had it. "Sarita Consta, the holodrama star."

"My older sister. I used to do stunt work for her. When she switched to comedy, working for her became just too boring."

Leia nodded, sympathetic. "I felt the same way when Han switched to comedy."

Han glowered at her. "Hey."

Tarth cleared his throat. "The last of your supplies will be here in a few minutes. You have clearance for both speeders to leave the space-port district."

"That'll give us time to switch to camouflage gear." Leia turned back toward the *Falcon.*

Tarth continued, "But where are you going to begin your search? It's a big forest . . . and the Skywalkers never checked in by comm."

Leia pointed. "North. They're somewhere north."

"Ah. Well, that's not exact, but at least it's an answer."

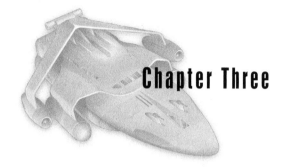

Chapter Three

THE DOOR SLID SHUT BEHIND JAGGED FEL, SEALING THE GALACTIC Empire's Head of State into his embassy quarters, and he breathed a sigh of relief.

Alone. After a day of negotiations with representatives of the Galactic Alliance, appearances at public events, carefully managed interviews with the press, hypercomm exchanges with ministers and functionaries back home in what most people referred to as the Imperial Remnant, he could use some time alone. It was almost as relaxing, as energizing, as time with Jaina . . . but sadly, they could not spend every waking hour together.

He tugged at his dress uniform, popping the seal of the tunic all down the right side of his chest, and felt trapped heat ebb away from him. It was also good not to be in perfect form for the holocams. A well-muscled man of just under average height, he knew he was good looking; the press here and back home often said so. His dark hair and close-trimmed mustache and beard helped give him a brooding look, though he seldom brooded. A lock of white hair emerging at his hairline, just where he'd picked up a scar in years past, gave him a touch of distinction. His choice of dark, militaristic dress clothes added to the impression of a vital leader with valuable wartime experience.

But it was all for show. He mostly wanted to be in a pilot's jumpsuit, flying against an enemy he could shoot. Sadly, that was no longer his life.

He stood there for a moment, eyes closed, breathing slowly to settle and center himself, and reminded himself of the biggest single word in his life: *duty.*

His sense of duty, instilled in him by his father and every facet of the Chiss society in which he'd grown to adulthood, was with him always, but it was sometimes so devoid of a sense of accomplishment, of any sense of reward, that he felt hollow.

He was the most powerful individual in the Galactic Empire, and yet so often he merely . . . negotiated, taking, in turn, hundreds of people and trying to persuade each one to tilt his own individual balance a little away from self-interest and a little toward the needs of the Empire. It was often like trying to herd hundreds of greased mouse droids, each one programmed by a different maladjusted child. And at the end of the typical day, he usually felt as accomplished and successful as if he had, in fact, spent hours wallowing with those greased mouse droids.

He heaved a sigh, expelling the last of the day's frustrations, and moved through his quarters—through the receiving room with its comfortable furniture, then into the antechamber that gave access to most of the rooms of his suite. He bypassed the door into his bedchamber and moved on to a smaller, narrower portal, one that only his voice could open. He addressed the hidden voice sensor at the top of the door. "Nek and nek."

The door slid up, revealing a small chamber almost fully occupied by a black, ball-shaped apparatus the height of a human male: a starfighter simulator. A ladder was affixed to the side facing the door, and it led to an open hatch on top. Energy restored, Jag trotted up the ladder, his heels clanging on its durasteel steps, and dropped through the hatch into the pilot's chair beneath.

This simulator was able to duplicate any model of TIE starfighter or similar craft produced since the original TIE fighter, but its default setting was one of Jag's favorites, the Chiss clawcraft, and as he settled in place the front screens lit up, arranging their view into an accurate simulation of the clawcraft's forward viewports.

"We'll start with a mixed-squadron attack, give me sixty percent Y-wings, twenty percent X's, twenty percent A's . . ." Jag strapped on the helmet and reached for the face mask. "Range of pilot skills from green to elite, even distribution." He pressed the face mask to his face.

It smelled odd, sweet.

Instinctively, he threw it from him, to his feet. "Abort, abort."

The hatch, moving into closed position on its hinges above his head, did not hesitate or reverse direction.

From his boot holster, Jag drew a small, powerful blaster, something like the type referred to as a hold-out or throwdown weapon, but much more expensive, much more reliable. He fired once at each hinge. Blaster bolts flashed against the machinery, some of the energy ricocheting away; the rest imparted hundreds of degrees of heat, blowing away sections of metal, superheating the rest. The air in the enclosed space of the simulator became much warmer. The hatch stopped in a half-closed position.

The face mask began hissing. Jag scrambled to his feet and launched himself up through the narrowed exit, careful not to come in contact with the superheated portion of the hatch, and made it atop the simulator.

He dropped to the floor on the side away from the ladder. As he did so, the door into the chamber shot up and open. Jag peered around the circumference of the simulator to see a stormtrooper in full white armor step into the chamber. The man, unaware of Jag's location, raised his blaster rifle, aiming it up toward the hatch.

Jag leaned out far enough to aim and opened fire. His first shot hit the trooper in the center of the chest plate, sending the man staggering back. His second hit the same spot; his third, the helmet. The trooper fell with a clatter of armor. "Lock open," Jag said, and there was an obedient *clunk* from the door mechanism.

Jag had to think, and had little or no time with which to do so.

Gas in his simulator, probably sleep gas. The enemy goal, then, was to capture him, but whether this was for ransom or just to kill him later was unknown. It probably meant the trooper's blaster rifle was set to stun. Small comfort, that.

This was an inside job. Neither his outer door nor the door into the simulator chamber was forced, and no alarms had been triggered. It was reasonable to suppose that the entire sensor and alarm setup for his suite was disabled, meaning that he could shout forever without being heard. No help would come.

More kidnappers would, though. They'd want more than one conspirator to carry him out of his quarters. So . . .

He glanced up at the ceiling. He didn't know what was situated directly above this room, but he was about to find out. He aimed at the ceiling and began pulling the trigger.

As shot after blaster shot hit the ceiling, one spot blackened, deformed, and gave way completely. Jag watched the energy meter on the blaster's butt count down as he fired, but before the charge was quite depleted he was rewarded with the faint sounds of a shriek and a curse from overhead. Then the wail of an alarm filled the air.

Another stormtrooper appeared in the doorway, already aiming at Jag. Jag pulled back, putting the body of the simulator between himself and the newcomer, and the stun bolt, a wavering flash of blue, hit the side of the machine. Jag felt a tingle as the simulator's skin conducted some of the energy into him, but only a fraction of the charge reached him.

The simulator, like the cockpit ball of a TIE fighter, was spherical, and Jag had something that no armored stormtrooper did: flexibility. He went flat on the permacrete floor, peering under the curve of the simulator hull, and had a clear view of the trooper's legs up to the knees.

He fired once into each kneecap. With a howl, the trooper turned and fell flat on his face. Jag couldn't hear whether there were more enemies coming—deafened by blaster shots and by the alarm, he wouldn't have heard if an entire regiment of troopers was marching toward him. So it was a risk, but Jag scrambled forward under the curve of the simulator, reaching the downed trooper, and set his near-empty hold-out blaster down. He grabbed the man's rifle and swung it around, aiming out through the door where he could now see about a quarter of his antechamber and the first downed trooper, who was still unmoving. Jag switched the weapon from stun to kill.

Two more troopers moved into view, heading his way but separating as they came—Jag guessed they were part of a small formation fanning out as they approached. He fired at the one on the left, who would have had an easier time ducking out of sight. But Jag's shot caught him in the unarmored inner thigh, spinning him down to the carpeted floor. The man's scream choked off before he fell. The second trooper threw himself to the floor, narrowing his profile considerably, and opened fire. Jag rolled to position himself more fully behind the body of the nearest trooper, and that trooper's body caught the one stun bolt that came near. Jag fired once, twice, three times, and the trooper in the next room lay still, his helmet a charred, smoking mess.

In a conversational tone, not loud enough to be heard over the alarm and through trooper helmets but loud enough for the nearest suite microphones to pick up, Jag said, "Door, unlock. Door, disengage all safety governors. Door . . ." He waited before issuing another command, and wriggled backward, dragging with him the trooper he was using for cover.

Two troopers appeared in the doorway, side by side, clearly having leapt into place from outside Jag's field of view.

Jag said, "Shut."

The door slammed down, hammering both troopers to the floor. The door, not meant for use as a weapon, bent and accordioned around its two victims.

Jag shot one trooper, then the other, in the neck. He said, "Door, open." The ruined remains of the door rose, jamming in the up position with half its length still in view.

Then there was more blasterfire, a lot of it, and Jag could see the antechamber being illuminated as if by a fireworks display, but only a couple of blaster bolts entered the simulator chamber; one burned through the side of the simulator and the other ricocheted from the walls, flashing back into the antechamber.

The blasterfire stopped. The alarm cut out, leaving a ringing silence in Jag's ears. Finally, he heard, "Sir? Sir, are you here?"

The voice, normally soft-spoken, now held both worry and rage. It belonged to Ashik, formally known as Kthira'shi'ktarloo. Ashik was a Chiss who was Jag's devoted assistant, attendant, and head of personal security. And who, no doubt, was probably more agitated at a possible failure of that last duty than Jag himself was.

"I'm fine, Ashik." Jag stood, winced at the smell of burned flesh and armor, and smoothed his tunic. "Hold your fire." He ducked and stepped through the doorway, blaster rifle in hand.

The antechamber was a ruin of eight or nine downed stormtroopers; blackened, destroyed furniture; and fumes. Still standing were Ashik and a complement of Imperial security men and women. Ashik's blue face was set in anger; his piercing eyes were hard, and his full lips pressed together.

Jag nodded at Ashik. "Yes. I'd like some answers. Right away."

Answers were slow in coming.

The first stormtrooper Jag had shot, the first of six he had killed, was no stormtrooper at all, but Lieutenant Oln Pressig, Ashik's dayshift opposite number. The other armored intruders were also, in a sense, fakes; they had all seen active service with the Galactic Empire, some of them as long ago as before the Yuuzhan Vong War, and all had either been discharged dishonorably or had entered dubious professions after their tours. In the last few weeks, all had traveled to Coruscant on funds transferred to their accounts from a dummy company on Borleias, which had been in Imperial hands since the Second Galactic Civil War.

The guards outside Jag's quarters were alive, felled by stun bolts. After recovering, they told Ashik that they had been approached by an armored trooper carrying and broadcasting proper credentials, and had been gunned down.

While Jag's theoretically more secure embassy chambers were being cleaned and repaired, he relocated to the hotel suite he often engaged in order to spend time with Jaina. Jaina sat while Jag paced. "It's all pretty much according to formula."

On the sofa, maddeningly calm in contrast with Jag's nervous energy, Jaina looked confused. "Whose formula?"

"Oh, there's got to be a book or file somewhere. *Conspiracy, A*

Methodology, by Emperor Palpatine, annotated by Ysanne Isard, with a foreword by the Warlord Zsinj. The bestselling resource for plotters for the last three decades. Don't you think?"

Jaina smiled. "Probably."

"Chapter six, I'm sure, is all about covering your tracks in case the assassination attempt fails. Insulate cells of operatives. Make sure anyone acting as contact for two or more cells can be quietly killed or spirited away when things go wrong." Jag stopped against an outer viewport, one that was mirror-reflective from the outside, and put his palms up against the cool transparent metal.

"You could be safer," Jaina said. "This suite isn't as secure as it could be. Neither is your embassy."

"What, return to the *Gilad Pellaeon?* Hide out on my Star Destroyer? I have to project confidence and courage."

"Well, then you need to strike back. But whom?"

"The Moffs. It had to be."

"All of them?"

"No. One, two, three at most. Probing at perceived weaknesses."

"Lecersen would be in the best position to take advantage of the situation if you . . . were killed."

Jag nodded. "But I doubt this was Drikl Lecersen. It's crude by his standards. And I think that an attempt like this would mean that he had given up."

"Given up?"

"Given up on getting rid of me in a more elegant manner." Jag turned back toward Jaina. "Let's face it, he really believes that my relationship with you is a weakness, one that is potentially harmful to the Empire. He hasn't come near to exploring all the ways he can cause me trouble." He saw Jaina wince, and he took a step forward, hands up in an apologetic gesture. "I didn't mean it that way. I know it's not a weakness."

"Are you sure?" There was just a trace of uncertainty and hurt in Jaina's voice. She was not a woman prone to insecurity, he knew, so for her to ask such a thing suggested that this thought had been preying on her.

He nodded. "I'm sure. It's change. I'm trying to change the way the Empire thinks of itself, of Palpatine, of the way the Moffs have done things for generations, of the Jedi. People who try to effect change are lucky if they aren't . . ." Jag hesitated. He'd meant to say, *aren't put to death by stoning,* but he realized almost too late that Jaina would still be upset by Jag's close call. "Lucky if they have any success at all. Lucky if they're remembered fondly."

Jaina did relax again. "You won big tonight, though."

"Yes, I'm still alive."

"More than that. One of the nasty little rumors floating around about you is that my Jedi powers are all that have been keeping you alive—that I'm your secret backup bodyguard corps. But tonight I was nowhere around. You took out six armored veterans trying to kill you. That's very, well, Imperial."

Jag snorted. "My deputy minister of trade, perishable goods, was in the suite above mine. I shot her in the foot while she was entertaining a guest. Not so very Imperial."

"Well, that's not what everyone is talking about."

"Good." Finally somewhat calmed, Jag moved across to sit beside her. "I just don't know if I can pull this off, though. Hold things together long enough for the Empire and Alliance to reunite, and beyond. Effect any sort of change."

Jaina shrugged. "Think about what you *have* accomplished. You've saved lives. You've maintained the honor of the Fel family name and brought it into a new generation. And you've shot a deputy minister in the foot."

Despite himself, he grinned. "Couldn't let that one go, could you?"

"You could start a whole new Imperial custom. 'Dance, fool, dance!' *Zap, zap, zap!* 'Ow, my toe!'"

"Just keep quiet, will you?"

DATHOMIR SPACEPORT

The two-vehicle caravan got under way as soon as Han and Leia finished changing into camouflage.

Han took the pilot's seat in the faster, nimbler ruin of a sports-speeder. Leia and Dyon joined him. The others, Yliri piloting, took the cargo speeder. Leia directed them northward, following her vague sense in the Force of where Luke must be.

Luke's presence was steady and distant, and Leia had no sense that he was in immediate danger. But this feeling was not as accurate or specific as a homing beacon, and Leia could follow it in only a meandering, imprecise fashion, now correcting more to the northwest, now to the northeast.

The two vehicles moved through the Dathomiri rain forest at what, to Leia, seemed a maddeningly slow rate. They flew at an average of three or four meters above the forest floor, the sports vehicle in front, both pilots being very careful not to scrape against tree branches and conceivably knock passengers free. The cargo speeder sometimes had to stop, backtrack, and circle to find passages when Han's speeder could easily navigate shorter routes, but Yliri did seem to be a more-than-competent pilot.

Occasionally Leia would get flashes of other presences in the Force: Dathomiri forest predators lying in wait as the two speeders passed. No attacks came, and she assumed that most wildlife on this planet would steer clear of tangling with humans and other humanoids, so many of which here carried deadly weapons and made use of Force powers. None of these brief Force flashes was familiar to her; none carried the unmistakable stamp of Luke or Ben.

A couple of hours in, Leia's sense of direction failed her. She could still feel her brother in the Force, but her perception of him was divided; he was distant, but his emotions were near, lingering in this area, probably because of some encounter. "I've lost him," she told Han.

He thumbed the dilapidated speeder's comm board. "Mark this spot for a possible muster point, then commence spiral search. Report anything out of the ordinary."

Yliri acknowledged and her speeder banked away to starboard, beginning its spiral pattern. Han banked to port. Their two spiral searches would overlap to a considerable degree, offering double coverage to the area Leia most wanted to search.

A short while later, when the two speeders had come within view of each other for the third time, Leia saw the cargo speeder halt. There was discussion among the four people aboard, then Tribeless Sha dropped over the side, landing nimbly on the forest floor four meters down. She looked right and left, then set off at a trot to the right, a course that would carry her past the red speeder's current path. When she'd moved forty paces, the cargo speeder followed at a slow pace.

Leia activated her speeder's comm. "What's happening? Over."

Yliri's voice came back, "Sha spotted blood on a bush. Now she's spotted rancor footprints. She's tracking back to where the beast was injured. Over."

"Thanks. Out."

Within a few minutes, Sha had found the spot, ground that was charred everywhere as if by a broad-ranging but not very intense fire. Within a hundred meters of it were two wrecked speeder bikes. Tarth looked over the registration numbers engraved in their engine compartments and gave Han a nod.

Han sighed. "Luke and Ben are going to lose their deposits."

Leia elbowed him in the ribs. "Not funny. Where are they?"

"Hard to track." That was Sha, one of the few times she'd spoken since she'd been hired. She gestured to the northwest, at a distinct angle from their previous course. "That way. There's another set of tracks. Dathomiri woman, I think." Her hand transcribed an arc, then ended up pointing in the same direction. "Went off at an angle, then went that way, too."

"Who was leading and who was following?" Leia frowned. While she didn't like the idea of anyone tracking or trailing Luke and Ben, she knew that her brother might merely be allowing an enemy to do so.

Sha shrugged. "Impossible to tell. Too long ago."

"Can you track them?"

Sha nodded. "Yes. But slow. Walking speed."

"Let's do it, then."

"Electronics are fried." That was Tarth, still rummaging around in the mechanical insides of one of the speeder bikes.

Han frowned. "How's that again?"

"Electronics are fried. Both speeders. I also found a comlink by the other one. Burned clear through and discarded."

"Char marks on the ground where they were?"

Tarth shook his head. "The same as all around, but nothing to suggest they were grounded when it happened."

Sha said nothing, but the look she gave Han was a question.

"Electrical attack of some sort," Han told her. "But electricity is most damaging when its target is in contact with the ground. If the two speeder bikes were shot out of the sky with an electrical attack while they were moving . . . well, that's a lot of power."

Sha nodded. "Lightning Storm. A spell cast by the Witches. Some Witches. All Nightsisters."

Leia took a step forward before she'd realized she had. "Nightsisters? I thought—I was hoping they were all gone."

Sha shook her head. "Never gone. They hide, they heal, they return. If their numbers are few, they come for your children." For just a moment, her usually expressionless mask fell and she looked bleak. Then that look was gone, wiped away by a blankness any sabacc player would envy, and Sha turned away.

Han gripped Leia's shoulder, gave it a reassuring squeeze. "The Nightsisters are their Sith." His voice was a grim whisper.

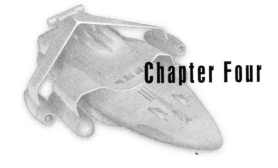

Chapter Four

CHIEF OF STATE'S OFFICE, SENATE BUILDING,
CORUSCANT

ADMIRAL NATASI DAALA, ONE TIME IMPERIAL NAVY OFFICER AND NOW
head of the executive branch of the Galactic Alliance government, sat
back in her chair and pondered whether she wanted to call in Wynn
Dorvan. Daala felt a flash of exasperation; there were times when she
just wanted things to be orderly and clear-cut. And Dorvan always
seemed to have something for her to think about that made things the
opposite. Still, he was such an efficient assistant that she had to make
allowances. It was, after all, the civilian way of doing things.

And she wanted to remain on good terms with him. With a little
guidance, he would make a superior chief of staff someday . . . once he
accepted the notion of having greater authority and responsibility.

Trusting the secretarial software built into her comm system to
scrub weariness out of her tone, she said, "Wynn? A moment of your
time please."

"Certainly, ma'am. I'll be right in."

She took one last look around her office, at its calming purity of Imperial white furnishings to match her uniform. She brushed strands of her long red hair out of her face, tucking them behind her ears in a likely-to-fail bid for neatness.

The door slid open to reveal Dorvan. While he often was the harbinger of things complicated and messy, he himself was not. He was, as ever, alert and precise, his brown hair currently immaculate, reminding Daala of her own momentarily untidy state. From the left breast pocket of his tailored suit jacket poked a curve of brown fur striped with orange—the neck of his pet chitlik, named Pocket.

She gestured toward a chair and he eased into it, crossing his legs and looking up expectantly at her.

Daala went straight to the point. "Wynn, even after two years, this process of civilian rule is sometimes bewildering. So, where in military life I'd normally issue a command and later on ask a colleague what he thought of it in hindsight, sometimes here I need to gauge opinions before things are decided. A lot of different opinions. From different people."

"That's actually pretty common among civilian leaders with any sense." Dorvan settled back in his chair, permitting himself to relax slightly. His own expression was curious, just a little wary. "Ask away."

"This whole struggle with the Jedi. Do you think I'm—do you think my tactics are sound?"

He considered his answer for a moment. Dorvan always considered everything. "Admiral, when the holocams are recording, I'm behind you one hundred percent."

"I know you are. They're not recording now."

He sighed. "I trust the Jedi to put the needs of the people first. To arrive at the right answer, even if it's by trial and error. I think you're pushing too hard. You can have them either as allies or subordinates, but not both. You seem to have decided that their proper role is subordinates."

She nodded. "I have. Though not *my* subordinates. The government's. So I have to bring them into line."

"I would choose a different approach . . . but you're the boss. I back you all the way."

"But you don't think I can pull it off."

"Palpatine did. For a while. At a cost."

Daala whistled appreciatively. "Nicely struck, soldier. Where do you hide that vibroblade when you're not using it?"

"Pocket keeps it quite handily in her pouch. She's a useful pet."

"You think I'm becoming Palpatine, then?"

"No ma'am, I don't. I wouldn't be working for you if I did. I'm saying your *tactics* are similar to his, and could be perceived as such by the general public and your enemies."

She gave him a brief smile she didn't feel. "Well. I appreciate your candor."

"It's my job, ma'am."

"That'll be all."

He rose and left. When the door slid closed behind him, Daala continued to sit, unmoving, now unaware of her errant hair, and pondered the course of action she was taking.

DATHOMIRI RAIN FOREST

Tribeless Sha emerged from a screen of bushes like a phantom, no noise heralding her arrival, and Han, seated on the hood of the red speeder, jerked in surprise; caf sloshed from his cup onto his wrist. The sudden burn caused him to jerk again, more violently this time, and the full contents of his cup dashed across Carrack's armored legs.

The big man gave Han an admonishing look and moved around to the far side of the grounded speeder as if putting it between them for cover.

Han shrugged an apology. "Sorry." He rubbed at his stinging wrist. "Her fault."

Leia moved forward and gave Han an amused smirk before turning to Sha. "What did you find?"

"Many tracks." Sha gestured toward the northwest. "The woman tracking your brother precedes him. Again and again she cuts across his path, becoming clumsy and obvious when she does so. She always heads northeast. He sometimes follows a little while and sometimes not. He always returns to his northwest course."

Yliri, stretched out on a blanket on the broad hood of the cargo speeder, laughed. "She's trying to draw him off, and he's not having any of it."

Sha nodded. "You are a tracker?"

"Not like you. But I've done some hunting." Yliri rolled onto her side, facing the others. "So what is she trying to draw them toward?"

Sha shook her head. "Away from. Another set of tracks. An entire clan at least, and many rancors. Heading toward Redgill Pass."

"Huh." That was Dyon, who had been working diligently at their small campfire, situated on bare spongy ground between the two landed speeders, warming caf and packaged meals. "Wait a second." From one of his vest pockets he drew a datapad and spent a few moments tapping in commands. Finally, he turned his screen around so the others could see it; on it was displayed a simple, colorful two-dimensional map. Most of the map was green, with some irregular black dots indicating mountains and bluish lines and blobs indicating bodies of water.

He pointed at a lake situated between two mountain peaks. "Redgill Lake. Also Redgill Pass. It's a choke point for northward passage. The valley beyond has another pass farther north, meaning it's easy for clans to defend."

Tarth's face fell. "So there could be a battle coming. One clan fortifies itself up there to fight another one."

Dyon nodded.

Han made a derisive noise. "And this woman, one of the scouts for a clan about to go to war, deals with two dangerous Force-using pursuers by trying to lead them astray? Does she belong to Clan Nice? No, it's something else."

Leia looked up through the trees, their branches meeting more sparsely above this clearing, and at the sky beyond. Sunlight slanted in at a steep angle, suggesting the lateness of the hour. "We're not going to catch up to them tonight, I take it."

Sha shook her head. She moved to the campfire and sat cross-legged beside it. Dyon handed her a cup and poured caf into it from the pot resting on a folding metal grill set up over one low portion of the fire.

"Then let's sleep." His wrist no longer stinging, Han moved over to get his own cup refilled. "We'll start at first light and see how long it takes us to catch up to them. Two-hour watch shifts: me, then Leia, Dyon, Sha, Tarth. Carrack and Yliri, you'll pull last shift together; I want twice as many eyes open and Carrack's weapons ready in the last shift before dawn."

Carrack nodded approval, but Yliri laughed. "I knew you were famous, but I didn't know you were so bossy."

"Corellians are natural leaders, sister. You should know that."

Leia rolled her eyes, but her smile took the sting out of it.

ABOARD THE MILLENNIUM FALCON, DATHOMIR SPACEPORT

C-3PO hovered, as was his nature, at the entrance to the cockpit while Allana had her encrypted comm conversation. She might, after all, need reassurance or a glass of milk at any moment.

The golden droid could hear the little girl's side of the conversation, with Queen Mother Tenel Ka's voice reaching him as a series of buzzes. Voices across the comm speakers had to be easy to understand by those in the pilot's seats, but the speakers had recently drifted out of register, as they did from time to time. C-3PO suppressed a sniff— or, rather, a synthesized sound identical to a sniff in both characteristics and meaning. *His* speakers never became misaligned, and if they did, he'd see to their repair immediately. It was no wonder the *Falcon* was constantly breaking down. Such shoddy maintenance . . .

Allana's conversation was winding up. "I will . . . I won't . . . Don't worry, I have Anji . . . I'm not bored." Even the droid could sense the lie in the girl's words. "I love you, too. *Falcon* out." There was pride in the last two words; clearly, she felt very adult in remembering to add them.

The little girl rose from the pilot's seat and turned back to face C-3PO, her red hair so like her mother's, her serious expression so like her grandmother Leia's. She gave the droid an unfriendly look. "You don't have to listen to me all the time."

"To do my job effectively, young mistress, I do. And I am very, very good at my job."

"Most of the time, I guess."

She sighed, clearly upset about something, then stepped over to Anji, who was curled up on the copilot's seat. She sighed again, then began to stroke the nexu's fur. Anji responded with a welcoming purr, but Allana did not seem to notice. She merely stared out the cockpit canopy, shaking her head at some little-girl sadness that C-3PO could only guess at.

"Come now, you mustn't worry about your physical welfare," C-3PO said. "Artoo and I are quite capable of keeping you tidy and well fed."

Allana whirled on him. "I'm not a *kid,* Threepio!" she said. "I can keep myself tidy, and I *know* how to use the food synthesizer as well as you do."

Anji raised her head and cast a wary eye on C-3PO, obviously appraising whether she needed to test the effectiveness of her bite restrainers on him. C-3PO did his best to ignore the ungrateful feline and kept his attention focused on Allana.

"Well, then, I'm afraid you'll just have to tell me what's wrong," he said. "I certainly can't fix it if you make me guess."

"*You* can't fix it at all," Allana complained. "They forgot."

"Oh, come now. Perhaps Captain Solo *is* prone to forgetfulness, but that's not the case with Princess Leia," C-3PO replied. "Whatever it is, I'm sure she left instructions for me to arrange it on her behalf."

Allana's eyes lit up. "Really?"

"Of course," C-3PO said. "What is it that you're thinking of? Her offer to teach you how to play dejarik?"

Allana stepped over to him. "The rancor!" she said. "Grandma promised me that the next time we were on Dathomir, I could ride a rancor!"

A surge of static shot through C-3PO's central processing unit. "Oh dear, perhaps they *did* forget," he sniffed. "I'm afraid no one said anything to me about *that.*"

Allana scowled at him. "I thought droids couldn't lie."

"I didn't *lie,*" C-3PO replied, suppressing an electronic sniff. "I was merely . . . *mistaken.*"

"About Grandma never forgetting?" Allana demanded. "Or the part about leaving instructions to take me rancor riding?"

This time C-3PO did not suppress the sniff. "Clearly, you need some alone time. I will go about other duties. Please call if you need me, mistress."

C-3PO moved aft, his microservos whining as he walked. He suspected that the girl's question was not actually a verbal jab, probably just a child's inquisitiveness, but considering the other strong Solo traits the girl possessed, he couldn't be sure.

As he traveled the curving passageway that gave access to the *Falcon*'s main deck, the droid reached the passageway to the starboard-side loading port and saw that the boarding ramp was down. But R2-D2, his astromech ally of so many years—he couldn't even remember their first meeting, so it had to have been prior to a memory wipe—was rolling up the ramp, and the ramp was rising into place, keeping the nighttime spaceport at bay. "Well, what have you been up to?"

R2-D2 wheetled at him, in the musical, very data-dense code of astromechs.

"Exploring? What's to explore? It's a patch of mud spattered with permacrete habitations. I've seen more promising sites on the underside of a shoe."

The astromech wheetled again.

C-3PO stopped where he was to stare at his comrade. "Ah. So at a spaceport, a place where ships come and go all the time, you have seen . . . a ship. How observant."

Wheetle.

"So what if the mechanic hurried to close the hangar door when he saw you watching? Humans can be very self-conscious, you know. Thank the Maker that we don't suffer from such ailments."

Wheetle.

C-3PO offered up a synthesized sigh. "The tail end of a Sorosuub yacht. Might I point out that there are about as many Sorosuub yachts out there as there are piranha-beetles on Yavin Four?"

The astromech's tweetling took on an irritable tone.

"No, I won't investigate with you. We're not to leave the young mistress alone." C-3PO shook his head in worry. "Frankly, Artoo, I don't know what our Masters were thinking, leaving that poor child here alone with no one but us to protect her. We're on Dathomir—

don't they realize what happens to Force-sensitive girls on this planet?"

R2-D2 answered with a long, low buzz.

"I most certainly *do* have something to worry about!" C-3PO replied. "Sometimes I think you have all the sensibility of a rolling dustbin and could be replaced by one. In fact, I insist that you stay here with me. I may need you to defend the ship."

Tweetle-blatt.

"No, the best defense is not a strong offense. The best defense is a strong *defense*. And that means staying put, protecting Mistress Allana, and not letting her get into trouble, which is her genetic predisposition. As it would be yours, if you had genes." C-3PO shook his head sadly and continued heading aft, secure that he had, in fact, sorted R2-D2 out for once.

SECURITY SERVICES SHOOTING RANGE, SENATE BUILDING, CORUSCANT

Fifty meters down the narrow black-walled lane, the gleaming silver droid went from stillness to an athlete's run in an instant, hurtling toward Chief of State Daala.

Daala, dressed in baggy, comfortable exercise wear in blue, drew her blaster pistol from a shoulder holster and aimed in a single, practiced motion. By the time she put her sights on the droid, it had covered half the distance between them. She took an extra moment to aim, allowing the droid to close to ten meters, a distance at which the grin on its skull-like facial features was evident, and then she squeezed the trigger.

Her shot took the droid in the chest—upper right pectoral, had it been a human. The shot turned that section of silver skin black. The droid spun, its beautiful running gait interrupted, and Daala fired again, a snap shot that took the droid in the left side, blackening its hide there.

The droid spun down to the glossy black floor and slid to within three meters. As it did, Daala aimed one last time, carefully, and put a bolt into the thing's temple.

The indicator screen built into the lane wall beside Daala flashed with the word KILL. Below it appeared more words:

REPLAY TASK

ANALYZE RESULTS

RESET

CHANGE PARAMETERS

EXIT SIMULATION

Instead of issuing one of those commands, Daala stepped aside and nodded for her companion to take the firing position.

General Merratt Jaxton, Chief of Starfighter Command, dressed like Daala for this practice, stepped up and adjusted his orange-toned goggles. A human male of average height, gray-haired and dark-eyed, he had the sort of squarish build and facial features that the civilian population expected and found reassuring in its military leaders. Like most of the current generation of high-ranking officers, he had come to his position in the power vacuum that had resulted from the end of the Second Galactic Civil War. The change in GA government had left innumerable careers like the droid before them—blackened, prostrate, and failed—and people like Jaxton, efficient war-hawks with spotless records, had stepped up and assumed power.

He looked down at the fallen droid. His voice was a touch rough, lightly flavored with the accent of long-lost Alderaan: "You let it get too close."

Daala shrugged. "You go for the center of mass first. Put them down, *then* put them out. If you go for the kill shot right away, you, well, die."

"Nonsense." Jaxton turned to the control board. "Change parameters. Red Rage addict, enhanced to ten. Reset."

The droid leapt to its feet and trotted back to the fifty-meter distance spot. As it reached the spot, vents protruding from the walls blew out a quantity of white fog, engulfing the droid. The fog dissipated almost immediately, and with it disappeared the three black marks on the droid's skin.

The droid turned back toward Daala and Jaxton, then became still. Jaxton grinned. "Go."

The droid moved toward them.

Jaxton drew the blaster pistol on his right hip. As the barrel came up into line, he fired.

The bolt took the droid in the center of the forehead. The droid's head snapped back, then its body fell.

It had taken two steps. It slid forward another two meters, then lay still.

"Impressive." Daala wasn't really impressed. She had known too many ex-starfighter-pilots who were far too proud of their shooting skills. In the field, show-off tactics like Jaxton's would get a soldier killed. But she managed to keep the boredom out of her voice. "You must practice all the time, day and night."

Jaxton paused, doubtless wondering if her statement was a jab at his recently divorced state. "Not *that* much." He stepped aside.

"Reset." Daala stepped up.

The droid rose, returned, was engulfed in fog, and stood gleaming and ready.

Daala did not set it into motion immediately. "I've been hearing things. About, well, restlessness."

"Are we on the record?"

"No."

"Natasi, I'm your wingman. Always. You know that."

"Certainly." Actually, she didn't; she had never been close to Jaxton, had barely known him before he became a military chief. But he could be telling the truth.

"But, yes, there are mutterings. About you."

"So, what's going on—"

At the syllable *"go,"* the droid charged Daala.

Grimacing at both her mistake and the inconvenience of the interruption, Daala raised her pistol and fired. At forty meters, the bolt took the droid in the crotch. The droid curled into a ball as it fell and lay still.

Daala blinked. It really had been her usual center-of-mass shot, but she'd squeezed the trigger just a trifle prematurely as she raised the pistol, and the results looked much more effective than her shooting skills usually warranted.

"Nice."

"Thank you. Reset. So, why are there mutterings?" She stepped aside.

Jaxton didn't immediately move to take her place. "In my opinion, the people in the officer corps don't think you're protecting their interests or furthering their ideals. Not the way they, we, expected you would."

Daala frowned at him. "Across the last couple of years, I've restored the strength and responsiveness of the military to a degree that exceeds analyst expectations."

"Granted."

"I've taken steps to bring the Jedi into line. The Order has been beheaded—Luke Skywalker is chasing the ghost of his dead nephew around the galaxy, and his replacement is familiar with and friendly to our outlook."

"Yet the Jedi still struggle with you."

"For now."

"And one of them, Gilad Pellaeon's murderer, is still at liberty."

"That's a civilian case, and it takes civilian time. Tahiri Veila will be convicted. She'll be executed. It just takes time."

"Well, perhaps some other lesson can be taught in the meantime. I'm thinking of a criminal who would be subject to military, not civilian, law."

"Who?"

"Cha Niathal."

Daala blinked, honestly surprised. Admiral Niathal, a naval lifer from Mon Calamari, had been in Daala's own position, sharing Chief of State duties with Colonel Jacen Solo—or, as he later chose to be called, Darth Caedus. As Caedus had become more and more destructive, Niathal had sought to curb his excesses, eventually turning on him. She now lived in retirement on Mon Calamari. "Merratt, you may not have looked at the records of her actions as closely as I have. It's hard to accuse her of anything but a mistake, the mistake of trusting Jacen Solo."

"The very same mistake Luke Skywalker made, and was convicted for."

"But Cha Niathal is *one of us.*"

"I agree, and I would not want to see her come to harm. Even to interrupt her well-deserved retirement." Finally he stepped up to the firing lane. "Go."

The droid lurched into motion. Jaxton let it get three steps into its run before raising his blaster and shooting it in the head. He lowered the weapon. "But the thing is, in reviewing her actions and deciding to head off a legal case against her, you've opened yourself up to charges of tampering. Of, in a sense, pardoning someone in your exact position in the hope of setting a precedent—in case you mess up. Thus the loss of faith. The muttering."

Annoyed, Daala shook her head. "So I should arrange to prosecute Niathal just to shut up whiners?"

"You'd be surprised at how many and how powerful those 'whiners' are. And the idea is to prosecute, not persecute. Find three military judges who are impartial, not swayed by public opinion, and well respected by the armed forces. Have them sit on the court-martial. They'll acquit, Niathal will go home, the masses will stop muttering."

"I don't like it." Daala thought about shooting the droid a few more times to rid herself of her annoyance, then decided against it. "Reset. Exit simulation."

"Of course you don't. But like it or not, you're waging a campaign against the Jedi. Until it's resolved, any other action you take becomes one front of a two-front war. That's not good, especially when the second front is your own people."

Chapter Five

THE SOLO EXPEDITION SET OUT AGAIN JUST AFTER DAWN. SHA LED THE way on foot, following and interpreting the scant signs of travel left behind by Luke, Ben, and the mystery woman who was pacing them. Han's and Yliri's speeders followed sedately, some two hundred meters back, using Sha's comm signals for navigation.

Only a few minutes into their travel, Leia sat up in her seat. "I feel Luke."

"All of a sudden?"

"He's . . . he's . . ." Leia frowned, concentrating. "He's submerging himself in the Force. Looking for something. I think he's been concealing himself from the Force. Ben, too." She closed her eyes and tilted her head. "Now he can feel me. Now he knows I'm here. He's calm. No danger at the moment."

"That's something, then."

Leia looked off slightly to starboard of their current direction.

"Let's pick up Sha and head toward Luke at speed. I think, if I can maintain contact with him, we can save a lot of time."

"Whatever you say."

DATHOMIR SPACEPORT

Morning sun streamed in through the viewports of the *Millennium Falcon,* but in the engineering compartment, the only available light was from ceiling glow rods.

It was there that Allana found C-3PO sitting behind the curved shell of the hyperspace module. She hopped out from the shadows like a monster from a children's tale and stood over the golden droid, her hands on her hips. "Where's Artoo?"

"I'm sure I don't know, mistress." His hiding place discovered, C-3PO rose awkwardly to his feet. "Around, I assume."

"Around where?"

"Around . . . here. I assume."

She scowled up at him. "You're lying again, Threepio. Anji and I have looked all over the *Falcon.* He's not here. If he was, Anji would have found him. And you've been hiding from me."

"I would never do that, Mistress Allana."

"Then what were you doing here?"

"Two years, four months, and three days ago, Master Han dropped a credcoin here in the engine compartment. He was never able to find it. Since then, it has emerged at times of high-stress maneuvers, rolling about and clattering. It's quite maddening, really. If I could find it—"

"You're still lying." Allana's tone was more disappointed than accusative. "If Artoo was doing something that was all right, you'd tell me. So he's doing something sneaky and he could get hurt."

"Droids don't get hurt, little one. Just damaged."

"And sometimes kidnapped and tortured and taken apart. That's not hurt?"

"Well . . . not technically."

"Are you going to tell me where he is, or am I going to talk to you *all day long?*"

C-3PO offered up a simulated sigh. "He went out last night after we tucked you in bed. He hasn't returned. Though I'm sure there is no cause for worry."

"Where did he go?"

"I am not sure. But at one point he was raving about seeing a ship in one of the domes hereabout. He probably went to investigate."

"Well, let's go find him."

"No, miss. Either there is no problem, in which case he will return to us, or there is danger, in which case we are under strict orders not to expose you to it. Why, if you were to be harmed, Master Han and Mistress Leia would find themselves a whole new Wookiee to pull my arms and legs off."

"But you're not doing anything!"

"I am monitoring Artoo's preferred comm frequencies. That is all I can do while remaining here."

Allana stomped in frustration, then turned and ran to the top of the *Falcon*'s boarding ramp. It was in the up and locked position. She reached high and hit the wall control to lower it.

The control panel *clunk*ed to acknowledge that it had been activated, but the ramp did not lower into place.

"Threepio!"

"I'm sorry, mistress. Orders, you know."

DATHOMIRI RAIN FOREST

Their opponent, Luke knew, had superior knowledge of the Dathomir wilderness, superior tracking skills, and Force powers that, while probably not greater than Luke's, might be better adapted to this environment.

So Luke set about to change the rules.

The woman who was pacing them, constantly trying to slow and divert them, had now established a standard operating procedure. She would maneuver herself to one side or another of Luke and Ben's path and either set up some sort of trap to inflict a minor injury on them or lay down a false trail to lead them astray. Several times, only the Jedi's

Force awareness allowed them to dodge whipping branches, avoid venomous serpent nests, or keep from slipping down an unexpectedly slick slope into a river.

Setting up traps or stomping through the forest like a drunken bantha took time and a greater interaction with her surroundings than she might have experienced while doing simple tracking. So it was then that Luke should be able to find her in the Force.

With Ben on guard for both of them, Luke sat on a flat rock and sank into a Jedi meditative trance. He opened himself to the Force fully for the first time since embarking on this quest. He cast around, trying to become one with the rain forest. If he did this properly, he would be able to feel minute changes, little areas of damage, that would give him some hint of his opponent's plans and location.

And he felt . . . Leia.

The unexpected contact nearly jolted him out of his trance, but he calmed himself and sent his sister a touch of reassuring emotion, the Force equivalent of a smile. Then he turned back to his task.

Distantly, he felt animal life across a wide area grow alarmed and alert as they detected a deep rumble in the ground; but it was only a minor tremor, a natural occurrence causing no damage. He gave a little shake of his head and turned his attention elsewhere.

Scars in the forest . . . a new one-family settlement south-southeast, near the spaceport, a plot of ground laid bare by fire, a prefab permacrete hut now being erected there. He could feel other scars, tiny ones close by caused by the feet of rancors ripping at the forest floor, big ones in the distance caused by migrations of hundreds of beasts or people.

And then there she was. Her booted feet bruised grasses and lichen growing on rock outcroppings as she strung cord, turning a patch of ill-balanced boulders on a hillside into a dangerous deadfall.

She was unhappy about that, Luke could tell, unhappy that this trap was so much more dangerous than the previous ones. She didn't want to hurt them. She wanted, absolutely *needed* them to go away.

Luke felt her tense. He backed away on his contact. More dimly, he could sense her looking around in sudden paranoia, but her emotions gradually settled.

She had sensed him but not identified him. Her control of the Force was limited in certain areas, clearly.

Sure now where her rockfall trap lay and where she intended to wait, Luke withdrew and opened his eyes.

He looked up at his son. Ben stared at him, a worried expression on his face.

"What is it?"

"You're pale, Dad."

"Am I?" Luke tried to get a sense of his condition.

He was tired, more tired than he should be after such a mundane effort in the Force. Clearly, he was not yet recovered from his exertions in the Maw. He needed days of uninterrupted rest, and he wasn't getting them.

Well, that was all right. He could go on for some considerable time this way.

He rose, demonstrating, for Ben's sake, more vigor than he actually felt. "Let's go."

"Did you find the crash site?"

"Eh?"

"It occurred to me after you went into the trance. The Sith girl crashed her ship out there somewhere. I assume that would have left the kind of damage you were looking for."

"It would have, yes." Luke frowned. "But I found no sign of the crash."

"Maybe she crashed into a lake. Then there'd be no surface damage."

"And that would be a good reason why the search party found no sign of the site." Luke turned toward the northwest. "Let's find her and ask her."

Within the hour, they had the Dathomiri woman's rockfall trap in sight. The ground here rose into mountain foothills, and the eastern slope of a narrow pass, cut in some distant time by a now vanished creek, was dense with irregular white stones.

The woman's sabotage of that slope was not visible. Whatever arrangement she had made with trip cords was well hidden.

Luke and Ben lay on a jagged slab of rock a few hundred meters from the pass. They had crept up on the area so quietly and carefully that Luke believed the woman lying in wait could not have detected them. Still, the minutes they spent surveying the area offered them no advantage. They'd have to deal with the trap directly and physically.

"I have our tactic." Ben's voice was unexpectedly deep and mature.

"Yes?"

"When the rocks fall, we get out of the way."

"Thank you for reducing our task to its basic components. Come on." Luke rose and began trotting toward the rockfall.

He could not feel the woman in the Force. She had to be concealing herself. No, more than that. If she was nearby, she could not even be watching the rockfall. To watch it would be to experience increased anticipation as her intended victims approached, which was likely to tip off Force-users . . . and she had to know that her opponents were well versed in the Force. So she would be nearby, but would pay no attention until she heard the rocks fall.

Luke and Ben crossed the distance from their hiding place to the pass with its snare in moments.

"Not so muggy here." Ben's tone was cheerful, and it did not sound forced.

"Eh?"

"Making conversation." Ben lowered his voice to a conspiratorial whisper. "Sounding natural."

"Of course." With his next step, Luke's foot landed on a rock that shifted under his weight.

If his senses in the Force had not been tuned to detect any stirring, any remote hint of danger, he would not have felt the tripping of the trap. Far over his head, boulders perched on an overhang leaned out and dropped toward their heads. Luke could feel other, more subtle shiftings take place in the rock wall to his right, but so far the only threat came from that first set of rocks, now gathering speed and building kinetic energy.

Luke leapt up and to the left. His feet came in contact with the rocky slope there, the one on which he had detected no sabotage. He felt rather than heard Ben leap and land beside him.

The slope here was almost vertical, but with a push in the Force Luke sprang up along it, climbing an easy six meters. He dropped back-first onto a ledge. Ben settled in beside him.

They watched several tons of rocks plummet past them, hitting all along the pass and to either side of where they had just been standing. More stones on the facing slope slid free and toppled into the pass, clattering down among the others.

"Three stages of fall," Ben said, his tone still conversational.

"Very sophisticated. Now let's find her."

They opened themselves to the Force, seeking the woman.

Luke made an unhappy face. "Uh-oh."

"Miscalculated, didn't you?"

A rancor scrambled into the pass through the entrance Luke and Ben had just used. It carried a gnarled wooden club that must have weighed two hundred kilograms. On its back and neck was a saddle, in which sat a stout blond woman of middle years. She wore glossy black hide garments, and her expression was furious. For the rancor to have appeared there, presumably in response to the triggering of the trap, it must have been concealed very close by. Perhaps it had been cloaked by the Force.

Another rancor appeared down the pass in the opposite direction, thirty meters away. It had no club but carried a metal shield like the first one the Jedi had encountered. Beside it, on the ground, ran the woman Luke had seen the previous day, she of the Lightning Storm, and the rancor's saddle carried another woman, so like her as to be a sister, though this woman's garments were tan and her dark hair was streaked with bands of white. The woman on the ground looked dismayed; the rancor rider was smiling as though she relished the scrap to come.

Three more women, dressed in a fashion compatible with the others, appeared at each end of the pass, arriving at a dead run, surefooted. Luke felt a tickle in the Force and looked up. A third rancor was now reaching the summit of the hill where the Jedi sat. This beast was riderless and unarmed, but bigger than the other two.

Luke turned to his son. "When I spotted the woman, she didn't have these reinforcements."

"Embarrassing, isn't it?"

"A bit."

"What would one of your old Masters tell you at a time like this?"

"Never mind that now." Luke turned toward the woman they had been following. He called out to her, "A pleasure to meet you at last."

Looking grave, she opened her mouth to reply. But the woman in the rancor saddle above her gestured, and a sudden wind howled along the pass, plucking Ben from his perch and sending him tumbling down the slope.

With a sigh, Luke released the Force technique that was holding him in place and followed his son.

"Hurry, hurry." Leia's tone was urgent.

Han, grim-faced, could not manage any more speed; the airspeeder was at its flat-out maximum. But he could shave off microseconds by taking chances. Veering right and left to avoid the thinning trees, he now came within centimeters of scraping off hull paint against tree bark.

In the seat behind them, Dyon made a strangled noise audible over the engine shriek. Han paid him no mind. The boy clearly needed some excitement in his life. This was it.

They shot past the last of the trees onto rising, rocky ground and topped a low slope. Han's eye was drawn first to the huge rancor standing atop a nearby hill, roaring down into the gap below. "Oh, stang."

Leia shook her head. "The rancors aren't the problem."

"*Rancors?* Plural?"

"There are Witches here."

Their angle of approach brought them in line with the opening into a rocky pass, and Han could suddenly see what Leia was talking about. Farther down the pass, Luke and Ben, the former in white garments, the latter in black, were leaping side-to-side at the bottom of the pass, dodging head-sized rocks swirling around them. The stones were a cyclone of blunt weapons that could easily crush their skulls. A rancor with a rider stood at either end of the engagement zone, accompanied by three or four Witches of Dathomir. The women gestured, clearly keeping the potentially lethal stones moving with their Force spells.

Han angled so their approach was straight toward the pass entrance. The combatants hadn't seen them yet. Perhaps the noise and confusion of the fight would keep them distracted for a few crucial seconds. "We're outmatched."

"Why aren't Luke and Ben using their lightsabers?" Leia held hers at the ready but unlit, her thumb on the ignition button.

The Witches and rancors remained unaware of Han's speeder as he entered the pass. He killed forward thrust, slewed to port, and kicked the repulsors to full strength, skidding the speeder bottom-first toward the nearest group of enemies.

With any lesser pilot, the maneuver would have caused the speeder to slam nose-first into the pass wall, killing everyone on board. Han couldn't see but could feel as his bottom-mounted repulsors went from hammering at empty air to hammering at obstacles. There were shrieks as Witches were abruptly propelled out of the way. The wrong-angle deceleration pressed Han deep into his seat.

Then they came to a sudden, spine-compressing stop. The engines kicked off. In the moment he had before gravity took over, Han decided that only a handful of pilots could have pulled off such a maneuver. Himself, Jaina, Luke, Wedge, Tycho. That was it.

Leia and Dyon leapt free. They went to starboard, which was almost straight up into the sky. Each leapt to a different side of the rancor. Then the speeder fell leftward, sliding down the calves of the rancor legs it had fetched up against, falling two or three meters, and crashed onto the rocky floor of the pass.

Han's breath was jolted from him. But the instincts of a pilot finding himself in a crashed vehicle—*get out, get clear*—took over. Though dazed, he rolled out of and away from the speeder, coming to his feet, off-balance and face-to-face with one of the Witches, a redhead who perhaps looked angrier than any woman Han had seen, Leia excluded.

Someone shot her; a stun bolt took her in the face and she fell out of sight. Who had done it? Oh, that's right, *Han* had; now he saw the blaster pistol in his hand, saw the charge meter click down by one. Leia had insisted that he switch over to stun bolts. He so seldom did that.

Farther up the pass, Luke and Ben were now moving in concert, gesturing to turn back the reduced wave of flying boulders. Ben launched himself through the air, a perfect flying side kick, and took a dark-haired Witch right in the solar plexus. The woman went down.

Closer at hand, Leia, her lightsaber lit, and Dyon, unarmed, leapt right and left, crossing each other as they did, striking at nearby Witches.

The closest rancor turned, roared down at Han, and raised its club.

"Oh, stang." Han crouched, gauged which way would be the best to leap.

A blaster bolt—no stun bolt, and bigger, more explosively powerful than any that came from one of Han's blasters—took the rancor in the center of the chest. The site sizzled and turned black. The rancor, wounded but not impaired, staggered back from the impact and howled again, now looking far past Han.

Han hazarded a look backward. In the distance, just topping the nearest rise, came Yliri's cargo speeder. Beside her on the front seat, half standing, his rifle braced on the windscreen, was Carrack. Sha and Tarth held on for dear life in the backseat.

Han looked up in time to see the rancor bearing down on him, but it was charging the oncoming speeder. Han leapt out of the way. The rancor's furious gait, he saw, was jarring the Witch in its saddle, preventing her from aiming whatever spell she was weaving. As the rancor passed, Han aimed a shot up along its back, hitting the Witch at the base of her spine.

Yliri's speeder headed straight for the oncoming rancor, then sideslipped left and abruptly gained altitude. The rancor swung at it, but the beast's club missed its bottom by meters. The speeder climbed the slope of the leftward hill, toward the larger rancor standing there.

Carrack's second blaster bolt hit that rancor, a forehead shot that staggered the beast. Then Yliri's speeder topped the hill, slewing around in a smuggler's reverse that brought its relative speed to zero. Its left rear panel hit the stunned rancor in the back of the head, a deliberate maneuver, no accident.

The rancor's arms flailed and an almost comic expression of dismay crossed its face. Then it fell down the hill slope toward the pass below, carrying a landslide of rock and scrub with it.

Farther down the pass, Luke gestured as if making an upward palm strike against the empty air. Meters away, the farthest rancor stumbled backward and fell, landing full on its rider.

Ben gestured to Leia, saying something Han couldn't hear. Fresh from having hammered a Witch one–two–three with snap-kicks to the midriff and leveling her, Leia switched off her lightsaber. She flicked it toward Ben, a toss that should have only carried it a meter or two, but the weapon flew straight into his outstretched hand.

Ben ignited it and placed the tip of the glowing blade mere centimeters from the throat of the woman he'd kicked.

And that was the fight.

Chapter Six

THE OFFICE, OUTFITTED WITH RICH, TRADITIONAL WOOD PANELING AND furniture, had a chameleon-like quality Moff Lecersen appreciated. Though it belonged permanently to no Imperial representative and was assigned to any high-ranking official as needed, it was made to be customizable in seconds. The aide of the admiral or general or Moff using it would enter, slide a datacard into the slot on the desk, and the transformation would begin. Holodisplays on the walls would glimmer to life with the VIP's favorite images; for this meeting, Lecersen had chosen vistas of space docks and orbital vessel construction platforms. The datacard would supply information on preferred ambient temperature, scents, white noise, available entertainments, the array of beverages to be stocked in the small cabinet bar, and more. In extremely expensive hotels, the information would also dictate the hue and apparent texture of color-changeable carpets and walls.

All that information took only moments to impart. Then the aide, if he knew what was good for him, would spend the next hour scanning for listening and recording devices. A pity that this task couldn't also be relegated to a datacard.

With the air cooled to his favorite temperature, the walls gleaming with demonstrations of military might in the making, Lecersen smiled a sand panther's smile across his temporary desk at Haydnat Treen, Senator from Kuat. A lean, imposing woman of about eighty standard years, she wore gold-and-brown robes in a very up-to-date Kuati style; her silver-blue hair peeked out from beneath her golden scarf. She held a saucer and cup of very thick, very strong caf with aristocratic grace, and the smile she directed at Lecersen was just like his.

"You'll imagine my surprise," he told her, "when I conducted a private investigation into the recent kidnapping attempt on our Head of State and found no evidence implicating any of the usual suspects."

"The Moffs, you mean?"

"It would be disingenuous of me to say otherwise. Yes, of course. The Moffs."

"Did you look into your own affairs?" Treen asked. "Perhaps this *was* one of your plans, made while you were sleepwalking."

"Well, sleepwalking would explain why it was so crude, so thoroughly botched."

She did not rise to the bait; she merely sipped at her caf.

"So a deeper investigation was warranted." Lecersen continued. "Fortunately, one of the Borleias banks used for the transactions had a duplicate set of books—the second set being the sort one never shows the government—and that had not been so thoroughly scrubbed. The flow of credits led back to a Coruscanti vehicle importer, which led to a Kuati construction firm, which led . . . to you."

"Oh, my. Your accusation positively rends me. I think I'm going to swoon."

"Please do. I know you'll make a graceful display of setting the caf safely aside as you collapse. I look forward to seeing it."

Treen did not swoon, but continued to smile.

"So," Lecersen said, "I have to ask, why does a Senator from Kuat want to kidnap the Imperial Head of State?"

"Well, he's handsome, isn't he?" Treen gave him an admonishing look. "No, truthfully, it's because I want you to be Emperor, of course."

"Ah. I see." Lecersen blinked. That was not the answer he expected. In truth, he had not expected any sort of confession from her. Now that he was getting one, he had to figure out what to do with it; he had no jurisdiction in Kuat or here, and so might have to hand over evidence to the GA authorities.

Unless there really was something in it for him, of course. "No, actually, I don't."

"I'd be happy to enlighten you. Would you accompany me to the Kuat embassy?"

"Would I find myself drugged, with a bag thrown over my head?"

"Of course not. I want our next Emperor to look upon me with gratitude and respect, not irritation. But, please, do bring all the security forces you wish to. Just make sure"—she dropped her voice to a conspiratorial whisper—"you trust them absolutely."

Half an hour later, accompanied by two security men bound to him by debts so profound that he could trust them absolutely—well, nearly absolutely—Lecersen walked with Senator Treen down the marble-lined halls of the Kuat embassy. Arches led to side passages and function rooms, most of them dim and silent. The creamy, blue-veined marble that decorated every surface, Lecersen knew, could, if salvaged and sold, buy him a brand-new Star Destroyer.

"I had been a Senator for one year when Palpatine came to power," Treen told him. "Do you know what his greatest mistake was?"

"Making you angry with him?"

Her smile returned. "In a sense. Oh, the first years of the Empire were glorious. Taxes increased, sadly, but our planetary economy boomed as ridiculous Republic regulations were trimmed away. No, his mistake was in silencing the voices of planetary leaders. It would be like a general suddenly saying that no one of colonel rank or below could ever speak or communicate with him again. When Palpatine suspended the Senate, I knew madness had him in its grip."

"Very interesting," he lied.

She led him and his agents through an arch into a side chamber. The glow rods along its ceiling came on as they entered. The walls were covered with holopanels, each displaying, at five-second intervals, a changing sequence of still recordings of Kuat and the early days of Palpatine's Empire: flotillas of Kuat-built vessels, public appearances by the dark-cloaked Emperor and Darth Vader, the construction of massive complexes.

The Senator heaved a deep sigh. "I miss the Empire—in its original, benevolent form. And I think you can bring it back to us."

"I'm touched by your faith. But kidnapping Jagged Fel would not make me Emperor."

"No, but it would be the first step. And the other steps are mapped out. Masterfully, irresistibly mapped out."

"Tell me."

"First, the Fel boy has to be eliminated because he cannot preside while the Galactic Empire experiences reunion with the Galactic Alliance."

"I would have thought that you'd be opposed to reunification."

"Oh, no. The resurgence of a powerful, healthy Empire depends on it."

"Everything you say is a surprise . . ."

"If the reunification takes place under Fel, then Fel gets the credit. If Fel disappears or dies, his successor gets the credit. And who is more likely to succeed him as Head of State than you?"

"Fair enough. So I'm Head of State, and reunification occurs, and I'm now the *second* most powerful individual in the galaxy—a very distant second behind the Alliance Chief of State."

She nodded amiably, clearly pleased that Lecersen understood. "Now, bear with me. A couple of years ago, Natasi Daala came to power. Wretched woman. We're still suffering from her effects on the Empire."

Lecersen snorted. "Because of her, half the Moffs are women. I have a hard time believing that a Senator from Kuat would object to that."

"I don't, but that would have happened anyway. Eventually, inevitably. I'm talking about this ridiculous compulsion to promote nonhumans far, far past their level of competence. She clearly has no sense. Another reason why Fel must go, of course. Despite his ancestry, he's Chiss on the inside. Not at all human."

"Ah." Lecersen withheld comment. This woman, though speaking the beliefs of millions of traditional Imperials, was beginning to sound more and more like an advertisement for antipsychotic drugs.

"Anyway, Daala has done something useful for us. In the wake of the Second Galactic Civil War, she promoted, and the Senate enacted, the most recent Emergency Powers Act."

"Which gives the Chief of State enormous temporary executive powers that she can use unilaterally . . . but the Senate can, if it disagrees with her, choose to freeze government spending and lock her down tight."

"Not quite." Treen's smile became knowing, confidential. "First, a clause that *I* made sure was included in the final form of the act states that the Chief of State cannot suspend the Senate. Second, it is not the Senate itself that can tie her hands by freezing the budget, it is the Appropriations and Disbursements Committee. When the act is invoked, control of the existing budget goes to them, and they continue to control financial acquisitions and spending."

Lecersen frowned. He was, at last, beginning to sense the shape of Treen's plan. "Wait a moment. You'd need . . ."

"We'd need a majority of the Senators on Appropriations and Disbursements. We'd need the Chiefs of the Armed Forces, who also receive special powers if the act is invoked, and could see to it that the entire budget of the Galactic Alliance went where it needed to . . . so that order was imposed. And we'd need a Chief of State who could be trusted to do the right thing.

"Now, imagine this course of events. Imperial Head of State Fel disappears, or dies, or is deposed. It may take nothing more than catching him in the right circumstances with that Jedi lover of his. Perhaps he's bought her a moon or something. Moff Lecersen becomes the new Head of State, perhaps only temporarily."

Lecersen nodded. "Go on."

"A crisis erupts. Somewhere. I'm working on some useful potential crises. Perhaps you can, too. Advisers placed close to Chief of State Daala recommend invocation of the Emergency Powers Act. Enough pressure, enough anxiety, and she will invoke it. But the situation gets worse and worse, public approval for Daala plummets—I'm working on that, too, and she's giving me all the help she can with this Jedi situation—and ultimately she must resign. A new Chief of State must be appointed, even temporarily. And some of the biggest power blocks in the Galactic Alliance, including Kuat, her allies, and the newly re-turned Empire, have a candidate in mind."

"Haydnat Treen."

"Chief of State Treen, if you please."

"But there's rather a large hole in your plan. Appropriations and Disbursements. And the Chiefs of the Armed Forces."

"A hole? Ahem." She cleared her throat, as loud and obvious as if she were performing on stage.

One of the wall holodisplays, floor-to-ceiling in height, slid aside, revealing a chamber beyond. In the new doorway stood a man.

He was tall and impossibly old. His hair was thin and white, his skin like flimsi stretched tight over bones. He wore a well-tailored suit that did little to conceal the cadaverousness of his build. He walked for-ward at the slow, deliberate pace of a man who did not care that he might be making others wait, and who did care that a misstep might cause a bone-shattering fall.

Reaching Treen and Lecersen, he extended a frail hand to the lat-ter. "Moff Lecersen." His voice was whispery and thin.

"Senator Bramsin." Carefully, Lecersen took the older man's hand and shook it.

Fost Bramsin was the Senator from Coruscant and had been, off and on, for decades. His most recent interruption in service had been during the years Coruscant was undergoing Vongforming during the Yuuzhan Vong War. Since the return of the New Republic to power, he had resumed his Senatorial post, diligently seeing to the orderly and efficient distribution of tax funds throughout the budget.

"I am surprised to see you here," Lecersen continued.

"Pendulums," the old man said.

"Pendulums," Lecersen repeated.

"The last war was a disaster." Bramsin paused, considering his words. "A disaster that would never have happened in an orderly soci-ety. The new government is also a disaster. Imposing ever-tightening controls as Palpatine did in his last years. Enacting reflexive, poorly thought-out laws. It must stop."

"I agree."

"I want to see order—*sensible* order—restored before I die. Are you the one to do it?"

"I believe I am."

"See that you are." Bramsin turned away and began his slow walk back the way he'd come.

"He brings us a majority of the Senators on his committee." Treen's voice was a whisper, one that probably did not carry to the old man's ears.

"What about the military chiefs?"

"We have Starfighter Command and the army. We're working on the navy."

"And—so we're clear, so there are no unspoken assumptions— what do you want? Other than order restored."

"Grand Moff of the Corusca sector. And four dinners with you."

Lecersen suppressed a laugh. "Four? Why not fourteen?"

"Because if, in four dinners, I cannot convince you that you should propose to me, and that I should be the first Empress of the reforged Empire, then I will have to acknowledge that I have failed . . . and that I must be content with just the status and wealth of the galaxy's most powerful Grand Moff." She gave him a familiar pat on the cheek. "You and your men can, I am sure, find your way out." She turned and departed.

Lecersen just stood for a long moment.

This could work.

CHIEF OF STATE'S OFFICE, SENATE BUILDING, CORUSCANT

It left a sour taste in Daala's mouth, but General Jaxton had been right. Rumblings of disapproval were increasing in the armed forces. The situation called for sacrifice. Still, a sense of unease tugged at her as she waited in the hypercomm chamber for her technicians to put the call through, and that unease would not be dispelled, no matter how meticulously she set her organized military mind against it.

The communications officer on duty, a dark-furred Bothan, looked up and caught her eye. "I've reached her assistant." His tone was as neutral and cultivated as that of any Bothan with political aspirations. "They're putting us through now. Ready to go live in five, four, three . . ." He held up the appropriate number of fingers as he counted down, and went silent for the final two numbers, counting them off with fingers alone.

The reception zone of the chamber, a circular open space with holocomm projector antennas directed at it from the ceiling, glowed into life, a swirl of colors, then stabilized into a brilliant three-dimensional picture. Most of the volume of the zone seemed to be occupied by clear blue water; fish, bright yellow with black vertical stripes, darted back and forth in small schools.

In the center of the image floated a Mon Cal female. She was dressed in a simple white robe, a garment better suited to the surface than underwater. Life-sized, she turned slightly to look straight at Daala, regarding her steadily. In her gaze was none of the hostility that Daala usually experienced when dealing with Mon Cals or Quarren, a hostility stemming from her military actions against their planet years ago.

"Admiral Daala." Niathal's voice had the curious, echoing tone characteristic of an underwater speaker. "I am honored."

Daala inclined her head, one peer acknowledging another. "Admiral Niathal. Thank you for taking my call. Is this your home?"

"A quiet spot near my office. When my assistant received your call, he had a portable holocam setup run out to me."

"Very accommodating." Daala knew that she herself did not look anywhere near as calm or rested as Niathal. Dressed in her formal white admiral's uniform, upright with military bearing, brilliantly illuminated by the holocam lights ringing her, she knew she had to look like some grim, glowing supernatural harbinger of danger.

Which she nearly was. She continued, "I also appreciate your agreeing to see my emissary."

"Yes . . . Our appointment is for tomorrow. Which is why it is surprising to hear from you today." Niathal did not sound at all surprised.

"Admiral, at your meeting tomorrow, my emissary will serve you with documents. A subpeona and summons to return immediately to Coruscant."

"To face trial, I should imagine."

Daala nodded. "The principal charges come down to gross dereliction of duty—"

"In that I failed to recognize Colonel Jacen Solo's gradual descent into a pattern of behavior that eventually included genocide and crimes against all sapient species."

"Yes." Daala felt a wash of sympathy for the disgraced officer. She allowed some of that sympathy to show on her face. "I've called, one officer to another, one Chief of State to another, as a show of respect, and because if any of this were to catch you by surprise, it would be . . . inappropriate. I suspect that you'll be able to beat, or at least reduce, the charges. The public can be convinced not to demand blood. What they *will* demand is acknowledgment of mistake."

Niathal sighed. "There we have a problem. Well, I have a problem. Because the actions they find most egregious, my supporting Solo in his efforts as Chief of State, cannot in any way be considered a mistake."

Daala found herself to be startled. "Even now? At the distance of several years?"

"What *is* a mistake, Admiral?" There was a touch of rich, self-aware humor in Niathal's gravelly voice. "It is a decision in which one or more of the factors is known to be dangerous, or poisonous, or compromising, but which we calculate will not keep us from achieving our goals. But when there is no foreknowledge of such factor in evidence, can it be called a mistake? If you walk out on an empty field and the ground suddenly gives way beneath you, and there was no way to predict it, was any part of your decision making a mistake? No." Niathal turned her body side-to-side, a Mon Cal effort to mimic a human head shake. "There was no way to predict that Jacen Solo would become what he became. Therefore, no mistake. And if I do not fight back with a vicious but smooth-tongued lawyer on the one hand, and hang my head and admit to a nonexistent mistake on the other, the public will not forgive. It will have its blood. This trial will be a fiasco, an embarrassment to the navy, a battle that every participant can lose."

"I'm sorry." Daala actually was, but she kept her tone professional, unyielding. "I have no choice."

"But I do."

Daala narrowed her eyes, looking intently at her predecessor. "And what choice do you make?"

"To do exactly as you ask. If you wish me to come to Coruscant, I will."

Daala nodded. "Thank you, Admiral."

"Thank *you*, Admiral. For the advance warning."

Daala glanced at her communications officer. The image of Niathal faded from view, just as the hologram of Daala in all her uniformed brilliance would have faded from the water before Niathal.

Saddened, Daala turned away from the broadcast area and headed back toward her offices, oblivious to her usual retinue of bodyguards and functionaries. Niathal's words had rattled her just a bit, because they were true; in politics, as in military planning, it was possible to do everything right, to make no mistake that could be predicted, and still fail. Still be crushed. And Niathal, if she chose not to play the game of the repentant offender . . .

. . . chose not to *lie* . . .

Would be destroyed.

Chapter Seven

TEN MINUTES AFTER THE FIGHT WAS DONE, THINGS WERE MUCH MORE
settled.

Nine Witches of Dathomir sat or lay on the stony ground, their
hands tied behind their backs—all but the rider of the second rancor,
she of the tan skins and streaked hair, who had sustained a break to her
right forearm when her mount fell on her. Her injured arm had been
splinted by Yliri; she had refused medical treatment from Dyon. She
had not been tied but had been disarmed. The expressions worn by
the Witches ranged from furious to professionally neutral.

The three rancors were huddled farther down the pass, licking their
wounds. The biggest of them was also the most seriously damaged,
with a forehead burn and numberless cuts and scrapes sustained during its tumble down the rocky slope.

Tribeless Sha stood with Han, Leia, Luke, Ben, and Dyon. "They are the Raining Leaves Clan. Very traditional, women in charge. They suffered a disaster about ten years ago, no one of the clan talks about it with outsiders. But we think their senior Witches all died then. We are now well north of their territory; I do not know why they are here."

Luke put on a cheerful expression. "Then let's ask them."

"They will not tell you. Traditional, as I said."

Luke turned and moved toward the captured Witches; the others followed. He stood before the black-haired woman who had been pacing him and Ben all this time, but it was the woman with the broken arm who spoke first: "If you kill us, the rancors will eat you whole. Only our will keeps them at bay."

Luke gave her a look of mild reproach. "I think you know that three rancors are no match for three Jedi, much less the sort of people who travel with Jedi. But thank you for the warning. We actually have no intention of killing you. In fact, this woman"—he indicated the black-haired Witch—"has been very cordial, in a way. Until this ambush, she'd tried several times to dissuade us without harming us."

The woman with the broken arm turned a scornful look on her near twin, as did a lean, blond-haired Witch, whose green-red-yellow diagonally striped hide garments suggested a venomous serpent was their unwilling donor.

Luke continued, "Why did you switch tactics?"

"You would not be dissuaded." The black-haired woman looked regretful. Her voice was throaty and low, like that of a back-alley cabaret singer. "You could not be allowed to proceed."

"Why?"

She did not answer.

Luke sighed. He sat before her. "If we don't talk, we're not going to find common ground. Let's start with introductions. I'm Luke Skywalker."

That got a reaction. The Witches exchanged glances. Pressing his advantage, Luke continued, "And here are Leia and Han Solo, my sister and brother-in-law, and my son, Ben. And, presumably, Han and Leia's escorts."

"I am Kaminne Sihn. I am head of the Raining Leaves Clan." With a nod, she indicated the woman with streaked hair. "My sister,

Olianne, our war-leader." She looked in turn to the woman with the viperous garments and the stoutest Witch. "Halliava Vurse, chief trainer of scouts, and Firen Nuln, trainer of rancors."

Olianne, suddenly urgent, leaned close to her sister. Luke could barely hear her words: "Do not be moved by who they are. It does not matter who they are."

"It does matter." Kaminne's expression became thoughtful. "In a way, these events would not be taking place without Luke Skywalker. I can declare him and his friends counselors."

"Do not."

Luke remained silent. The argument seemed to be leaning in his favor. He decided not to put any influence into the Force; these women might have enough sensitivity to detect manipulation on his part.

Kaminne nodded, decisive. "I so decree." She fixed Luke with a stare. "You may untie us now."

"Thank you. Please continue." Luke made no motion to rise.

"You are now part of this meeting of clans. As counselors, you bear some responsibility for its success or failure. It would not do for you to show up with the leaders of the Raining Leaves in bonds, in your custody."

Luke considered. He sensed no duplicity in the woman's words. She was clearly jockeying with him for power in this situation, but if he kept her as a prisoner, he might do more harm than good.

He looked up at his companions. "Sha?"

Sha moved behind the line of prisoners and, one by one, cut their bonds. While she was about that task, Luke rose and moved a few steps away with his comrades. "You know what I like about coming to worlds so backrocket that no one watches the news broadcasts?"

Han shook his head. "What?"

"No one ever says, *You look taller on the 'Net.* Say, you didn't bring any tools, did you? Replacement circuitry, soldering gear? Our lightsabers are out of commission."

Han nodded. "There's a kit in what's left of my speeder, and I think Carrack, the Friendly Giant, has a kit."

"When we get to a spot where we can camp, Ben and I will get to work."

Kaminne, absently rubbing her wrists, moved up to them. "We will see to the injuries sustained by our rancors, then we can move out."

Luke gave her a smile. "That sounds good."

"You know, from all the stories told of you, I thought you would be taller."

Han's speeder was a lost cause, trampled by the rancor it had hit, damaged beyond any hope of repair. Yliri's was functional, having suffered only minor damage to a rear panel. Luke, mindful of the status and prickly nature of his new Dathomiri associates, elected to ride in the cargo speeder. Its seats and generous cargo bed accommodated the Skywalkers, the Solos, the other offworlders, Sha, and the Sihn sisters. Yliri piloted it at a pace that would not leave the remaining Witches and their rancors behind.

"This gathering is, in a sense, your doing," Kaminne told Luke.

He gave her a surprised look. "How is that? I haven't been here in years."

"But when you did come here, you changed things. That is what they say of Luke Skywalker. Wherever he goes, things change." There was a touch of sadness to Kaminne's voice. She did not look at Luke or even at the rising, hilly terrain in the direction she faced, but into some distant region of the past. "I was a baby when first you came to Dathomir, and your deeds were often spoken of around the fires. Some of the clans experimented with new laws, freeing their menfolk. Later, when you commanded that a Jedi school be raised here, it accepted any who were strong in the Force, not just girls, which was a very different way of doing things."

Luke nodded. Traditionally, the clans of Dathomir were matriarchal and matrilineal, with the males often slaves or little more. "So change came."

"Yes. Not evenly. Not predictably. Sometimes not peacefully."

Luke felt a little prickle of danger, of hostile intent, as a raising of hairs on the back of his neck. He turned and caught Olianne in the act of glaring at him from the rear of the cargo bed. He had the sense that if she had the opportunity to creep up on him with her knife, she'd not just kill him, but skin him as well.

He forced himself to ignore her.

Kaminne, apparently unaware of the exchange of glances between Luke and her sister, continued, "With some clans, the bolder and stronger men would escape and live in small groups out away from the women. This had been going on as long as there have been people on Dathomir, but their numbers increased in the years after your visit. Some of these men would make raids on the clans, striking when there were few or no Witches about, stealing supplies . . . sometimes even stealing mates from among the women who had no powerful arts."

Luke offered her a sympathetic expression. He'd had reports of such events cross his desk in the years when there was a Jedi school here. "You've had reason to suffer from raids like this?"

"Worse. The Raining Leaves remained traditional, old-fashioned, through these times. But ten years ago, there was an uprising by our men. Not all of them, but many. They struck with cunning and ferocity, cutting down the most experienced Witches during the deepest hour of night. No Witch still in our caves survived that night. My mother, my aunts, my oldest sister . . . Some of us were away from the caves, out hunting or on distant errands. Returning, we got wind of the uprising. We used our arts and attacked, cutting down the men. Not one over the age of ten years survived. My father fell, too, even though he was blameless. In a week, we had lost two-thirds of our people and all of our most experienced Witches."

Olianne's voice, mocking and harsh, floated forward from the rear of the speeder. "So what is it like to be a hero, Skywalker? Shall we name our boy-children after you, in your honor?"

Luke turned to regard her again. "I'm sorry for your losses. But I don't teach that sort of violence. The Force doesn't encourage it. It was a desire for vengeance, a dark emotion, that prompted both your slaughters . . . not me."

"He is right, Olianne." Kaminne stared at her sister until Olianne dropped her gaze, and Luke could finally see some of the quiet strength of character that Kaminne had to possess to be chief of this clan.

Kaminne turned forward again. "That was the start of the hard years. Relearning years. There were man-tribes out there that were actually larger than the Raining Leaves, and stronger. But there was also one man-tribe that did not attack, that was willing to trade, and eventually more than trade. The Broken Columns." Kaminne's expression softened. "Over the years, we have come to a new custom. Each year the two clans convene north of Redgill Lake. We camp in each other's company. We stay a month. Marriages are made, marriages that last a year. The next year, when the two clans convene, we give the boy-children over a certain age to their fathers and introduce the girls to them, so that they might know their kin."

"And this is where you are going now." Luke thought it over. "No wonder you didn't want outsiders along."

"It is more than that. This year, we convene to negotiate another kind of marriage—a marriage of clans. Raining Leaves and Broken Columns becoming one. If we can come to terms, I will marry Tasander Dest, their chief, and it will be a marriage of more than just a year."

"Tasander Dest." Luke frowned. "Surely that's not a Dathomiri name."

"Hapan. The Hapans have had a compound on Dathomir for many years. Their old Queen Mother was Dathomiri, and their current one is half Dathomiri. Tasander was brought here as a boy by his father and chose to stay when his father left."

Leia, sitting on Luke's far side, leaned in. "Do you have any children? By Dest or another Broken Column?"

Kaminne shook her head. "For years I could not. It is a problem that runs in my family, except in my mother. Olianne, too, is childless. But when we began talks of this union with the Broken Columns, I went to the doctor at the spaceport. She said it was a reversible condition and gave me medicines."

"I was going to recommend that, but you're ahead of me."

Kaminne shook her head. "We are not stupid. Ours is a hard life, but it is one we choose, not one we are just too foolish to avoid. When our spells are insufficient, we find other ways. Some of our warriors have blasters now and know how to use them. We have comlinks and beacons. Changes, all changes brought on since you first came here."

Leia smiled at her. "I know about changes. Some are bad, some are good, and when you look back on your life, you will probably approve of the ones you yourself brought on." She leaned back in her seat.

Luke decided to change the subject. "My son and I are looking for a girl, not Dathomiri, who crashed her ship somewhere north of the spaceport." He felt Ben, back in the cargo bed tinkering with Han's tool kit and his lightsaber, perk up.

Kaminne's face became blank, a sabacc player's neutral expression. "Yes. Vestara is her name. She is with the clan."

"We need to take her back." Luke glanced skyward, suggesting a return to space.

"Oh. How many of us are you willing to kill to do this?"

"Kill? We have no intention of killing anyone."

"You have no authority here. You may not just take her. She will not want to go with you. She is *with the clan* now—Olianne mentors her and may choose to adopt her."

"Oh." There was a sinking feeling in Luke's gut. All of a sudden they knew where their quarry was . . . and she was, in a sense, farther away than ever. "Well, perhaps she'll be willing to talk to us."

"Perhaps."

QUARTERS OF CHIEF OF STATE NATASI DAALA, SENATE BUILDING, CORUSCANT

A chime woke Daala—three mellow, musical sounds—and her eyes snapped open. The alarm always awoke her the first time it sounded; as with most military lifers, she slept very lightly.

But this wasn't her preset morning alarm. The musical notes indicated a live communication from Wynn Dorvan, and that meant something urgent was up. She cleared her throat to make sure she did not sound sleepy or raspy. "Speak."

"You have a priority communication from Elyas Caran." Dorvan's voice was unusually subdued.

Elyas Caran was the emissary Daala had sent to Mon Calamari. She checked her chrono and did some quick math. It would be midmorning in the time zone where Admiral Niathal lived, so Caran would have been in the admiral's company for half an hour or so. A live holocomm message from him did not bode well. "Is there some reason you can't pipe the transmission into my chambers?"

"I don't think you want it transmitted anywhere yet. I think you need to see it full-sized, in the comm center, before anyone outside your staff does. We need to be thinking about how to respond." The faint hiss of comm transmission vanished as Dorvan ended the call.

Daala was up in an instant. This was not like Dorvan, and this was not good.

Dressed in tan sweat garments suited to a workout and a blue robe, Daala walked into the communications chamber where, a day earlier, she'd spoken with Niathal. The reception area was already showing the live transmission from Mon Calamari. Two steps in, she began to understand what she was seeing. Her pace slowed as she approached the wavering three-dimensional image.

Elyas Caran, a lean, graceful man dressed in pearl-gray and blue garments cut like a military dress uniform, had elegant features creased with middle-aged lines and a shock of jet-black hair that suggested he was a much younger man. Daala knew he dyed his hair; she didn't know whether this was from vanity or a diplomatic urge to suggest vitality. Caran stood in the foreground of the transmission image.

The background was dominated by a water tank, three meters high, its floor-to-ceiling transparisteel surface curved. The water within was a beautiful green-blue.

In the center of the tank was Cha Niathal. She wore her admiral's uniform. Her eyes were open and fixed. She was not entirely unmoving; little invisible eddies in the water stirred her uniform, caused her arms and legs to sway oh so slowly. The skin of Niathal's face and hands was a curious color, more reddish than the previous day, and Daala wondered distractedly if the hypercomm's color correction was set correctly.

Clearly, Niathal was dead. Daala felt a sudden ache, as though she'd swallowed a sharp rock and it had gotten lodged halfway down her throat.

Caran took a deep breath as if bracing himself for the bad news he was delivering. "It was done sometime this morning. When I arrived, her assistant came in to tell her I was present . . . and found her in this state." He gestured up at the top of the tank, toward something the holocam did not include in its image. "She apparently ran a gas feeder line into her tank. Carbon monoxide. A painless method."

"Did she . . . did she leave any indication as to why?" Daala knew the reason. She knew why she herself might have done exactly the same thing if she had been in Niathal's position. Any protracted legal defense would harm her extended family, the navy. But Daala had to know what words Niathal might have left, since they would be the last expression of Niathal's legacy.

Caran offered Daala a smile of mixed sympathy and sadness. "She left a note."

"Read it, please."

The diplomat did not fetch out a datapad or a piece of flimsi. He quoted it from memory. "'This has been done with honor, without error, and by my choosing. Niathal out.'" He glanced down at the floor, a moment's reflection.

The stark simplicity of those words seemed to make the stone in Daala's throat grow larger and sharper. She ignored the pangs. For now.

Caran met her gaze again. "What do you . . . want done?"

"Bring her here. Let those who asked for her blood see what they have achieved." *And,* she told herself, *we will see who is sorry and who rejoices, the better to know our enemies.* "Then we'll return her to Mon Calamari for a funeral with full military honors."

"I'll make it so."

The image wavered more sharply and then disappeared.

Shaken, but unwilling to let anyone recognize the fact, Daala spun on her heel and marched from the communications center, not making eye contact with anyone there. Once in the hall, she couldn't entirely keep the tears from coming. With a casual gesture, she dashed them from her eyes and continued, stiff-backed and stone-faced, to her quarters.

Chapter Eight

IT TOOK ALLANA SEVERAL HOURS TO FIGURE OUT HOW TO ESCAPE THE *Falcon*.

Some of her plans, she eventually acknowledged, would not have worked very well. Such as hiding in the *Falcon*'s smuggling compartments until C-3PO panicked, assumed that she'd escaped, and lowered the boarding ramp to go look for her, whereupon she would make a dash for the ramp and run past him, laughing. The problem with that one was that it might take hours for the droid to notice her absence, and hours more of searching before that moment of panic came, and in all that time she'd need food, drink, entertainment, and refresher breaks.

Instead, after failing to conceive of an escape plan that might work, she eventually hit on the notion of playing one of the ship's instructional programs, one that taught correct ship maintenance procedures. It was in that ancient Corellian Engineering Corporation ship's-tour tutorial, in less than an hour, that she was reminded of the tiny lift that gave mechanics access to the topside hatch and the equipment on the *Falcon*'s top hull. Minutes later she confirmed that C-3PO, having also forgotten about that exit, had not programmed it to ignore her commands.

As the shadows began stretching across the spaceport grounds, Allana sneaked herself and Anji into a storage compartment, found a coil of flexible cable, and took it to the tiny lift. She waited until she was sure that she could hear the droid's puttering and monologue commentary emerging from the far side of the ship, and she activated the lift. As she'd hoped, it smoothly carried her and the nexu upward, the top hatch opening before them, and in a moment they stood atop the *Falcon*, staring at Dathomir's sun as it began to dip, oversized and golden, below the western horizon.

She wrinkled her nose. Rain forest smelled bad. Her other grandmother really came from *here*?

Now was the scary part. She tied one end of her cable to a strut, adding hitch after hitch to her knot because she knew her rope-tying skills were not very good, and then dropped the remainder of the coil over the side. She leaned over to look. The ground seemed a long way down. But Anji just took one look and jumped, landing on the ground as lightly as . . . well, a nexu.

Allana focused her attention on Anji and thought, *Sit.* Anji yawned and stamped her feet, waiting. Close enough. Allana took a moment to make certain she remained undetected. There was someone in that skinny ship on the other side of the *Jade Shadow* standing in the hatch—a tall man and his lady friend, Allana thought—but they were in the shadows and it was hard to tell whether they were looking in her direction.

When she did not hear anyone's voice raised in alarm, she grabbed the cable, sat down on the hull, and scooted along until her legs dangled over the edge. Then, alarm and excitement mixing in her, she allowed herself to slide over the edge, repositioning her hands so they would not scrape across the hull's edge, until all her weight was supported by her hands.

Well, that wasn't good. That was a lot of work. She was strong for

her size, and had been encouraged to exercise by her very active
grandparents, but she wondered if she would actually be able to climb
all the way back up.

It didn't matter. If she couldn't get back into the *Falcon* on her
own, she'd just have to alert C-3PO and face the music that much
sooner.

She half climbed, half slid down the cable, gasping as a slide of too
great a distance seemed to cut into her palms. Then, suddenly, she was
standing on the ground next to Anji, her arms a little tired.

She looked at her palms. They had been abraded almost shiny by
the cable, but there was no blood. She felt soreness but not real pain.
She looked up at the mountainous height she had descended,
shrugged, and turned to look out over the spaceport.

It was darker now than before. Lights were coming on atop many
of the permacrete domes in the compound. A smell of cooking food,
some sort of meat being roasted, drifted her way from one of them,
and her mouth watered.

How would Grandpa Han find R2-D2? He'd rely on instincts,
meaning that he'd go toward whichever place looked most interesting.
Allana had met very small children who thought that way, and she
wondered how Han managed to win at so many things when he
thought like a small child. She wasn't sure it would work for her.

Jaina's boyfriend Jag talked about methodology and grid patterns,
which were just grown-up terms for making sure you looked at everything in order. She looked around, mentally dividing the grounds into
quarters, and wondered which pie-slice to start with.

And, oh yes, there was the Force, which Leia, Jaina, and Allana's
real mommy used all the time. She wondered if the Force would tell
her anything. She was a little frightened of it, since it had led her to
where a scary thing had talked to her on Kessel. But R2-D2 was missing, and she wasn't willing to be frightened right now.

She thought about R2-D2, how she missed her astromech friend
and how everyone would miss him worse if he never came back. Then
she turned due north and began walking toward the domes in that direction. Anji quickly padded out ahead of her and disappeared into the
shadows. Allana wasn't worried. She could still feel Anji in the Force,

and she knew that Anji wouldn't stray very far from her. After all, Allana was Anji's friend, and friends didn't run off into the jungle without each other.

NORTH OF REDGILL LAKE, DATHOMIR

The odd grouping of one cargo speeder, three mounted rancors, and four Witches on foot rounded a spur of Redgill Lake just as dusk was settling. Spread out before Luke and his party was a large encampment, a gathering of nearly two hundred individuals in two distinct areas separated by a few meters of unoccupied ground.

Luke's party had, of course, passed by several hidden sentries on their way here, especially in the last few kilometers. Luke had felt them out there, concealed, observant. So had Kaminne, and she had offered hand signs, a different one at each location, and Luke's party had passed unmolested.

Now, as they came within a hundred meters of the encampment, curious Witches from the near portion of the camp and equally interested men from the northern portion moved their way. Luke could sense suspicion and even hostility, especially from the women.

And one touch of alarm, quickly suppressed. He looked back and forth, trying to pinpoint its source, but could not; it had vanished before he could get a fix on it. He altered his perceptions and could feel his own blood among the people, but in the thick of the crowd it was impossible to pinpoint its exact location. Still, he had reason to be certain that the Sith girl was nearby, watching.

Kaminne sprang forward from her seat to land on the hood of the cargo speeder. She spoke loudly, projecting like a trained orator. "I bring good words. The men who have been following the trail of the sisters of Raining Leaves are not enemies. I have met them and now bring them before you as counselors to this conclave. You have all heard the name of Luke Skywalker. It is he who sits behind me."

A murmur of voices rose from the assembling crowd, and Luke felt the emotions shift—the suspicion did not exactly diminish, but it was joined by interest and curiosity.

"With him is his son, Ben, and they have been joined by the lady Leia Solo, her mate, Han, and others. I have granted them safe passage among us." She looked down at Yliri and gestured for the Corellian woman to guide the speeder to a spot a few meters from the waterline, near one of the campfires.

Han sighed. "So I'm just 'her mate.'"

Leia gave him an innocent smile. "Always have been. Fetch me something good to eat, would you, mate? And then you may treat yourself to a few drippings of soup."

Carrack gave Han a sour look. "Hey, at least you got a name. Me, I'm just 'others.'"

The speeder grounded where Kaminne indicated. Its occupants piled out and were quickly surrounded by curious Dathomiri. Kaminne stayed atop the hood and offered an abbreviated account of her efforts to lead the Skywalkers astray before she realized who they were. Luke, for his part, smiled, shook hands with those few Dathomiri who came forward to meet him, and kept his attention open for the Sith girl.

She was out there, at a greater distance than before, in the densest part of the Raining Leaves crowd.

A man moved through the crowd toward them, distinct from the others because of his height—he stood eye-to-eye with Han—and his features, which were exceptionally handsome, ideally suited to the stage or to holodramas. Some of the Raining Leaves women before him moved out of his path only grudgingly, resentfully. As he came close, Luke could make out blond hair, eyes the same blue as Redgill Lake when they had first spotted it a couple of hours ago, and garments that were an odd mix of Dathomiri hide vest and boots combined with offworld trousers in a distinctly civilized shade of purple.

Luke extended a hand. "Tasander Dest, I assume."

"Master Skywalker." Dest's voice was flavored with the refined accent of the Hapan noble families. "A pleasure to meet you at last." His attention wandered to the speeder hood, where Kaminne now told of the scrap between the Witches and the offworlders in the pass. Her tone made it sound as though the exchange had been a romp rather than a potential tragedy.

"Kaminne told us what this gathering was for." Luke gestured across the group. "You have some interesting challenges ahead of you."

"So do you, if you're here for anything other than watching tribal customs. The clans have not changed their ways much since you first came to this planet."

Luke shrugged. "So how do we get them to open up?"

Dest smiled, an expression that exposed what seemed to be a broad panorama of perfect teeth. "The Games start tomorrow. Win some of them. You gain respect, others will talk to you. I'll be competing. Beat me at something . . . if you can." The good cheer in his manner seemed to rob that statement of all the arrogance that should have come with it.

Half an hour later, once Luke's party was settled down at a new camp-fire of its own, Kaminne led Luke and Ben across the campgrounds to a dark patch of ground near a stand of trees.

"Nice place for an ambush," Ben told her.

Luke gave his son an admonishing look, but Kaminne merely smiled. "I only plan one ambush a day. And today's was not so success-ful."

With the mood eased, Ben changed the subject. "I know this is your family business, but it also relates to what my father and I are doing here, so I was sort of hoping to ask a question."

Kaminne's expression went from amused to neutral, unreadable. "Go ahead."

"Why has your sister taken such a stong interest in the Sith girl? She's known her for, what, a day or two and is already considering adopting her?"

Kaminne didn't answer immediately. Clearly she was considering her answer, deliberating how much to tell, how much to withhold. "A few months ago, Olianne's only child, Sesara—she was eight—died of a fever. When Vestara stumbled out of the forest, helpless, nearly in a state of collapse, into the midst of Olianne's hunting party, and all but fell into Olianne's arms, something about her plight touched my sis-ter's heart. It is as simple as that."

Luke exchanged a look with his son. Ben's thoughts were so easy to read at this moment, no skill in the Force was called for. *What an interesting coincidence that Vestara should first find the clan member who might be most sympathetic to her situation. But was that a matter of luck . . . or foreknowledge?*

From ahead, they could hear conversation—just the rise and fall of speech, two female voices, resolving within moments into comprehensible words. The first voice was recognizable as Olianne's: ". . . not have to speak with them."

The second voice was lighter, younger. "I want to."

"You were running from them before."

"I was alone before. Now I am among family."

The voices stopped. Luke knew that neither he, Ben, nor Kaminne had made noise on their approach, but Olianne and the Sith girl probably had very acute senses.

And Luke could see them now, Olianne's outline with her distinctive hair illuminated by moonlight, a slighter, leaner silhouette standing beside her. As they came within a couple of meters of the two women, Luke got a clear look at the girl without environment suits or attempted murder getting in the way.

She was a teenager, about Ben's age or a trifle younger, slender, with long straight hair that looked as though, out of the moonlight, it would be a light brown. Her eyes were dark. There was no fear or apprehension on her face; in fact, she seemed to be wearing a half smile until Luke realized that the expression was an illusion, caused by the small scar at the corner of her mouth.

Luke gave Olianne a courteous nod. "Could we have some time alone with this young woman?"

"No."

Luke restrained a sigh. "Very well." He gestured toward the ground. "Shall we sit?"

Kaminne did, followed by Luke and Olianne. The teenagers were last to take their seats.

"I'm Luke Skywalker. This is my son, Ben."

"I know." The girl gave a little shrug. "I am Vestara Khai."

"And you are a Sith."

"I . . . was."

Luke raised a brow. "You are no longer."

"Now I am Raining Leaves."

"Then if you've chosen to abandon your Sith ways, you wouldn't mind telling us all about your former life."

Vestara's illusory smile became real. "No matter how I regard myself now, my friends are my friends and my kin are my kin. Shall I tell you all about them, so you can go to them and slay them?"

Luke shook his head, dismissing her protest. "All it takes to do evil is to stand aside while others do it—when a single word from you could have stopped it."

"It's also hard to talk of them without, in some sense, calling to them. Summoning them. Do you want me to summon them to this place?"

"Yes." Luke kept his voice matter-of-fact. "If that's what it takes."

"I do not wish Olianne hurt. Not her, not my new clan."

"She's lying." Ben's tone was exasperated. Luke did not have to look at his son to know that Ben was rolling his eyes.

Luke wanted to tell his son, *Of course she's lying. Yet you can learn almost as much from the lies as you can from the truth.* But he did not. Instead, he let Ben feel a flash of irritation, and outwardly ignored his son's interjection. "For one who is anxious to be free of the Sith, you fought alongside your companion with exceptional dedication."

"Of course I did! To do any less than your best effort at any time is to invite punishment. Is it not so with your Jedi?"

Luke ignored the question. "What can you tell us of your homeworld?"

"Nothing."

"And your plans, your aims? Whatever brought you to the Maw cluster in the first place?"

Vestara shrugged. "Nothing." Vestara leaned toward Luke. "Just let me be. Let me stay among the Raining Leaves. Stop chasing me."

"Where did you crash your yacht?"

She blinked as if surprised to be asked a question she could choose to answer. "It was in the middle of the jungle. I don't know where. All the instrumentation was out. After the crash, I wandered for hours before Olianne found me."

"Where's your lightsaber?"

"It was in my cabin when I began my landing run. When the crash happened . . . there was nothing left of the cabin. I couldn't find any sign of my gear."

"Are you done?" Olianne did not sound so much worried for Vestara as annoyed with Luke.

Luke considered his answer, but Ben spoke first. "Olianne, this girl is a Sith, and that means she's pure evil. She's like a thermal detonator rolling around your camp waiting to go off. When she does, you and all your clan—"

"Evil?" Vestara practically sputtered the word. "Being Sith has nothing to do with good or evil, any more than being Jedi does."

Ben glared at her, outraged. "How can you say that? People become Sith and they do nothing but evil—"

"Oh, I suppose that explains your Jacen Solo, whom we have heard of—"

"It does. He was Sith."

"He was Jedi, and you know it!"

"He became Sith," Ben insisted.

"Be quiet." Luke spoke softly, but put some extra emphasis on his words through the Force. All four of those near him leaned away as he spoke.

He returned his attention to Vestara, but Olianne spoke first. "Not these Jedi nor any Sith can take you away from us. You need feel no fear." She leaned over to embrace Vestara.

Knowing that they were not likely to glean anything more that night, Luke rose, gave the Dathomiri women a little bow, and led Ben back toward the offworlders' campfire.

Once they were far enough away that the women could not hear them, Ben, irritated, kicked a stone. "She's playing them. Like they're a sabacc deck. A children's sabacc deck."

Luke gave his son a disapproving look. "She played *you* exactly the same way. She drew you into an argument that was all emotion, no logic. And since she's Sith and you're Jedi, that means she won hands-down."

Ben was silent for a long moment. Then he kicked another rock. "Yeah. I know."

DATHOMIR SPACEPORT

Spying, Allana concluded, was mostly boring.

In the holodramas, a spy would hide herself where she could watch an important door, and a minute would pass, and something would happen at that door, and the spy would have an Important Clue.

But here, though she hid herself well among hedges that gave her a good view of the front door of one of the domes, a minute could turn into fifteen or thirty without anything happening. Anji would come back and curl at her feet and fall asleep. Allana would wait some more, then finally grow frustrated. She'd get up and trot to another vantage point . . . and wait there for an endless amount of time in which she learned nothing.

Well, not *nothing*. She learned that the dome nearest to where the *Falcon* and *Jade Shadow* were parked was a communications center. She could have guessed that by all the antennas, including hypercomm antennas, that crowded its roof, but it was good to catch a glimpse of the dome's interior through a briefly opened door and see lots of comm equipment and one bored-looking man about Ben's age yawning on duty there.

Another dome, the largest, turned out to be a hostel. People wandered in and out all the time, and through the constantly opening door Allana could see a cramped lobby like many she had visited. It was from this dome that all the intriguing food smells emerged.

It occurred to her that if R2-D2 had been looking for a yacht, he wouldn't find it in a hostel.

That gave her something to think about. A space yacht would only be parked in some kind of dome. Not in a restaurant, not in a playground, not in a hall of records.

She decided to wander past the front doors of all the domes and read the signs this time. And it was the fourth sign she read, affixed to one of the largest of the domes, that bore the words, MONARG'S MECHANIC WORKS.

She set herself up a little nest among a stack of two-hundred-liter hydraulic fluid drums, waited half an hour, and sighed. Spying was dull. She hoped she'd find R2 soon.

The viewports of the dome were, at their bottom rims, about four meters above the ground, far too high for her to see into. But she gave the fluid drums around her an experimental push. They moved easily; they were clearly empty. Of plastoid construction, they were also very light.

Her heart racing, she picked up and carried a drum to the dome, carefully placing it directly beneath one of the viewports a quarter of the way around the dome's circumference from the door. Scrambling atop it was no challenge, but she was still too low to see in. So she brought up another, placing it flush against the first one, and brought a third. That one took some work, because she had to lift it to rest atop the other two.

Now she could scramble up, and as she stood, wobbling, atop the third drum, she could peer in through the viewport.

Most of her view was blocked by a curtain, but it was tattered. There were holes and gaps she could see through.

She saw the gray tail end of a yacht. It looked a lot like Uncle Lando's, but older and more beaten-up.

There were droids all over the place, small spindly ones. Most of them did not walk on legs; they glided around on wheeled tripod rigs. Most seemed to be rolling trays or racks for tools and parts; each had two skeletal arms and a sensor station where a head should be, and stood about a meter and a half tall.

There was a man present. Allana did not see him at first; he moved into her field of view from someplace along a wall. He was tall and gaunt, wearing a stained gray jumpsuit. When he turned to track and speak to one of the rack droids, Allana saw that he had a patch over his left eye.

There was no sign of R2-D2, but along one wall in the shadow of the yacht was a blue drop cloth draped over something that could have been an astromech droid. It did not move, and Allana was struck with the sudden worry that her droid friend was hurt or dead. She'd have to find out.

"Miss Amelia? May I inquire, where are you?" C-3PO's voice seemed to erupt from the pocket where Allana kept her comlink.

Allana ducked. Even as she did so, she saw the man's head begin to turn up in her direction.

She hadn't heard much noise from within the dome; even a hydrospanner dropped on the permacrete floor had barely been loud enough for her to hear. So the man probably hadn't heard much of C-3PO's voice. But Allana was suddenly afraid and didn't want to count on that. She scrambled down the drums as fast as she dared and ran to hide among the drums she hadn't moved. Then, finally, she activated her comlink. "I'm right here," she whispered.

"Here, where, precisely?"

Should she tell C-3PO now? No, she needed to do that once she could trick him into coming with her. Which might mean tomorrow. "I'm playing hide-and-seek."

"Ah. Am I to find you, then?"

"Yes. But don't hurry. I have to, uh, hide better. Count to a thousand."

"Very well."

The door into the dome had not opened. Her heart in her throat, Allana sneaked back to the dome and carefully brought the three drums to their places in the stack, then raced across the spaceport grounds to the *Falcon*.

The climb up was twice as hard as she had imagined, and if she'd had to do it with arm strength alone, instead of shimmying with both arms and legs, she never would have made it. When she got to the top, Anji gave a little yowl from the ground behind her. Allana peered back over the edge and frowned. She hadn't thought about how her nexu was going to get back onto the *Falcon*.

But Anji was determined not to be left outside. She cocked her head and studied the rope for a moment, then extended her claws and began to climb up just like Allana had. If her claws hadn't been safety-dulled, she probably would have made it a lot quicker than Allana had. As it was, Anji's feet kept slipping until she learned to catch the knots between her toe pads, and then she clambered right up. Within a few minutes Allana was hauling the coil of cable up to the top hull, standing on the tiny lift, and descending into the *Falcon*.

C-3PO found her as she was preparing for a sanisteam. "I say. You aren't hidden at all well."

"I got sweaty and bored. I'm going to clean up."

"Excellent idea. And I'll prepare you a nice snack for afterward. For being so cooperative today."

She just smiled at him.

Chapter Nine

WITH HER FORK, DAALA PUSHED SOME BITS OF FOOD AROUND ON HER plate, silently cursing her chef. The man was as good a personal chef as any government leader might need, but his choice of seafood for tonight's meal was a grotesque reminder of Admiral Niathal's suicide. Daala took a moment to calm down, to remind herself that her chef was not in the loop of government secrets, could not have known about the hypercomm transmission Daala had seen with Niathal's body so prominently displayed.

She pushed her plate away and gave her dinner companion a look of apology. "I'm sorry. I'm not very good company tonight."

Nek Bwua'tu, Chief of Naval Operations for the Galactic Alliance, a gray-furred Bothan, gave her a lupine smile in return. "The Chief of State does not need to apologize for having troubled thoughts. Only if your conscience were as easy as a cub's would I be suspicious and worried."

"Can we talk business?"

"Yes. Particularly if it will help."

"Have you heard any recent, I'm not sure what to call them, rumblings among naval personnel suggesting that I'm not being tough enough on enemies of the state?"

Clearly not disturbed by, or not recognizing, any resemblance between his dinner and a recent topic of conversation, Bwua'tu speared a well-grilled cephalopod on the tines of his fork and popped it into his mouth, chewing as he considered his answer. "Yes," he finally told her. "In the last few months, there has been more grumbling. About the Jedi especially. Colonel Solo, Pellaeon's killer, and most recently about the crazy Jedi."

"And what do you think?"

"I think that some sort of special-interest group is keeping those flames burning high. I don't object to the Jedi being brought in line, you know that, but I don't believe that they're as far out of line as the grumblers are saying. I think they're basically a beneficial force with the Alliance's interests at heart."

"But whatever the reason for the grumbling, if it continues to grow, it could damage this administration's efficiency."

"Conceivably."

"Niathal's death was a tragedy. But speaking pragmatically, it also deprives us of the relief of pressure that her trial—and eventual acquittal—would have offered. I'm going to need to take some very visible steps to do that. To reassure the grumblers."

Bwua'tu offered her a noncommittal grunt.

"You don't think so?"

"I don't have the sense of what it takes to ride herd over a huge, mostly civilian government, and simultaneously over different departments of the armed forces, the way you do. The way you've learned to since you became Chief of State. I hear grumbling, my thought is to tell them to pipe down and do their jobs. Are you contemplating a move on the Jedi?"

It took some of Daala's considerable self-discipline to refrain from twitching. Again Bwua'tu seemed to have peered into her thoughts. Of course, he was a master military strategist, her superior in that capacity, but it was still unsettling. "Yes."

"I recommend against it."

"Why?"

"I think there's a risk of alienating them, as Colonel Solo did. We want the Jedi to be a well-integrated Alliance resource. Too much pressure, too much overt action, runs the risk of turning them into a completely uncooperative element."

"You wouldn't offer that advice about, say, an elite military unit."

He shook his head. "No, I wouldn't. But then, commandos don't usually have super powers or a tradition that goes back to the very beginnings of the Old Republic."

"But it's commandos the civilian population should admire and respect. More than they do the Jedi." She frowned, considering.

Bwua'tu grinned again. "You're going to use the Mandos, aren't you? To send against the Jedi!"

Daala's voice turned sharp, as if Bwua'tu's mind-reading exercises had been meant to hurt her feelings. "Now, cut that out."

"If you wish."

Finally, she smiled at him. "Sorry. I'm just touchy. Are you staying tonight?"

"If the invitation's open."

"You know it is."

JEDI TEMPLE, CORUSCANT

Kyp Durron swept into the Masters' Council Chamber, moving so fast that his robes gapped open at the front and swirled around his feet like a cloak. He didn't hate being late, but he did hate people thinking he was lazy. At such times, speed was called for.

As he entered the Chamber and began to make his way toward his designated chair, he saw that a hologram of Jaden Korr, a live hypercomm transmission, was in the process of addressing the assembly. Korr, a man of Coruscant and onetime apprentice of Kyle Katarn, was far too serious for Kyp's taste, but had conducted a long and impressive career as a Jedi Knight.

Korr was saying, ". . . evidence is not overwhelming, but it is growing, and continues to point to a resurgence by the Black Sun. And there are odd elements to it, such as graffiti found in garbage dumped by the hijacked ships, graffiti that suggests the existence of some sort of cult . . . one that venerates Xizor."

That drew some murmurs from the assembled Jedi. Prince Xizor, a member of the Falleen species and head of the Black Sun criminal organization forty years earlier, was long dead . . . or, at least, long believed dead.

Master Kenth Hamner asked the question that leapt to everyone's mind. "Is there any chance that Prince Xizor is still alive?"

Korr's hologram shrugged. "I've seen no evidence of it. Zero evidence. But if any *piece* of him survived, and some sort of Black Sun cultists got their hands on a cloning chamber . . ."

"Yes, yes." Master Hamner seemed unimpressed with the theory. "Check it out, of course. Do you have all the resources you need?"

"For now."

"Very good. Thank you, Jedi Korr. Temple out."

Korr's image wavered and disappeared.

Hamner turned back toward the main body of Jedi and picked out one by eye. "Jedi Saar. Do you have a report on your ongoing investigation?"

"I do." Sothais Saar, the man who came forward at Hamner's summons, was a Chev—outwardly human in appearance but albinoid. He was tall for a Chev, with blue eyes not commonly found in his species, but his heavy brow was characteristic of his kind. His hair, cut short, was black on top but lightened in an even manner farther down so that it was a light brown at his temples and down to the back of his neck. He wore dark robes that were stylishly cut by contrast with conservative Jedi tastes, and as he stepped out in front of the chairs to face Hamner, he hooked his thumbs in his belt like a backworld advocate ready to argue a case before a jury. "My task for the last several months has involved assembling a comprehensive report, as comprehensive as circumstances allow, on the subject of slavery as it is practiced in the galaxy, both officially in regions not controlled by the Galactic Alliance and unofficially within certain less regulated regions of the GA." He spoke with the voice of an advocate or natural politician.

"I won't bore this assembly with a recitation of numbers, but I will discuss trends. In regions such as Hutt-controlled space, slavery of members of sapient species continues unabated. And since, in the last several years, the Jedi Order has increasingly acknowledged its definition as a force benefiting the Old Republic and its successor states, our efforts to diminish slavery outside the Galactic Alliance have decreased in number and effectiveness. While we jockey with the GA government over issues related to use of GA resources outside GA borders, slave populations that once thought of the Jedi Order as their last hope now increasingly face the disappointing realization that they are being left to their own fates . . ."

Kyp tuned him out. Kyp was far from indifferent to the young Jedi's cause; he'd been a slave miner himself decades ago, on Kessel. He would be happy to go anywhere and practice "aggressive negotiation" on slavers. He just wasn't as interested in paying close attention to a speech that seemed less about informing the Jedi and more about irritating Kenth Hamner, who was in charge of the Order at this politically conservative time.

Kyp felt someone moving toward him. He looked up to find Jaina leaning against the back of his chair.

She pitched her voice as a whisper. "Xizor, huh? Why is it that dead enemies can't be content to remain dead?"

Kyp shrugged. "I'll ask Exar Kun the next time we're out drinking together."

"Funny man."

". . . full text of my report, titled *An Inquiry on Surviving Slavery Practices in the Aftermath of the Second Galactic Civil War,* is available in the Temple Archives. That's the simple version; I'll have the annotated and cross-indexed version available in about three weeks."

Hamner's voice was inexpressably weary. "Thank you, Jedi Saar, for your extravagant efforts on this cause. We certainly recommend that everyone acquire and familiarize themselves with your report." He took another look around, spotted Kyp, and abruptly straightened. "This concludes the primary portion of this meeting. The continuation of this meeting is limited to Masters and those we have asked to remain behind."

As one, the Jedi Knights and apprentices not among the invitees rose and began to file from the Chamber. Jaina remained.

Master Hamner waited until the last of those departing had passed beyond the Chamber door. He pressed a button on his chair arm, and the door slid into place and locked. "Master Durron, report readiness."

Kyp cleared his throat. "Our StealthX squadrons are currently at seventy-two percent operational readiness. By current estimates, in two days they'll be at ninety-one percent, which is likely to be a peak. To get a better proportion of fully operational Exes, we'd need to lay out credits in such a way that the government and press couldn't possibly not notice."

"This one says we launch now. Let the other percentages join us in two days."

Master Hamner looked as though he were repressing a pained reaction. "Thank you, Master Sebatyne. And launch where? To the Maw? We don't know where these new Sith are."

Saba Sebatyne did not seem in the least daunted. The reptilian Jedi Master stood, restless. "Launch for a staging area where the government cannot interfere with us. Where they cannot record and track us. Let us go dark, stealthy . . . and *now*."

"In two days, we may have reestablished contact with Ben Skywalker or the Solos. We may know much more than we do now. We wait." There was no mistaking the martial tone of command in Hamner's voice. "We'll maintain the same subterfuge we have been using: Most of the Masters will remain clear of the Temple except during these meetings, so as to avoid the appearance that we're up to something. Master Ramis, the rotation of our most experienced Jedi pilots back to Coruscant is continuing as planned?"

Octa Ramis merely nodded.

"And still no evidence in the Archives for this hitherto unknown branch of Sith?"

That set several heads to shaking. Hamner sighed. "Very well. Let's get back to it. Thank you, everybody." He pressed the button on his chair arm again, and the Chamber door slid open.

Kyp caught Jaina's eye before he headed for the exit. "Stay close to the Temple. When we launch, I want you in a StealthX."

"Count on it."

NEAR REDGILL LAKE, DATHOMIR

Ben woke early, predawn. He hadn't had much sleep; he'd stayed up late with his father, working on their respective lightsabers, and they had been rewarded with two fully functioning weapons before they turned in, shortly after midnight.

Ben could have slept longer, but his thoughts and sleep were troubled. He sat up where he'd slept, a couple of meters from the offworlders' campfire, wrapped his blanket around him, and thought, hoping to soothe his worries, to be as detached and reflective as a Jedi should be.

When Darth Caedus, his own cousin Jacen Solo, had died, predeceased by Jacen's Sith mentor Lumiya, and when his Sith apprentice Tahiri Veila had shown no sign of wishing to follow the Sith traditions, Ben had hoped it meant that the Sith were finally gone for good. Oh, of course there had been suggestions otherwise: the continued existence of Ship, the Sith meditation sphere he himself had once commanded; rumors of lingering, dying Sith communities out in the galaxy somewhere. But he could ignore them. They weren't in his face, waving lightsabers.

That had changed with the arrival of the Sith strike team in the Maw cluster. Most of the Sith whom Ben and Luke had fought had been at about the level of training of experienced Jedi Knights. Luke had described Vestara Khai's female companion as being at the approximate level of a Jedi Master. Ben didn't feel lucky enough to hope that the strike team had been the last representatives of this new Sith Order.

So there were Sith again, and part of him, the younger Ben who had been tortured and nearly turned by Darth Caedus, was still a little afraid of them.

Death didn't frighten him. Becoming like Jacen Solo . . . that was another matter.

A couple of meters away, Luke sat up, fully awake, serene. "Your emotions betray you."

Ben gave him a scowl. "*Your* emotions wander around short-sheeting beds and putting everyone's hands in bowls of warm water."

Luke grinned. "Would you please stop saying things like that?"

"Sorry. I just get tired of hearing the same old phrases, the same old way, year after year. I think that's why Master Yoda mangled his Basic for the archival recordings. After nine hundred years, he was sick of hearing the same old things the same old way. Use the same cliché phrases too long and people stop hearing their message, you know?"

Luke blinked, considering. "You may be right."

"So, Dad, what's our plan for this morning?"

Luke rose, discarding his blanket. "Making breakfast."

"Not actually the work of strategic genius I was hoping to hear."

Luke grinned again. "No, but if we don't eat, I won't be capable of much strategic genius later in the day." He headed off toward the supplies.

As Dathomir's sun rose, the camp began its preparations for the day's activities. Groups of men and groups of women, seldom mixed, moved out into the grassy fields surrounding the lake, hammering marker stakes into the ground, flattening grasses along racecourses, situating targets, corralling sturdy green-and-yellow lizards.

Firen Nuln, trainer of rancors for the Raining Leaves, perhaps having lost a bet or finding herself in line for minor punishment, came to join the offworlders at their campfire. "I am to answer questions. If you have any." Her tone was disinterested. Clearly it was a duty she did not relish.

Ben exchanged a glance with Han and shrugged. "Sure. Um, what sorts of competitions are you having?"

"Many. Footraces, riding-lizard races, rancor races, speeder bike races for those who have them, shooting competitions with pistol and rifle, accuracy with spear, wrestling, boating, swimming, riddling—"

"Riddles?" Ben couldn't keep surprise and even a little scorn out of his voice. "You have a competition for telling riddles?"

Firen nodded. "Of course."

Ben held out his two hands about a third of a meter apart. "What's this big, weighs forty kilos, and eats people?"

Dyon, leaning against the cargo speeder and watching the preparations in the fields, shook his head without turning. "That's not how it's done. Among the Dathomiri, and among most people with an oral history tradition, riddles take a very different form. Yours would go something like, 'I am less than the length of a man's arm. Yet my weight would cause a grown man to stagger should he carry me a full day. And when that day is done, it is a grown man I will have for my meal.'"

"That's a lot more involved than the way I asked it."

Firen nodded. "Yet it is more dignified. Less like a child's game when it is phrased as Dyon did." She looked restless, uncomfortable. Finally, she added, "What *is* so long, weighs forty kilograms, and eats people?"

Ben gave her a look that was all innocence. "An Ewok in a lunch box."

Han snickered.

Dyon turned to give Ben an exasperated look. "You see, that's not funny because there's no local context. There are no Ewoks on Dathomir, and no lunch boxes except at the spaceport."

"It could be adapted." Firen frowned, considering. "Perhaps a kolef lizard in a wineskin."

"Loosen up, Dyon." Han stretched, his joints popping. "It was funny."

Dyon shook his head. "You won't win any of the competitions with that attitude."

Han looked startled. "Win? We're not competing!"

"In fact, you are," Firen said. "You must compete—the adults among you, anyway—if you are to hold the respect of the clan members."

A slow grin spread across Han's face. "Well, now, that's a different story!"

Firen nodded. "First, of course, you must declare which of the divisions you will compete in."

"Men and women, I assume." Leia, adjusting the top layer of her Jedi robes, sounded only so interested, but Ben wasn't fooled.

"No." Firen shook her head. "Women and men compete against each other. The divisions are those with the Arts and those without the Arts."

"Force-users and non-users?" Ben looked out over the field again. Sure enough, where competitors were gathering, every group had both men and women but seemed to be dominated by one gender or the other rather than having an even mix. He guessed that the groups with more women were the Force-users, and those with more men the non-users.

"As you would say it, yes. It must be this way, for in competitions between those with the Arts and those without, those with the Arts almost always win." Firen gestured, not toward the fields, but toward a bare patch of lakeside beach where wood for a large fire was being placed. "There is where the riddling and other competitions will take place. Those are among the few where those with the Arts and those without can compete with each other."

"It seems very well thought out." Luke, sitting cross-legged on the speeder hood, was doing some final adjustments on the hilt of his lightsaber. "I suppose there would especially be a lot of talk if *I* don't compete."

"Oh, yes." Firen sounded sure. "All will wonder if you have grown feeble, or if you merely scorn our traditions."

"Guess I'd better compete, then, so they'll know neither is true." Luke gave his brother-in-law a look. "You, too, Han."

"But I *am* feeble."

Leia snorted. "Right. You mean lazy."

Han looked at Firen, an appeal for help. "Tell me that there's a wine-tasting competition."

"No."

"Solving navigation problems?"

"No."

"Bragging?"

Firen sighed. She turned away and headed back toward the Raining Leaves encampment.

When the call went up for the first competition of the morning, the short footrace for those with the Arts, Luke went out to join the competitors, and most of the offworlders went out to cheer him on.

Ben did not. He stayed in the shadow of the cargo speeder and began dealing with items he had traded for or borrowed in the earliest hour as the camp was rousing.

A green Broken Columns cloak, suitable in these temperate foothill elevations, went over his black garments, and a brown hood hid his too-visible reddish hair. He slid the clip for his lightsaber to the back of his belt and put a large sheath knife, borrowed from Carrack, where the other weapon normally hung. Now anyone looking at him would still, in moments, be able to discern that he did not belong to the Raining Leaves or Broken Columns, but he was not instantly obvious as an offworlder or Jedi.

As he was putting on his impromptu disguise, he sneaked the occasional look at the athletic field, specifically at the crowd around the competitors. Olianne was there, and, as Ben and his father had guessed she might, she was keeping a close eye on the offworlders.

Vestara was near Olianne, but not always; she drifted along the edges of the crowd. Ben got up and moved as nonchalantly as he could toward the race's audience.

As he walked, a woman of the Raining Leaves bellowed the rules. All competitors were to race the length of the field, round a marker post, keeping it to their left side, and return to the starting line. Afterward, a longer race would be run, eight laps. Then the two races would be repeated by those with no Arts.

As the recitation of rules came to an end, Ben found himself at the back of a press of onlookers. Three meters ahead of him, at the front of the crowd, was Vestara. Olianne stood a dozen meters to the right of Vestara, separated from her by onlookers.

A blaster fired into the sky was the signal for the race's start. Ben saw his father and three others, two Dathomiri women and one man, draw out to an early lead. Luke did not move to the front; the Raining Leaves trainer of scouts, Halliava Vurse, was ahead of him. Ben doubted she'd remain there; Luke, ever strategic, was doubtless pacing himself.

Vestara withdrew a couple of steps into the crowd, which put her directly in front of Ben. Then she turned to look at him. She showed no surprise at finding him there. "Good morning."

"If you say so."

"You don't think it is?"

He frowned. "Whether it's good or not isn't relevant."

"It's always relevant. Will your morning be worse if your father loses?"

"He won't lose."

Over Vestara's shoulder, Ben saw the racers as they returned to the starting line. Luke was clearly drawing on the Force and gaining ground—but so was Halliava. The Dathomiri woman stayed a good two meters ahead of Luke and crossed the finish line first. The audience erupted into cheers.

Vestara smiled. "So. Better? Worse?"

"The same." Ben struggled not to show the irritation he was feeling. "I'm not here to watch the races. I'm here to talk to you—"

"—without my adoptive mother seeing—"

"—about your pack of lies from last night."

"Oh. What did you think of them?"

"So you admit you were lying to us, to Olianne?"

"Happily. Come on, let's watch the long race." She turned and moved back to the front of the crowd.

Feeling awkward, Ben followed, pushing himself up to the front beside her. "What are you actually doing here?"

"Wait, wait, wait." Vestara gave Ben a scornful look. "You haven't told me which of my statements were lies."

"They all were."

"No. First, my name. Vestara Khai. A lie?"

"I don't know. And I don't care. If Vestara's not your name, it's a convenient tag. Anytime I say 'Vestara,' my father will know who I mean."

She nodded. "That's a good point. And an even better dodging of my demand. So, what was my next lie?"

Ben thought back to the previous night's conversation. "You denied being a Sith."

"No, I said that I had *been* a Sith, and that I was now of the Raining Leaves."

"You're still a Sith."

"From a certain point of view, perhaps. But by the laws of the Raining Leaves, I am not. So, no lie. What's next?"

The athletes participating in the long race were lining up. Luke and Halliava were among them. The blaster sounded and they began to run, their pace somewhat less ferocious than in the short race.

"You said you wouldn't talk about your friends and family because it would get them hurt."

"Another truth. You certainly want to hurt them. Where, exactly, is my pack of lies?"

"You just *admitted* they were a pack of lies."

"Perhaps I lied."

Ben found himself gritting his teeth. Her smart-mouthed evasions were really getting on his nerves. He wondered what Luke would have done if he, Ben, had ever—

The realization that he'd given his father precisely the same sort of responses on innumerable occasions hit Ben like cold water in his face.

Above the sound of onlookers cheering, he heard Vestara laugh at him.

"You lied about where you crashed." Ben knew this was true; he put the confidence he felt into his voice.

She considered, her head tilted to one side. "You know, I think you're right. I did."

"Where did you crash?"

"Oh, I'm too good a pilot. I've never crashed in my life."

"Another lie."

She laughed again. Then she pointed. "Your father's doing quite well."

She was correct. Again, Luke and Halliava were at the head of the racing pack. They were first to reach the starting line and round the post there. They headed back toward the far post, another lap completed.

Vestara looked contemplative. "These are a fine people, Ben. I think my kin could learn from them. Would you prefer that not happen?"

"I'd prefer that the Sith not learn anything except how not to be Sith."

"And what have you learned from me?"

He considered. "The Jedi have a saying. *The future is always in motion.* Sometimes it's said garbled because of one eccentric old Master.

From you, I calculate that the Sith equivalent is *The truth is always in motion.*"

"Interesting. And if I say, *I hope your father wins,* am I telling the truth, lying, or just aiming at a moving target?"

Ben shook his head and turned away.

Chapter Ten

LUKE WON THAT RACE, COMING IN METERS AHEAD OF HALLIAVA, WHO
in turn was meters ahead of the third-place finisher. Halliava was less
than half Luke's age, but his ability to draw on the Force at a consistent level clearly surpassed hers, and he raced across the finish line, his
pace undiminished, to the cheers of the onlookers.

Luke rejoined his son at the fringes of the crowd and toweled off
with a cloth from the cargo speeder. He gave his son a significant look.
"Anything?"

Ben, back in his customary black—he did not want Olianne or others to become accustomed to seeing him in more concealing garments
when he was with his father—shook his head. "She's the conversational equivalent of a monkey-lizard on too much caf. Here, there,
everywhere, and it's impossible to pin her down."

"Pity."

"She did say something about liking the Dathomiri, wishing her
people could learn from them. It was innocuous . . . but it kind of sent
chills down my spine."

Luke looked around. "That's good. Good awareness on your part. And if we can figure out what she wants to learn, maybe we can determine a weakness in her Sith Order. What do the Dathomiri have that the Sith don't?"

"Unique Force abilities. Interesting mating habits."

Luke snorted.

"Dad, is it true that Teneniel Djo tried to marry you against your will?" Teneniel Djo, mother of Tenel Ka, had been a Witch of Dathomir.

"If *marry* is the word, yes. So be careful who you smile at around here. I'm not ready to be a grandfather. Or even a father-in-law."

"Don't worry. What are my prospects here? A bunch of women who are used to ruling their men, and one Sith girl."

Ben spent time in the shadow of the cargo speeder, using macrobinoculars borrowed from Carrack to spy on Vestara.

But, blast her, she didn't do anything suspicious.

She watched the competitions with interest and enthusiasm. She spoke often with Raining Leaves, especially Olianne, and not infrequently with Kaminne and Halliava.

Vestara chatted and cheered, was warm to some and chilly with others. She moved with a dancer's grace that was at odds with the slight awkwardness of any young woman her age.

She was, to Ben's increasing aggravation, like most teenage girls he had met. Nothing about her screamed *Sith.* She was not surrounded by a miasma of evil, not even by the sort of implacable drive and focus that had been characteristics of Jacen Solo as he became darker.

Ben wished intensely to find some personal reason to dislike the girl, and couldn't.

He was distracted by a competition—by Han Solo stepping up to the front of a crowd of competitors. Belatedly, Ben realized that it was a blaster pistol competition for those without the Arts. He had been hearing the slow, rhythmic blasts of methodical shooting for some time.

Now Han stood at the front of the line as targets, small clay plates, were stood on end in brackets atop ten wooden posts.

The clan members setting up the targets had barely gotten to a safe distance from them when Han drew and began firing. Unlike the previous competitors, he shot from the hip. His shots came so fast that Ben could barely distinguish between them. In less than three seconds all ten plates were smashed into expanding clouds of clay and gas. Han grinned, twirled his blaster on his finger, and reholstered it.

Ben smiled, too. Han was taking a chance that the reduction in accuracy he'd suffer from firing so fast would be more than offset, if he cleared his targets, by the dismay his show would cause in other competitors.

And he was right. Ben saw faces fall among the other shooters. Many in the audience cheered the ostentatious display of skill.

Tasander Dest, leader of the Broken Columns, stepped up, seeming not at all disheartened. The organizers of the event set up ten new targets. When they were clear of the posts, Dest drew and fired just as Han had. Ten targets exploded into clay fragments.

Han made an unhappy face. Ben snickered. It was good for his uncle to run up against people who could give him a hard time.

There was, to Ben's surprise, a speeder bike race. Enough members of the Raining Leaves and Broken Columns had acquired the vehicles, whether by trading or stealing Ben didn't know, to warrant such a competition. There was only one race, for those without the Arts, and eight competitors lined up to participate. Ben supposed that there were not enough Force-users with speeder bikes to hold a heat.

As the speeders roared from the starting line, Ben realized that something was working at him. Nagging him. He pulled down his macrobinoculars and thought about it. Something he'd missed? He was still bothered by Vestara's claims of having lost her lightsaber. He couldn't imagine losing his that way, but questions put by Luke and Ben to members of the Raining Leaves made it clear that Vestara had come into their company with nothing but the clothes on her back, with no way to have carried a concealed lightsaber.

No, although that question did concern Ben, it wasn't what was eating at him. He tried to drift away from thoughts and puzzles, to feel the ambient flow of the Force through him.

There was malevolent intent at work here in the camp.

He could feel it, a faint tinge of malice, very scattered, very diffuse. He immediately thought of Vestara, but, to his surprise, even resuming his observation of her through the macrobinoculars, he did not feel that it emanated from her.

And as the sun rose higher, that sensation grew, even though it became no more focused.

Near noontime, Ben greeted the other offworlders and Tribeless Sha as they returned for the midday meal. "I saw you shooting," he told Han. "How'd you do?"

"First place, of course. Seventy of seventy." Han's tone was matter-of-fact. "That fancy boy from the Broken Columns came in second, sixty-nine of seventy." He jerked a thumb toward two of their companions. "Carrack and Yliri tied at sixty-eight, and they had a shoot-off to break the tie. Yliri smoked him."

Carrack scowled. "I don't practice much with pistols. If a target is close enough to be in pistol range, I've fouled up somehow with my rifle."

"Excuses, excuses," Yliri said cheerfully. She held up a medallion, circular and about five centimeters in diameter; it was of yellow porcelain, had the image of a pistol on it, and hung from a leather thong. "They give out awards."

Han held up his. It was glossy black and had apparently been carved from onyx and then polished rather than fashioned from clay. "I think I'll win six or eight more and have a complete set of coasters."

Tarth and Sha took over the maintenance of the campfire and the pot of stew over it—Ben's ostensible reason for staying at the camp all this time—and the others settled down to eat. Luke, Leia, and Ben sat apart, a Jedi cell.

"Do you feel it?" Luke asked.

Leia and Ben nodded. Leia glanced toward her husband. "It has something to do with him."

"Really?" Luke sounded surprised. "He hasn't been here long enough to give anyone reason to harm him—"

"That doesn't take Han very long," Leia assured him.

"—meaning that it may have something to do with his relationship with Dathomir from before. When he theoretically won it gambling."

Ben shook his head. "If it were just him, maybe. But I'm feeling malice that's more widespread."

They quieted for a minute as Tarth and Sha moved among them, distributing bowls of stew. Ben ate, surprised at how hungry he'd become just from hours of spying. He himself had assembled the stew from ingredients provided by the Dathomiri and scavenged from the supplies brought by the offworlders. It was largely made up of Redgill fish, sliced tree tubers from the rain forest, and tart clusterfruit leaves, all seasoned by Ben to spicy Corellian standards. He had to admit that it had turned out pretty well.

Then he felt just a trickle of alarm and wondered if, somehow, the stew had been poisoned while he wasn't looking.

Luke and Leia felt it, too. It appeared that Dyon did as well; the man's head snapped up, and he looked around.

Leia rose in a smooth motion and walked over to her husband. "Don't move, Han." Her voice was pleasant enough.

He stopped with a wooden spoon halfway to his mouth. "You want to remember me just like this, right?"

"Sure." She leaned over him, past him, and grabbed at something on the ground. "Oh, no, you don't."

When she straightened, she had a serpent in her hand, gripping it just behind the neck, and it was in the process of coiling around her arm. It was mostly green, with red and yellow bands decorating it. The color scheme was one of warning.

Han came upright as if he were a puppet yanked to his feet by an overly energetic child. His stew splashed across Carrack's legs. He spun around, somehow keeping an eye on Leia's snake while also scanning every meter of ground near him. "What the . . ."

"Kodashi viper." Sha's tone was flat, but her eyes were big. "Most poisonous serpent in the rain forest. It bites you, you die in minutes, no antidote. But they're good to eat."

Leia displayed the serpent to Sha. "Are they found around here?"

Sha shook her head. "It's too cold here at night."

"It was directed." Luke kept his voice low, but everyone at the offworlders' camp heard him. "That's what we were feeling. It was directed through the Force—"

There was a cry from elsewhere in the camp, a man's cry of pain and dismay. It was so visceral that it brought the rest of the offworlders to their feet, and they craned their necks to look in the direction of the noise. It came from a campfire in the Broken Columns camp, and they could see, at this distance, a group of men standing in a circle, some of them bending over, swinging burning brands at something on the ground. Finally, one of them drew a blaster pistol and fired. The others waited for a moment, then backed away and turned their attention to something on the ground a couple of meters away, something Ben could not see.

Luke, Ben, and their companions headed in that direction, as did scores of Dathomiri . . . and then there was another cry, again a man's cry, from elsewhere in the Broken Columns camp.

Half an hour later, what had been mystery and puzzlement had been revealed as tragedy.

At the same time the serpent in the offworlders' camp was coiling to strike at Han, five more kodashi vipers were preparing to strike elsewhere in the camp—all in the Broken Columns area. One had been speared before striking, but the other four had been successful. Four men, all winners of various events at these games, had been poisoned, had suffered agonizing pain from the serpents' neurotoxins, and had died within minutes. Gone were the winners of the speeder bike race, the wrestling, the long footrace, and the spear-throw, all for those without Arts.

Within minutes a man of the Broken Columns—bearded, burly, dressed in tan leather vest and kilt—moved out to the gap between the two camps, only meters from the offworlders' campfire, and began to shout. "It was them!" His voice, grating and deep, was loud enough to carry to every corner of the camp. He pointed into the center of the Raining Leaves encampment. "They say they want to unite, but they mean they want us as slaves again. They'll kill any man who stands out above the rest—"

"Liar!" That was Firen, trainer of rancors. She ran out into the gap between camps, redness and an expression of anger suffusing her face.

She charged the shouting man and, despite his effort to twist away, struck him an open-palm blow to the chest. The impact took the man off his feet and sent him to the ground.

Ben headed that way. Women and men from all over the campsite also moved in the direction of the altercation.

The bearded man, despite the raw power of the blow that had taken him down, rolled away from Firen and stood in a single graceful motion. Though somewhat bent over from the obvious pain in his chest, he was fully functional, and his hand fell on the hilt of his sheathed knife.

Ben put on a burst of speed, though his experience slowed down as his sense of time distorted.

In what seemed like exaggerated slow motion, the man drew his knife, which had a double-edged blade that was probably thirty centimeters long. He held his left hand, his empty hand, before him, his knife hand drawn back, as he stepped toward Firen.

And then Ben was upon them. He drew his lightsaber, ignited it, and struck all in a single motion. The glowing blade hit the man's knife just ahead of the crossguard. The noise of energy blade meeting steel was almost musical as the lightsaber sheared the knife in half. Ben deactivated his weapon and took half a step back before the bearded man and Firen could even react.

The bearded man, stunned, looked down at his ruined weapon. Firen, her angry expression unchanged, now kept an eye on Ben and drew away from him.

Luke was there, too, all of a sudden, in their midst. When he spoke, his voice was nowhere near as loud as the bearded man's, but it seemed to carry just as far. "Tell me. Who thinks for the Broken Columns?"

Onrushing Dathomiri were now skidding to a halt. Eager a moment ago to mix it up with other tribesmen, they seemed far more wary of assaulting armed Jedi. One man cried out, "What do you mean, who thinks for us? You mean, who speaks for us."

"No." There was considerable scorn in Luke's voice. "Clearly, this man *speaks* for you. It's just as clear that he doesn't think at all."

"I spoke the truth." The bearded man hurled the knife hilt down between them. "No man of the Broken Columns would send vipers against us. Killing our own champions. It was them." He pointed variously among the Raining Leaves gathered around, and his finger stopped when it found Halliava. "It was her! She even dresses in kodashi colors."

Halliava fixed the man with a look of mixed irritation and pity. "Many of us do. Some of *you* do. Their stealth and power are to be admired. But would I dress in their colors and then send them against you, implicating myself? I'd have to be as stupid as you. Besides, who among us could control so many snakes at once?"

That question did make them think. Tribesmen and tribeswomen began looking around for a likely suspect. As often as not, their attention became fixed on the Jedi.

"That's an easy one to answer." The speaker was Tasander Dest, just arriving. He stepped out into the open space, joining the Jedi, the bearded man, and Firen. Kaminne Sihn was right behind him.

He clapped the bearded man on the shoulder. "Drola, think about it. Who has the Arts to command the serpents? Who wants to return things to the way they were generations ago? Who would be happy for brave men to die and for Raining Leaves women to take the blame?"

Drola didn't answer immediately. His mouth moved as if he were reluctant to speak. Finally the word came: "Nightsisters."

"Yes, Nightsisters. The Nightsisters have caused a tragedy today. The Skywalkers have prevented us from having a second one."

Kaminne now addressed the crowd. "We will double the guard tonight. If you see or feel anything strange, untoward, report it to a clan leader or chief."

"Tonight we will have funeral rites for the fallen, and tomorrow, special games in their honor." Dest's tone became more forceful. "We *will* watch out for each other, Broken Columns for Raining Leaves and Raining Leaves for Broken Columns. And in giving us a common enemy, the Nightsisters will find that they have furthered our union of the clans, not prevented it." He turned as if to speak privately with Kaminne, all but telling the gathered onlookers, *You are dismissed.*

Conversations rose among those gathered, but Ben was relieved to feel a lessening of tension. The rear edges of the crowd began to turn away, people drifting back toward the campfires.

Luke stepped in close to Ben. He pitched his voice low enough that it would not carry beyond the two of them. "Nice work with the knife."

Ben shrugged. He returned the lightsaber to its clip. "The arm would have been an easier target. But it's kind of clear that there aren't lots of prosthetics to be had on Dathomir."

Dest and Kaminne moved in their direction, but Luke spoke first. "So, where are these Nightsisters?"

Kaminne gestured out among the departing crowd. "Some live in the forests and mountains in small groups. But these days, the majority are among us. They keep the fact that they are Nightsisters a secret. They are better these days at concealing the effects that dark uses of the Arts have on their flesh. It is said that all clans have a few Nightsisters among them. And sometimes there are Nightsister gatherings." She looked unhappy. "It seems that there is such a gathering now, and that it wants to prevent this union of clans."

"New ways threaten them." Dest seemed matter-of-fact about it. "I guess we'll just have to keep shooting them."

OFFICE OF THE ASSISTANT TO THE CHIEF OF STATE, SENATE BUILDING, CORUSCANT

Wynn Dorvan paused before reentering his office. He had to brace himself for the remainder of his encounter with the Jedi waiting for him. Seldom had Dorvan encountered a personality that was simultaneously so strong, so focused, so . . . dull.

But Dorvan was a professional. He put on a pleasant smile he didn't feel and walked toward the door. It rose to admit him to his private office.

In a chair, his back to the door, sat Sothais Saar. The Chev Jedi did not visibly react as Dorvan entered.

Dorvan moved past to resume his seat behind the desk. "The Chief of State regrets that she cannot join us, but reiterates that she, too, is an enemy of slavery both within and outside the Alliance." He glanced at Saar to gauge the Chev's reaction to these perfunctory words.

Saar was asleep, slumped in his chair, his head lolling to one side, his eyes closed.

Dorvan looked at him in surprise. He smiled, amused. Never before had he caught a Jedi napping—in this case, literally. It was all he could do to keep from laughing. "Jedi Saar?"

"Eh?" Saar jerked and his eyes opened. He looked around as if confused.

"Obviously, the Jedi schedule is one of long hours and uncertain timing."

"Uh, yes." Saar looked at him as if Dorvan had suddenly grown a third eye—as if only half recognizing him. The Jedi seemed to compose himself rapidly enough, though. "I should be going."

"Without hearing what the Chief of State has to say?"

"No, of course not." Saar twisted to glance at the door, as if half expecting to see Daala standing there. He returned his attention to Dorvan. "Perhaps you could walk me out and tell me as we go."

"Of course."

As they left the office and headed toward the lift accessing the main entrance level, Dorvan tried again. "Chief Daala wants you to understand that she is as devoted as anyone to eliminating the remnants of slaver mentality from the galaxy."

"Yes, yes." Saar fidgeted, and as soon as the door opened to give them access to the turbolift, he darted inside.

Dorvan followed. "But she does have many other demands on her attention and resources, of course."

"Of course. Main level." The turbolift doors dropped into place, and the lift descended.

Dorvan felt a flash of impatience. Saar normally played the verbal-politics game with skill and enthusiasm. Now it seemed he couldn't be bothered. "So perhaps you could put together a proposal for a cooperative effort between the Jedi and the government, using resources of both, for her to evaluate. Achieve both our ends. Perhaps engender a greater feeling of cooperation between us than we've experienced recently."

Saar turned to look at him, a stare of evaluation. Dorvan felt unsettled by it. It was as if the Jedi were staring through a magnifying lens at him, discovering for the first time that Dorvan belonged to a hitherto unknown species. But he merely said, "Good idea."

The turbolift stopped and the door shot up. Saar stepped out into the building's main entrance hall. To the right, a hundred meters away, was sunlight. Between here and that exit were innumerable cross-corridors, doors into offices, bustling politicians, ambling protocol droids.

Saar set off at a rapid walk in the direction of the exit. Dorvan struggled to keep up with him. "Jedi Saar, let me speak frankly. Tensions between the Jedi Order and the government are damaging both. It behooves us to go out of our way to find common ground. To calm things down before something sparks a tragedy. Before our differences become irreconcilable. If the heads of both groups cannot find this common ground, perhaps lower ranks can. Yes?"

"Yes." Saar sounded not in the least interested.

And it was then, finally, that Dorvan realized what he was seeing, what he was hearing. The realization was almost like being hit by a stun beam—though in this case, it was a wash of fear rather than energy.

If he was right in his guess, he was in more danger at this minute than he had been in years.

But he had to know.

He thought back over recent events, over the odd behavior of other Jedi, and finally he said, "You're probably wondering what I've done with the real Wynn Dorvan."

If Dorvan was wrong, if Saar's behavior had some more innocuous explanation, Dorvan could explain the comment away as a figure of speech.

Saar stopped and spun to face Dorvan. Suddenly his lightsaber, unlit, was in his right hand. His eyes were wide—not with fear, but with the awareness of a man ready to enter combat, taking in as much visual data as he could.

Dorvan stopped, too, uneasily aware that a single wrong move might lead to his death. He felt as if a heavy weight were resting on his chest. It was difficult to breathe. "Jedi Saar, I'm unarmed."

Saar seemed to disappear. Dorvan blinked and realized that Saar was still before him, now a dozen meters away and running at such speed that he appeared to blur as he headed for the exit. There was a shriek as the Jedi brushed past an aide carrying a precariously balanced stack of datacards; the cards went flying in an arc, clattering to the stone floor of the hallway.

Dorvan grabbed his comlink. "Lockdown, lockdown!"

Those words, broadcast by his comlink, triggered an instant and automated response in the building's security system. The sunlight ahead suddenly narrowed as blast doors began a rapid close-and-seal. A low, bone-rattling alarm tone began cycling.

The blur that was Jedi Saar suddenly became even harder to focus on as he raced to the exit, diving through the closing doors when there was less than a meter's gap between them.

Dorvan cursed.

"Dorvan, this is Captain Brays in security. What is—"

"Jedi male, Chev, leaving main entrance, dark robes, is a mad Jedi. Repeat, mad Jedi. Bring all resources to bear to track him. Do not confront him unless you have the resources necessary to take down a Jedi Knight."

"Understood."

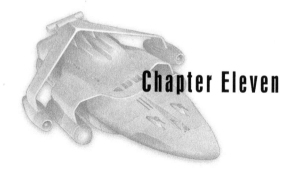

Chapter Eleven

JEDI SAAR RACED ACROSS THE PLAZA BEFORE THE SENATE BUILDING. He had to get away from the broad open space and had to do so fast, before the inevitable stream of security airspeeders launched to follow him. He couldn't keep up that Force-boosted running speed for the entire distance. He slowed to a rate that was merely that of a championship runner.

Ahead was the security station that screened all pedestrians and speeders entering the plaza from that direction. The agents in it would just now be receiving the alert. He raced past, ignoring the cries of the helmeted workers. The station's automated defenses, designed to detect and bring down vehicles coming in from the other direction, could not impede him as he passed by.

Now he was on the street beyond, a street thick with pedestrians. It would take him a mere second to shuck his cloak, perhaps grab a gaudy tunic from a passerby, making himself visually distinct from the image he'd presented to the Senate Building holocams—

He almost gasped in relief. Ahead of him, departing from a hired airspeeder and awkwardly handing credcoins to the driver, was Master Cilghal. She would know what to do, she—

It was not her. In the seconds it had taken him to cross most of the thirty meters separating them, Saar realized that the Mon Calamari female he was facing, for all that she was identical in garb and appearance to Master Cilghal, *was not Cilghal.*

He stopped. He heard a *snap-hiss* and realized that he had ignited his lightsaber without meaning to. Its blue-black blade glowed as it stretched like a teacher's pointing tool. Pedestrians exclaimed, changed direction, drew away from the two Jedi.

The driver of the hired speeder hit his thrusters and sped away, scattering Cilghal's credcoins. They clattered to the permacrete pavement and rolled in all directions.

The Mon Cal Jedi looked steadily at Saar. "Jedi Saar, I suspect I know what you are experiencing."

"What have you done with Master Cilghal?"

The false Cilghal blinked at him, each eye blinking separately, as she considered her answer. Finally, she nodded, as if coming to a decision. "I know how this conversation progresses. There is no point to it. You cannot be reasoned with." She reached for her lightsaber, drew it forth, ignited it.

Saar leapt toward her.

Their blades came together in a spectacular clash of sparks and *pop-zapp* noises. Those few people surrounding the scene who had not already drawn back did so now, in a hurry. A moment later the hum of the lightsabers was drowned out by the sirens of oncoming official vehicles.

Saar threw a quick series of blows, intended to draw his larger, clumsier opponent into an ever more extravagant series of blocks, the last ones pulling her out of line or off-balance. But she *wasn't* clumsier. She fought like a Jedi Master, lightning-fast, anticipating every attack, not being fooled by feints.

He backflipped to put a few meters' distance between them, but when he was upside down and facing away from the false Cilghal, he felt a pulse of Force energy from her direction. He was hurtled forward into the granite facing of the closest building. With his own use of the Force he tried to slow his rate, to soften the impact, but to no avail. He hammered into the building edifice.

The last thing he saw was the street pavement above his head sliding down to meet him.

CHIEF OF STATE'S OFFICE, CORUSCANT

Daala looked up as Dorvan walked into her office. Her expression was hard, but there was concern in her voice. "Are you all right?"

"I managed not to impale myself on his weapon while we were talking." Clearly upset, he flopped down into a chair without waiting to be asked. "I'm mostly mad because the lockdown *I* called for didn't even slow him down but it kept me from getting here for half an hour. What does security say?"

"He ran into Jedi Master Cilghal, dueled with her her briefly, and was flattened like a bug. She commandeered a passing commercial speeder and took him back to the Temple." She glanced down at the monitor on her desk. Her eyes flicked back and forth as she read an update. "The Coruscant Security officers I dispatched to the Jedi Temple are there now and have issued an order to the Jedi. They must turn over Jedi Saar within the hour or there will be consequences."

"*Will* there be consequences?"

"Oh, yes. Definitely, yes."

JEDI TEMPLE, CORUSCANT

The news about Jedi Saar's madness and the Coruscant Security officers parked on the Temple's front steps circulated with the speed of comm traffic. When Jaina swept into the medical ward, the first thing she saw was news coverage of the event on the chamber's main monitor. It showed an aerial holocam view of the Temple, uniformed security officers and Jedi guards standing stiffly, meters apart, in a temporary standoff.

Cilghal or Tekli had switched the sound off. Jaina turned to Cilghal, who was bent over the unconscious form of Saar. The Jedi Knight lay on his back on a hovergurney, the device currently settled on the floor. His tunic was off, and he wore a monitor ring on his brow like a headband. His eyes were closed; his wrists and ankles, shackled to the bed. There was a formfitting blue plascast on his nose.

Jaina moved up beside the Jedi Master and Shul Vaal, Jedi medic and Cilghal's aide, a middle-aged blue Twi'lek whose unhurried movements and soothing manner made him seem the island of calm at the center of any storm of chaos. "Same as the others?"

Shul Vaal nodded. "Paranoia and hostility. No manifestation yet of Force powers he should not possess. Master Cilghal gave him a concussion and a broken nose."

"I had to end the fight quickly." Cilghal sounded gruff, even defensive. "Sometimes to heal, you must first hurt."

Jaina grimaced. "In just a few words, you've summed up my love life. Anything I can do?"

Cilghal nodded. "Prep a shuttle. Before the government gets the bright idea to examine every vehicle leaving the Temple, I want to get Jedi Saar offworld and to the Transitory Mists."

"Will do."

Several levels down in the Temple, Jaina walked into one of the building's civilian hangars. The chamber was broad and deep enough to host a ball game, and the ceiling was ten meters high, to accommodate repulsor takeoffs and landings. Two *Lambda*-class shuttles and a number of airspeeders and speeder bikes were in place there. Both shuttles had their wings locked in upswept position. One had a panel off at the engine section, but the mechanic, a woman in Jedi robes, was leaning against the fuselage, watching the same news coverage on the wall-mounted monitor. She gave Jaina a distracted nod. "Jedi Solo."

"Jedi Tainer. Is the other shuttle fit to fly?"

Tyria Sarkin Tainer nodded. A woman of about Leia's age, she was lean and blond. It was said that in her youth she'd been a raving beauty, but now her looks had more of an all-mother appeal to them. Her sleeves were pinned up and her arms were spattered with dirty lubricants from fingertip to elbow. "I can have this one up and ready for you in half an hour, too."

"No need, one's enough." Jaina glanced at Tyria's befouled hands. "I think I'll handle the sign-out myself."

Tyria nodded. "The smart choice." She turned back to the engine compartment. "Don't ever marry a mechanic. Over the years, you pick up a lot of training, whether you want to or not. And then you're stuck on motor pool duty whenever you can't avoid it."

"I *am* a mechanic. And I like motor pool duty." Jaina moved over to the desk by the door and began typing into the console there, checking out the other Lambda. How would she describe the mission for the records? Something dull and Jedi-like to allay suspicions. *Delivery of practice lightsabers to Corellia.*

It was said that Tyria would never make Master owing to deficiencies in her command of the Force, but she was an excellent flier, hence her current assignment to the Temple. When the StealthX squadrons rose, she'd be in the cockpit of one—

Jaina felt the other woman tense. She looked up. "What's wrong?"

Tyria was once again looking at the monitor. "It looped."

"Eh?"

"The recording just looped. There was a little stutter and then it went back to the recording of several minutes ago. But it still says LIVE BROADCAST." She pointed to the lower right-hand portion of the monitor screen.

Jaina looked. The screen did say what Tyria indicated. It could have just been a mistake by the news provider's technical personnel, or . . .

Jaina extended her senses into the Force, settling as quickly as she could into a meditative state that would make her more sensitive to thoughts of anger or vengeance, intrusion or attack . . .

There was nothing close, but as her range of attention broadened, she felt a quiver of anticipation, felt eyes trained against the Jedi.

She grabbed her comlink. "Comm center, this is Jedi Solo."

A man's voice answered. "We read you, Solo."

"Tell Master Hamner possible attack imminent." She didn't bother to add recommendations for security or defensive procedures. Hamner was ex-military. He didn't need such advice and might resent it.

"Will do."

Tyria grabbed solvent-soaked cloths from the pavement at her feet and began degreasing her arms.

Jaina, still half in her meditative state, moved back out into the hall.

If she could get more of a fix on the contradictory emotions she was feeling . . .

She heard a succession of *clunk*s as numerous exterior doors on this hangar level were remotely shut.

A teenage apprentice, black-haired and old enough to carry a lightsaber, moved out into the hall from the main starfighter hangar. He didn't waste time asking what was going on. Obviously he felt something, too. "Should I go up to the Main Hall?"

"Yes." Just outside the Main Hall, at the main entrance, was where those security agents waited. "But . . . No. Wait here." Jaina shook her head. She felt *something* amiss, not just distant emotions suggesting imminent attack.

A wail cut the air, a keening alarm. The Temple lights flickered for a moment.

Jaina heard no direct sounds of conflict, but her comlink suddenly came alive with traffic. "Alert, alert, Main Hall under attack. The doors are compromised—"

"State enemy strength and disposition." That was Master Hamner, his voice icy, under complete control.

"It's Mandos." The young Jedi speaker sounded overly excited.

Jaina cursed. Mandalorians. The government wasn't just serious, they were being *smart* and serious.

She turned toward the distant turbolifts, but a nagging presentiment kept her from moving in that direction. She pinned the apprentice with a look. "What's your name?"

"Bandy Geffer, from Bespin."

"Apprentice Geffer, get to a hardwired intercom away from any outside wall. That's your position until I say different. Keep your comlink in hand and if it cuts out, give me a shout."

"Yes, Jedi Solo." He spun on his heel and raced off.

Tyria appeared in the nearest doorway, her arms clean, her unlit lightsaber in hand. She paid Jaina no mind. She looked down the corridor as if gauging the strength of the walls, then looked up, examining the rafters and other architectural elements of the corridor's high ceilings. "I hate defending a position."

"Me, too."

The door that Apprentice Geffer had emerged from, the door into the StealthX hangar, rattled in its frame and there was a muted *boom* from beyond it. Jaina nodded. It would be shaped charges, simultaneously blasting several entry holes for commandos. She raced past the shuttle hangar, was unsurprised to hear Tyria running right behind her. "Inform control. Second attack prong is *here.*"

"There's static on the comlinks now! I'm on the intercom."

"Report the comm loss, too." The two Jedi ran past the main door into the StealthX hangar. At the next corridor intersection—beyond it were the turbolifts for this level and, at a wide point in the hall, the coordinator's desk where Apprentice Geffer was now sitting—Jaina turned and lit her lightsaber. Tyria joined her; her blade came alive with a *snap-hiss.*

The door into the StealthX hangar blew out, instantly transformed into innumerable chunks of durasteel ranging from the size of pebbles to the size of starfighter helmets. At the same instant four places in the wall, two on either side of the door, blew out. And from each hole emerged a Mandalorian warrior, distinctive in their modern armor with classical helmet designs. They were as anonymous as Imperial stormtroopers and yet more individual than Jedi, each set of armor having its own color pattern, its own unique helmet contours.

They turned toward the Jedi. There were no preambles. The foremost Mando gestured and smoke trails, a cluster of them, jumped toward the Jedi—mini rockets.

Jaina and Tyria leapt about two meters. With an exertion of the Force, even as the Mando was aiming, Jaina caused the largest section of wall debris to fly up in front of the commando's outstretched hand. A wave of mini rockets slammed into the debris and detonated. The blast disintegrated that debris but blew the firer and the two commandos closest behind him off their feet.

Tyria nodded, approving. "Nice."

"Thanks."

Tyria looked back toward the apprentice. "Report five-plus Mandos. Tell them to consider sending reinforcements."

"*I'll* reinforce you—"

Tyria's voice turned sharp. "Abandon your post and you'll be tasting my boot from a direction you *never* expected."

The fourth Mando, blaster rifle in hand, darted diagonally forward. He crossed in front of the fifth commando, and as he passed, Jaina realized that the fifth commando had fired a second spray of mini rockets, using his comrade as a visual block. It was a beautifully timed stratagem. At the point Jaina realized more rockets were incoming, the spray was already too widespread—the rockets were already past the debris—for her to use the same defense.

Tyria leapt to her right, putting her around the corner from the oncoming missiles. Jaina charged straight at the Mandos.

She twisted and let a mini rocket pass by no more than three centimeters from her body. It and the other projectiles slammed into walls, floor, and ceiling behind her, causing the floor to rock. A gust of heated air from the explosion overtook her.

And then she was in their midst, in the middle of the pack of Mandos, where they'd have to fire precisely or not at all to avoid harming their fellows. Three of them were rising, unhurt. One of the two still standing drew a short vibrosword, holding it in a reverse grip, and launched himself at her.

She watched the other one who was still on his feet. Sure enough, he used the direct assault as a distraction, waited half a second, and fired at her from what looked like a line-throwing forearm attachment. But what came at her was a flexible projectile that broadened, expanded into a net.

She grabbed at it with the Force, exerting herself against it as if it were a bad idea, and flicked it into the path of the vibrosword wielder. It wrapped around him.

Nor did Jaina let go of it then. She maintained her mental grip on the net and yanked it through one of the holes in the wall. That Mando went flying, and the one who'd cast the net, still attached to it by a line, was hauled off his feet. He went flying after his comrade, the sudden lateral movement causing him to drop his blaster rifle.

Three left, but the other two were unhurt and would be back in a moment—perhaps with reinforcements.

The three were on their feet now. One turned away from Jaina, facing back down the corridor, and threw up his arm just in time to catch Tyria's descending lightsaber blade on it. The *beskar* from which his crushgaunt was made withstood the impact of the green energy blade, and he was not wounded. But the crushgaunt was scarred and the sheer force of Tyria's blow drove him back a step.

Jaina spun between the other two, chambering her weapon, ready to kick. One of the two Mandos, a female, wore a rocket pack and ignited it, carrying her up and away from Jaina. That was all right; she was not Jaina's original target. Jaina leapt, and her kick took the other commando in the side of the head. It was certainly not powerful enough to damage the *beskar*, but a lot of kinetic force was transmitted through the helmet, rocking the man's head. He staggered away.

Tyria's lightsaber found an unarmored chink in her opponent's plating. She drove the blade, point-first, into his inner thigh. He made a strangled noise, took two jerky steps backward, and fell as the smell of burned flesh joined that of explosives residue. But another commando, the one who'd launched the net at Jaina, leapt out from the hole in the wall and swung at Tyria before she could react. His gauntleted fist took her in the jaw. Jaina heard the *crack,* saw the jaw deform, and suddenly Tyria was down, unconscious. The odds abruptly went from two against five to one against four. Or three and a half, if the concussion she was sure she'd given one Mando counted for anything.

There was a new *boom* from farther down the corridor, back toward Apprentice Geffer and the turbolifts. Jaina nodded, comprehending. Another handful of Mandos would be leaving the StealthX hangar the same way these had, using explosives to bypass doors, moving laterally in directions the Jedi wouldn't normally prepare for.

Now the only thing between this second unit of Mandos and the turbolifts was one apprentice. She saw Geffer's desk slide through the intersection, picking up speed, propelled by the boy's use of the Force, and a split second after it vanished from sight down the cross-hall she heard it destroyed by mini rockets. Apprentice Geffer, grimly determined and frightened all at once, stepped out into the intersection, his lightsaber lit.

Jaina swore to herself. She could not retreat to help Geffer. She had to hold here or they'd both be flanked. But the apprentice was no match for experienced Mandos, especially Mandos who had clearly trained and prepared for conflict with Jedi. She had to hope he'd last a few seconds.

The flying Mando female fired down at Jaina with a blaster pistol. Jaina sidestepped the barrage of shots, making it look clumsy when in fact it wasn't, and launched herself at the commando who had taken Tyria out.

The turbolift door opened and Raynar Thul stepped out into the passageway. He saw an apprentice, lightsaber glowing blue in his hand, facing down a side corridor. Down the main corridor, Jaina Solo was squared off against three Mandos, one of them flying. Correction, four Mandos: another one, casting off ruins of a net, charged out through a hole that used to be a doorway.

Raynar strode forward, told the apprentice, "I'll take this," and turned toward the apprentice's subject of attention.

Subjects. Five more Mandos moving forward through the ruins of some furniture and what once had been sections of wall. They hesitated when they saw him.

For once, people seeing him were not hesitating in the face of his well-healed yet widespread burn scars—but because he was a more formidable enemy than they'd expected to confront.

He ignited his lightsaber and pointed it at them. "I am Jedi Thul," he told them. "I have not fought for real in many years. I should be a pushover. Come get me."

They fired—blaster rifles, mini rockets, a flamethrower. It was a co-ordinated attack, each firing to cover a different portion of the hallway, the gout of flame straight down the middle.

But Raynar had used the moments of his speech to begin some Force trickery, grabbing at a panel of durasteel wall knocked free by the explosions that had put the Mandos' entry holes into the wall. As they fired, he yanked the panel and held it floating before them.

He knew the panel wouldn't last a second against their barrage, knew that it wasn't close enough to them to reflect concussive force back toward them. But in much less than a second he ran forward and leapt.

Fire hit the panel and smoke roiled up from the point of impact. Mini rockets hit it, blew it to shrapnel, and added their own smoke to the visual confusion.

Raynar sailed past above the smoke cloud, using it as cover, executing one lazy flip as he went, and landed behind the two rearmost Mandos.

As their sight line cleared, they saw what Raynar saw: the young apprentice still barring their way, once again alone. They exchanged glances—were probably exchanging comm traffic as well.

With his free hand, Raynar grabbed the arm of one of the two rearmost Mandos, a female with a mini rocket launcher. Before she knew he was there, before she could tense and pull away from him, he aimed her arm at two of her comrades and triggered the weapon.

Mini rockets emerged, traveled a few meters, and slammed into a *beskar* breastplate and a rocket pack.

The detonation of the rocket pack dwarfed those of the mini rockets. Raynar was staggered back by its force and felt bits of shrapnel cut into his face, chest, and arms; felt himself battered by an unhealthy amount of heat. *Pity. More work for the plastic surgeons.* He shook his head, clearing his vision.

All five of his opponents were down, but three were moving, rising to their feet and assuming defensive positions. He stepped forward and swung, cutting through a blaster rifle before it could draw a bead on him.

A line wrapped around his ankle. The commando who had launched it yanked, pulling him off-balance. His free arm flailed around and his attacker's crushgaunt caught it . . . and squeezed.

Raynar felt and heard his left arm break above the elbow. The jolt of pain was almost enough to cause him to black out. He swung his lightsaber, glanced it off his attacker's upraised forearm, and brought it down to cut through the line that gripped him. But that Mando still had a hand on Raynar's broken arm . . .

The apprentice was suddenly there, racing through the trio of Mandos with Force-augmented speed, striking down at the leg of Raynar's attacker. The blow was a slash aimed at the back of the man's knee. A trained Jedi Knight would have thrust rather than slashed, bypassing all armor at that vulnerable spot, but the boy still connected, his blade cutting through centimeters of cloth, skin, and muscle before being arrested by the armor at the sides of the man's knee.

The Mando did not cry out but he did fall backward, losing his grip on Raynar's arm.

The other two Mandos had reflexively turned in response to the boy's arrival. They'd taken their eyes off Raynar. Fighting down the pain and the effects it could have on control of his powers, Raynar exerted himself through the Force. The helmet of one of the Mandos jerked and flew upward, yanked clean off the man's head, then inverted and came down again, hard. The *thoonk* of the metal against the man's head was gratifying in a way Raynar knew he should find inappropriate. That Mando fell.

The apprentice turned and rained lightsaber blows down on the commando he'd injured, pressing his advantage, giving no mind to the other enemies present . . . trusting Raynar to deal with them.

There were new *boom*s from around the corner and down the main corridor. So Jaina was still up, still fighting.

The other fully functional Mando before Raynar, the woman whose mini rockets he had triggered, spun against him, a bare vibroblade in her hand. She thrust; he dodged. He riposted with his lightsaber; she caught the blade on her gauntlet, allowing the blade to skid harmlessly away. Raynar focused on her, could not pay attention to the apprentice's fight, though he could hear the *zat-zat-zat* sounds of lightsaber blows raining quickly yet ineffectively against Mandalorian armor.

Raynar feinted with a high-to-low lightsaber slash but spun out of the false maneuver into a side kick that caught his opponent in the helmet, at the jaw. He spun again twice more, kicking twice more, his spinning momentum maintained by the Force, and connected each time. On the third blow, his target crashed to the floor and lay unmoving.

The spinning also caused Raynar's broken arm to flail around uncontrolled. It hurt, and a groan escaped him. But he'd been hurt worse, far worse. This level of pain wouldn't debilitate him.

The apprentice was now backing away from his crippled opponent, batting away blasterfire as fast as he could swing his lightsaber. Raynar gestured, used the Force to levitate the Mando, and then slammed him down onto the floor again and again.

Normally that wouldn't take out an armored commando, and it

didn't this time, either. But the injury to the man's leg made the impacts hurt him far worse than they would have otherwise. And Raynar just lofted the man and slammed him down until the Mando fell unconscious.

Panting, Raynar looked at the apprentice, who was breathing even harder. "All right, you'll do."

"Sir, your arm—"

"Yes, make me a sling, would you?" Raynar tucked his left hand into his belt, partially immobilizing the arm, then trotted toward the intersection, trying to catch his breath as he went.

Jaina's battle had gone silent. That was either very good or very bad.

Raynar peeked around the corner. Down the way, walking toward him, carrying Jedi Tainer, was Jaina Solo. Her robes had burn marks but she seemed unhurt. Raynar stepped out and gave her a nod.

Jaina did not look happy. "This level is indefensible. There are holes where the StealthX hangar exterior doors should be. There may be more Mandos massing outside." She swept past him on her way to the turbolifts.

He followed. "Let's go up one level, lock down the lifts, and hold there."

She nodded. "How'd the new boy do?"

"Not bad. Not so good at taking orders. I remember when you were like that."

She finally grinned. "Still am."

An hour later, it was clear that the raid on the Temple was both a failure and far more damaging to the Jedi than the government could have guessed.

The assault on the Main Hall, which had involved Mandos firing ranged weapons into the hall from fixed positions outside, was, Master Hamner announced, nothing but a feint. "The real attacks came at the hangar level and through the food warehouse areas. Commandos entered with enough explosives and electronics subversion gear to open indefensible passages throughout the Temple and cripple all our communications and coordination. But fast thinking and an early alert from Jedi Solo meant we were aware of the possibility of flanking maneuvers and could counter them."

No Jedi had died. Losses among the Mandos were unknown; follow-up Mando units had retrieved their fallen comrades. Government forces were now situated around the Temple, preventing traffic from moving to or from the edifice. Mobile artillery emplacements were trained on the main entrance and all known secondary entrances.

Kyp Durron, who had led the defense at the food-preparation level, brought the news to Jaina. "The StealthX launch is scrubbed. No way are we going to be able to get them out of here unseen."

Jaina, sitting alone at a table in the mess hall, using a datapad to compose her report, scowled at him. "They're the stealthiest vehicles in the galaxy."

"In space. In atmosphere, the repulsors and thrusters still make noise . . . and Master Hamner is certain that the government has directional mikes aimed at every exit. If they hear starfighter engines powering up . . ."

"They'll power up their mobile turbolasers and blow the StealthXs out of existence by sight, one by one, as they leave the hangar." Angry, Jaina sat back. "We can't reinforce Uncle Luke. We can't do anything about the Sith or the Maw."

"We can't even get Jedi Saar offplanet. The sneaky ways we have to get into and out of the Temple without being seen presume that the parties involved are cooperating."

Jaina sighed. "Any word from the government?"

"Demands for our surrender. Master Hamner's on the arrest list, me, you, Thul, pretty much anyone they recognized or recorded during the assault. And Saar, of course. How are Thul and Tainer?"

"Up and around. In casts." Jaina became contemplative. "It was good to see Raynar in action again. He was . . . almost . . . normal."

"We'll let him be abnormal. These are abnormal times."

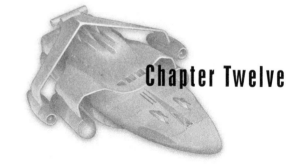

Chapter Twelve

NIGHT HAD FALLEN. ALLANA HAD BEEN FED, HAD COMPLETED HER studies, had been tucked into bed by C-3PO.

Now that he was gone, she rose and dressed again, this time adding a dark hooded jacket to her ensemble to make her harder to see in the dark, then got Anji and crept to the mini lift. Just as they had the previous night, they exited the *Millennium Falcon* and descended to the ground. Just as the previous night, Allana saw someone standing night watch in the needleship berthed near the *Jade Shadow*. This time, the silhouette seemed to be that of a woman, sitting alone in the cockpit and barely visible behind the canopy. Allana didn't like the way that made her feel—like the woman was watching her. But wasn't that the way she always felt when she disobeyed?

Instead of heading straight for Monarg's hangar, Allana led Anji around in the darkness until she could see the *Falcon*'s cockpit. Through the viewport, she could see C-3PO, sitting in the copilot's seat, apparently studying the baffling array of controls on the main console.

Allana activated her comlink. "Threepio?"

The droid jerked upright. He looked back along the *Falcon*'s cockpit access corridor, and his voice came back across the comlink. "Yes, Miss Allana? Have I forgotten something? Would you care for a nice glass of water or milk, perhaps?"

"We can see you."

C-3PO leaned forward a little, as if to assure himself that Allana could not be crouching at the end of the corridor, out of his sight. "Oh, I doubt that very much. None of the bulkheads between us is made of transparisteel."

"But the forward viewport is. Turn around and look hard."

The droid did as commanded, swiveling in his seat, looking first at the monitor screens on the console, then peering out through the forward viewport.

Allana stood on tiptoes, stretched her hand as far above her head as she could, and waved at him.

The droid came to his feet. "Oh, my. Miss Allana, how did you get out there?"

"We walked here."

"I clearly must have forgotten to lock the exterior hatches. Yet I remember doing so. Did you decrypt the password? Thirty-four characters long and composed of a baffling array of illogical alphanumeric sequences. You would have to display skills far beyond those you have demonstrated in your studies."

"It doesn't matter. We're going out."

"No, no, you must come back inside. I'll be right out."

"We'll be gone by then. But you can find us at Monarg's Mechanic Works. We're going to rescue Artoo-Detoo."

"Oh, no, miss—"

She switched off her comlink and dashed out of sight of the cockpit viewports, knowing with a child's certainty that C-3PO would be along to sort things out if she couldn't rescue her other droid friend.

* * *

Moments later she stood once more in the shadow of the stack of lubricant barrels beside Monarg's permacrete dome. She knew she didn't have much time; though C-3PO walked comparatively slowly, it wasn't all that far from here to the ship.

She hefted an empty container. It was, in fact, *almost* empty; perhaps half a liter of fluid sloshed inside. She set that barrel aside for the moment.

With Anji shadowing her steps, she carried two others and set them side by side five meters from the shop's front doors, then brought forward the first one she'd picked up. Once she was adjacent to the others, she uncapped the container, upended it with the awkwardness inevitable when a child manipulates an object light enough to carry but too big to handle easily, and poured its contents out on the other barrels. Then she set this barrel beside them.

Now to commit a crime. She hesitated a moment because she was sure it *would* be a crime. But it was also the right thing to do, and whenever Han had to choose between obeying the law and committing a crime for the right reason, he committed the crime and said that it was because Leia made him do it for the right reason. Allana nodded, satisfied with that logic.

She pointed at the door beside the shop, then whispered to Anji, "Go sit."

Anji cocked her head and twitched her whiskers.

"Don't play stupid with *me*," Allana warned. "I know how smart you are."

Anji contemplated Allana's outstretched arm for a moment, blinked a couple of times, and trotted off—then stopped about halfway to the door and turned around to wait. Allana sighed. It would have to do.

From her pocket, she brought out the tiny welder she'd borrowed from the *Falcon*'s tool locker. She'd seen Han use it several times for minor tasks, but never for arson. She ignited it and held its flame to the liquid she'd poured out over the barrels. In moments they were ablaze.

She switched off the welder, collected Anji, then ran to stand beside the doors into the shop and kicked them several times, which resulted in a loud, metallic banging. Then she crouched down, pulling the garment's dark hood over her head and wrapping Anji under her arm.

There was no response. She watched the fire growing on the barrels and wondered if it would burn itself out or perhaps be snuffed by a neighbor before Monarg ever noticed. She wondered if Monarg was even in his shop. Perhaps she should have peered into his window again before trying this. But no, that would give C-3PO enough time to catch up to her and stop her.

Then the doors swung outward. The one nearest Allana hit her, not hard, and pressed her and Anji up against the rough permacrete surface of the dome exterior. Anji bent her legs, gathering herself to jump on the man, but Allana dug her fingers into the nexu's fur, holding her back.

Through the gap between door and jamb, she saw Monarg standing in his doorway as if thunderstruck. Then the man said a word that Han never, ever would use if he thought Allana was around. He turned and dashed back into his shop.

Allana frowned, unhappy. That hadn't worked right. He was supposed to run outside and hop up and down near the fire.

Monarg dashed out through the doorway, carrying objects in his hands. Allana thought she recognized one of them as a fire extinguisher, but he was visible in the gap for only a fraction of a second, so she could not be sure.

She scooted sideways and peered around the door. Sure enough, Monarg was holding a fire extinguisher, and she heard its *chuff* as he began spraying its foamy contents across her fire. He was also looking around, paying as much attention to his surroundings as to the fire . . . and in his other hand was a blaster pistol.

Allana gulped.

But as Monarg moved around the burning pile, as he turned his face away from her and only his eye patch was visible, Allana dashed around the door and into his shop, still clutching Anji's fur so the nexu would stay with her, then immediately ducked to one side so he could not see her through the open doorway.

The shop was as she remembered from the other night, alive with the rolling and scooting little mechanic droids. All had trays of parts and tools incorporated into their bodies just above wheel level, and some carried more in their hands as well. The droids did not react to her presence.

Dominating the center of the dome was the yacht. It was now a fiery yellow-orange, its many hull dents either pounded out or made hard to detect by the new color scheme. The yacht was far too big to have been brought in through the doorway Allana had used, but the shop had a larger sliding door at the far end, directly ahead of the yacht's bow.

Over against the far wall, not far from that door and beside a desk and computer console, was the blanketed mound Allana recalled. She led Anji over to it, keeping a wary eye back toward Monarg, making sure they never moved fully within his sight. As they reached the desk, the smell of fresh-brewed caf, strong as a Wookiee, assailed her nose and drove away the odors of paint and fuels; Monarg's cup was there on the desk, just poured and steaming.

She lifted the edge of the blanket draping what had to be her droid friend.

And it was. R2-D2 stood there, silent, unmoving, his indicators unlit.

"Artoo?" Allana's voice was almost too faint for her to hear. Was he dead, at least as dead as droids could be? Then she saw the restraining bolt plugged into the droid's torso.

Of course he couldn't wake up or answer. Monarg was stealing him. He had to keep the droid quiet so he could flush the droid's memory and reprogram him.

Allana grabbed the restraining bolt and tugged at it. Her small fingers slipped from the rounded piece of metal. She grabbed and yanked again, more fiercely, with the same result.

Desperate, she looked back over her shoulder out the doors. Monarg was still in sight, his back to the dome. The fire was out, the fire extinguisher was at his feet, and his blaster pistol was in his hand. He looked back and forth, his posture suggesting that he was very, very angry.

A mechanic droid rolled past Allana. She saw tools on its rack, one of them a set of hydraulic gripper-pliers. She snatched the tool, letting the droid speed harmlessly past.

Monarg was turning now, back toward the dome.

Allana pushed Anji under a workbench, then moved up next to

R2-D2 and let the blanket fall across them both. A moment later she heard, over the noise of busy droids, the sound of the doors shutting . . . sealing her in the shop with Monarg.

She moved as quietly as she could, making sure not to shift the blanket at all. She clamped the pliers onto the restraining bolt and began tugging. It still refused to come free.

She did not hear Monarg again until a few moments later, when the chair to her left creaked. She bit her lower lip and continued tugging. She could feel how curious and excited Anji was getting, like she thought they were playing a game. Allana tried to make Anji feel how serious she was, but that only made the nexu nervous.

C-3PO should be here by now. R2-D2's bolt should come free. Nothing was going right. That seemed to be the way it always was for Grandpa Han, too.

She heard Monarg's voice, a surprisingly smooth, mellow tone. She had expected him to sound gruff and mean. "Yes? What do you want?"

There was no answer. But a moment later the blanket concealing her was yanked aside. Monarg, seemingly as tall as a giant and twice as menacing, stood there, a mechanic droid beside him. The droid was pointing with one spindly arm at her, and as she came fully within view of its optical sensors it shifted so that it was pointing at the pliers.

Monarg grabbed her arm, yanking her away from the astromech. "*You.* You set the fire."

She screamed, a high-pitched wail of distress, and kicked him in the shin. Then Anji jumped on his shoulders and tried to chomp the back of his neck. Her bite restrainer kept her teeth from closing quickly enough to break the skin, but the surprise of feeling the mouth of a nexu cub around his neck made Monarg scream and release Allana's arm. At the same moment, the mechanic droid nimbly plucked the pliers from her hand and sped off back toward its intended task.

Monarg whirled in a circle, then reached up behind his head and grabbed Anji. If her quills hadn't been safety dulled, they would have gone right through his hand. But as things were, he grabbed the scruff of her neck and pulled her off, then slammed her head down on his workbench—*twice*—and tossed her onto the hangar floor several meters away.

Anji landed with a pained yowl, then rolled back to her feet, whirled back toward Monarg and . . . staggered three steps before she collapsed in a whimpering heap.

Allana kicked Monarg in the shins again. "Bully!"

Redness suffusing his face, Monarg turned back to her and glared with his one good eye. "You're going to pay for that, little girl." He had to speak loudly. Allana realized that it was because she was still screaming.

She stopped screaming, grabbed Monarg's cup from the desk, and dashed its contents into his too-close face.

He roared like a wounded Wookiee and staggered away from her.

She threw the caf mug at him. It bounced off his left shin, directly above where she'd kicked him, then dropped to the permacrete floor and shattered.

Monarg straightened and glared back in her direction, but his eye could barely open, and the way he turned his head, like a short-range sensor dish trying to pick up an incoming target, told Allana that he could not see her. She almost cheered.

Then the hangar door bang closed again. Allana glanced over to see if C-3PO had finally arrived, but the droid was nowhere to be seen. In fact, she didn't see anyone near the door, just two shapes that she might have been imagining disappearing into two dark corners. One looked big and male, and the other small and female, and then they were gone.

Allana didn't know who they were—or even if she had really seen them—but she *did* know that if they weren't C-3PO, they probably weren't on her side. She looked around for something else to throw at Monarg—something big enough to knock him out so she could rescue R2-D2 and Anji and get out.

Monarg flipped the patch up from his other eye. The orb he revealed was durasteel gray with a glowing yellow optical at the center. That was inhuman enough, but then it extended out four centimeters from his eye socket, telescoping and pointing straight at her. Monarg lunged at her.

Allana screamed again and darted aside. He froze where he was and turned, his head swiveling, the telescoping eye swinging independently.

And yet he did not see her, not in those first few moments.

She understood. The prosthetic he had for an eye was a micro-optic, designed to make very tiny things, such as delicate circuitry, easy to see and evaluate. With his normal eye out of commission, he had to look for her as if peering down a narrow reed. She ended her latest scream with a gulp and backed away.

He spotted her again and came after her, but his leg slipped out from under him—almost like somebody had pulled it—and he fell down.

Allana ran, hitting and ricocheting off one of the mechanic droids, and rounded the stern end of the yacht. It smelled like fresh paint. She wondered if she could find a container of paint to dash into his prosthetic eye. She peered back the way she'd come.

He had lost her again. His head and eye turned this way and that. As a mechanic droid passed near him, he reached out, seized it, assured himself by touch that it was not a little girl, and let it go.

Monarg made a strangled noise loud enough for her to hear, then raised his voice. "Headache mode!"

Every mechanic droid in the shop slowed its pace. The rumble of wheels across permacrete and servos moving arms immediately muted. A near silence fell across the shop, broken only by faint whirs, quiet metallic clatters, and Anji's soft whimpers.

Allana gulped again. If she had to creep to avoid being heard, it would take her so long to get back to Anji and R2-D2 that Monarg was sure to hear her again . . . or maybe the pain of the caf would wear off and he could use his real eye again.

But maybe . . . She looked at all the droids gliding around her. Even at reduced speed, they made pretty good time.

She crouched down into a ball and rolled onto the carry-tray of a droid passing her. It was a simple move, acrobatics much easier than some Leia had taught her, and she felt very proud of herself as she rolled up to a sitting position, having made almost no noise at all.

The droid carrying her rolled back the way she'd come, straight toward Monarg. Allana made an unhappy face, fearing that she'd have to kick the man again. But as the droid neared the man, he grabbed it, determined by touching its head-sensor area that it was one of his, and let it go. It moved past him a few meters, then suddenly veered off toward a set of side tables, almost as if someone had turned it off. Allana did not question her good luck. She just rolled free and stayed low, partially shielded by tables.

Why didn't Monarg command his droids to surround her and hold her in place? Obviously, it was because he couldn't. Their spindly bodies didn't have a lot of room for processors. Probably they knew only how to go places and fix things.

Another droid rolled past Monarg, was confirmed by him as a droid, and was released. It rolled on toward R2-D2. Allana moved forward and slid into its carry-rack as it passed.

This rack was full of tools. It was not comfortable to sit on, and she could not help but make a little noise as she situated herself on it. She saw Monarg turn back toward the noise, his eye stabbing around, seeking her.

Between her feet, she saw a metal file that looked like it might be able to pry R2-D2's restraining bolt loose. She snatched it up. Then an idea occurred to her. She picked up the hydrospanner beside her knee and flung it as far as she could toward the tables she had so recently hidden behind. It came down on the floor with a series of clangs as it bounced to a stop.

Monarg's head snapped in that direction. The droid Allana rode stopped, then reversed direction and headed off toward the spanner. Allana rolled free and came up in a crouch. She was now only a few meters from R2-D2. She moved as quietly as she could to stand before him.

Monarg reached the vicinity of the hydrospanner, vainly looking for the source of the noise, and inadvertently kicked the tool. His extensible optic pointed straight down at it.

Allana turned away from him and managed to get her improvised pry-tool jammed under one edge of the restraining bolt. She began tugging at it. It came a few millimeters free. She looked back again.

Monarg now had the hydrospanner in his hand and was looking around in its vicinity. The droid Allana had ridden last rolled up to him and took the spanner from him, returning it to its tray. Then its head swiveled around, detecting Allana, and it rolled toward the girl.

Frantically, she returned her attention to the bolt and tugged harder. Another few millimeters—

A shadow fell across her, and Monarg's hand clamped across her arm again. He yanked her away from the droid. Allana heard the clang of her pry-tool hitting the floor.

Monarg hauled Allana off her feet, holding her at arm's length so she could not kick him. The optic pointing out of his eye socket, looking around as if it had a mind of its own, made things even worse. She screamed again.

He waited for her to run out of breath.

And waited.

She didn't so much run out of breath as realize that her arm hurt. She choked off her wail and thrashed, trying to break free of the man's grip, but he seemed to be as strong as a loader droid.

"The problem with little girls," he told her, "is that, unlike droids, they can't be memory-wiped and reprogrammed. Meaning that if I let you go, no matter what you promise now, someday you'll tell on me."

She glared at him, wishing that she could make one of her own eyes scary. "I'm not going to promise you anything. I *will* tell on you. You stole Artoo."

"Yes . . . I think you need to see the inside of a trash compactor."

Allana heard feet shuffling toward her out of the hangar's dark corners. Monarg must have heard them too, because his prosthetic eye began swinging back and forth, peering into shadows.

Allana struggled, swatting ineffectually at the arm by which he held her. She opened her mouth to tell Monarg that he was in a lot of trouble, but it was not her voice she heard next.

"I say, I think you should unhand the little girl. If you do not, I will be forced to thrash you."

Chapter Thirteen

MONARG'S EXPRESSION CHANGED TO INCREDULITY. HE SWUNG AROUND toward the doors and the source of the new voice.

C-3PO stood there, the doors open behind him, his posture as awkward and unthreatening as always. But his voice was stern as he addressed Monarg. "I assure you I am not jesting, sir. It is time for you to release the girl. If you wish to avoid unpleasantness."

"I thrive on unpleasantness." With his free hand, Monarg rubbed his caf-abused eye and opened it wider. The skin surrounding it was red and it could not open fully, but it was clear to Allana that he could see again.

Monarg cleared his throat. "Seal up shop."

The doors swung closed behind C-3PO, trapping him inside the dome, and Allana heard the sound of automatic bolts engaging.

Undeterred, C-3PO took a few steps toward Monarg. "I am now in the process of loading a comprehensive package of unlimited-class total-combat maneuvers, the use of many of which constitutes a felony on most civilized worlds."

"Protocol droids don't fight." Monarg dropped Allana. She landed on her feet, rubbed her arm where his grip had pained her, and then scampered to one side, into the shadow thrown by the SoroSuub yacht.

Anji was still in the middle of the hangar floor, whimpering. Every time she tried to get up, she could only stagger a few steps before she seemed to get dizzy and fell down again. Allana didn't know how she was going to get her friend out of the hangar. The nexu was still just a cub, but she was already too big for Allana to carry.

Monarg advanced on the droid, his movements graceful and decisive. Allana winced. C-3PO was clearly in for a horrible beating, and she had no idea what he'd been thinking when he challenged Monarg.

The mechanic droids had slowed to a halt when Monarg had called for the shop to seal up. Now they constituted a silent audience, their head sensors slowly swiveling to track their master as he approached C-3PO.

Monarg stood before the golden droid, towering over him, and glowered down at him. "Have you finished loading your fighting program?"

"Well, frankly, no. It's a large package, and I'm having to debug and compile certain portions of it on the fly."

"Unfortunate for you." Monarg put one hand on C-3PO's chest and shoved.

The golden droid staggered backward, slammed into the sealed doors, and slid to a sitting position on the floor. "You are no gentleman, sir."

"I'm aware of that. It doesn't cost me any sleep." Monarg advanced and kicked, a powerful blow that connected with the side of C-3PO's head.

His head rocked and the glowing lights of his eyes dimmed for a moment. "Oh, dear."

Allana had to stop this, now. C-3PO couldn't endure much of this sort of pounding. He'd be in pieces in moments. Monarg kicked at C-3PO again, this time so hard that he spun himself around in a complete circle and fell on the floor. He screamed in surprise and rolled to his knees, then whirled around to glare at Allana.

"Did you do that?" he demanded.

"Do *what?*" Allana replied.

Monarg only shook his head and stood up, turning back to C-3PO. Allana dug out her comlink and switched it over to the emergency services channel. But no one responded to the words she whispered into it—there was only a hiss.

She glared at Monarg. He thought of *everything.*

Well, not everything. The mechanic droid nearest her had a tray full of tools, and one of them was an extra-long, extra-heavy hydrospanner. Perhaps if she had that, and sneaked up behind him . . . Surreptitiously, she began moving toward that droid.

A few meters behind her, lights came on all across R2-D2's torso and dome-like head. They did not indicate actual consciousness, not at first. The sequence in which they flashed was like a language to astromech engineers, who could talk at length about what power-up and self-test each sequence indicated.

But as R2-D2's start-up sequence activated his memory and reasoning centers, he began assembling data very fast—far faster than a waking human could.

Across the dome C-3PO had brazenly entered in his search for answers, the man who had attacked him was now in the process of swinging him around by his legs and slamming the golden droid into walls and permacrete flooring.

The restraining bolt Monarg had plugged into R2-D2 was now on the floor a few meters away, discarded. That was good. Anji was in the middle of the hangar floor, staggering around in circles. That was bad.

Allana was creeping up toward the man, a large tool in her hand, going from table to table and making use of them as available cover. R2-D2's threat analysis matrix marked it as a virtual certainty that she was going to attack the man. It was nearly as certain that the attack would fail.

Comm frequencies were being jammed. R2-D2 had several messages waiting, all from C-3PO and Allana. One from C-3PO was most recent, and was marked HIGHEST PRIORITY. He reviewed it in the milliseconds he waited for his motivators to come online completely.

"I say, Artoo, I've sent you a wake-up command. With the luck

I usually experience, it has probably had no effect, but if it has penetrated, please be aware that I am probably now in the process of being destroyed. This is chiefly a delaying tactic on my part, in the hope that you can awaken in time to rescue me, or, more importantly, Miss Amelia. I've attached the psychological profile of my assailant, as stored by the computer system of local law enforcement authorities . . ."

R2-D2's motivators came fully online. He immediately sent an emergency situation report to Zekk and Taryn Zel, then settled himself into wheeled tripod configuration and rolled forward almost silently.

Monarg was now folding C-3PO backward, exerting more and more pressure, threatening to snap the droid in half at the spine. The smile on Monarg's face was curiously friendly. Clearly, he was enjoying himself.

R2-D2 had traveled no more than five meters when he received a response indicating that Zekk and Taryn were aware of the situation and monitoring it from inside the hangar. He found this perplexing, since they had not yet made their presence known to Monarg. The solution to this puzzle came to R2-D2 a millisecond later, when he recalled the order *he* had been given not to reveal their presence to Allana—or even C-3PO. Obviously, they were operating deep undercover and needed to remain in hiding as they rendered assistance.

R2-D2 vectored to the right to stay as much behind Monarg as possible during his approach. He rolled past Anji, then Allana, who gave a little gasp of surprise as he shot by.

The astromech opened an external access plate and extended one of his many tools, an arc welder. He adjusted its electrical output to voltage and amperage that were less efficient in metal welding and more effective against living tissue. As he rolled up behind Monarg, he chose a target area—left buttock, a large and, for the moment, comparatively stationary region—and touched his welder to it, discharging current into it.

The results were . . . gratifying. Monarg seemed to leap straight up into the air, and the volume of his screech made him sound like the opening tones of a planetary alert siren. C-3PO crashed to the floor, straightening into something like his normal configuration. Monarg landed beyond him, clamping his hands over his buttocks, and spun to look at his new attacker.

R2-D2 extended his welder in what he thought might look like a menacing pose and rolled past C-3PO toward the human.

Monarg ran, limping, along the curve of the wall, away from the droids. The astromech ignored him and rolled up to the doors. He extruded his datajack and inserted it into the wall plug beside the doors.

Normally, it would take several minutes to crack the security on this dome. It had taken that long when R2-D2 had entered for the first time. But Monarg, knowing that the astromech was helpless, had not bothered to change his codes. The doors unbolted and swung open. R2-D2 swiveled his head to look at his companions and tweetled at them.

C-3PO, struggling to his feet with a great whining of his servos, nodded. "I agree. Miss Amelia, Artoo suggests that we leave now. At a running pace."

Allana raced over to Anji and buried a hand in her fur, then led the cub toward R2-D2 and C-3PO. A mechanic droid reached for her stolen hydrospanner as she passed. Barely looking at the droid, she swung the tool at it without even thinking, just reacting to the sense of danger. The blow was as effective as Monarg's kick to C-3PO had been: the droid's head rocked, and the droid fell over.

She reached the doors. "I was right." Then she and Anji were through, into the darkness beyond.

"Yes, you were right." C-3PO waddled after her.

"You were wrong."

"If I had teeth, I would be gritting them at this moment. Yes, I was wrong."

R2-D2 issued a final command to the dome, then rolled in the wake of his friends. The doors closed behind him; as they locked, R2-D2 heard the distinctive sound of a blaster pistol being discharged, its bolt hammering into the thick durasteel of the shut door.

The astromech knew that the lockup command he had issued would not delay Monarg for long, but any delay would help—especially the way Anji was staggering about. In addition, the comm center commands he'd issued would keep the man from calling for support for some time, and that could be even more important.

"Do you really have an ultimate fighter program?"

"Oh, no, miss. I'm certain that a child of four could outwrestle me on my best day."

"Then we'd better hurry up and get Anji aboard the *Falcon*," Allana said. "She doesn't look very good, and I don't think Monarg would be very nice to her if he caught us again."

"I should think not," C-3PO agreed. "While pursuing you, I did access local files on our friend Monarg and his arrest record. He has a habit of becoming inebriated and engaging in unscheduled combat events involving his neighbors. I ran his behavior against a psychological analysis and prediction package, and came up with a profile of, as they say, "buttons to push" in a variety of situations. When I entered the dome and saw that Artoo was inert but freed of his restraining bolt, I took steps to awaken him and then keep our host's attention on myself while Artoo awoke."

"That was a good plan."

"Thank you, miss."

"I wish all your plans were that good."

C-3PO merely sighed.

As they ran, waddled, and staggered up the *Millennium Falcon*'s boarding ramp, they heard the doors of Monarg's dome slam open.

Allana looked, anxious, at R2-D2. "Can we keep him out?"

At the top of the ramp, the astromech waited until Anji had stumbled past, then sent a localized comm signal to the *Falcon*'s computers. The ramp rose into place and locked. He tweetled at C-3PO.

"Artoo says, um, no. Or, rather, only for a few minutes. We face an angry, determined mechanic with a shop full of tools. In addition, his is the most successful local mechanic's shop, and his arrest record, which reveals that he is never more than locked up overnight for his drunken rampages, suggests that he is in very good favor with the local authorities."

"So what do we do?"

"We get on the comm and threaten him with legal action if he continues his aggressive behavior, of course."

Allana glared at C-3PO, then ran up to the *Falcon*'s cockpit.

"Grandpa and Grandma will know what to do." She jumped up into the pilot's seat and looked over the alarmingly complex comm board. Since Han and Leia had adopted her two years ago, Han had, with the mixed pride of an owner and a grandfather, shown Allana every detail of the ship's controls. He had done so again and again, had even let her take the yoke for brief periods of time and complete simple flying tasks.

Now she knew what to do. She activated the comm board, waited for a confirmation that it was live and receiving all local and satellite broadcasts normally. She switched the board to the preset for her grandparents' normal frequency and activated the mike. "Hello? Uh, this is *Millennium Falcon*. We need to talk to Han and Leia right away."

There was no answer.

"Please? Anji's hurt."

"Don't forget to say 'over,' miss."

"Please, over? Hello? Please call. He's going to be coming for us soon."

There was no answer.

BESIDE REDGILL LAKE, DATHOMIR

Ben was wrapped up in his cloak again, but this time it was for warmth rather than disguise.

All his life, he'd heard his father make amused but highly critical remarks about meetings. How they wasted time, how they usually constituted a forum for people to air complaints but not resolve things.

And this meeting was an example of exactly that. Clan leaders of both the Raining Leaves and Broken Columns, and the offworld "counselors," sat around a campfire built beside the lake and talked. One Raining Leaves woman, gray-haired and lean to a point just short of emaciation, had the floor—meaning that she held the gnarled, skull-topped staff indicating that she was the only person other than clan chiefs allowed to talk at the moment. "Clearly, *Shattered Chains* is no different from *Broken Columns*. It speaks only to the men's tribe and ignores the Raining Leaves. It is a ridiculous suggestion."

Several of those gathered, especially the men, raised their voices in protest, but Kaminne and Tasander waved them to silence, pointing at the speaker's staff. Those who had objected raised hands, reaching toward the woman, and she reluctantly yielded the staff to a black-bearded Broken Columns man.

He stood. "No name can please everybody. We have to decide and enforce our decision. We can't worry whether every member of both clans is satisfied. I say—*Rusted Fetters*."

Another raising of unhappy voices, another raising of hands.

Ben sighed. He wished Tribeless Sha were here. Of all the people at this conclave, she probably had the most perspective on clan customs and was not influenced by loyalty to either clan. But he had not seen her in several hours.

The question of what name to give the united clan seemed like one of secondary importance, but Ben had learned since joining the camp-fire council that the union simply could not take place until it was re-solved. And the way the two sides argued partisan perspectives, while pretending they were trying to help everybody, was a crime.

He stared into the fire, built higher than Carrack was tall, and frowned. Perhaps it *was* a crime, and perhaps it should be solved like a crime.

Motive, means, opportunity. Those were the staples of determining who had committed a crime. Once you knew who had a reason to commit it and what that reason was, who had the resources necessary to commit it, and who had the opportunity to commit it, the answer was close at hand.

With this crime, that of supporting one tribe's naming agenda over the other's, means and opportunity were not in question. But motivation—what reason did the two clans have to support names that referred only to themselves, that elevated them over the other? Ben suspected that it was nothing more than a lack of imagination on their parts—that, and a lack of understanding of what their clan names rep-resented.

He thought about it while more futile discussion raged. Then, in a lull while members of both clans glared among themselves, he raised his hand.

Olianne, who had just been speaking, looked annoyed but handed him the speaker's staff.

He rose. Several people looked confused that he would be talking. His father merely looked amused.

"Can I take it that the name *Raining Leaves* sort of speaks to your place in the world—you live in the forests, under open skies, you want to make reference to nature?" Ben looked from Raining Leaves member to member as he spoke.

Firen Nuln nodded, though she looked a little uncertain. "The name is ancient, so we do not know what the members of the clan council were thinking when it was chosen. But, yes, that's the belief."

Ben turned to Tasander. "And *Broken Columns*. I kind of get the sense that the name is saying, *We break with the traditions of the past that made us slaves.*"

Tasander nodded. "That's exactly right. Columns representing society as it was before. A failed way of living."

"Then I have a suggestion." Ben drew a breath as he composed his thoughts. "'I am as ancient as time and yet constantly newborn. Nothing lives without me, and without me there is no hope. Yesterday's children smiled at me, and tomorrow's children will as well.'" He stopped and glanced around, silently inviting the gathered clan members to solve his riddle.

They were silent for a moment, then Kaminne looked startled. "The sun."

Ben nodded. "Right. Older than nature itself on Dathomir. But new each day. So it sort of combines the symbolism of your two names."

There were murmurs, mostly approving, from the gathering. Firen, a thoughtful look on her face, raised her hand. Ben passed her the staff and sat down again.

Luke leaned over to whisper in his ear. "Not bad."

"Gave 'em something to think about, anyway."

"And you invoked one of their own customs to do it. Politically savvy of you." Luke leaned back.

Ben smiled, cheered by the praise, then returned his attention to the assembly.

Within a quarter of an hour, Tasander and Kaminne, after huddling together, proposed *Bright Sun Clan* as a name for the united group.

There were objections, but fewer than for the other names—and none suggesting that *Bright Sun* favored one clan over the other.

Halliava pointed skyward as that discussion continued. "That's a good sign."

Ben and the others looked up. There, flitting around in broad circles, was a glowing object, a tiny one; it gave off a little yellow light that intensified and faded at irregular intervals like a malfunctioning glow rod.

"Sparkfly." That was Drola of the Broken Columns. "You don't usually see them when it's this cool out."

"Look, another." Kaminne pointed to a different quarter of the sky, where a second sparkfly flew its erratic course.

The gathered Dathomiri seemed cheered by the symbolism of the pretty insects, and within a minute many more sparkflies had joined in the aerial display. Then the sky seemed alive with them, sparkflies by the hundreds, and Ben could see men and women of both clans all over the campsite craning their necks to stare up at the glowing patterns the insects made.

A sparkfly descended to alight on a man of the Broken Columns not five meters from Ben. The man froze, nervous, as the long-winged, translucent insect walked from his elbow to his wrist, the luminous glow produced within its body ebbing and rising in the same rhythm as those of the sparkflies overhead.

Then the insect's tail end dipped and brushed against the man's wrist. A large spark erupted from the tail and a patch of his skin, a centimeter in diameter, blackened. Smoke rose from it and the man yelled, swatting the insect away.

That seemed to be a signal for the other insects. Streams of light poured down from the sky, the sparkflies remaining in coherent patterns until they reached an altitude of one or two meters from the ground. Then they spread out randomly, seeking the Dathomiri, stinging with their high-temperature sparks.

Shouts and screams erupted from all over the encampment. Ben saw two sparkflies buzzing in toward him. He flicked a finger at each, thumping the insects away. They circled and went off in search of easier prey.

Suddenly his father was by Ben's side. "Nightsisters again. Can you feel it?" He swatted a small cloud of sparkflies away from his face. The insects hurtled into the ground. Some immediately flopped over back onto their feet and took to the air again.

Ben put his hand on the hilt of his lightsaber but restrained himself. Swinging a live lightsaber around in this environment, with pained and panicky Dathomiri now beginning to run in all directions, veering randomly in their efforts to elude the stinging insects, could prove fatal. "I can't."

"Focus, son. Or keep them off me while I focus."

Ben opted for the latter. Luke closed his eyes and relaxed into a meditative posture—a choice that looked strange, surrounded as he was by the chaos of flying, stinging insects and fleeing, shouting tribe-members. Ben kept near him, circling his father, swatting sparkflies away from Luke and from himself.

A gout of flame rose from someone nearby, spreading out into the sky, and waved about, incinerating an entire cloud of the sparkflies. Smoke rising from the flames spread through the air, and Ben saw sparkflies enter the smoke cloud and immediately grow disoriented.

He glanced at the source of the flames. It was Carrack, struggling into his armor while being beset by at least a score of sparkflies. In one hand he held the nozzle of a flamethrower, which, despite his state of distraction, the big man directed toward the thickest clouds of sparkflies in his vicinity.

Luke's eyes snapped open. He turned toward the trees surrounding the encampment—toward the very stand of trees where they'd had their meeting with Olianne and Vestara the other night. "They're out there, scattered, several of them. But I can feel a couple of them very clearly."

"Let's go."

Together the two Jedi set out at a dead run, zigzagging to avoid fleeing clan members and pursuing sparkflies.

Wielding a blanket dipped in lake water like a flexible club, Han stayed near Leia and tried to keep the sparkflies off her. He'd been fairly successful. She had a burn mark on one bicep, and he had one on his forehead. She walked through the camp as if unaware of the sparkflies near her; her attention was on the larger clusters high in the sky. To Han, it seemed that the insects would make attack runs against targets on the ground, then rise into the air, regroup, and begin new runs. It was eerily similar to starfighter attack patterns. It didn't remind him of insect behavior at all.

Where Leia watched, turning her attention from cluster to sparkfly cluster, the insects would waver and break formation. But she did not seem to be able to sustain this effort against them, and they would inevitably regroup.

She shook her head. "They're under tight control. Very organized. I wish Valin Horn were here. He used to be very good at this sort of thing."

"Keep them off me! I need help!" That was Carrack, still dividing his time between his armor and his flamethrower.

Han glanced at Leia, and she nodded. Together they trotted over to the big mercenary.

Carrack thrust his weapon, a long rod with a trigger at one end and a nozzle at the other, attached by tubing at the trigger end to a large metal bottle that was currently dragging on the ground, into Han's hands. The big man had burn marks on both cheeks, but most of his armor was on. "I just need a few seconds."

"You got 'em." Han took the weapon. Not bothering to ask for advice or instructions—that would have been unlike him, after all—he aimed the nozzle up toward the nearest large cloud of insects and pressed the trigger.

A gratifyingly bright gout of flame erupted from the nozzle and shot into the cloud of sparkflies—into and through, jetting on for another fifty meters or more. It illuminated the camp from one end to the other.

Leia took Han's blanket, rolled it into something like a lash, and cracked it like a whip, here swatting three sparkflies out of the sky, there one. "Maybe a little *less*, dear."

"No, I like it this way." Han let off the trigger, aimed, and fired again. Once more the camp was bathed in hues of red and orange as insects were vaporized out to a distance of fifty meters.

A broad grin spread across Han's face. "Why haven't I ever gotten one of these for myself?"

Leia shot him an incredulous look before returning her attention to keeping the insects off the three of them. "Because it would be like letting children play with thermal detonators."

"I *like* it." Han swung the nozzle around, causing the gout of flame to curve across the sky, sweeping insects away as it reached them. "I have a *flamethrower.*"

"Blast it, Carrack, see what you've done?"

Carrack jammed his helmet down. Han heard a sudden hum of machinery as the helmet locked into place and systems all over the armor booted into life.

Carrack picked up the oversized blaster that lay at his feet and began a slow turn, eyeing the distant fringes of the trees. "Infrared active. Han, don't put the fire in front of me, you'll blind me."

Han, his grin unabated, swiveled so that his flame scoured the air mostly above and behind Carrack. "What have you got?"

"Stationary figures in the forest, deployed at positions thirty to forty meters apart. Women, all of them. I've got two males moving toward their line, but not straight toward any of the women. Oh, it's the Skywalkers."

Han saw more and more of the Dathomiri running into the lake, despite the chill of the water. They waded out until they could stand upright with only their heads protruding. The tactic did not seem to be working: sparkflies dived at them, settling on their scalps, stinging and burning them through their hair, and more were clustering out there by the hundreds with every passing minute.

He glanced at his wife. "You can use the Force like a big public address system, can't you?"

"I can make myself heard, yes."

"Tell the ones out in the lake to duck under the water at the count of ten. Then count down."

"You in the water!" Leia didn't seem to raise her voice above the Senatorial projection and volume she'd been able to employ since she was a teenager, but her voice somehow carried to all corners of the camp. "When I call 'zero,' go beneath the water! Ten . . . nine . . ."

Beside Han, Carrack raised his blaster rifle to his shoulder. He did not fire immediately, instead jacking a clip of what looked like small cylindrical grenades into the bottom. A rectangular optic screen flipped up over the weapon's usual sights, and Han could see images displayed on it, human-shaped silhouettes in a light green. Carrack was murmuring, barely audible through his helmet: "Target one, one five seven point three meters." He swiveled just a bit, and a new silhouette appeared on the display. "Target two, one three four point two meters."

"Two . . . one . . . zero!"

Han saw the heads of the Dathomiri in the lake go under the water. He aimed down and swept his flame across the water's surface. His blast incinerated hundreds if not thousands of insects, and smoke rising from the spot baffled and dissuaded more sparkflies descending in their wake.

"Away." Carrack fired and immediately racked the grenade launcher attachment on his weapon. He adjusted his aim and fired again instantly. "Away." He aimed. "Away." He fired.

He got five shots off before the first shell detonated in the distance.

Even for a Jedi, Ben decided, running full-tilt through a forest in pitch blackness was a bad idea. He grazed off one tree, stinging his shoulder, and crashed through a thornbush before the first pain of scratched flesh registered on his nervous system. Ahead, Luke seemed to be doing better, but not well; Ben heard his father smack a low-hanging branch, and the man's startled exclamation was a word that Ben would never have thought to hear him say.

Another few steps and Ben tripped over something that felt like a log made of meat. He hit the ground in a graceful roll and rose. "Stang."

"You all right?"

"I'm fine." Ben took a couple of steps back and reached out for the object that had tripped him. He had a bad feeling about it.

His hand encountered a face. Its skin was cold. "Dead body here."

"Our adversaries are concealing themselves in the Force. A reversal of focus. The closer we come, the more diffuse my awareness becomes—oof!" With Luke's exclamation came a thrashing of branches and a tremendous *thud*.

"Dad!" Ben charged toward the noise.

Then there was more noise, a lot of it. Fewer than thirty meters away, ahead and to Ben's left, an explosive detonated. Instinctively, Ben went flat to the ground. A moment later another explosive went off, ahead and to Ben's right.

Seven more explosives went off at intervals of about a second, each farther from Ben and Luke. When it was done, Ben raised his head. He could see a stand of trees burning not far away, another burning off to his right. "Dad?"

"I'm fine." Straight ahead, the darkness was briefly interrupted as Luke's lightsaber ignited at an altitude of about four meters. Ben saw it move, cutting through what looked like a series of vines. Then it, and presumably Luke, dropped to the ground. Ben didn't hear Luke land, but the lightsaber stopped in its descent.

Ben got to him. "What happened?" In the lightsaber's glow, he could see his father's face. Luke looked unhurt.

Luke gestured with it up into the air. "Net trap. Big stone counterweight. There were also some spikes with a gummy substance on them, probably poison, in the netting, but I avoided them. The trip wire and net were set up where the trees were thinnest, right where someone running out from the camp would come."

"Great." Ben tried to focus his attention on the Force, but either he was too rattled or the enemies were farther away.

"They're moving." Luke's tone suggested neither happiness nor disappointment. "I think this situation is done."

Chapter Fourteen

CARRACK FIRED NINE TIMES. HALFWAY THROUGH THE SEQUENCE, the first shell exploded in the distance. When he'd fired his final shell and waited for it to detonate a few seconds later, he turned to Han. "One for each of 'em." He raised his weapon and sighted in through the infrared optics. He swung the weapon in a slow, broad arc. "They're all moving. Well, seven, anyway. So are the Skywalkers. I'd better hold off firing any more until things go stationary again."

"Um." That was Leia. She caught Carrack's attention and pointed up.

Over their heads, in five separate groups, the sparkflies were clustering.

Carrack looked up. "Not good."

"Not good for *us*." Han gave the mercenary an injured look. "You're in armor."

"The armor has gaps. Gaps that are big doors for bugs."

"Leia? Lake?"

She nodded and bolted toward the water's edge.

Han followed. He pointed the flamethrower nozzle straight up and held the trigger down.

He needn't have bothered. All five groups of sparkflies descended on Carrack.

Han skidded to a stop and swiveled, sweeping the sky over Carrack with his gout of flame. His aim was good. Perhaps two-fifths of the insects went away.

The rest swarmed Carrack, clustering upon him, adhering to him. The big man was suddenly alive with lights as every one of the insects, it seemed, tried to burn its way through his armor. Han heard the man yell in pain as sparkflies got through gaps in the joints.

Carrack wasn't standing still, either. He'd bolted after Han and Leia toward the lake edge. Even now, with hundreds of thousands of the things on him, weighing him down and hindering him, he moved at a walking pace, but his speed was slowing.

"Han, get ready." Leia threw her sleeves back and gestured toward Carrack.

Han let off the trigger and swung the nozzle around toward the lake.

He'd guessed right. Leia spun, exerting herself through the Force, and Carrack was suddenly airborne, on a ballistic trajectory toward the water.

The instant he hit, Han cut loose with the flamethrower. His gout of fire swept along the flight path of Carrack's tormenters, not just catching the ones that had stayed with the big man all the way to the water but also incinerating those that lagged behind. In an instant the greatest population of attacking sparkflies was gone.

A moment later Carrack stood up in the water. He looked around, his movements stiff, and popped the helmet from his head. There were at least a dozen burn marks around his neck, and he looked miserable. "Medic."

The remaining sparkflies dissipated into the night sky. The Dathomiri and offworlders began to assess damage and figure out what had happened.

Nobody had been stung enough to perish, but several were badly injured, Carrack the worst of them. The burns at his knees, elbows, armpits, and neck were enough to send him into shock. Yliri and a healer of the Raining Leaves tended him, wrapping his burns in clothes soaked in a plant infusion the Dathomiri said was good against burns.

Han looked over the wounds as Carrack was being bandaged. "He needs bacta."

"That means the spaceport." Dyon had one black burn spot on the tip of his nose, now bandaged, and another on his right forearm. "None of the clans has bacta reserves."

Clan members straggling out of the forest reported that those who had headed off in search of the attackers had run into traps—nets, spikes, deadfalls, poisonous animal traps. It was there that the fatalities began to add up, two women of the Raining Leaves, three men of the Broken Columns.

And two Nightsisters. Luke went from the site of Carrack's first grenade explosion to each one in turn. At the first two, he found bodies—fragmentary bodies—of Dathomiri women. Kaminne, Tasander, and other representatives of both tribes went out to look. Olianne identified the woman at the first blast site as Hacina of the Red Mud Potters, and no one could identify the other. By no stretch of the imagination was either supposed to be here, so far from her clan lands. "Which," Dyon said, "means Nightsisters. I suspect that Carrack's grenades killed these two before they even felt the danger. But the first couple of explosions alerted and scattered the others. The survivors sent the insects against Carrack for revenge."

Ben led a search party back to the body he'd tripped over. In the light of Dyon's glow rod and the torches of the Dathomiri, they recognized that body as well.

It was Tribeless Sha. She had a stab wound in her back, and her throat had been slashed. Her eyes were open, her expression vacant. Solemn, Luke stooped to close her eyes.

"She's cold," Ben said. "She's been out here for quite a while."

Kaminne's expression was sympathetic. "She must have stumbled across some of the Nightsisters as they were setting up traps, and they killed her."

Ben shook his head. "As good a tracker as she was? She comes out here, sees something odd going on, hunkers down to watch—and *they* sneak up on *her*?"

Luke shrugged, an *It's possible* gesture. "They had the Force on their side, Ben."

"Yeah, I suppose. But something doesn't feel right."

His father gave him a half smile. "Well, I've learned to listen whenever someone like Corran Horn said something like that. I'd better learn to do the same with you. Trust and follow your instincts, Ben."

"Thanks, Dad."

They returned to camp in time to hear Han and Leia react to beeps from their comlinks—beeps indicating a message received and recorded. Han pulled his comlink out and activated it.

Allana's voice came over the miniature speaker. "Hello? Uh, this is *Millennium Falcon.* We need to talk to Han and Leia right away. Please? Anji's hurt."

C-3PO's voice, faint, could be heard next: "Don't forget to say 'over,' miss."

Allana continued, "Please, over? Hello? Please call. He's going to be coming for us soon."

Han paled. The change to his complexion was visible even in the firelight. He activated the transmitter on his comlink. "Han to *Falcon,* Han to *Falcon.* Come in, Amelia. Over."

There was no answer.

ABOARD THE *MILLENNIUM FALCON,* DATHOMIR SPACEPORT

"We could call the spaceport guards." Allana kept her voice hopeful. There had to be an answer that would keep Monarg away from her, and she hadn't exhausted the full range of adults-coming-to-her-rescue options yet.

C-3PO, now in the copilot's seat, sounded less sure. "Analysis of recent events, local records, and other probabilities suggests that any involvement of local authorities will result in the *Millennium Falcon* being seized and you being held to compel the surrender of Master Han and Mistress Leia. The likelihood that local authorities know their true identities, and are merely waiting for some authorization or provocation to move, approaches a certainty."

"Speak Basic, Threepio."

Something moved into the field of Allana's vision on the ground before the *Falcon*'s cockpit. It was Monarg, his expression clearly unhappy even in the limited light being cast through the forward viewports. With him were some broad-shouldered men in festive garments, likely friends of Monarg's rounded up while dining or drinking in the spaceport's limited facilities, and a rolling gantry—a mechanism that was half droid, half metal stepladder.

Monarg held up what was in his hand, an industrial-strength cutter-welder. He pointed at it, then pointed at Allana. Finally he walked around to the *Falcon*'s side, out of Allana's sight, followed by his companions.

"Not good, not good, not good." C-3PO sounded distinctly worried. "I calculate that even with the *Millennium Falcon*'s formidable armor plating, a tool like that, competently utilized, will allow him to cut his way through in a matter of minutes."

R2-D2 rolled in, back from his errand retrieving Allana's escape cable and sealing up the topside hatch through which she and Anji had made their exit. He tweetled.

"Artoo mentions that there is an antipersonnel blaster cannon situated very near the loading ramp, which is where that scoundrel is preparing to make his assault on our armor."

The astromech tweetled again.

"Oh. I was not supposed to convey that information to you. In no way was he recommending that you activate the antipersonnel weapon and annihilate our tormenter." C-3PO turned toward the astromech. "Of course, we can't use it, either, so why mention it at all?"

Tweetle.

"No, it's not a part of my programming that I've ever endeavored to overcome."

Allana looked over the ship's controls, momentarily overwhelmed by their number and complexity. She looked for something, some button marked REPEL BAD MEN, anything that would get her out of this jam.

There was no such button, and when she looked out the cockpit canopy again, she saw two more figures running toward the *Falcon*—a tall broad-shouldered man and a female companion—and they were both wearing coats with hoods pulled up to cover their heads. Didn't bad people always try to hide their faces?

Allana looked back at the control board. No, there was no single button that would help. But there was . . . all of them.

Allana was a very good student when the subject was interesting, and the *Falcon* was very interesting.

Tentatively at first, she began flipping switches in the ship's power start-up procedure.

"Mistress Allana, what exactly are you doing?"

R2-D2 tweetled.

"I know that, you rolling trash collector, but I'm giving her the conversational escape route of plausible deniability. Mistress Allana, please don't play with the power activation controls."

"I'm not playing. Go get me some pillows."

"Now is scarcely the time for a nap."

"I need the pillows because I'm short. The chair is too big for me. Please go get me some pillows so I can save us and keep them from hurting Anji anymore. There are more bad guys coming—I saw them!"

"Yes, miss." The protocol droid hopped up and waddled out of the cockpit with unseemly haste.

He was back in less than a minute and, under R2-D2's direction, as Allana continued her distracted, meticulous series of switch and control activations, arrayed them behind her on the pilot's seat so she could lean back against something solid while still handling the controls. "Artoo, we are all doomed."

Allana glanced at the astromech. "Can you plug in to the computer?"

He tweetled an affirmative. He extended his datajack arm and slotted it into a plug near the comm board.

Monitors and readouts all over the control surfaces were now lighting up, many of them with notifications of an imminent hull breach at the loading ramp.

What was next? Oh, yes, a checklist. She didn't know the checklist. Well, she knew one item. "Passenger, buckle in."

"Oh, dear."

Tentatively, even fearfully, she put her hands on the yoke. No, that wasn't right. First, the repulsors. She activated that system, diverting most of the *Falcon*'s motivator energy away from thrusters, and then gripped the yoke again. Distantly, she heard cries of alarm from the vicinity of the loading ramp—then she felt a big bump and heard a sharp bang.

"Oh dear," C-3PO said. "That sounded like an explosion."

Gently, as carefully as she could manage with her too-small hands, she pulled back on the yoke.

The *Falcon* lurched nose-first into the sky. Reflexively, she shoved on the yoke and the nose came crashing to ground again, jarring Allana nearly out of the seat, sending a metallic clanging noise throughout the ship.

R2-D2 tweetled.

"Artoo reports that Monarg's cutting torch exploded as he was trying to light it," C-3PO said. "We appear to have taken some hull damage, but the rest of the intruders have fallen off."

"Good." She tried again, even more gently this time, pulling up on the yoke as well as back.

The *Falcon* rose, wobbly, into the air. The repulsor system whined like an uncertain adolescent.

Perimeter lights all around the spaceport's fences brightened into sun-like luminescence and swung around to train on the *Falcon*. Allana was momentarily dazzled by the unwelcome brightness, but the polarized transparisteel of the viewports darkened. She blinked against the spots before her eyes.

The comm board lit up. "Dathomir Spaceport to *Naboo Duckling*, please state your intention."

"Tell him we're leaving."

"Oh, dear. Um, Naboo Spaceport, this is the *Dathomir Duckling*. We are departing."

"Return to your berth at once. You have not filed a flight plan or received clearance to depart."

Allana glanced out her starboard viewport. *Jade Shadow* seemed so very close. All she had to do was twitch the wrong way and the two ships would crash together. "If they won't protect us against big, ugly, mean droidnappers, we're leaving."

"Our captain wishes you to know—"

"I can hear your captain. What is she, ten years old?"

Allana felt a flash of pleasure. Ten! They thought she was ten. She pushed the yoke forward a touch. The *Falcon*, nose-down but completely off the ground, began floating toward the fences ahead. "Tell them I'm twelve."

"Tell her it doesn't matter how old she is. I will personally guarantee that she'll be tried as an adult if she does not set that wreck down right where it is and surrender to our security team."

"I don't think I'll pass that along. The young miss is a child in command of concussion missiles, and I think that her temper at this moment could best be described as uncertain. In addition, she has legitimate grievances against your spaceport administration, which I can enumerate."

Allana pushed just a trifle harder, and the *Falcon* gained forward speed. The brilliantly lit fence came toward them at an alarming rate.

R2-D2 tweetled.

"Our astromech friend, who should know such things, calculates that we're actually a couple of meters too—"

The *Falcon* drifted over the fence. *Mostly* over the fence. The landing skids caught the flexible wire-weave construction. Electricity sparked in all directions from the points of contact. The skids caught the fence material, but the *Falcon* was unslowed. With each passing moment, a twenty-meter stretch of fence on either side yanked free of its support posts and was dragged along behind the ship.

Finally there was a shudder through the *Falcon*. The nose dipped farther but did not come to ground again. The engines strained, and then the ship lurched and resumed her speed of a moment before, leaving in her wake a tremendous gap in the fence.

"Artoo reports obstruction cleared. I calculate the total cost to repair damages at—"

"I don't care."

"That doesn't include punitive compensation, pain compensation, sentimental value compensation assuming that the fence serves as a treasured memento to someone—"

"I don't care. I just want to know how long I'm going to be grounded."

R2-D2 tweetled.

"The odds say fifty point four two Coruscant years."

Allana flew for a while at treetop level. For her, this meant flying with the comforting noise of treetops scraping their way to oblivion along the *Falcon*'s lower hull. While that went on, she was sure that she was far enough above the ground. But R2-D2 pointed out via C-3PO that this tactic would allow pursuers to find her without effort once dawn broke, so she gained a little altitude.

At R2-D2's urging, she changed direction several times, eventually heading east into marshy territory characterized by very tall trees, festooned with moss, with open spaces between their trunks. Then, in a harrowing five-minute exercise in trial and error, she brought the *Falcon* to the ground. The crunch of landing, reduced by the softness of the soil, was not too alarming, and only a few diagnostic screens came up with damage alerts.

"Artoo points out that, if we are to elude pursuit, it might be best if we deploy the camouflage covering, which will help conceal us from aerial observation. It does mean walking about on the ship's top hull."

Allana nodded, feeling old, wise, and as successful as one can be when facing a punishment destined to last more than half a century. "I can do that."

BESIDE REDGILL LAKE, DATHOMIR

Han was still screaming into his comlink, demanding to know how Zekk and Taryn could have allowed someone to fly off in the *Falcon* with Allana and the droids aboard, when Leia's comlink beeped.

She answered it immediately. "Jedi Solo."

"Leia?"

"All—Amelia! Are you all right? Where are you?"

C-3PO's voice was next. "Actually, that's a lengthy story."

And it was. It went on long enough for Han to sign off with Zekk and for the Skywalkers to come over and eavesdrop, and between Allana and C-3PO it was recounted in enough detail that Han, pale, gave in to a sudden urge to sit on the ground. "She *flew* the *Falcon*."

Leia glowered down at him. "Hush. It sounds like she did quite well." She spoke back into the comlink. "Amelia, sweetie, have Artoo transmit us your coordinates. We'll be back there as soon as we can. Very, very soon."

"All right."

"I love you."

"I love you, too."

"Solo out." Leia looked among her comrades. "How do we want to handle this?"

Yliri, standing uncertainly nearby, stepped up. "We should load Carrack onto the cargo speeder. I'll take you to your ship, dump the speeder's memory so spaceport security can't use it to track you down. Then I'll take Carrack in to the spaceport."

"That'll probably be best." Leia sighed. "I hate leaving before things are resolved here."

Luke shook his head. "You have to."

"I know." There was a beep from the pouch at Leia's waist, though her comlink was still in her hand. She dug around in the pouch and came up with her datapad, which she flipped open. "Artoo is also forwarding your mail, Ben. Your datapad hasn't been picking it up."

"Yeah. My datapad is a lump of charred circuitry. Can I borrow yours?"

"Keep it. I'll get another one on the *Falcon*."

In minutes they had the unconscious Carrack and the shell-shocked Han loaded aboard the cargo speeder. Tarth Vames also boarded, apologizing for abandoning the party, explaining that he could do more good smoothing matters over at the spaceport. Then Yliri accelerated the lot of them southward.

Luke sighed. "Circumstances and the Nightsisters seem to be winning. Not one of us died and yet we're down more than half our strength."

"More bad news." Looking unhappy, Ben snapped the datapad shut. "I got a message from Jaina. There was a government raid on the Temple. Daala sent Mandos to do the job. No casualties, but it's a mess."

Luke took a look around, noting Vestara's location—beside Olianne, at the Raining Leaves' chiefs' campfire. Ben felt better knowing that Vestara had not been close enough to hear their exchange.

Ben whistled to himself. "I've got it. I wish I'd thought of it before."

"Got what?"

"How she's managed to hide her lightsaber and other gear. And maybe even what she's doing here. Part of it, anyway."

"Enlighten me."

"We know she didn't crash. The yacht at Monarg's shop that Amelia and Threepio were talking about has to be hers. Same model and antiquity. She leaves it behind to be fixed, maybe so she can escape in it later."

"Good. And?"

"She moves around in the wildlands to keep us moving, keep us guessing. And either her stuff is back with Monarg, or . . ." Ben looked off into the darkness beyond the encampment. "Or the first Dathomiri she ran into weren't Raining Leaves, but Nightsisters. Sith and Nightsisters go together like caf and cream. Her stuff is with them. She gave them the intelligence they needed to execute this attack."

Luke thought it over and shook his head. "Maybe she did encounter them first. That's not unreasonable. But we know that every clan has a Nightsister or two secretly among its members, so they didn't need her for the intelligence you mention."

"I guess not. I just want to blame her for something."

"Figure out what she's really doing and blame her for *that*."

"Yeah. Good plan."

Chapter Fifteen

HAN SWITCHED OFF THE WELDER AND LIFTED THE NEARLY OPAQUE goggles from his eyes. He stood in the starboard-side loading ring of the *Millennium Falcon,* the hatch open to the moist night air beyond. The armor-grade durasteel patch he'd just applied to the *Falcon*'s exterior hull was no thing of beauty, but it would maintain hull integrity in space and undo all the damage caused when Zekk had used the Force to sabotage Monarg's cutting torch. Han nodded, satisfied with his work.

"A little sanding, a little paint, and you'll never know it was touched."

Han jumped and turned to glare at the speaker. Leia stood a couple of meters back along the access, atop the end of the boarding ramp, which was in its up position and locked into place. "Keep sneaking up on me when I'm using power tools, sister, and there's going to be one amazing accident someday."

She grinned. "I waited until you'd shut it off. This time."

"The kid asleep?"

She nodded. "I kind of had to reassure her that we weren't going to ground her until she was our age."

"I wish you hadn't done that. I wanted to keep our options open." Han stepped away from the hatch and hit the button to close it. It slid into place and locked with a reassuring *thump*.

"I'm already making her wait until the next time we're on Dathomir to ride her rancor," Leia said.

"Oh yeah, the *rancor.* I forgot you promised her she could ride one."

Leia's brow shot up. "That wasn't exactly *me,* you know."

Han shrugged and smiled. "It is the way I remember it."

He took Leia's arm and walked with her up to the cockpit, depositing welder and goggles in a locker en route. "And how's the nexu?"

"I think she'll be fine. Lots of bruises." Leia said.

C-3PO loitered in the cockpit, his body language more than usually uncertain. "We are all sealed in, sir?"

"All sealed." Han flopped into the pilot's chair, which was now empty of Allana's pillows. "You and Artoo have finished all the cosmetic fixes?"

"Artoo's handling the last of the panels that popped free during our most distressing landing, sir. Otherwise your diagnostics boards are showing all green, I believe the expression is."

Leia took her customary seat in the copilot's chair. "Threepio, why didn't you inform us when Artoo first went missing? A lot of this trouble could have been avoided."

"Oh, dear, I knew this topic would arise. I was under specific instructions from Artoo not to disturb you unless a certain amount of time passed without further communication from him. I assume he felt that his investigations might take some time. And as I'm quite familiar, from decades of suffering the consequences, with his tendencies to initiate activities without anyone's go-ahead, I acquiesced. I truly do regret that this led Mistress Allana into harm's way."

"Not your fault." Han sighed. "Heredity and environment are to blame, just like usual."

Leia gave him a close look. "Usually it's enough for you to say *It's not my fault,* without actually coming to a conclusion about what *is* to blame."

"Yeah, well. Unusual times. Threepio, go ahead and knock off. We'll let you know when we've figured out what to do."

"As you say, sir."

Han waited until the golden droid waddled his way aft. "I hate to say it, but we've got to go back to Coruscant."

"I know."

"If Daala's mad enough to throw Mandos at the Jedi—at our *daughter*—we've got to do something about it."

"I agree."

He gave her a narrow look. "Since when did you become so agreeable?"

"Since when did you become so responsible?"

Han glanced over his shoulder toward the aft sections of his ship. He couldn't see her through intervening bulkheads, but Allana would be back there now, asleep, at peace. "Since we got another chance— and I'm not making the same mistake again."

"Oh, I think I can count on you to foul up this time, too." There was no real sting in her words, just amusement.

"Now, that's the disagreeable girl I married." He grinned at her and turned around to begin a preflight checklist. "You want to call Luke and let him know?"

"No."

He glanced at her, puzzled.

"Just being disagreeable." She leaned forward to activate the comm board.

CORUSCANT

Somehow, while Daala wasn't looking, the funeral of Admiral Cha Niathal had been transformed into a morning procession to be followed by a public service scheduled for broadcast on major news services.

In her quarters in the Senate Building, Daala struggled to straighten her freshly pressed white dress uniform jacket while keeping her comlink and datapad in hand and watching the coverage of the pre-procession preparations on the wall monitor. "So Coruscant Security signed off on the procession itself. But, specifically, who?"

The voice from her comlink was male and sounded defensive. "Well, it's spelled three different ways on three different forms. It appears to be something like Captain Koltstan."

"And is there a Captain Koltstan in Coruscant Security?"

"No, ma'am."

"Then that's not the name. Find out who it *was*. And who paid for the transportation and for the drum line and for the security deposit." Her door chimed to announce the presence of a visitor—and since it was a chime and not a query from a security agent, it was someone with standing authorization to enter. "Come."

The door slid up and Wynn Dorvan walked in. Seeing the rows of buttons on Daala's dress jacket unfastened and the jacket gaping open over her undershirt, he turned his back with an unobtrusive grace that suggested he had, in fact, dropped in to study the Super Star Destroyer holo prominently framed on the white wall before him.

"Oh, don't be an idiot."

"Ma'am?" That was the voice on her comlink.

"Not you. You, go away and get me answers. Daala out." She flipped the switch on her comlink with enough force to break a device built to less than mil-spec standards. She hurled the comlink onto an off-white sofa, then threw the datapad after it. "Any more delays and I'm going to be late to the procession." She got to work on her buttons. "What is it?"

Dorvan hazarded a look over his shoulder, then turned to face her. "Security estimates that the threat level for the service is rising."

Daala blinked. "I was just speaking with security."

"Yes, with their investigative arm. I'm talking about the arm that handles protection of high-profile targets such as, oh, you."

"And they're estimating increased danger for high-profile targets?"

He shook his head. "No, just for you."

She finished with the top buttons and turned to look at a blank section of wall. "Mirror."

The wall panel slid aside, revealing a full-length mirror. Daala couldn't stand the notion of having such a testimonial to vanity on display at all times, but she did need one for any self-examination before a public appearance, and having one hidden behind a wall panel was her compromise. "Would you be more specific?"

"Your public approval rating has been dropping since the announcement of Niathal's suicide, and Security thinks someone might take a shot at you during the service. It's that simple."

"Niathal was on Most Hated lists as recently as—"

"As recently as the day before her death. Now she's being looked on as a noble officer who took a blaster bolt for the squad. And you're the officer who attacked Mon Calamari a while back."

"So it's dissident Mon Cals and Quarren we have to worry about?" She swept her hair up, freeing strands from her collar, and let it fall into place against her back again. "What do you think—loose, braid, or up?"

"That's a very girlie question coming from you."

"That's why I'm asking *you*. I have no idea what the right answer is."

"Braid. But don't go. It's not just Mon Cals and Quarren. There are Mon Cal sympathizers, crazy Confederation holdouts, anti-Imperial extremists, Niathal admirers, Darth Caedus admirers . . ." He shrugged, apologetic. "Security considers the individuals who might want to harm you an unorganized and irrational threat, but numerous enough that they're taking it seriously."

She stared at him, trying to keep frustration from showing on her face. "I can't win here."

"No, you can't."

"If I show up, crazies get to take a shot at me. If I don't show up, I'm the insensitive Chief of State whose callousness led to Niathal's death and who can't spare the time to acknowledge her."

"You're right." Dorvan spread his hands, palms up, a *What can I tell you?* gesture. "So if you're going to lose anyway, I'd prefer that you lose and be alive, so we don't have to attend two admiral funerals back-to-back."

Daala breathed a long sigh. "Do you have any good news for me? Public reaction to the raid on the Jedi Temple?"

"Still hostile. The Jedi are now being looked at as trying very hard to take care of their own problems, such as the Solos taking the mad Jedi off to be cured, and we look stupid for not being able to stop them."

"You mean *I* look stupid."

"Using the Mandos is being interpreted by the armed forces as a sign that you don't have confidence in their abilities. Special forces are especially offended."

Daala rolled her eyes skyward, as if seeking aid from a Super Star Destroyer parked in low planetary orbit. "Is there some force I'm not aware of? Some massive conspiracy devoted to the destruction of the career of Natasi Daala?"

"Every politician I've ever met has asked the same question about his or her career at some time. The answer is usually no." Dorvan looked thoughtful. "Which means, of course, that it's sometimes yes."

Daala returned her attention to him. "All right. I'll remain in my offices and deal with any of thirty lesser crises. But I need something to divert public attention from me. Just for a day, or a week. Build a fire under the prosecutor's office and get them hopping on the Tahiri Veila case. Make sure every development is well covered by the press."

"I'll do that."

"And make sure everyone knows that she's an assassin, yes? That, unlike me, she actually *killed* an admiral? That she's not a sweet young orphan who sells baked goods door-to-door?"

"I'll try to remember that part." Dorvan spun and headed for the exit.

From the chilly safety of her gleaming white office, Daala watched Admiral Niathal's funeral events on her monitor.

Niathal was laid out in a transparisteel display casket mounted atop a repulsorlift-based flat-topped vehicle that moved at a serene pace from its starting position at the Mon Calamari embassy grounds toward the distant Plaza of the Founders, the great circular public gathering place erected in the wake of the Yuuzhan Vong War. The procession was, of course, aerial—a marching event would have to take place down in the dark, dank surface levels or along winding, narrow elevated pedwalks high in the air, neither of which promoted a sense of somber elegance—and so all participants rode speeders of various types, mostly fully enclosed dark vehicles suited to politicians.

Immediately before and after the casket craft were large barges carrying units of the Galactic Alliance Navy Drum Corps. As the procession moved along Coruscant's permacrete canyons, they played a martial percussive rhythm that echoed off the skytowers. It was a stirring performance suited to Niathal's career and temperament. It sounded like distant thunder organized into music.

After the drum corps craft came the dark airspeeders of the attending ambassadors, officers, and other important beings who had regularly dealt with Niathal in life. It was a long train of vehicles.

The procession cruised at one of the standard traffic altitudes, a height where civilian pedwalks were common, and the walkways along the entire procession route were thick with citizens. Daala saw not just faces but also signs in that throng, some of them hand-printed placards, some flashing diodes on thin sheets of flexiplast. One read GA OUT OF MON CALAMARI. Another flashed THE GREAT CURRENT WELCOMES YOU. A third, its lettering black and blocky, read DAALA, MURDERESS.

As the procession continued, the velvety tones of holocaster Javis Tyrr floated out from the monitor, describing the action. ". . . passing Medway Avenue. The drum corps has begun, I believe it's a percussion arrangement of 'Tialga Hath Fallen,' a traditional Alderaanian air about a warrior-queen who makes a stand against impossible odds so her children can reach safe haven. Yes, that's it indeed, and you can hear the polyphonic tones of the sequential bells substituting for Alderaanian flutes in this arrangement. Just passing under the midlevel Medway Avenue pedwalk, which you can see is raining silver flimsi confetti down on each vehicle in a constant downpour—ah, I'm given to understand that this is symbolic of tears, this would be the tears of the admiral's non-aquatic mourners, since the natives of Mon Cal do not cry—is the vehicle carrying Jagged Fel, Head of State of the Galactic Empire. There are reports that Fel faces increased political opposition within the Empire, so it's very generous of him to take a day off from interplanetary matters to pay his respects to the fallen admiral. Next is the vehicle of the Mon Calamari embassy, notable for its liquid-filled rear compartments and topside entrance hatches. Curb weight of the Mon Cal vehicle in its liquid-filled configuration is in excess of thirty tons, and it can only set down on specially reinforced landing pads owing to its high kilograms-per-square-centimeter ratio. Next . . ."

Daala muted the sound. While she would not object to a drum corps participating in her own funeral, the thought of her ceremony being *narrated* bothered her to a degree she had not anticipated. Just the notion of someone like Tyrr participating in any capacity was disturbing. She would not have wished it on Niathal.

The procession finally reached the Plaza of the Founders. The casket vehicle and the first thirty or so speeders turned to starboard and began a slow spiraling approach to the center of the plaza, where temporary stages and landing pads had been erected. The casket vehicle landed on the tallest pad. The other speeders set down in a series of semicircles, looking like parentheses bracketing the stages, and participants streamed out from them to ascend the construction.

An elegant middle-aged man, fit but prematurely white-haired, wearing the dress uniform of a Starfighter Command general, took the central stage's lectern. The words GENERAL TYCHO CELCHU, GA STARFIGHTER COMMAND (RETIRED) flashed up under his face as he began speaking.

Daala sighed and cradled her head in her hands. Of course it would be someone like Celchu. He'd worked with Niathal during her final years in office and retired when she had, but he had not dealt with Jacen Solo and was untouched by Solo's corrosive legacy. He was a good speaker, popular with both enlisted and officer ranks. He would make a speech that would cause the listeners to resent even more bitterly the loss of Niathal. People visiting Niathal's memorial would have only to touch a button on the marker stone to have the address pop up before them in holographic form, preserved forever.

Daala sighed. Nothing was going right.

Nothing was going right.

Chapter Sixteen

THE MORNING AFTER THE SPARKFLY ATTACK, THERE WAS A DIFFERENCE in the atmosphere at the clan conclave. Even though he was an outsider, Ben could feel the difference, in part because of his sensitivity to the Force, in part through simple observation.

Men and women of the two clans were more alert, suspicious. That wasn't good, because members of each clan were naturally more suspicious of the other. But there was also a new pride in their walks and voices. They'd weathered two Nightsister assaults and were still together, still advancing toward their mutual goal. Ben could see a growing conviction of their inevitable success in their eyes.

Of course, if he could, so could the Nightsisters. They would be angry at having been driven off, angrier at having lost two of their own. They would retaliate, and soon. If they waited very long, the tribal unification they opposed would take place.

None of which was Ben's concern right now. He wanted to catch a murderer. For Sha's killer was assuredly a Nightsister, and if he could identify her, it could lead him to other Nightsisters.

That morning, while more athletic events were conducted and funeral rites for the victims of the kodashi viper bites were planned, he wandered the campsite and asked questions. *Was Sha among you yesterday? How did she act? What did she say? Do you know who she spoke to before coming to you? Do you know where she went after leaving you?*

He got some answers. She was asking about the children of the Raining Leaves. *Asking what, specifically?* Just their names and ages.

Frustrated, at midday he returned to the offworlders' camp. He was not the first there; Dyon was already on hand, cooking their midday meal. Dyon, turning lizard cutlets wrapped in transparisteel foil atop bare ashes, grinned up at him. "You're a very dull boy, Ben. You know that, don't you? There are lots of Force-using girls around here who have still not paired up."

"Oh, be quiet." Ben sat, his back to a large rock. "No, don't be quiet. Tell me what you know about Tribeless Sha."

"Huh." Dyon frowned, thinking back. "Her name was Sha'natrac Tsu. She was originally of the Blue Coral Divers. But the clan put a death mark on her."

"Why?"

"The Blue Corals had a feud going with the Scissorfists, who were named for a kind of big, lumbering crustacean. The Blue Coral Divers were one of the new breed of clans, women and men ruling jointly, and the Scissorfists were former escaped slaves from a variety of clans and some women who'd joined them. Both clans lived near the sea. It was one of those feuds that went on for years; a handful of clan members on either side were lost every year to ambush, or just disappeared."

"Got it. Two clans not smart enough not to kill each other."

"That's basically it. Anyway, in one of those rare fits of sense that the Dathomiri clans sometimes have, the feuding groups had a diplomatic meeting to try to work out their differences, and Sha was part of the party, and she fell in love with a Scissorfist."

"Oh, no, not a love story."

"And one with a sad ending, too. The peace talks went badly, the two clans went back to warring, and Sha and her mate, who hadn't made any secret of their relationship, were suddenly traitors because they wouldn't agree to kill each other. They ran off together and were exiled. They ended up moving to a site not all that far from the spaceport, well out of the hunting ranges of their former clans. This would have been about seven years ago."

"So? Tragic ending?"

"So about five years ago, she starts hiring herself out to patrons at the spaceport, as a guide. She accepts courier jobs, hunting jobs, spying jobs, and seems to prefer the ones that take her farther and farther away from her home grounds, especially if they give her the opportunity to meet clans she hasn't run into before. When people ask about her husband, she says he's dead and she's going to kill whoever killed him. She doesn't say more than that, though."

Ben glared at him. "That's it? That's the whole story?"

"That's the whole story as far as anybody but Sha knew it, yes."

"You really know how to make these epics come alive, Dyon. How is it that you didn't become a historian?"

Dyon waved him away. "Don't be sarcastic to the man cooking your food."

"Actually, that's good advice." Ben fell silent. Dyon's story did suggest that perhaps Sha had stumbled across the killer of her husband. Still, the tale raised more questions than it settled. Who had killed her husband, and why? And how would the specific questions she was asking lead her to that person?

Something nagged at Ben, something Sha had said when they'd first met.

That was it, words about the Nightsisters. *They hide, they heal, they return. If their numbers are few, they come for your children.* And she'd looked so sorrowful, but only for an instant.

Ben stared at Dyon. "That's it. They took her daughter."

"What daughter?"

"Yes, what daughter?" That was Luke, settling into a cross-legged sitting pose beside the fire.

"I think Sha had a daughter, and the Nightsisters stole her." He explained his thinking.

Luke accepted a mug of caf from Dyon and shook his head. "That's pretty tenuous, Ben."

"I'm trusting my instincts. Yeah, it's tenuous, but it explains a lot if it's true. She and her Scissorfist husband are living away from their persecutors but also away from the protection a clan normally offers. They have a baby, everything's good. Then one night the Nightsisters come. Suddenly her baby's gone and her husband's dead. She hires herself out on missions that finance her while she searches for her kid." Ben looked around, visually scanning the Raining Leaves camp. "And she found something. Maybe one of the Raining Leaves told her, *There was a baby like that. But I don't want to talk out here in the open. Someone might hear. Let's take a short walk into the Trees of Imminent Doom.*"

Luke frowned. "You're being awfully flip about a woman's death."

"Sorry. Investigator humor. I heard a lot of it when I was with the Galactic Alliance Guard. Anyway, it would help if I could pin down the dates a little more precisely."

"I might be able to help with that." Dyon went fumbling through his many vest pockets and eventually brought out a scuffed, sturdy-looking datapad. "Luke, can you take over the fire for a few minutes?"

"Of course."

Dyon began tapping commands and queries into his 'pad. "It's nice to have comm repeaters and satellites. I can access the records at the spaceport. I mean, you're used to that sort of thing on Coruscant, but here . . . Um, Sha Tsu and Vagan Kolvy are first recorded as visiting the spaceport seven years, one month ago. The husband has no more visits after five years, ten months back. Five years, eight months ago, Sha lists herself as available for scouting, guiding, hunting activities."

Ben thought about it. "So in all probability, they took her baby—"

Luke shot him an admonishing glance. "Her *theoretical* baby."

"They raided her theoretical campsite, murdered her theoretical husband, and took her theoretical baby just over five years, eight months ago." He scanned the campsite again. "It would be pretty hard to introduce a new child into a clan like this, wouldn't it?"

Dyon snapped his datapad shut. "No, but it would be hard to do it unobtrusively. These people lead a hard, low-calorie existence, so nobody has a pregnancy that goes undetected because of extra weight. There's some exchanges of members among clans, so it's possible, say, for you to have a cousin over in the clan next door, and that cousin dies and you adopt her child. But everybody knows that the child originally came from another clan."

"Huh." Ben accepted a piece of foil-wrapped meat from his father and tossed it from hand to hand to keep it from burning his fingers. "After lunch, I think I'm going to start asking new questions."

His father grinned. "And when someone asks you to talk to her among the Trees of Imminent Doom?"

"I say yes, and close my eyes and pucker up for a big kiss?"

"There, that's the Skywalker survival instinct at work."

Ben was true to his plan. After the midday meal, he wandered the camp again, asking new questions. *Is this your child? How old is she? Daughter of one of the Broken Columns, I take it? Does she have any friends her own age?*

It was nightfall before he came across any answers that interested him.

With a special wrestling event, honoring those that had fallen to the snakes, loud in the distance, Ben stared down at a little black-haired girl, who stared solemnly back up at him. "This is your daughter?"

Halliava, winner of the short footrace for those with the Arts and other competitions, gave him a wide smile, a proud smile. "Yes. This is Ara. Ara, this is Ben. He's from far away, and he's a boy-Witch. Give him proper greetings."

The girl raised a chubby hand, palm toward Ben. "Welcome to our fire. We have bread and meat and water."

Halliava's prompt came as a whisper: "I am called . . ."

"I am called Aradasa Vurse."

Ben returned the salute. "I am called Ben Skywalker."

"Are you really a boy-Witch?"

He nodded. "But we call ourselves Jedi. Some Jedi are boys and some are girls, and the Arts we know are a little different from yours."

"Oh." Suddenly shy, Ara grabbed and clung to her mother's thigh, but she did not turn away from Ben.

Ben gave Halliava a friendly smile. "She's, what, four?"

"Five and a season. She's small for her age." Halliava shrugged.

"You can never tell how fast they'll grow. I'm tall, and her father was very tall. We used to jest that he was half rancor."

"*Was* tall?"

"He died before Ara was born. He was a warrior of the Broken Columns. We wed at the annual conclave six or so years ago, and parted at conclave's end. When next I heard word of him, he had died in a fall, climbing tall trees to plunder nests of their eggs."

"I'm sorry."

She shrugged again.

"I heard the circumstances of her birth were difficult, too."

Halliava gave him a little quizzical frown. "Who said that?"

"I forget. My father was telling stories around a campfire. Before I was born, my mother carried me around from battle to planetary disaster and back again, and one of your Raining Leaves wanted to top that story."

"Oh. Well, yes. I was saddened by Dasan's death and had told no one I was expecting his child. I went on one last long scouting expedition for the clan, knowing that soon after my return I would begin to show . . . but when I was at the farthest point on my trip from home, I slid into a ravine and broke my leg. I nearly starved, which I think is what has left Ara so small. It was not until after she was born that I was able to return to the Raining Leaves."

"Clearly, you're a strong woman."

She gave him another smile. There was no guilt or duplicity evident in it. "There are no weaklings among the Raining Leaves."

He waved at Ara. "Nice meeting you, Ara."

The little girl gave him another salute, but turned it into a wave halfway through.

Ben turned and, with a last cordial nod to Halliava, moved on to the next campfire. There he'd continue the deception that he was meeting as many clan members as possible, the better to understand their ways.

Halliava's story was unlikely but possible. Dasan of the Broken Columns had indeed died a month after the clan conclave six and a half years before, though no one could remember him wedding Halliava; still, not all such unions were officiated or remembered.

Halliava had indeed departed on a lengthy scouting mission three months after that conclave and had not returned for months, now with the baby Ara in her arms.

Blast it. Ben didn't want his suspicions to be correct. He rather liked Halliava. And maybe he *was* wrong. He'd have a better sense of whether he was right if something befell him to end his investigation—a plausible accident or a murder attempt.

He reminded himself that he did need to survive if he was to achieve his goals: justice for a dead woman and the uncovering of a nest of Nightsisters. Nightsisters, and perhaps Sith in collaboration with them.

Chapter Seventeen

CORUSCANT

TAHIRI VEILA STARED OUT THE TINY VIEWPORT OF HER DETENTION cell, staring at the late-afternoon traffic streaming past at a slightly lower altitude. Thousands and thousands of people swept by in their airspeeders every hour. And if they knew that Tahiri Veila, murderer of Admiral Gilad Pellaeon—an officer and leader remembered as affectionately by the Galactic Alliance as by the Empire—stood behind this viewport, some would probably try to put a blaster bolt though the transparisteel.

She knew she did not look like a killer. Tall and blond-haired, attractive though she did not enhance her looks with makeup or glamorous clothes, bearing curious faint scars on her forehead from events a lifetime ago, she looked like the sort of athlete who'd won championships early and then retired to a life of endorsing breakfast foods while smiling at the holocams. But it had been a long time since she'd smiled.

She turned to her visitor, who was seated at the end of the bunk that—aside from an unpartitioned refresher unit—was the only furniture in the tiny room she now called home.

The visitor gave her an understanding nod. "It's difficult to understand because it's based on logic that is alien to all rational minds. It's attorney logic, legal logic."

His name was Mardek Mool. A Bith, he had the elongated cranium and epidermal cheek-folds of his species, and huge dark eyes that watched Tahiri as though he expected her to fly into a rage and use a Force-choke on him. It did not bode well for her case, she knew, that her own public defender seemed to believe her capable of a senseless, cold-blooded murder just because she was frustrated. Still, Mool was competent, dedicated, and good-hearted, and he seemed determined to do the best job he could for her. Given that the courts had denied her the services of Nawara Ven, on the grounds that his relationship to the Jedi Order posed a conflict of interest, Tahiri supposed she ought to be glad to have Mool.

She moved away from the viewport. The transparisteel automatically darkened as she sat at the opposite end of the bunk from Mool. "So explain it. They arrest me on charges of complicity and murder, crimes of which I'm clearly guilty—"

"Don't ever say that. Not out loud, not to yourself, not when you're alone, not even when you're asleep. You're not qualified to judge whether you're guilty."

"Thank you for that vote of confidence," Tahiri said dryly. "They accuse me of these crimes, they tell their side of the case to the press as if they're hopping mad and lusting for my blood, all the while leaving me sitting in here for the longest time—in a medium-security detention center from which I could escape sleepwalking, by the way. And now, suddenly, they're pressing the courts for a trial date. I just don't get it. I don't even understand why *they're* prosecuting instead of the Empire, when the man I killed—"

"The man you're *alleged* to have killed."

"Stop that. Was an Imperial citizen and died on an Imperial world. I'd have thought that the Empire would have jurisdiction and I'd be tried there."

Mool sighed. "Tahiri, do you actually want to live long enough to figure out whether you *deserve* to live?"

She was silent a long moment, but she'd settled that issue in her own mind a while back, shortly before the security officers had come to arrest her. "Yes."

"Then you need to start doing what I say. You never say *I did it*—for a couple of reasons. A belief in your own guilt can show in your face, in your body language, more than you think, and can persuade a judge or jury of your culpability when everything else is perfectly balanced. And you never know when a government might have court permission to place listening devices in your vicinity. I do a sweep whenever I visit, and that might be good enough for now, but I'm not an expert and I won't always be around. They might not be able to convict you with the resources they already have. Don't give them any more."

"All right. So I'm . . . not guilty."

"You say it, but you still don't believe it. Meaning you think that every one of your decisions was of your own making, and that Jacen Solo had absolutely no influence over you."

"Well, of course he had some influence over me."

"How much?"

"It's impossible to quantify."

"Correct." He gave her an approving nod. "I think it was more influence than even you are able to recognize. He preyed on your insecurities. He isolated you, making himself the sole point of reference for your worldview, which means your ethics and understanding of right and wrong. He may have used Force abilities on you, abilities you never saw being employed. Tahiri, every one of us wants to believe that he or she is mentally competent at all times. But nobody is sane at every moment of his life, not a soldier or pilot who has killed and seen friends killed throughout a career, not a Jedi who struggles with lightside and dark-side issues all her life, and not a teenage girl who saw the love of her life die and who later got to be led back into his presence again and again by his charming brother. Where, in the middle of all that, do you even have a chance to be consistently sane?"

Tahiri felt a stirring of hope. But to accept Mool's explanation would mean surrendering her belief that she'd always been in charge of her own thoughts, her own decision making. That would be an awful conclusion to come to.

Fortunately for her, Mool turned the subject back to her other questions. "As to why they arrested you, then let you sit in a medium security facility—they *wanted* you to escape."

Understanding dawned for Tahiri. "Because if I fled, I'd convict myself."

"Not only that, but you'd probably seek help from your friends, putting *them* on the wrong side of the law, too. And why did the government talk mean and then sit on the case? You always talk your best game so that the opposition can never point to a statement you've made that suggests a weakening of your position or a lessening of your righteous fury. But then they sat on the case because time was on their side. The longer things take, the more credits it costs you, the more stress it puts you under . . ."

"The more I'm likely to give up or escape."

"Very good. Now, why not let the Imps try you? They might have done that. They *still* might. But the GA *does* have the right. Pellaeon was accorded GA citizenship for life because of his tenure as Supreme Commander of the Galactic Alliance Defense Forcce. As to why they've suddenly turned up the heat under this case, I can only guess, but I think it's because Chief of State Daala needs something to distract the press from Admiral Niathal's death."

"So I'm just a game piece being moved around to convenience them. There's no offended sense of justice at work here, not really."

Mool clapped his hands as if applauding a superior sports play. "And if they aren't pursuing justice, why are you willing at all to submit to justice?"

A wave of cold anger washed across Tahiri. For a moment she wasn't sure how to handle it—suppress it like a Jedi, draw strength from it like a Sith? She chose neither, letting it settle on her, letting it turn the tone of her voice brittle and sharp. "So what do we do?"

"I begin assembling medical witnesses who can testify to the mentality of someone experiencing undue influence from a manipulative authority figure. I begin aggressively promoting a change of venue for the trial—"

"Why?"

"Because the one person in the galaxy who has the most experience with the Sith is prohibited by law from coming back to Coruscant to testify."

"Luke Skywalker."

"Correct. And we are very eager for him to testify, not only because of his breadth and depth of knowledge, but also because the public is experiencing a growing sympathy for the Jedi, and when I announce that Grand Master Luke Skywalker *must* testify in order for the trial to be fair, the prosecution case will experience more resistance from the public. Meanwhile, you need to remember that phrase you just used about being a game piece, and whenever you're in public, put on a face reflecting how that feels, because you were also Jacen Solo's game piece, and that's why you're in trouble. Tahiri, you really were a victim. You need to understand it, and the public needs to understand it."

"All right. I'll try."

"Nobody wants to think of herself as a victim. You'll have to try very hard to overcome that reluctance." Mool rubbed at his cheek folds and looked away from her for a moment.

"You've got more bad news."

"I hate dealing with Jedi. Hard to keep secrets." He looked at her again. "I think you should reconsider the deal."

"*What* deal?" Tahiri asked, putting some ice into her voice.

Mool flared his cheek folds. "The only deal I've brought you." Shortly after becoming her public defender, Mool had brought her an offer from someone inside Daala's government: If she would become an informant and gather evidence of Jedi crimes against the Galactic Alliance, she would be sentenced to a short term in a minimum-security facility of her choosing. "I've been led to believe that the offer remains open—and it may be your only chance of avoiding a death sentence."

Tahiri glowered. "I've given you my answer on that," she said. "I'm not changing my mind."

Mool sighed and nodded, then said, "In that case, I think you need to consider where you might find a more suitable advocate."

"You're *quitting?*"

Mool shook his head. "Not a chance."

"Then why?"

"Because I've been in this business for a few years now," Mool said. "And that's long enough to know you need someone who's been in it for a few *decades*. As much as it pains me to say it, I'm not the best being to handle a high-profile case like this. It's a different game than the one I usually play. To tell you the truth, if you're determined to take this trial, I won't even know the rules we're *really* using."

Tahiri sighed, then looked across the cell at her refresher unit and nodded. "At least you're telling me the truth," she said. "That counts for more than you know. Thank you."

"You're welcome," Mool said. "I just wish I had more to offer. I want to help you—I truly do."

"The truth is enough, Mardek." Tahiri turned and gave his knee a grateful squeeze. "Give me that, and you give me everything."

Chapter Eighteen

LUKE'S BACKFLIP WAS PERFECT. AT ITS APEX, HIS HEAD WAS HIGHER THAN it would have been if he were standing. He came down in a slight crouch, already in a defensive posture, and barely stirred the dust as he landed. There were whoops of appreciation from the crowd surrounding the fighting ring.

Firen was close upon him, having charged during his flip, and she struck just as he came down, an open-palmed blow to his chest, what was clearly her favorite move. He got his right wrist against hers before the blow hit and forced it to the side. Her blow missed his chest by six centimeters at least.

And his parry left him in perfect position for a riposte. His own counterblow, also open-palmed, caught Firen on the point of the jaw. There was no *clack* of teeth meeting teeth; her mouth was clenched shut when he hit. But her head rocked and she staggered backward.

And her left hand came forward, opening, releasing a cloud of dust and sand into Luke's face, blinding him.

He stumbled back, hearing cheers from the Raining Leaves in the audience. He shook his head, but his vision didn't immediately clear.

This was bad. He was Firen's superior as a fighter, having trained in more styles on more worlds than she had fingers and toes, but he'd forgotten that Dathomiri unarmed contests were no-holds-barred, with no rules against using weapons of opportunity. Firen hadn't cheated. She'd outwitted him. And she'd be coming for him— *now.*

This time his flip was a forward one. He heard his opponent pass beneath him, unable to stop her forward rush, and heard her offer up a colorful Dathomiri curse.

Luke more than heard her. He found her in the Force.

He landed awkwardly—*deliberately* awkwardly, as though not being able to see had caused him to over-rotate. He stumbled forward a couple of steps, then steadied himself and furiously scrubbed at his closed eyes.

He could feel Firen charging. Now she was almost silent. She was as fast and predatory as a Dathomiri lizard.

But he knew where she was. As she came within range, he lashed out with a side kick, his left heel connecting with her midsection, stopping her in her tracks. She uttered an "oof" that sounded like it accompanied all the air from her lungs.

Luke pivoted on his other foot, lashing out with a spinning kick that connected just below the first one. The blow took Firen off her feet. He heard her hit the dust. And in the Force, he could dimly envision her, facedown, struggling to rise.

He got beside her and bent down, wrenching the arm she was using for support up behind her back. She fell toward him and thrashed, but he kept one hand on her elbow, one on her wrist, and the leverage he applied held her in place.

He heard the crowd begin to chant, counting down from ten. In that ten-count, Firen was unable to free herself. After "one" came a mass cheer and shouts of dismay, but the fight was done. Luke released his grip, stepped back, and went to work again clearing his eyes.

"Here." It was Ben's voice. Luke reached out and was handed a waterskin. Grateful, he poured some of its contents across his eyes. He blinked, his sight restored. "Thanks."

Firen stood a couple of meters away. She looked unhappy. Seeing his gaze on her, she turned toward him. "There's nothing worse than being beaten by a man."

Luke grinned. "You mean a *lowly* man?"

"Well . . . Kaminne says we should no longer use that phrase."

"There's having a rancor fall atop you."

She thought about it. "You are right. That is worse." She stepped forward and extended a hand. "Well fought, lowly man."

"Well fought, traditionalist oppressor."

"Stop it, you two." That was Kaminne, stepping forward, but there was no censure in her tone, and she was smiling. She turned to face the crowd. "So in the weaponless combat for those with the Arts, champion for this year is Luke Skywalker of the Jedi."

Members of both clans, though mostly Broken Columns, came forward to congratulate Luke, and Tasander gave him his first-place winner's medallion. Then, inevitably, the audience began to dissipate, most of its members headed off to the next staging ground, the next event.

Luke took a look around then glanced skyward to check the position of the sun. Midafternoon. He wondered if tonight would bring—

"Yes, they will."

He glanced at his son. "What?"

"Yes, the Nightsisters will attack tonight." Ben lowered his voice to a conspiratorial tone straight out of a holodrama. "Your thoughts betray you."

"I'm going to shake you so hard . . . I'm certain that you got nothing through the Force about my thoughts."

"Not everything is the Force, Dad. First you looked off in the direction where we had our traps and bodies and so forth the other night. Then you scanned the tree line all around, but not the lake. So you were thinking about avenues of approach toward the camp, which meant enemies, which meant Nightsisters. You checked the sun, which, since it's usually there, means you were really estimating time until sundown, so you were asking how much time minimum we had before the Nightsisters attack."

"Maybe it wasn't such a good idea to let you train with the Guard. You think you might be happier dispensing caf or sketching caricatures?" Luke breathed a sigh. "All right, why do you think they're going to attack tonight?"

"Because Dyon got a very interesting communication on his comlink while you were in the semifinals."

They took the short walk back to their campfire, where Dyon was clearly expecting Luke. At Ben's nod, Dyon took a look around to make sure no one was in hearing distance. "Yliri contacted me a little while ago."

"Good." Luke was anxious for word from the spaceport. He knew Han and Leia had gotten offworld without incident, but didn't know how things had gone with the rest of those who had departed.

"Anyway, I think there's something going on there."

Luke gave him a quizzical look. "At the spaceport?"

"No, between Yliri and Carrack. She was so worried about his injuries, so insistent about accompanying him back. She's clearly been tending him night and day. I think some sort of romance sprang up while they were here. Of course, a conclave like this is just the place for it . . ."

Ben sighed. "Dyon? Speeder bikes?"

"Oh. Right. Earlier today, the spaceport sensor station picked up speeder bike transponders, three of them, arriving at a broad meadow west of the spaceport at different times."

Luke shrugged. "So what? I understand that there are speeder bikes with several of the clans now."

"So they were arriving from different directions. Suggesting different clans. And a lot of the speeder bikes get modified when they fall into clan hands, their transponders being disabled, because the clans have a natural dislike of people being able to track their movements. So if three speeders with transponders converge on a site, it means there were probably more than three there at the time."

Luke nodded. "Where do their signals say they are now?"

"That's just the thing. They were there for a little while, then the three signals winked out, all within two minutes of one another."

"Which suggests," Ben broke in, "that they were sitting around waiting, and someone said, *You* have *all disabled your transponders, haven't you?* And three of them with the brains of monkey-lizards said, *What are transponders?* And then they fixed the problem."

Luke thought about it. "So you're calculating that the Nightsisters decided they needed reinforcements, and more Nightsisters are coming in on speeder bikes."

Ben nodded. "Sure, there are other explanations. But I'm kind of naturally suspicious."

"Well, being suspicious seems to work for your uncle Han." Luke looked around, scanning the campsite. "If you're right, they've more than replaced their losses, and we haven't replaced ours."

Dyon nodded. "It's never a good idea to let the enemy choose the battlefield."

Luke moved off toward the camp's center of activity: the competition ground where Kaminne and Tasander would now be officiating a new event. "Let's talk to someone about moving the camp."

Tasander, who, like many noble Hapan males, came from a family line with a tradition of piracy, and Kaminne, who had kept her clan together and alive across ten hard years, didn't require much convincing. The problem was simply one of logistics.

"A full packing-up and moving-out can't take less than an hour." Kaminne thought about it. "Though we could announce it as a run to safety. Five minutes to get to your camp and grab what is most important to you, five more minutes to muster, and then move out, leaving behind everything not absolutely crucial. But where do we go? Add marching time, and there's only so far we can get before night falls and we're vulnerable."

Tasander glanced to the northeast. "There's a hill a few kilometers that way. It's off the trade paths. Very ugly, unpromising hill. Steep-sided, rocky, and barren. But there's nothing up there to burn and it's very, very defensible."

Kaminne nodded. "Water?"

"Nothing to drink up there, unfortunately."

"We'll have to fill up every waterskin and other container before we move out. More time, unfortunately. And whose is the standard?"

"Huh?" Tasander seemed stumped by that one.

Luke was, too. *"The standard?"*

Tasander gestured around. "This is not one campsite. It's two. Broken Columns distinctly over here, Raining Leaves distinctly over there, each under its own standard, or clan symbol. Oh, three camps now, with you offworlders right in the middle. But that hilltop, small and irregular as it is, can't be partitioned off as easily. So it will be a Broken Columns camp or a Raining Leaves camp, but not both. One clan will be there at the sufferance of the other . . . and won't like it, which undercuts our morale and chain of command. So, which is the hosting clan? Whose standard do we fly?"

Luke let a little durasteel creep into his voice. "Jedi. It's a Jedi camp. Dyon, I need you to make a standard. Quickly."

Dyon nodded. "Done."

Kaminne glanced at Tasander, then looked at Luke again. "Raining Leaves agree."

"So do Broken Columns." Tasander scratched his chin, so obviously and theatrically an *I'm thinking now* gesture that it was difficult not to laugh. "We still need one member from each clan to accompany the Jedi to claim the site and plant the standard."

Though Kaminne was opening her mouth to answer, Ben interrupted her. "Halliava and Drola."

Kaminne gave him a curious look. "Why?"

"They're both young and popular, they've both won several matches. They're both unmarried. Gives people something to speculate about."

Kaminne shrugged. "Good enough. Halliava and Drola, then."

"But don't tell them what this is all about. Let's confine information as much as possible." Ben kept his tone light, as though this were a reasonable request but not a critical one.

"As you wish." She glanced at her fiancé. "Let us begin."

"Let's."

Together they trotted off toward the current competition, unarmed combat between those with no Arts.

Luke gave Ben a look he tried, and failed, to make an admonishing one. "You're getting very sneaky, Ben."

"I get that from Mom. And maybe from the Skywalkers, too—Leia's your sister. Sneakiness just skipped you."

Dyon shook his head, confused. "I don't get it. What was sneaky?"

Ben gave him an innocent look. "It's a teenage thing. You wouldn't understand."

Not too surprisingly, Dyon had on his datapad some information on the Jedi and the Galactic Alliance. Using familiar symbols on the 'pad as a frame of reference, he quickly worked up a flag that would serve as the Jedi standard for this mission. On a large square of tan cloth, he painted in black the bird-like symbol that had served as the basis for much New Republic and Galactic Alliance heraldry. Over that stark image he painted two crossed lightsabers, both lit, one with a green blade, one with a blue.

Ben, watching over Dyon's shoulder, nodded approval. "That should do the job."

"I'll blot it so that it doesn't drip while we're carrying it. But otherwise it's ready to go."

Within minutes of the standard's completion they joined Luke, as well as Halliava and Drola, both of whom looked perplexed and testy at being taken from the games, and set out for the hill Tasander had described. He'd given Dyon accurate information about its location, so all Dyon had to do was check his datapad against satellite coordinates every few minutes. Half an hour after setting out from the Raining Leaves/Broken Columns camp, they emerged from a particularly thick stretch of trees in view of the hill.

It was indeed unpromising looking. It was a forty-meter-high slab of black rock thrust up from beneath Dathomir's surface in ancient times and only slightly worn down since. Jagged edges jutted up at the sky, with little greenery growing from its upper slopes. The southwest slope was gentler than the others, meaning that it required only ordinary athletics to climb, not extraordinary efforts. Ben could see that the top was broken, angled terrain, a place where it would be hard to find a comfortable place to put down a bedroll. He hoped it didn't rain tonight.

The five of them, all in good shape and unhurt, climbed the slope in a matter of minutes, then stared down along the valley toward Redgill Lake. In the late-afternoon sun, the lake waters glinted in rippling bands of blue and yellow-orange.

Drola blinked. "Well, it's pretty. But not pretty enough to miss the rock hurling. I think I would have won this year."

Halliava snorted. "Would you have started with the rocks between your ears?"

Unruffled, he shook his head. "No, with the granite ball you call your heart."

Luke smiled. "You have something more important to do than throw rocks. We need you as a witness." He gestured, and Dyon handed him the long wooden pole to which the new standard was attached. Luke raised the standard high. "I claim . . ." Then his voice trailed off. A thoughtful expression on his face, he lowered the pole so that its butt end rested on the hilltop stone.

Ben gave his father a concerned look. "What is it?"

Luke shook his head. "I can't do this. If I claim this hill, however temporarily, it becomes a Jedi facility. Right?"

"Right . . . oh." The terms of Luke's conviction prohibited him from creating or visiting Jedi facilities.

Luke held the standard out to Ben. "You have to do it. I don't think I can even be here."

"Where will you be? Down at ground level with no support?"

"No . . . I'll station myself at about the halfway mark down the hill. You just claim the hilltop and we'll be fine."

"He cannot." That was Halliava. She still looked perplexed as to their intention, but she seemed certain of something. "With you gone, there is only one Jedi here. Meaning you have no greater claim than Drola, Dyon, or myself. We cannot bear witness to this because our claim is as great as yours."

Dyon made a strangled noise. He turned to Luke. "You think it's bad dealing with planet after planet, each with a different form of government and constitution? Imagine a place where, if you cross a creek, you've got a different form of government, different customs, and no constitution, since there are few or no literate people there to write one. Welcome to Dathomir."

Luke just grinned at him and handed his son the standard. "Ben, you're the one with the sneaky genes. Fix this problem." He turned and began descending the slope.

"Great." Trust his father to shoot Ben out of his own cannon.

He looked at his three remaining companions, and an idea occurred to him. He propped the standard pole against his shoulder and began fishing in his belt pouch. In moments he found what he was looking for, a five-credit coin of Coruscant minting.

He flipped it to Dyon, who caught it. "Dyon, I'm hiring you. I can't make you a Jedi, but I can employ you for the Order. As a consultant."

Dyon looked sorrowfully at the coin, then tucked it away into one of his vest pouches. "I've sunk pretty low. Selling myself for five creds."

"That's life with the Jedi." Ben glanced at the Dathomiri. "Now do the Jedi outnumber the Leaves and the Columns?"

Drola nodded. Halliava considered, then nodded as well.

Ben held the standard up. "I, Ben Skywalker, hereby claim this hilltop, from an altitude of twenty meters up, for the Jedi Order." He looked at the Dathomiri. "Will that work? Dramatic enough?"

Halliava shrugged. "You must mention your witnesses."

Drola pointed to the pole he held. "And then plant the standard so it can stand by itself."

"I hereby make this claim in the presence of Halliava Vurse of the Raining Leaves Clan and Drola—Drola—"

The bearded man scowled. "Kinn."

"Drola Kinn of the Broken Columns Clan." Ben looked around for some loose rocks with which to prop up the pole.

"If you are going to fumble with my name, I should at least go first."

"You're a man. You go second. Ben, are we done? I want to return to camp."

Ben gave Halliava an apologetic smile. "No, we have to wait here. Kaminne and Tasander want that, too." He rested the pole against a vertical rock face as high as his shoulder and began piling loose stones against it to hold it in place.

Drola tried to make his voice sound reasonable. "They *did* say that."

"Oh, be quiet. We never should have taught your kind to talk."

Ben grinned. Halliava's tone was not biting, not genuinely angry. She was just bantering. As contentious as things had been in the camps during the conclave, he liked the sound of that.

He felt a sudden stab of guilt. Maybe Halliava *wasn't* the Nightsister here. He didn't want his constant scrutiny of her to cause offense or to make others mistrust her if she were actually innocent.

But he still couldn't tell her the truth, not when she might be able to convey it to distant Nightsisters. Not when he didn't know.

His task complete, he straightened. "Welcome to Camp Jedi. Now we wait."

Chapter Nineteen

THEY DIDN'T HAVE A LENGTHY WAIT. AN HOUR AFTER THEY FIRST achieved the summit, Ben saw the first clan members straggling out of the forest. Tasander was at their head. As more and more emerged from the trees, Tasander directed some to climb the hill, others to begin moving along the tree line surrounding it. Within a short time, men and women were reaching the summit and setting up bedrolls and, where possible, tents; those below were emerging from the trees with hastily cut poles whose ends they began to sharpen with long slashing blades.

Ben gulped. Suddenly it struck home. They were indeed at war, preparing fortifications to defend themselves. He'd been born during a war and had fought through others as a boy and an adolescent. Now it was war again, however small its scale. He wondered if he was always to be involved in some war or another. Then he thought back over his father's history and knew the answer.

His father was visible, too, halfway down the hill. Luke sprang from stone to stone, landing, rocking back and forth on each perch, leaping to the next one within reach. Ben knew what he was doing: testing the terrain, giving himself home-field advantage should enemies come against him.

Ben heard Drola and Halliava asking the newcomers if they knew the reason for all the commotion, and finally getting their answer. *We're fortifying against the Nightsisters.* Now, if Halliava was one of the Nightsisters, she would find a way to communicate the news to her fellow conspirators. But as Ben watched her from the corner of his eye, she did not immediately dash off on some pretext of an errand. Grim-faced, she met and took her daughter from Olianne, then set about erecting her own camp.

Ben found Dyon sitting on a boulder overlooking the southwest slope, tapping away on his datapad. "What're you doing?"

"Composing a chronicle of the day so far." Dyon didn't look up, and his tone indicated that he was concentrating mostly on his document. "I'll be sending it to Yliri and updating it as the night progresses."

"Why?"

"I could die tonight, Ben. Die alongside people who barely know me, a long way from home. I'd like for the people who care about me to know why."

"Oh." As if suddenly deflated, Ben sat on a boulder nearby. "I'm sorry."

"For what?"

"Sorry that we asked you for help. Well, that Han and Leia did, and that we asked you to stay behind."

"Don't be." Dyon left off his typing for a moment to look at Ben. "You know that, when I was younger, I wanted to be a Jedi. That I was tested and did some training."

"Yeah."

"I washed out. Not good enough with the Force. I understood, but it still came down to being told that I just wasn't good enough. Not valuable enough."

Ben winced. "That's not what it meant."

"I know that, but on an emotional level, that's *exactly* what it meant. Well, that's all right. I found other ways to make my life worthwhile. And now, just these last few days, I've been able to give the

Jedi—the *Grand Master* of the Jedi—help that he couldn't get anywhere else." He shrugged. "If I die tonight, I want people to know that I didn't go out thinking there was no value to my life." He turned his attention back to his datapad and began typing again.

Ben turned to look over the last several dozen clan members straggling in from the forest.

As with Dyon, any of them might die tonight. Just because they wanted to take their clans, to take their culture, in a new direction, one of their choosing. He felt cold anger settle across him, anger for those like Jacen Solo and the Nightsisters and the Sith, those who valued their own goals so far above the very lives of ordinary people like—

"Water?"

He turned. Vestara stood before him. Around her neck was a leather strap supporting a crude leather container, a bucket of sorts, holding water; it rested against her hip. She dipped a long-handled wooden ladle into the water and offered it to him.

He took it, drank, returned the implement to her. "Can I ask you something?"

"I'll only lie. That, or tell the truth."

"Where'd you get the credits?"

"What credits?"

"Enough credits to get your yacht fixed."

She smiled and shook her head. "I have no such fortune, and I have no yacht, and I have authorized no repairs."

"There's really no point in lying. We found the yacht in Monarg's shop."

"That's not my yacht."

"Well, let's say the one that's yours by right of salvage, since it was abandoned in the Maw and you retrieved it."

"Still not mine."

He sighed.

"Really, Ben." She returned the ladle to the bucket. "You shouldn't tell people you consider your enemies what you're thinking. Didn't your parents teach you *anything*?" She turned away and headed for a cluster of Raining Leaves a few meters away.

Ben shrugged. Sure they had. But maybe he hadn't learned quite enough.

CORUSCANT

So much for transponder codes.

The *Star Tripper*—an alias for the *Millennium Falcon* that Han had *thought* no one else knew—had barely entered Coruscant orbit before a pair of *Aleph*-class starfighters had appeared out of nowhere and started to follow her down. To Han, the choice of escort craft suggested they were more of a courtesy than a guard detail. Heavily armed and armored, Alephs were well suited to picket duty, but couldn't hope to keep up with a ship like the *Falcon* if she decided to run.

Leia spoke a few words of confirmation into the comm board and switched off the transmitter. "They've given us landing coordinates. In the plaza outside the Senate Building."

Han grimaced. "So they want a show for the media—but it can't be of an arrest." He jerked a thumb toward the aft, roughly in the direction of the Alephs. "If they want to arrest us, they would have sent something that could catch us."

"Probably," Leia said. "But I sent for Jaina, just in case. She has clearance to meet us, to take charge of Allana and Anji."

From the passenger seat behind Leia, Allana piped up, "She's bringing Master Cilghal, right?"

"Anji's condition isn't critical any longer," Leia said. "She'll be fine until you and Jaina take her to the infirmary. Master Cilghal will just need to run a few tests, then she'll probably send you both home to rest."

"You're sure?"

"Pretty sure," Han said. "But it's better for Cilghal to wait for you in the infirmary, so she can have everything ready to start the tests."

"I guess that makes sense," Allana said. "But she'd better be ready. Anji doesn't like having a headache."

As they approached the Senate Building, Han could see that there was indeed a crowd, made up of well-dressed politicians, brightly dressed holocasters surrounded by their crews, and uniformed security officers. They were all waiting around the perimeter of the *Falcon*'s designated landing zone. The fact didn't improve his disposition. It was bad enough having to face crowds, any member of whom might be someone he owed money to—well, that was the old days. Now any member of a crowd might be an old enemy or a killer paid by an old enemy. Even when times were good and people cheered, he didn't much like crowds. It was worse at times like these. Jeers, subpoenas . . . it always irked him. He smiled. It didn't wear him *down,* of course. It just irritated him.

They came to a smooth landing at the designated spot, which was ringed with security speeders and journalist vehicles. Han and Leia went through a very abbreviated checklist and power-down, then mustered at the top of the loading ramp with the droids. After instructing Allana to wait aboard with Anji, Han hit the button to lower the ramp.

As it touched down, as the Solos and their droids began to move down its length, their greeting party stepped into the shadow of the *Falcon*'s hull and stopped a few meters down the ramp. In among a small group of Coruscant Security officers and troopers were Daala and her aide, Wynn Dorvan.

Han gave Leia a glance, a faint twitch of his eyebrows, acknowledgment that he hadn't expected the Chief of State to be on hand personally for their arrival. Leia's microscopic shrug said she hadn't, either.

Allana, standing inside the hatch behind them, called, "Hey, Jaina!"

Han looked toward the back of the crowd and saw his daughter arriving, a somber and striking martial figure in traditional Jedi robes. He waved, but then broadened the gesture to include the crowd. There was a low cheer from onlookers not in government uniform and not otherwise occupied.

The Solos came to a stop at the bottom of the ramp. Half comically, Han put his wrists together and offered them, in turn, to the closest three security troops.

"Oh, don't be ridiculous." Daala stepped forward. She extended her hand to shake Han's, then Leia's. "Yes, there is a warrant out for you, but it's not being executed today."

Once free of Daala's grasp, Leia glanced at her hand, as if doing a quick count of her fingers, then returned her attention to the Chief of State. "Well, that's promising . . . but if I may ask, why not?"

"Because some problems require complex solutions, and, sadly, arrests and convictions aren't always complex." Daala looked past their shoulders, up toward Allana. "And you must be Amelia Solo."

Allana's voice held no trace of awe or intimidation when she answered, "I'm supposed to wait here. I have a hurt nexu."

"A . . . *nexu?*" Daala's eyes widened and returned to the adult Solos. "Her pet?"

Han shrugged. "She's good with animals." He looked around, still trying to figure out what Daala's game was, then said, "Well, thanks for coming out to meet us, but it's been kind of a long trip. If you don't mind, I think we'll just—"

"*After* our meeting, if you don't mind." Daala wasn't requesting. Her gaze drifted back up the ramp toward Allana. "Will Amelia and her nexu be joining us?"

Han glanced over at Leia, who merely shrugged and said, "No, her sister Jaina is here to collect her."

Daala followed their gaze to where Jaina stood behind the Coruscant Security lines. "Ah. Well, I hope young Amelia has a good day with her sister."

Dorvan waved at the security troopers nearest Jaina and indicated that they should let the Jedi approach. In moments, after a flurry of quick embraces, Jaina was boarding the *Falcon* to collect Allana and her nexu. Han and Leia were swept up in Daala's retinue and headed for the Senate Building.

They settled into her gleaming office. Only the Solos, Daala, and Dorvan were present. Daala pressed a couple of buttons and the door slid shut. "I'm recording, by the way. Not to have evidence for a trial, but to have a record of any agreements we might reach."

Leia smiled. "Still, it wouldn't be in our best interests to admit to any shooting sprees or smuggling actions."

"I suppose not," Daala said. "But we aren't here to discuss plea deals."

Han stirred, restless. "So why *are* we here? I was kind of looking forward to getting bailed out in time for dinner. A meeting could go long and ruin my evening."

"And mine." Daala sat back, a posture that looked almost relaxed. "Here's what I want. I'd like the two of you to take an offer to the Jedi Order, and perhaps help me resolve this thing."

"Acting as advocates for *who*, precisely?" Leia asked. "I'm sure you don't expect us to represent you."

"I expect you to do what's best for the Galactic Alliance," Daala countered, a bit sharply. "Which happens to be helping the two sides resolve their grievances with each other and return the Jedi Order to its longstanding role as a government resource. As long as you're making progress toward that goal, the government will overlook your recent crime spree in helping several criminally insane Jedi escape the planet. If you actually succeed, the case will be dismissed."

Han scowled. "If you expect us to sell out to dodge a few trumped-up charges, save us *all* some time and just arrest us now."

Daala sighed and rolled her eyes toward Dorvan. "I *told* you this would never work."

Dorvan raised a hand for patience, then turned to the Solos. "Your suspicion is understandable," he said. "But that's not what the Chief is asking. She's just looking for someone to help cool tempers, present her case, and see if there aren't some reasonable accommodations that *both* sides can make."

Han looked back to Daala. "Reasonable accommodations?" He allowed a crooked smirk to creep across his mouth. "Things must be getting pretty hot in the Chief's seat, huh?"

Daala's eyes grew hard, but Dorvan admitted, "Particularly since Cha Niathal's funeral. It's beginning to interfere with the state's other business."

Han and Leia exchanged a look, and he gave her a little shrug signifying consent. "There's a problem, though."

"Yes?"

"Leia's a Jedi. Doesn't that sort of slant our outlook in your eyes? Make us sort of biased?"

"Absolutely." Daala leaned forward again. A small smile crossed her face. "Han Solo, you've held a commissioned rank in the New Republic armed forces."

"Uh-oh."

"The privileges and rights of which carry over into the Galactic Alliance. And in times of Alliance crisis, which this is, the Chief of State, as commander in chief of the armed forces, can return retired officers, even those not in the reserves, to active duty."

Han sank back into his chair and covered his eyes with his hand. "Don't say it."

"Sorry, but I must. I'm returning you to the rank of general and assigning you the responsibility of searching for a *reasonable* solution to our mutual problem. Unless you'd like to formally resign your commission, which I will take as a sign that you don't want this assignment or the clemency that comes with it, in which case I *will* have to execute the arrest warrant."

Dorvan cleared his throat. "We realize that you don't care for the public at large to know that you have ethics and would in fact try to fulfill your duty to the Galactic Alliance here. So the exact terms of this deal won't be revealed. Just an announcement that former Chief of State, Jedi Leia Solo, and Alliance hero and scoundrel Han Solo are making an effort to resolve the disputes between the government and the Jedi."

Han peered at his wife. "Did he say *scoundrel?*"

"He did."

"It's gotta be *wildly popular scoundrel* or it's no deal."

"So recorded, so noted." Daala looked between them. "So do we *have* a deal?"

"I don't see how, in good conscience, we can refuse." Leia leaned forward to extend a hand. "It's a deal."

Daala shook it, then shook Han's. "General, you'll need an aide."

"I have one. See-Threepio." It pained Han to say those words, but he'd rather keep any government-appointed military attaché out of his business.

"Ah, your protocol droid. Of course." Daala glanced toward her assistant. "Dorvan has prepared a small briefing sheet that outlines what I'm willing to offer."

Dorvan withdrew a single sheet of handwritten flimsi from his tunic pocket. "There are no identifying marks, of course. Should it fall into the media's hands—"

"It *won't*," Leia said, plucking the sheet from his grip. "We've handled delicate negotiations before."

"Good," Daala said. "Let Dorvan know if you need any resources to aid your efforts. And please send me a daily update on your progress."

The words sounded like a dismissal, so Han rose, as did Leia. Uncomfortably aware of his renewed responsibilities, Han threw Daala a sloppy salute, one suited to a wildly popular scoundrel, and turned for the door.

He and Leia did not speak until they reached the main exit and emerged into sunlight. "So . . . what the blazes?"

Leia shook her head. "She's in trouble. She needs to make it look like she's looking for a solution."

"*Is* she?" Han asked.

"I guess we'll know after we read this," Leia said, flicking the flimsi Dorvan had given her. "Either way, though, we stay out of jail and she makes herself look a little less unreasonable."

They angled toward the *Falcon*. It was shut up tight, but still had security troopers posted around it. "Is this something we can actually pull off?"

"Maybe. All I can say is, it's better to be out here trying than in prison not trying."

Chapter Twenty

AN HOUR LATER, DORVAN REENTERED DAALA'S OFFICE. AT HER GES-
ture, he sat.

She took a moment to look up from her monitor and the formwork
she was handling. "What?"

"The story about the Solos has hit the press and the news sources
already have polls in the field to gauge the public reaction."

"I'm . . . I'm shocked, Wynn."

He ignored her sarcasm. "In preparation for this meeting, and for
other events that would involve the press, I recently set up some
checks and monitors of news sources and public feedback sources.
One of those checks and balances involves minute examinations of
daily and hourly planetary net archives."

Daala fully turned away from her monitor to look at him. "That's a
nontrivial expense for your office. And I know I didn't authorize it."

"I didn't go through my office. Or yours. I called in some favors."

"And in an hour you've found out something?"

"Nothing substantial. But I have determined that press releases about you, when the news sources auto-disassemble and restructure them before having newswriters work on them for stories, are being filtered and massaged in a pretty consistent fashion. Consistent regardless of news service . . . or even the news service's political orientations and alliances."

"I actually have next to no understanding of what you just said."

He sighed. "All right. We issue a press release. It goes out over the planetary net and is part of low-priority packets fired offworld on the HoloNet. Every news service gets it. A computer program breaks it down, does an interpretation of its official language, runs a check against keywords for relevant recent and historical events, and splits the results up so that a live copywriter can rewrite and reformat it into the story a newsreader will deliver during the regular broadcast news."

"I love it when a man can translate gibberish into Basic. Well done."

"In the case of the press release about the Solos volunteering to resolve issues between the Galactic Alliance government and the Jedi Order, the following changes and adaptations are being made to the story in every news source we've sampled." He began counting on his fingers. "One. The Solos didn't offer this service. Chief of State Daala asked for their help. Two, news sources hostile to you tend to use the word *hapless* to describe you at this point, while those ostensibly friendly to you use the word *embattled*."

Daala frowned. "Consistently."

"Consistently. Three, the phrase *former Chief of State* is removed from the description of Leia Solo, replaced by *Jedi Knight*. Four, Han Solo—"

"Did you actually use the phrase *wildly popular scoundrel* for him?"

"Of course. Part of the agreement. But it appears as a quote from the subminister for trade with Corellia. 'Most people know Han Solo as a wildly popular scoundrel, but he's actually a savvy, tough negotiator.' As I was about to say, though, that paragraph gets dropped from the story, replaced by a summary of Solo's exploits in combating evil political leaders such as Palpatine. Five, while we didn't make any reference to the Solos' relationship with Jacen Solo, we knew we didn't have to, that the press would add that detail. But they haven't."

"So. Solos anti-government, Solos Jedi, Solos good. Daala hapless, Daala evil, Daala bad."

Dorvan nodded. "That's it. You translate gibberish to Basic very well."

"Then let me be sure my translation is correct. You're saying that the forces that shape public opinion are biased against me."

"Biased in a way they're not biased against anyone else, at least as far as I've detected. Luke Skywalker gets praised or excoriated depending on the political outlook of the news source doing the reporting. So do specific planetary leaders, trade union leaders, major military figures. Not you. Daala bad. Oh, by the way, a former Imperial Navy lieutenant you had court-martialed is about to release a memoir. *Into the Maw: Black Holes, Egos, and Other Forces That Devour Lives.* Guess who it's about."

"What would it take to engineer this?"

"Well, it could be a natural reaction. All of these prejudicial changes are within limits experienced by other political and military leaders. Meaning that if it's a conspiracy, they're being careful not to exceed effects that other leaders have experienced. But it would take software modification at the three or four sources of news-parsing programs starting years ago. It would take analysis of public opinion and the forces driving it going back at least as long."

"I've only been Chief of State for two years!"

"So, if this *is* a conspiracy, it was set up a long time ago for an eventual goal, not for the specific goal of hindering or ruining you in particular."

"Wonderful. I just happen to be the person in the sights when the Death Star's main weapon is first brought online."

"Correct." Dorvan lowered the hand he'd been counting on and raised the other one. "Want to hear my analysis of polls that have just been put out for the public to respond to?"

"No, I want you to fix this."

He smiled. "Ah, good. I'll need eight years and at least half a billion credits."

Daala shook her head. She was beginning to feel numb. "If I had that kind of money—never mind. What can we do?"

"The more people you enlist to help, the more likely it is that your enemies, if there are actually conspirators arrayed against you, will learn that you're on to them. I'd find one investigator who has all the skills you need, pay in large capital ships or small planets, and see if he or she can root out your enemies. In the meantime, make it harder and harder for them to cut your legs out from under you. Become a nicer and nicer figure in the public eye. Make the public like you."

She thought about it, then shook her head. Her voice sounded miserable, even to herself. "I can't do that. I can't be Wynssa Starflare."

"Who?"

"Before your time, child. A holodrama actress. Beautiful, perky, blond, shiny. I have to stick by my laser batteries and keep firing."

"All right."

"You want out?"

His smile showed teeth for a moment. "You may think I'm soft, but I stick to my laser batteries, too."

"I don't think you're soft. Just irredeemably civilian." She brushed her hair back from her face. "All right. Call in more favors, do what you can. I'll see what kind of revenue stream I can come up with for a top-notch investigator. And in the meantime, if the public is determined to think of me as a monster, I might have to give them a monster to remember."

Dorvan rose. "Eat your vegetables, children, or Admiral Daala will come for you."

"Just get out."

A SUITE AT THE GLEAMING FORTUNES CASINO, CORUSCANT

The turbolift door rose. Emperor Palpatine and his bodyguard, a headless Gamorrean, stepped off the lift. The guard on this floor, Darth Vader but only a meter tall, waved an electronic reader at the chest of each, noted that its diode continued to glow blue, and courteously waved them toward a set of golden doors inset in the black stone walls of this circular turbolift lobby. Palpatine and the headless thing approached the doors, which opened before them.

The suite beyond was the stuff of conspicuous wealth. The carpeting was transmutive, now graduating from a pleasing shell gray into a sky blue; the change began at the far side of the chamber, beside the wall-length transparisteel viewport, and graduated toward the doors through which they had entered. The walls were Kuati marble, white and veined with blue, but also inset with gilt flecks. The sofas and chairs were white and glowed faintly, both as an expression of their costliness and to warn anyone wandering through a pitch-dark suite of their presence. The central table, circular, with depressions all along its rim for drinks and game pieces, was of an artificial black marble veined in silver.

Across the end of one sofa lay what appeared to be a Wookiee, but it was flat, deflated, as if the creature's bones and organs had been removed, leaving only skin behind. At the round table sat a slightly oversized silver protocol droid with a human head, a thruster-pack-wearing clone trooper of six decades before, his helmet on the floor beside him, and a berobed female with the gray hands of a Neimoidian but the face of an elderly human female. A Neimoidian face, noseless and gray, as deflated as the body of the Wookiee, lay on the table beside her. A circular card-dealer droid scuttled around crab-like on the tabletop, and young, fit men and women dressed in dark garments were positioned along the walls. All looked up as the Emperor and his undead companion entered.

The Emperor gestured as if preparing to launch Force lightning. "Upon pain of death . . . deal me in."

The human/Neimodian clapped her hands together and beamed. "What a marvelous impersonation. Why have you never done this before, at social events?"

The Emperor shrugged. When he spoke again, it was in his own rich, mellow tones, not the Emperor's curdled voice. "One must be in the correct crowd to amuse with that impersonation, my dear Senator Treen." He glanced sideways at the headless Gamorrean, who bowed, then walked—cheekily, still in character, with a bounce to his stride accentuated by the foam suit he wore—to the wall, taking up a proper bodyguard's station there.

The Emperor took an empty seat, then reached up to peel his face off. He set the Emperor mask beside Treen's Neimoidian face. "That's a relief."

The protocol droid, Senator Bramsin, gave him a sympathetic look. "I know what you mean. I couldn't wait to get that monstrous mask off." He glanced at the clone trooper. "It must be hard for you."

The trooper shook his head. "Built-in cooling system. But it's hard to sit and even harder to stand up."

Bramsin nodded. "I now understand why I've never seen a protocol droid sitting down."

Senator Treen looked between the Emperor and the clone trooper. "Moff Lecersen, allow me to present you General Jaxton, Galactic Alliance Starfighter Command."

"We haven't met, but I recognized the general from the news, of course."

Jaxton gave Lecersen a little sand-panther-ish grin. "And from intelligence briefings, I would imagine."

Lecersen resumed Palpatine's oily tones for just a moment. "Such things are not spoken of."

The card droid flipped three cards, *thoop-thoop-thoop*, facedown to land neatly before Lecersen. The cards bore the emblem of the Empire on their backs. He smiled; how fitting. He picked them up and looked at their faces, surprised to discover that they were playing Chambers instead of sabacc. He held the Red Courtesan, Blue Destroyer Droid, and Red Imperial Guardsman.

Treen glanced at her cards with affected disinterest. "Fifty."

In silver letters, the words FIFTY THOUSAND CREDITS appeared on the tabletop before her, indicating her bet.

Jaxton glowered at her. "Some of us are public servants, you know."

"Oh, yes. Rescale stakes for the armed services, please."

The words before her changed to FIFTY CREDITS.

Lecersen set his cards down. "Match." The same bet appeared on the table before him. "So now I understand why this casino has had regular costume nights for so long."

Treen nodded. "Actually, I established costume nights years before ever hosting a meeting here, but with an eye toward this sort of gathering."

Jaxton, around the table to Lecersen's right, pushed his cards together as if closing a fan. He was clearly thinking hard.

Lecersen was amused. The ancient Imperial game was probably new to Jaxton, who doubtless wished he were holding cards from a children's deck, which would have all the values printed on them.

Finally Jaxton shrugged. "Match." The words representing the bet appeared on the table in front of him.

Bramsin, around the table to his right, rolled his eyes. "Hundred. So, what news?" His bet appeared on the table.

Treen did not bother looking at her cards again. "Match."

Then it was Lecersen's turn. "Match."

"Match." Jaxton offered a slight expression of disapproval. "I'm afraid that Admiral Bwua'tu is not proving as amenable as we had hoped."

Treen tossed out a card, the Red Clone Trooper Captain. "We always knew that his quirky personal ethics might make it difficult."

Lecersen tossed the Red Imperial Guardsman beside it.

Chambers was based on that most ancient of children's questions, "If so-and-so fought so-and-so, who would win?" A card tossed out by a player was presumed to meet with the card to its left in a private chamber, with the stronger card winning the presumed combat. But complicating the comparisons were choices of categories—Strength, Will, and Chance—and card colors, with blue trumping white, red trumping blue, and black trumping red. So Lecersen was in a superior position to Treen.

Jaxton hesitated, then threw out the White Clone Trooper Private, among the lowest-powered cards in the deck. "Well, it's more than that. My psychological warfare officer, who is doing analysis on Bwua'tu's mental profile based on the assumption that he's evaluating a captain of industry in the Corporate Sector—"

Lecersen snorted.

"—sees a pattern of loyalty to Daala that goes beyond the professional."

Bramsin set down a White Imperial Guardsman. It easily trumped the White Clone Trooper Private but did not trump Lecersen's card.

The dealer droid collected the four played cards. Its voice was the whisper of a quiet sports commentator. "Current hand, Round One. Two kills each to Lecersen and Bramsin. Please adjust bets."

"Stand fast." Treen fiddled with her cards as if nervous, which Lecersen knew she was not. "Bwua'tu remains your objective, General. What is your next step?"

Lecersen, in line to bet, interrupted. "Stand fast."

"Raise to two hundred." Jaxton looked unconcerned. "Time is substantially on our side. I'm continuing to make our choice for the next head of the navy into a combination of Thrawn and Mon Mothma in the public eye, and to determine what influences might cause Bwua'tu to resign. Sadly, he does not seem the sort for early retirement."

Bramsin seemed unworried. "Stand fast."

Treen nodded. "Stand fast on two hundred."

Lecersen stood fast as well. One more revelation of cards later, Treen had one kill, Lecersen one more.

On the third and final round of the hand, Treen raised the stakes to a thousand. The others matched. The Kuati Senator then tossed out the Blue Vizier, a powerful card. "And what if he can resist your efforts to retire him?"

Lecersen smiled and tossed out the Red Courtesan, whose Will value exceeded that of the Vizier.

"We'll find someone to kill him, of course." Jaxton played the Black Emperor, which trumped everything.

Bramsin offered a little sigh of vexation. He tossed out his card facedown, admitting that it could trump neither Jaxton's nor Treen's.

The dealer droid collected the cards. "One kill to Lecersen. Two kills to Jaxton, plus ten for a clean hand sweep. Final results for the hand, Treen one, Lecersen four, Jaxton twelve, Bramsin two. Launch proceeds to Lecersen."

Jaxton looked appreciative as the bet values blanked before the other players and his adjusted to FOUR THOUSAND CREDITS. He smiled at the others. "You shouldn't underestimate the new boy."

Chapter Twenty-One

IN THE DEAD HOUR OF THE NIGHT BEN SKYWALKER LAY AWAKE IN HIS bedroll, in one of the lengthy waking spells he'd experienced between short bouts of sleeping. He could have slept well despite the discomfort of thin bedding over hard stone, could have meditated himself to peacefulness despite the danger they were in. But part of him wanted to be alert, awake for any change.

And so he was when the trickle of dark side Force energy passed overhead.

It was a strange sensation. He visualized it as if someone held the end of a ball of yarn and threw the ball itself across the room, there to be caught by a friend, stretching a single strand of yarn between them. But here the yarn was Force energy far above his head, and it hung in the sky, unseen.

Ben rose noiselessly and stared up after it. He saw only stars, a brilliant sea of them, a vista you could only get somewhere hundreds of kilometers from cities and lights.

There was noise near him. He saw a woman rising, staring up as he had done. He could also feel her, strong and distinctive in the Force—Kaminne.

He returned his attention to the sky. He kept his voice quiet, barely more than a whisper. "Any idea what that is?"

"The start of a spell known as a control web. Known by some Witches as the Crawler's Perch, by others as the Guiding Net."

"What does it do?"

"It allows firm and difficult-to-interrupt control of animals over a broad area."

"Of course."

"They would have used one like it with the sparkflies. But this one is stronger, meaning that the animals they will send have stronger wills. They—"

She broke off as Ben felt another thread of Force energy pass overhead. The first one had moved southwest to northeast; this one moved southeast to northwest.

Kaminne offered a vexed sigh. "They are building it fast. There is no subtlety here as with the sparkflies, just speed. I'm going to rouse the camp." She turned and, with her toe, prodded at the dark shape of the woman sleeping nearest her.

Ben moved over to the southwest lip and looked down to where his father should be. He could not see Luke, but could feel him there, awake, alert.

In minutes, dozens more Force threads had passed overhead and the warriors and Witches of the two clans had been awakened. Now no new threads were being added, but Ben could feel the web of energy slowly descending, like an almost weightless net sinking through thick liquid.

Torches and glow rods were springing to gleaming life all over the hilltop. Ben noted that, though he was ostensibly owner of the encampment, the clan members turned to their individual clan leaders for orders. Tasander situated his warriors, spears forward and bows and blasters behind, as a wedge at the center of the southwestern slope. Kaminne split her force into two units and set up one unit, warriors ahead and Witches behind, to either side of Tasander's wedge. Reinforcements and nonfighters stayed to the center of the camp.

And nothing happened. There was no noise at all from the woods surrounding the hill; insect noises had ceased altogether. Now a murmur, increasingly nervous, sprang up from the Dathomiri.

Ben reached a conclusion and sprang up atop a rock. "Your attention."

The Dathomiri turned to look at him.

"What's happening now is what the Empire and Alliance call psychological warfare. *Why don't they attack?* you ask. Because they want you to get more and more nervous. They want your nerves to break. Are you going to let them do that?"

"Never." The voice was Drola's.

Others repeated his word. Drola's voice rose above theirs. "Cowards hide and wait. Warriors laugh at them." And he began to laugh, a forced and unnatural laugh.

More joined in, women as well as men, and the laughter rose. Ben imagined it flowing down the hillside and into the surrounding trees.

He hopped down from his boulder and found Dyon beside him.

"Good thinking, Jedi."

Ben shrugged. "My cousin became a master at psychological warfare."

"Your cous—oh."

Ben felt a twitch from overhead, as if a giant spider made of Force energy had stepped onto its web. Then, from the southwest, he heard a *thum-thum-thum* of footsteps—huge, heavy footsteps.

Down below, in the starlight and moonlight, three humanoid shapes broke free of the tree line and moved toward the hill at a run, a pace whose speed no human short of a Jedi could match.

Rancors.

"Bows, blasters, fire at will!" That was Tasander. "Spears, brace yourselves!" Kaminne was shouting similar orders to her warriors and Witches.

Far below, halfway between ground level and hilltop, a short line of green light gleamed into life—Luke's lightsaber.

Ben got his own lightsaber into hand, but held off from joining the spear line. Much as he wanted to be there to help resist the initial shock of the rancors' impact, he also knew that he'd be far more valuable plugging up the line if and where it began to fail.

From pockets in his vest, Dyon drew matching blaster pistols, small ones. He stood ready for the first rancor to top the crest of the hill ahead.

The imaginary Force spider took another step. Threads of Force energy were being depressed. Ben swore to himself, not wanting to be distracted from the events playing out below.

The rancors reached the bottom of the slope and hurtled upward, half running and half climbing, their pace barely slowed by the change in angle. As the rancors reached the halfway point, Ben saw his father's lightsaber swing with shooting-star speed. Then it disappeared as the central rancor's body interposed between Ben and Luke—but suddenly that central rancor was howling in rage and pain, climbing more slowly or not at all, being left behind by the other two.

Blasterfire and unseen bowfire rained down on the rancors. It illuminated them in brief glints of light but did not seem to slow them at all.

And suddenly they were at the crest, two of them, roaring. At first only their hands and heads were visible, then they heaved up, their waists at the hilltop.

The Broken Columns spearmen in the center and the Raining Leaves spearwomen to the sides surged forward, driving steel-headed weapons and improvised stakes into the bodies of the rancors. But the beasts continued forward and a second later both stood towering over the warriors.

And Ben could feel where those other Force threads were being tugged. He tore his attention away from the rancors and glanced at the opposite side.

Dyon aimed a blaster at the rightmost rancor. Ben caught his wrist and pushed it down again. He turned toward the fight. "Attack from the rear!"

No one heard. He put some Force energy into it. "Attack from the rear, reinforcements to the rear!"

Some heads turned, but in the tumult and confusion, no one responded.

Well, at least he had Dyon's attention. He gestured toward the northwest slope. "That way!" Then he himself bounced from rocktop to rocktop toward the east slope.

Before he reached it, a rancor heaved itself over the crest, moving as though precisely launched from some ancient artillery piece, and landed before him. It immediately reached for Ben, roaring.

He caromed off his last landing-rock and veered rightward, hitting and rolling across the uneven stone surface, and rose with his lightsaber glowing in his hand.

Now that he was close to a rancor, he could see, even in the dim moonlight, that the beast was swatched in patches of crude hide armor. Such armor provided almost no defense against a lightsaber's energy, but the rancors already had bones and muscles thick enough to make them hard to hurt. Ben slashed out at the beast's knee, splitting thick hide and skin, doubtless cutting into the kneecap, but the rancor merely howled and swept an arm before it. Ben leapt above his arm and the blow missed, but it filled the air with flying stones and camp goods. Something metallic rebounded from his skull with a deep *clank*. Sudden dizziness spoiled his acrobatic flip and he under-rotated, coming down hard on his heels, falling awkwardly onto his backside.

And there was that hand, reaching for him again. He rolled to one side, realized belatedly that his lightsaber was gone. The rancor's hand plowed through a tent beside the spot he'd just been sitting. He did a backward handstand and came up on his feet, shaking his head to clear the dizziness.

Ah, there was his lightsaber, still lit. The blade had fallen upon a leather tent and cut its way through the material. Ben gestured and the weapon flew into his hand.

The rancor took two steps and was in reach of him again. It lunged. Ben leapt forward, somersaulting between its legs, and stood out of the roll at the very crest of the hill. He turned to face his opponent.

It spun and lunged again. Ben skipped along the ridge of rocks along the crest, and it pivoted. Then he reversed directions, somersaulted past it, and lashed out at the back of its already injured knee.

He connected, a good slash. He couldn't tell if he'd hamstrung the beast, but as he rose he knew he'd succeeded at his objective. The rancor flailed and fell, toppling over the crest of the hill.

Ben watched it go. It rolled, crashing into outcropping after outcropping on its way down, creating a miniature stone avalanche. Then it hit the ground, rocks from the avalanche pouring down atop it.

Even then, it was not still. It rolled away from the stone downpour and struggled to its feet. Then it began limping back toward the trees.

Ben turned and found Dyon.

Dyon might not have been a Jedi, but he possessed the acrobatic ability of one. He leapt, he rolled, he spun, he rebounded, all the while firing into his rancor's chest and limbs and face with his small, underpowered blasters. The constant stream of fire from his weapons looked like energy from a blaster battery in miniature.

But that rancor did not fall and did not seem slowed, for all that its face and armored body were peppered with spots of char.

Still, it was slightly off-balance. Dyon executed a beautiful leap, a flying side kick that caught the rancor in the temple just as it was leaning slightly out over the far crest of the hill. Dyon bounced off from the impact and landed hard, rolling away from the rancor in an effort to stay out of its reach. The rancor wobbled but did not fall. Ben leapt in that direction, knowing he could not reach the beast before it regained its balance.

Then someone else was there, a slim figure, pale of skin, replicating Dyon's kick. This figure connected even more forcefully than Dyon had, and landed better, coming down on both feet in a well-balanced crouch.

The rancor uttered a moan of fear, then toppled. As Ben reached that crest, he could hear the beast crashing its way down that slope.

The slight figure was Vestara. She gave Dyon a hand up.

Dyon glanced at the number readouts on the butts of his weapons, then pocketed them. "Many thanks. That was well timed."

She brushed her hands together as if removing dust. "I finished my water duties, did some meditating and reading, then decided to come over here and see if anything interesting was going on."

Dyon snorted, amused.

Ben suppressed a flash of irritation. He looked back toward the southwest slope.

There were no rancors there. Dathomiri were standing at the edge, shaking spears and other weapons down toward the valley floor, and some were jeering, but there did not seem to be much conviction in their voices.

And there were bodies among them, injured and dead. Even in the darkness, Ben thought he saw six or seven. He headed that way.

And now, drifting up from the trees surrounding the hill, came the sound of laughter from many throats—brittle, female laughter.

At the lip of the southwest slope, the leaders held a hurried conference while the clan members tended to the dead and injured. Down the slope, Ben saw his father's lightsaber blade raised toward him in a wave of greeting and reassurance; then it disappeared as Luke switched it off to conserve battery life.

"Rancors." Tasander nearly spat out the word. "Of course they would choose an attack that would all but ignore our defensive advantage. Stupid of me to overlook rancors."

Kaminne shook her head. "We are vulnerable to them, yes, but not as much as if we were in a flatland camp. This was still the right choice."

Ben gestured to catch Firen's eye. "You're the trainer of rancors for the Raining Leaves, right?"

She nodded.

"Can we do anything to interrupt the way the Nightsisters are controlling them?"

"I think not. The Nightsisters have chosen their tactic well."

"Did you look over our situation before night fell?"

She nodded.

"So we know they can climb at points on the southwest, east, and northwest. Anywhere else?"

"Everywhere, really, but it will only be a fast climb for them there, and at one approach on the northeast." She thought about it. "The north they might not be able to climb at all. It is steepest, and we have been using that cliff as our latrine. Even rancors may be reluctant to brave it."

There were snickers from various chiefs and subchiefs.

Kaminne glanced over the edge. There was no longer any laughter from the forest verge, but there was no question that their enemies were still there. "I wish we knew how many rancors they have. Just the five?"

"At least twenty. Maybe thirty." Firen sounded unhappy, but she also sounded sure.

Tasander gave her a curious look. "How do you know?"

"Their growls as they approached. Rancors do not speak, but they have a complex set of sounds, many of which I know. The growls they offered meant 'Watch me fight,' and it was the tone used to command the attention of the pack. Not a single mate, not littermates, not a hunting party . . . an entire pack."

Ben did some quick mental calculations. He estimated that there were perhaps two hundred able-bodied combatants on the hilltop; perhaps another fifty too feeble, injured, or young to offer much strength. Against thirty rancors, even with Witches, those were bad odds. Witches usually took more time than Jedi or Sith to bring Force powers to bear.

But clan members and Jedi weren't their only resources. "I'll get in touch with Yliri by comlink. Hire her to bring out the *Jade Shadow* or Mom's starfighter. We can give the surrounding forest a soaking the Nightsisters will never—" He caught sight of Dyon, who was shaking his head. "No?"

Dyon looked sour, even in the moonlight. "The Dathomiri are learning more and more from other worlds. I tried to upload my latest update a few minutes ago. It was a failure; comm transmissions are being jammed. Probably they brought some more sophisticated comm equipment with the speeder bikes, maybe an offworld comm expert as well."

"Doubtless a woman." Drola sounded surly.

Tasander glared at him. "One more word that increases dissent in our ranks, Drola, and you get to go out and do some night scouting. Straight down a rancor's gullet."

Drola fell silent.

Tasander bent over and, with a rock, scratched a circle into the flat stone at his feet. He divided it into halves, then divided one half into three pieces. It was a crude pie chart. "We leave half our strength at this slope, since multiple rancors can come at us here simultaneously. Then one-sixth each set up at the other three approaches. Subchiefs, I want equal division of strength among the three smaller formations. Let's go."

The men stood. The women of the Raining Leaves did not; they looked at Kaminne.

She looked between them, surprised, and then her expression turned dark. "Until we say otherwise, Tasander speaks for me and I speak for Tasander. Anyone who doubts me, anyone who questions that, anyone who hesitates to see what the other leader says, gets to set up a forward perimeter. Forward of Luke Skywalker."

The women rose in a hurry to join the men.

Ben caught her eye. "Don't feel bad. Civilized politics are even worse."

"How so?"

"Incompetents don't automatically get killed right away. Sometimes they even get reelected."

Chapter Twenty-Two

As the new formations were moving into place, Ben felt another twitch against the web of Force energy. Dyon and several of the Witches felt it as well; he saw them turn to look skyward. He pitched his voice to carry, and did not have to add Force impetus to it in order to be heard: "Be ready, they're coming!"

They came, and in greater force this time. Five rancors hurtled toward the southwest slope, two each toward the three other climbable slopes. They were immediately illuminated by blasterfire, misses as well as hits, but their sheer strength and bulk, as well as the armoring effects of the hides draped across them, meant that the blaster bolts again failed to slow them. Each of the eleven monsters reached the bottom of the hill and began climbing at a terrifying rate.

Directly below Ben, Luke's lightsaber lit up. As the central rancor reached it, the blade swung back and forth, slashes so fast that they blurred together in Ben's vision. That rancor immediately slipped and, bellowing, began sliding down the slope again.

But the other four were past now, and reaching the summit.

Cyclonic winds whipped up around Ben. He could feel the Force power in them. They blasted past him, barely jarring him, and as the four rancor heads topped the crest, the winds flowed into them, howling.

One rancor lost its balance and plummeted. The other three, steadier and sturdier, made it to their feet and—despite ferocious blows from the spearmen of the two clans—began swinging at humans.

Ben ignited his lightsaber and bounded in. With a touch of the Force, he leapt clean over the ranks of warriors, passing nimbly between upraised spears, and came down directly in front of the rancor in the center.

It was in the act of grasping a Raining Leaves spearwoman around the waist. Ben lashed out with his lightsaber and caught the thing across the wrist. Its skin blackened and split, the wound instantly cauterized. It howled and dropped the woman, who immediately rolled to her feet and brought her spear to bear once more.

The rancor swung at Ben with its other hand. He leapt over the clumsy attack in a forward somersault. When his feet came into contact with the rancor's chest, he slashed at that surface as he kicked off again. His direction reversed, he continued through a backward somersault and came down on his feet where he'd stood only a moment ago.

The rancor clutched its chest, howling, and stumbled backward. Ben didn't need to add any Force tricks to be rid of this beast; unthinking, it retreated one step too far, its leg coming down past the crest and onto nothingness. Its expression changed from pain and anger to dismay as it fell, flailing its arms. Ben heard it go crashing down the slope. He didn't worry for his father, who would have no difficulty dodging one plummeting rancor.

That left three beasts, two to his left and one to his right. He chose the one to the right; if he could force its retreat, the clan members could close up that flank and concentrate their efforts against the two remaining.

As he prepared for a leap to clear the spear warriors in that direction, he saw the rancor grab one of the Broken Columns men, shake him just long enough for the man's shriek to cut off, and then fling the body out into the darkness well away from the hill.

Ben grimaced and leapt. His feet came down on the shoulders of a warrior—Drola, he thought—and he balanced there for a second, for the rancor's hand was coming down at the warrior. Ben slashed, catching the rancor in the webbing of skin between thumb and index finger, splitting it down to the beast's wrist. The rancor screamed, the noise as shrill and loud as a steam whistle, and took a step back.

Ben continued his forward motion, somersaulting to his feet in front of Drola. "Spears, together now!"

The warriors surged forward, men and women, hitting the rancor simultaneously all across its body from head to knee. Not all the blows penetrated its hide wrappings or skin, but all imparted kinetic energy. The rancor staggered back, fell on its rear end—and found that its center of balance was just a meter too far past the crest of the hill. It, too, toppled into darkness, and Ben and the warriors heard it crash its way down the slope.

Ben turned. The other two rancors on the southwest crest were being harried and forced backward by a combination of mass spear charges and winds from the Witches. Elsewhere on the hilltop, Dathomiri men and women were collecting themselves, improvising bandages, kneeling over the dead and badly injured. The rancors that had attacked the steeper slopes were already gone.

Dead and badly injured—Ben counted at least twenty Dathomiri who lay still or moved so feebly that they clearly would not be able to return to the fight.

That was 8 to 10 percent of the active fighters. Not good. He sought out Firen, who stood with the Raining Leaves Witches at the southwest crest. "How many of the rancors have been put out of commission?"

She shook her head. "Maybe one."

"You're kidding."

"The first time, five came against us and five returned to the forest. The second time, eleven—all fresh, I think—came against us, and eleven returned to the forest. One was crawling and had to be hauled by two others, so it may not return to the fray. But even now the Nightsisters, if they follow the same habits we do, will be using their skills and their spells to bandage and heal their rancors, to raise their spirits and fire up their instincts for destruction."

"Where are *our* rancors?" That was Drola, anger and even suspicion in his voice.

"By *our* you mean those of the Raining Leaves." Firen shot the Broken Columns warrior an ugly look. "You men have none of your own. We released ours to graze before we came up the hill. Because they would take up too much room, consume too much food and water. Ours . . . are probably far from here, or may be among theirs, but I have recognized none so far."

Drola nodded. "How convenient that we are deprived of our greatest weapon against the rancors."

"We could not have known that they would send rancors against us!" Firen's hand curled into a fist. Little flickers of what looked like lightning crackled around it, making popping and snapping noises.

"Stop it." Kaminne forced herself between Firen and Drola. "If you have nothing to suggest that will improve our situation, then you have nothing to say." She looked between them, stared each down in turn.

"Nightsister!" That was not one cry but many from those at the southwest crest. Pushing through the crowd in that direction, Ben saw several Dathomiri raising blasters.

When he got to the edge, he could see their target. A single human-sized silhouette had emerged from the forest verge and was walking toward the hill. She held a gleaming pole taller than she was.

"Hold your fire." That was Tasander, so calm as to seem almost disinterested. "She carries the white spear."

Ben shot him a curious look. "Some sort of truce thing?"

Tasander nodded. "Not even Nightsisters attack a bearer of the white spear—that anyone knows of, anyway—because they would never again be safe when they carried one."

The Nightsister marched to the bottom of the hill slope, stopping where soil mostly gave way to stone. She plunged the point of the spear into the ground, then turned and, at a rate so slow as to seem insulting, walked back into the forest.

Ben saw movement on the slope—the white garments of his father made him dimly visible. Luke descended toward the spear.

Ben started down the slope, carefully picking his way among boulders and rock faces in the dark. By the time he reached the midway point, Luke had climbed to that altitude again, the spear in his hands. "How are you doing, Dad?"

"Just another ordinary day at the Temple." Luke seemed neither hurt nor winded. In fact, he wasn't even dirty. He held the butt end of the spear toward Ben. "There's a note attached."

Ben unwrapped it from the spear butt. It was a piece not of flimsi, but of tanned animal hide, the words painted onto it—recently, to judge by the tacky wetness of the paint—in crude block letters in Aurebesh.

It read,

> *To the Sisters of the Raining Leaves*
> *Kill, enslave, or drive forth the men with you and we will have no further quarrel with you. Do not, and you will die with them.*
> *So swear we all, the Sisters of the Night.*

Ben showed it to his father. "Not too bad. No misspellings. I think they used a ruler to keep the lines straight, like a first-timer in school."

Luke cast an eye up the hill. "How are they doing?"

"Lots of injuries, lots of deaths. I think we're losing the morale war."

"Do what you can to keep that from happening. As much as your fighting skills, that's what they need you for."

"I guess." Ben rolled the hide around the spear butt, tied it fast with the leather thong that had held it originally, and gave his father a quick hug before ascending the slope again.

At its summit, he offered the note to Kaminne and Tasander. They and some of the subchiefs gathered around could read, and news of the note's contents spread throughout the camp.

Kaminne pondered. "What's an elegant way to say *No, and we hope you die in misery?*"

Tasander shrugged. "My father used to say, *May the stinging insects of a thousand worlds seek out your moist places.*"

Kaminne laughed. So did several of the subchiefs, both Raining Leaves and Broken Columns. "Yes, say that."

Tasander lay the note facedown on the rock and, with Dyon's paints, wrote that response in a beautiful, flowing calligraphic hand. Once the paint had dried to the point it would not smear, he tied the note to the spear and handed it to Drola.

The others opened up a lane for the warrior. He started well back along the hilltop, ran forward, and hurled the spear with an athlete's skill. The gleaming shaft sailed out far past the hill, burying its head in the soft soil partway back to the tree line. A few moments later a silhouette emerged from the trees, retrieved the spear, and returned to the shadows.

A little while later, Ben felt the familiar twinge in the Force net above him. He didn't have to warn the others. Olianne was the first to raise a voice. "They're coming!"

Ben was surprised to see the same number of rancors as before emerge from the tree line and race for the hill. All eleven seemed fresh, unhurt.

"Fire at will." That was Tasander, and blasterfire joined arrows to hurtle against the rancors.

The beasts reached the hill's base and, as before, clambered up with terrifying swiftness. This time, though, the central rancor of the five on the southwest slope stopped when it reached Luke, not ignoring him as the others had, and began grabbing at him as the other four swept up around him on both sides.

The spearmen braced themselves. But as the four rancors came almost close enough to receive their thrusts, they halted. Instead of surging up to the crest, they began digging and prying at the boulders toward the top of the slope.

Ben didn't understand their tactic until it was too late. Tons of boulders, ranging from the size of a human head to the size of an airspeeder, dislodged by their efforts, clattered and rolled as a broad, deadly curtain toward Luke Skywalker.

"Dad!"

Luke, caught up in combat with a curiously defensive rancor, did not hear. Perhaps he felt a touch of Ben's alarm, but he did not recognize it as applying to himself. He did not look up, and Ben saw the curtain of stone sweep across him and the rancor, carrying both down the hillside with it.

Then, and only then, did the four other rancors clamber up to the top of the hill.

Below, Ben could see Luke's lightsaber, gleaming but now still, at the base of the hill. And four figures, women glowing with blue energy, raced out from the tree line toward his father.

Ben crouched to jump—not at any of the four rancors now clambering to their feet to his right, but down the slope, toward his father.

A hand fell on his shoulder, restraining him. He looked up to see Dyon shaking his head.

It played out like a conversation but with no words being spoken, the entire exchange one of understanding, transpiring in a fraction of a second—

My father is in danger.

If you abandon the hilltop, the Dathomiri may lose heart.

My father—

Your attachment, or your duty?

Dyon was right, and that truth wrenched a groan from Ben. He stood up and pivoted, the better to leap into the midst of the rancors.

A slim hand plucked the unlit lightsaber from his grip. Ben caught a fleeting glimpse of Vestara in motion, flashing past him, before she dropped over the lip of the hill, his weapon in her hand.

Luke never lost consciousness, despite the head-sized rock that grazed his skull and toppled him down the hillside. He rolled and slid, his acrobatic skills keeping him from some of the pounding he might have experienced, and he stayed ahead of the majority of the rockfall. But dazed as he was, he could not avoid all harm. A rock slammed into his chest and he felt a pop in his sternum. Another slab of stone gave way under his weight as he came down upon it and slammed back-first onto a moving stone surface, the world spinning around him.

He leapt free but traveled only three or four meters before he hit another surface. The blow knocked the wind out of him. Stones continued to slide and clatter down toward him, but most of them stopped short of his position. Dimly, he could see the rancor he had been fighting; it was now between him and the base of the hill, lying still, tons of stone atop it.

And he could feel danger above and beyond the natural peril posed by the rockslide. Dark side Force energy was headed his way. He rolled forward, putting another two meters between him and the oncoming rockslide, pressing sharp stony points into his back and neck and legs, and sat up to see four Dathomiri women limned in blue energy running toward him. As they saw him struggling to rise, two slowed their forward pace and lifted their arms, beginning a series of intricate weaving motions.

Luke raised his lightsaber and tried to stand.

Lightning, Force lightning, erupted from the two spell-weavers. It crackled toward him, lethal amounts of energy.

He caught both bolts on his lightsaber blade. At such times, the weapon of the Jedi was more than a concentrated and constrained shaft of energy; it was an extension of himself through the Force, and the blade held the Force lightning at bay. Residual energy reaching him caused his hair to stand on end and the sheer force of the attack drove him back, forcing him down again.

The two nearest Witches were only meters away, and now Luke could see two more rancors break free of the tree line and charge toward him.

This was not good.

Chapter Twenty-Three

THE NEARER WITCHES CAME WITHIN TWO METERS OF HIM, THEIR ARMS raised and weaving spells in new patterns. Luke struggled to rise, could not do so against the press of the lightning and his own dazed condition.

Then there was a *thump* to his left as Vestara landed atop a flat stone the size of a tabletop. She was within reach of the nearer Witch on the left. She swung the lightsaber in her hand—blue, not the red one she'd wielded in the Maw—at that Witch.

The Witch, a redheaded woman of middle years with purpling blotches on her face, shifted the aim of her spell-weaving. Air superheated in a channel from her to Vestara. The Witches doubtless would have called it fire, but it was plasma.

Vestara took it on her lightsaber blade. She twisted, bracing herself on her right foot, and pivoted into a side kick. The blow took the Witch in the midsection, and Luke could hear ribs break. The Witch staggered back, her plasma attack sliding off sideways to play harmlessly against boulders and loose soil.

Vestara's attack was more than a successful assault against one Witch. It distracted the others as well. The attention of the two lightning casters wavered. Luke felt the pressure against him falter just a bit—just enough.

He rolled rightward, carrying the lightning assault with him but deflecting more of its energy, and came to his feet—and more, leaping up and toward the nearest Witch to his right. His kick caught her in the chin. He felt bone break under his attack. The Witch fell back, her spell-weaving immediately at an end. She collapsed gracelessly and lay unmoving.

The ground shook as the onrushing rancors came near. They passed the two Witches in the rear. One headed for Luke, one for Vestara.

Luke traversed toward the right. The Witches' lightning stayed with him. Too late, the Witches recognized his tactic. The crackling streams of lightning crossed over Luke's rancor.

The lightning jittered over the beast's body, illuminating it. The beast stumbled in its run, falling forward. Its inadvertent dive brought it below the lightning bolts, which returned to harry Luke. But he caught them on his blade again, and the damage had been done: the rancor lay still, smoke rising from its back. Luke grinned at the Witches, a smile not of humor but of warning.

To his left, Luke saw the second rancor tripping over something, falling toward Vestara—

The *something* was the Witch closest to Vestara. Somehow the girl had redirected the Witch, perhaps with another kick or an exertion through the Force, and had put her beneath the rancor's feet. Now the Witch was down, trodden upon, and the rancor was in the middle of an awkward collapse.

Vestara showed it no mercy. With grace and speed worthy of a Jedi Knight, she sidestepped and brought up her blade in a blindingly fast slash. The blow intercepted the rancor's throat. The beast's shoulder came to ground centimeters from her feet.

One of the two rearmost Witches diverted her lightning to Vestara. The Sith girl caught it on her blade and was forced backward, taking slow steps and skidding slightly as the energy compelled her into unwilling retreat.

But that left only one on Luke. Pushing, summoning his willpower and technique in the Force, he walked toward his Witch at the same rate Vestara retreated before hers.

He felt the new attack in the Force before he detected its direct effects. There was a pulse of energy from all along the tree line. Then wind howled out of the forest and rushed against him, battering him, adding its strength to that of the lightning.

He couldn't advance against it, so he rooted himself in place. The wind tore at his clothes and his hair, caused him to squint and shield his face with his free hand. But he could not be put down, could not be pushed back.

He saw winds hammer at the two downed Witches. In a moment the currents caught them up. They rose to an altitude of a couple of meters, the skins they wore rippling and tattering in the wind, and then they hurtled toward the forest. The two Witches pouring Force lightning against him and Vestara also retreated, but they kept their feet and backed away until they reached the tree line and disappeared within it.

Still the wind kept up. Luke saw Vestara pressed up against a sheer rock face at the bottom of the slope.

Now the four rancors that had passed him descended, too. All had blood on them, and clearly most of that blood was not their own. As they reached the base of the hill, they broke into a run and were, moments later, lost in the shadows of the trees.

Then, and only then, did the winds subside.

He looked over at Vestara, who could finally move free of the rock face she'd been pinned against. He gave her a little salute of the lightsaber before he deactivated it. "I'm surprised you came to my aid. Considering the determination you showed when you and your mistress fought me in the Maw."

Vestara, too, deactivated her weapon—or, rather, Ben's, as Luke now recognized it to be. She shrugged. "We were enemies then. Now we have a common goal."

"Which is, exactly, what?"

"Defeat of the Nightsisters, of course. Do you wish me to stay with you?"

He shook his head. "I think Ben will need his lightsaber back."

Vestara began a graceful ascent of the slope. "If I were you, I'd cut off one of the rancor heads and prop it up on a stone. Give the others something to think about. To fear."

"Not my style." After a moment, Luke began climbing up after her, returning to his halfway point.

Ben watched the girl climb. Emotions struggled within him. Gratitude that she'd helped Luke. Suspicion as to her motives. When Vestara clambered over the hill crest, he extended a hand to help her up, and she took it.

"I suppose I should thank you."

She handed him his lightsaber and flashed him a knowing smile. "But you probably won't. You're too surly."

"Thank you."

"Think nothing of it. Nice lightsaber, by the way. Too bad its color is so unfortunate."

She moved away, back toward the nearest group of Raining Leaves Witches, and Ben hung his weapon from the hook at his belt.

He forced himself to turn his thoughts from Vestara. She was a problem, and likely a danger, but not the most pressing one.

Despite the fact that the Raining Leaves and Broken Columns had driven their attackers off again, despite the fact that three rancors lay dead or unconscious at the foot of the hill, the attack still constituted a loss for the clan members. Another dozen of them were dead, and more were injured. Morale was slipping, and the fact that Nightsisters had actually shown themselves, demonstrating that they would partic-ipate directly in the attack, was contributing to the clan members' gradual loss of faith. Ben moved to join the conference of Kaminne, Tasander, and their subchiefs; Dyon was also there. Ben sat on a flat rock at the edge of that gathering.

Tasander looked worried, more uncertain than before. "I'm open to ideas. I've led the Broken Columns through a lot of engagements, but nothing like this. Rancors, Nightsisters—I don't have any tactical experience with this sort of thing."

Kaminne didn't look any happier than he did. "Nor do I. Nobody does."

Ben frowned as something occurred to him. "Not true. I have."

Kaminne brightened. "This is like Jedi fighting you have done?"

"No, not Jedi fighting. Space navy battles."

Tasander gave him a curious look. "How's that again?"

Ben made a sweeping gesture that took in the entire hilltop. "Think of this emplacement as a Star Destroyer. Or a Hapan Battle Dragon, if you prefer." He pointed at a couple of Broken Columns warriors, holding blaster rifles, outside the subchiefs' gathering. "Those guys, they're your long-range guns." He pointed next at warriors with bows and blaster pistols. "Turbolaser batteries." He gestured at the nearest group of Witches. "Ion cannons and other specialized ranged weapons systems like proton torpedoes." He pointed at a cluster of Broken Columns men with spears and sharpened stakes. "Finally, your shields. And then the rancors coming against us are attacking starfighters."

Tasander. "All right. But in the wise words of my father: *So what?*"

"We're losing because our weapons and shield systems aren't coordinated. Let's say you get a group of Raining Leaves spearwomen on the left and one of Broken Columns spearmen on the right. A rancor pops up where the two groups join. It attacks, and they withdraw in slightly different directions, opening up a hole. Your shields no longer overlap, no longer reinforce each other. The rancor wades in, grabs and kills two or three people."

"I get it." Dyon nodded. "And your archers and blaster warriors. They're spreading their fire across all the targets at once. Hitting everywhere equally."

"Which is fine against human opponents." Kaminne, too, was clearly caught up in rethinking their tactics. "Not so good against rancors."

Tasander stood and looked across the hilltop, at all the disparate groups of warriors and Witches. "I think I have it. Kaminne, you trust me?"

"You know I do."

"Then let me reorganize things, and back my play."

Five minutes later, Tasander addressed the entire gathering of Raining Leaves and Broken Columns. He spoke loudly enough for those amassed before him to hear, but not so loudly that his words would carry clearly to the forest floor. "As before, we'll be in four units. The main unit, here, will be half our total strength, and the other three units, where they were before, one-third the remaining strength.

"The spearmen and spearwomen are designated Shield. You'll set up back from the crest. In front will be those with sharpened sturdy poles, and you'll brace them against the ground. *You are immobile.* You neither advance nor retreat without orders. You let the rancors come up over the crest and impale themselves on your weapons. Those with actual spears, you stand behind them and stab at vulnerable points—their faces, armpits, wherever their hide does not protect them.

"Bow and blaster bearers are designated Turbo, which is short for 'turbolasers.' You'll start out in front of the Shield formation. When targets come into view, you'll harry them at range. Then, when you hear the command 'Shields up,' you fall back behind the spear lines. Re-form there and wait until the rancors hit the Shield line. Then, and only then, you open fire again. And if your unit commander designates a specific target, everyone fires at that target until you hear 'Free fire' or another target designation.

"Witches, you start and stay behind the Shield line, and give the Turbo formation enough space to line up in front of you. Your unit commander will also designate one specific target, and you use your spells on that target until it's down or fled. And then your commander will choose a second target, and a third, and so on.

"All those who consider themselves sharpshooters are with the Snipers group. You'll be set up at points along the crest that are too steep for rancors to attack. You'll fire where your commanders tell you. Mostly at the rancors once they're on the top, but if your commanders spot a Nightsister, they'll point you to that new target."

Tasander fell silent, but Kaminne spoke up before any conversation arose. "We chose not to let the Nightsisters govern us. That means we live as a fighting force or die as individuals. Live or die—you choose. And understand, Raining Leaves and Broken Columns will be intermixed in these new groups. When you line up, if you look to the right and left and see one of your fellow tribemembers there, *you have failed.* I want to see you intermixed, Leaf–Column, Leaf–Column. And if I see you abandon a fellow who is not of your tribe, *I will personally kill you*. If Tasander does not kill you first. This I swear."

Now there was no chance of murmuring. No voice rose in the silence that fell after Kaminne's words.

She waited a moment more, then nodded, satisfied. "Return to your original positions. Your new unit commanders will tell you what to do."

Silently, even breathlessly, the members of the Broken Columns and Raining Leaves moved off to their positions.

Ben heaved a sigh. "Ever seen anything like this before?"

Dyon shook his head. "It's the sort of thing that could only happen on a planet like this."

"Do me a favor, would you? Since I'm supposed to stay up here for morale purposes."

"Sure."

"Go down and tell my dad not to do his usual thing of knocking out one of the rancors. The Nightsisters are starting to adjust to his tactic. We're going to throw some new tactics at them, so he should, too. Tell him to do whatever he wants—so long as it's something they haven't seen before, something they can't predict."

Dyon grinned. "Consider it done."

The loss of three rancors and injury to two Nightsisters had apparently caused the remaining Nightsisters to do some thinking themselves. The next attack did not come until an hour after the last one ended. Again Ben felt a twitch in the Force net overhead; again he and others raised the alarm.

But this time, only archers and blasterfighters crowded the crest of the hill. Ben, leader of the Shields at the southwest slope, stood among the pole wielders and did not move forward to see.

"Five of them—six, seven, eight!" That was the Turbo leader ahead, one of the Raining Leaves women. She sounded worried but not fearful.

The Turbos began firing.

Their concentrated fire lasted only a few seconds. Then their unit leader called out, "Shields up! Shields up!"

Ben pressed himself in close to the stake wielder to his left, a Raining Leaf. His change in position opened space between him and the pole to the right. Bow and blaster bearers streamed between them, flowed through the loose formation of spear warriors behind, and began re-forming. Ben stepped back to his original spot.

The ground shook and Ben saw rancor hands and heads top the hill crest. He raised his voice to be heard over the general clamor. "Shields, brace yourselves!"

Then the rancors heaved themselves up onto the hilltop and charged forward. Wielders of the braced poles aimed their sharpened ends at each of the five rancors in the front rank. The rancors hit; poles bent, one snapped. The rancors reached for men and women; spear fighters impaled their arms and hands as they grabbed. Ben lit his lightsaber and thrust it into a rancor knee all the way to its hilt.

"Turbo, center head, fire!" The women leading the Turbos was well chosen; her voice, shrill but commanding, cut through the tumult and was easy to hear.

Blasterfire and arrows poured into the face of the rancor in the center. In moments that face was unrecognizable. And yet the beast was not dead, not quite; howling, it staggered away, crashed through the line of three rancors in the rear, and toppled over the hill crest. The one Ben had kneecapped also staggered back, but only far enough to have its position in line filled by an uninjured rancor.

That left four in front, three behind. "Turbos, left center, face, fire!"

In moments another rancor staggered away, dying. Those remaining grabbed as viciously and as vigorously at the lines of spear and pole wielders, but the latter kept them from advancing and the former protected their fellow warriors.

And now the Witches entered the combat. A storm of assaults—lightning, hails of rocks, flashes of fire, bone-rattling sonics—hammered into the rancor line.

A rancor managed to get past prodding spears and sharpened poles to grab the woman to Ben's left around the waist. He swung, put extra effort into the blow. Despite the sheer mass of the rancor's arm, his lightsaber cut through the wrist, severing the hand entirely. The rancor stood straight up, looking at its cauterized injury, howling in dismay at the pain—and then its head ignited, set afire by a Witch's spell. Clutching its head, it hurtled over the edge.

All of a sudden, of the eight that had come against them, three rancors remained. For the first time, Ben could feel an emotion from them that was not pain or rage, and that emotion was fear.

The rancors retreated.

"Shields, hold fast!"

"Turbos, advance! Fire at will!"

Chapter Twenty-Four

LUKE SAT ON A FLAT STONE METERS AWAY FROM THE EASILY CLIMBABLE portion of the southwest slope. He was wrapped up head-to-toe in a dark blanket he'd had Dyon bring him. His lightsaber was still on his belt.

In the initial moments of the attack, he watched impassively as eight rancors clambered up, some only a few meters away. One, toward the center, lagged behind the others, looking right and left, clearly seeking Luke. But it never found him, and continued on past.

Already half into a meditative state, Luke allowed himself to sink farther into the Force, away from the present.

Now he could feel, even visualize, the Force energy net above him. But he didn't want the whole thing. Just a strand . . .

He followed that strand across the sky, then down, as it separated from the weave and became a single pure channel of Force energy, dark side energy. He followed it to the trees, to the ground.

There stood a woman. He could almost see her in his mind's eye— tall, strong, even beautiful in the savage fashion of the women of

Dathomir. Her hair was red like Mara's. That caused him a little twinge of sadness but did not thrust him out of his meditation.

Nor did it cause him to abandon his current objective.

Beside him, the pile he had made—a dozen fist-sized rocks—rose into the air. Higher and higher they went, until they reached the Force net, until they met the strand he had selected.

The Nightsisters were preparing tactics against Luke Skywalker. So be it. For the next little while, he would be someone else.

Because the mercenary Carrack had been effective against them, the Nightsisters had eliminated Carrack. So be it; for the next little while, Luke would be Carrack . . . in his tactics and in his role, at least.

His cloud of rocks now moved laterally, following the Force strand he had selected.

It curved downward as the strand did. In his mind's eye, Luke followed it while the rocks separated by a few handbreadths and picked up speed.

In the distance, he saw the tiny speck of the redheaded Nightsister. She rapidly grew in his mind's eye as the rocks neared her.

At the last instant, having some presentiment of danger, she looked up. Then the cloud of rocks hit her.

The image disappeared. The strand of Force energy stemming from the Nightsister instantly evaporated. The net above twitched and weakened.

Rancors began sailing down the slope to Luke's left. He opened his eyes to watch. First was one whose Force presence was already failing. Its face was a ruined mess. Next was a flailing, howling beast whose head was on fire.

Luke sighed. He did not wish their deaths. But where men and women chose to wield the Force to achieve unnatural ends, death always resulted.

A cheer rose from the Dathomiri on the hilltop. At first, it was ragged; then it rose in volume, strengthened.

Ben caught the eye of the Turbo leader. "How many did you lose?"

She shook her head as if unable to believe it. "None. You?"

"Two badly injured. No deaths."

"And they didn't get as far as our Witches." She turned, got the attention of an adolescent Broken Columns boy. "You, bring water around."

Minutes later, it became clear that their victory, while momentary, had been almost complete. Four clan members were hurt, one of them perhaps fatally. Four new rancor bodies were piled up at the hill bottom, three along the southwest slope and one on the eastern approach.

And Ben could feel his father down the main approach, calm, unruffled.

Dyon joined Ben at the hilltop edge. "The Star Destroyer *Hilltop* held up pretty well."

Ben nodded. "And now we find out what the enemy commander is made of."

In the next two hours, the rancors came against them three more times.

Seven members of the Raining Leaves and Broken Columns died. More were injured. Twelve rancors died. More were injured. In the last two engagements, not a single rancor coming against them was fresh; all had fought before, all had been hurt before.

Dyon, visiting Luke after each skirmish, relayed Luke's report that one Nightsister had fallen during each exchange. Luke didn't know how many had been killed, how many injured. "But the way your father shook his head," Dyon reported, "makes me think those Nightsisters are goners."

JEDI TEMPLE, CORUSCANT

Walking down the broad hall of the main entrance level of the Jedi Temple, Leia beside him, Han smoothed the hair at the back of his neck. He pitched his voice to a stage whisper. "Didn't we just leave this party?"

Leia shot him a curious look. "How so?"

"A bunch of people we sided with, encamped, surrounded by enemies . . ."

She shook her head. "There are big, important differences between the two situations."

"Such as what?"

"Here you can take a quick trip down the street and buy yourself a good cup of caf. Here the air is kept to a comfortable temperature."

Han brightened. "No sweating all the time. Sanisteam stalls everywhere." Then he sniffed. "Though it doesn't smell like everyone here is using them."

Immediately ahead of them, Kani Asari, a golden-haired apprentice who was currently serving as Kenth Hamner's personal assistant, glanced over her shoulder. "The government has shut off our municipal water, power, and waste pickup. We're running on backup generators and recycled water. Not enough for all the comforts of home."

Han gave her an apologetic look. "Sorry."

They reached the first set of turbolifts. Several had silvery straptape crossing and sealing their doors in broad x-patterns, indicating that they were out of service, but one was still functional. The apprentice took the Solos down several levels and conducted them as far as a conference room, but did not follow them inside.

Within the room were dark, comfortable chairs and tables, platters of refreshments—and Jaina, who rose from a chair as they entered. Leia hurried over to embrace her daughter.

Han waited his turn. "Nice of Hamner not to be here on time." When Leia released Jaina, he pulled his daughter to him. "How's Amelia?"

Jaina rolled her eyes. "Telling tall tales out of Dathomir. About rescuing Artoo-Detoo and fighting a one-eyed giant. She has Cilghal and the medical staff enrapt. Here, sit. Eat."

Han released her and did as he was told. "Our daughter thinks I'm a trained nek. Sit, eat, roll over. How about Anji?"

"Cilghal thinks she'll be fine," Jaina said. "It was just a concussion."

"And Jag?" Leia asked. "Seeing much of him?"

Jaina waited until Leia sat, too, then resumed her chair. "Not so much in the last few days. There was an attempt on his life—"

Leia nodded. "We heard about that on the holonews on the way home."

"—and between that and all the other reasons for him to be under scrutiny, he's having a hard time getting away from his duties. Though he's volunteered to support your negotiations."

Leia smiled. "So we can call him in."

"That's right."

"Yeah, sure." Han adopted his customary slouch. "Call him in so he can steal all your time. We *do* like to see our daughter sometimes, you know."

The door hissed open and Master Kenth Hamner entered. Han was used to seeing the acting leader of the Jedi Order flanked by other Masters, so his unaccompanied state made him seem strange.

Hamner gestured for them to remain in their seats, ignoring the fact that only Jaina had made any attempt to rise.

"Sorry to be late. Many issues are making demands on our time. Jedi Solo . . ." His attention was on Jaina, though that term of address applied equally well to Leia. "You can stay if you wish." He sat opposite the Solos.

"Thank you, sir," Jaina said.

Hamner produced a datapad and set it open on the tabletop before him. "So. What do you have?"

Han and Leia exchanged a glance, then Han said, "I'm supposed to be objective about this, so I'll be polite about it and just say not much."

"But maybe a start," Leia corrected. "She wants us to turn over Sothais Saar."

Hamner's jaw dropped. "She made a production out of meeting you at the Senate Building so you could bring *that* to the Council?"

"She promises not to put him in carbonite," Han said.

Hamner frowned, but it was Jaina who spoke next. "And hold him *how?*" she demanded. "You *know* that's a hollow promise."

"*Do* we?" Hamner asked.

"Yes, we do," Jaina insisted. "He has the Force, and he's *trained* to escape from places like MaxSec Eight. How are a bunch of GAS goons going to hold him?"

"The same way *we* do," Hamner replied. "With ysalamiri."

Han's brow shot up. "Hadn't thought of *that*." Normally, he wouldn't have admitted that, but he *had* given his word, as a general of the Galactic Alliance, to try to be objective. "But even if you give them some ysalamiri, Jedi are tough prisoners to keep."

"So are Bothan commandos," Hamner replied. "And Yaka assassins. GAS manages to hold *them* just fine."

"And if they *don't*?" Jaina demanded. "You'll be putting Sothais's life at risk."

Hamner's face grew stern. "Jedi Solo, I put the lives of Jedi Knights at risk every time I send them out on a mission. This would be no different—and it would be no less for the greater good. Whether you wish to admit it or not, it would be good for the Order and the entire Alliance for us to reestablish a functional relationship with the government."

Even Han had to admit that much was true. "So you're going to do it?" He couldn't believe he was asking the question with an open mind—and maybe he wasn't, because he still didn't think it was a very good idea. "You're *sure*?"

Hamner thought for a moment, then shook his head. "I'm willing to consider it," he said. "But she'll have to give us something in return. The Masters will never go for it, otherwise—and I couldn't ask them to."

The meeting fell silent for only a moment, then Jaina asked, "What about the Horns?"

"That would be nice," Leia said, "but I don't see her releasing them."

"Not *releasing*, necessarily," Jaina said. "But if we could get her to thaw them out."

"Yeah." Han was beginning to think this just might work. "That's fair. If Daala thinks GAS can hold one crazy Jedi, why not three?"

"And she would have to stipulate that they're *not* prisoners," Leia added. "That they're patients—and, as such, deserve the benefit of medical care—the Alliance's *finest* medical care."

"They already have the Alliance's finest medical care," Jaina said. "There isn't anyone out there better than Master Cilghal."

"But Master Cilghal and her staff have limits that the entire medical establishment of Coruscant does not," Hamner countered. "This might even prove advantageous to the Jedi—provided, of course, that we retain access to the patients."

"Yeah," Han said, nodding. "*That* seems fair."

Everyone fell silent again, and Han did not need the Force to realize that they were all growing excited about the possibilities. If Daala was telling the truth about wanting to work things out—or even if she was merely backed into a corner, as Dorvan had hinted—they just might have the beginning of a solution.

And that, of course, was when Jaina sat back and crossed her arms. "It might start out fine," she said. "Then Daala will renege. She'll refreeze them all, she'll deny their data to us, and she'll be holding all the cards. We'll have no recourse."

Hamner considered this, then shrugged. "And if that happens, what have we lost? One Jedi. But we will have no doubts left about her lack of good will."

Han was incredulous. "You have doubts *now?*"

"Han," Leia muttered. "*Objective,* remember?"

Jaina watched this exchange with a frown. "What's going on, you two?"

"Nothing," Han said. "I just sort of promised Daala I wouldn't torpedo this deal . . . well, at least not if it didn't deserve it."

Jaina rolled her eyes. "Dad, you can't trust her."

"We don't know that for sure. She might be trying to do the right thing." Han shrugged. "What do I know? I taught you to mistrust all politicians except Leia, and now that's coming back to bite me." He jerked a thumb toward Leia. "Talk to your mother."

Leia looked thoughtful. "Since Daala became Chief of State, we haven't put her word to the test. This would seem to be the perfect time to do that. Then we'll know for sure."

Hamner nodded in agreement. "It's about finding a way to work together when we *don't* trust each other" He turned a stony glare on Jaina. "Even the Sword of the Jedi should remember that much about negotiation."

Jaina exhaled and slumped back in her chair.

"I'm skeptical, too, Jedi Solo," Hamner said. "But we've got to start somewhere." He turned to Han and Leia. "Take this to Daala and see how she reacts. That will tell us something about how sincere she is."

Leia nodded, but did not rise. "Think we can spend a little time with our daughters first?"

"Of course." Hamner rose and turned toward the door. "Take all the time you wish. It's not like the situation is going to resolve itself without you."

Chapter Twenty-Five

THERE WERE NO MORE ASSAULTS. THE RAINING LEAVES AND BROKEN Columns sat where they were stationed, wrapped blankets around themselves, and fell into exhausted sleep. They slept in small huddles. Some slept sitting up, propped back-to-back. Sentinels stayed awake at the hill crest.

And dawn came. The clan members awoke sleep-deprived and aching, some injured, many mourning their dead.

Dyon approached Ben, who was assembling some food and water to take to his father. "I was able to upload the updates to my document."

Ben used a thong to tie the ends of his food-cloth together to make a simple bag. "Meaning the jamming is done?"

"For now."

Ben pulled out his comlink. "Hey, Dad?"

"Ben. Good to hear from you."

"Want some food?"

"I have some. I'm fine."

"We're about to have a meeting of the chiefs, subchiefs, and their favorite Jedi representatives. I'll give you a report when we're done."

The gathering of chiefs did not take long. Its events had apparently been scripted by Kaminne and Tasander. Each summoned a priest of her or his clan. With the priests presiding, the subchiefs, Ben, Dyon, and Vestara as witnesses, Tasander and Kaminne wed in a short, simple ceremony.

At the request of the two, Ben lowered the Jedi standard that still flew over the hill. Tasander and Kaminne raised a new one, just painted by Dyon. It showed a radiant sun in gold; small, beneath it, were the black base of a broken column and a green fern leaf.

Tasander called out, loud enough for all those on the hilltop and below it to hear, "With this ceremony, I disband the Broken Columns Clan, which I myself founded ten years ago. I am now Tasander Dest of the Bright Sun Clan. Should any former Broken Column wish not to live as a Bright Sun, he may come to me, found the Broken Columns anew, and go forth, leaving us forever."

Kaminne made a similar declaration for the Raining Leaves. She continued, "The conclave and the games that brought us together are over. We are at war, Bright Sun against the Nightsisters who have come against us. Last night, we learned how to drive them into retreat. Now we will learn how to destroy them."

Tasander called, "Uninjured scouts and hunters to the southwest lip. That's all."

But it wasn't all, because, with the formal ceremonies and announcements complete, clan members surged forward to congratulate the newly wedded couple. Kaminne and Tasander's façades of stern chiefly mannerisms broke as they received embraces, backslaps, impromptu gifts. To Ben's eye, no one seemed to be approaching them for permission to carry on the Broken Columns or Raining Leaves clan elsewhere.

"Well done, Ben."

Ben jumped. He turned to see his father standing behind him. "You shouldn't sneak up on a Jedi."

"Well, only a Jedi should sneak up on a Jedi."

"And *well done* may not be appropriate. All I did was point out where their tactics were disastrously bad. They came up with tactics that worked, Tasander especially." Then Ben gave his father a good look and laughed.

"What's so funny?"

"At least you're dirty now." He stopped. "Wait a second, should you even be here?"

Luke gestured at the Bright Sun standard. "This is no longer a Jedi camp. No reason for me not to."

"True. And I guess I'm out of a job as a landlord."

Luke accompanied Ben back to the southwest lip, and together they looked over the rain forest canopy below. "We're not done here—the Nightsisters are dark side Force-users, they may have been in contact with our Sith girl, and that makes this whole mess Jedi business—but we need to be thinking ahead. Such as how we either convince Olianne to hand Vestara over to us, or convince Vestara to come with us. And how we convince Vestara to tell us about her Sith, or at least isolate her so she can't get the information about the dark side power in the Maw back to her people, when we don't have a legal leg to stand on."

Ben nodded. "Try this. I go on a walk with Vestara into the forest. I mention that I have a datacard with the access codes for *Jade Shadow* on it. I turn my back on her. When she tries to put a knife into me, you jump out of the shadows and stop her. Then we've got her on attempted murder."

"I suspect she's far too bright to fall for a holodrama tactic as transparent as that."

"Yeah, I know." Ben kicked a loose rock over the edge, watched it clatter its way down to join the rockfall of the night before. "So we're back to figuring out what she's really doing here. Once we can make it clear that she can't accomplish that—or, let's hope not, once we figure out that she's succeeded, or even help her succeed—she'll be content to leave."

"So what's she after, Ben? You've now had several opportunities to talk to her."

"She gave you no clues when she helped you last night?"

"Unless her helping me was itself a clue. Why would a Sith want the Grand Master of the Jedi to survive?"

Ben shook his head. "I doubt that she wants you to survive. You killed her mistress. Our whole Order stands as an inevitable enemy to her kind. At best, she saved your life because she wants to kill you herself, not watch you die at the hands of savages."

"That's probably it. Vestara's first goal: deliver Luke Skywalker into the hands of her people. But what's goal number two?"

Ben sighed. "She made comments about admiring these people. I think she meant the Dathomiri in general. And, really, it makes sense. The Dathomiri may be nature-loving stay-at-homes, but I don't think there's a higher percentage of Force-sensitives among any population in the galaxy. That, and its isolation means new Force techniques, new ways of looking at things. We really need to get a new Jedi facility operating here, Dad."

"You're right." Luke frowned. "It was awfully easy for us to discover where Vestara's yacht was. I mean, Amelia's a clever girl . . . but should she have been able to find that ship?"

Ben shrugged. "But we know no message large enough to contain the Maw navigational data Vestara had acquired was transmitted offworld. So she's got to be thinking about how she gets offworld to join her people. And that means a ship. The only ships she could be confident would be on hand are her stolen yacht and *Jade Shadow*. And she's made no effort to get back to either one." Ben blinked as a new thought settled into place, an unpleasant one. "Unless . . ."

"Say it."

"She's shown no sense of urgency. Zero. None. Her time spent with the clans here feels an awful lot like a delaying tactic."

"Meaning?"

"She has no intention of returning to the spaceport for either ship. Because the Sith are coming here for her."

Luke gave an approving nod. "So when she got to Dathomir in the first place, she staged an approach that looked like it might end in a crash landing. But she really just landed."

"She sneaked into the spaceport, no harder for a Sith to do than a Jedi, and she struck a deal with the best mechanic in port. Here, take my ship, it's all yours. My asking price . . ."

"Is just enough credits to send off a hypercomm message. Very short, easy to encrypt and conceal, comparatively inexpensive to bounce around a number of comm stations to conceal its destination from investigators, and small enough that it couldn't contain the Maw navigational data."

Ben smacked himself in the forehead. "Because if only she has the nav data, the Sith *have* to come for her. She remains valuable. Good tactics for dealing with the Sith, even when you *are* Sith. So then she runs off into the rain forest to act as a diversion, to keep us away from the spaceport and Monarg."

"In the meantime, she really gets a good look at the Dathomiri and likes what she sees. She may even run into the Nightsisters first, as you speculated. So she could have been playing the Nightsisters against the Raining Leaves."

Ben looked around and spotted Vestara. She was seated with Kaminne and Olianne, and was holding Halliava's daughter, Ara, in her lap. They were chatting, laughing. Had they been dressed in modern clothes and surrounded by the trappings of a tapcaf, they could have been a gathering of family members anywhere in the galaxy. "Dad, if we're guessing right, time could be very, very short."

"I know. When the hunters and scouts move out, we need to have someone watching Vestara. Preferably both of us, trading off, so if she detects one of us, she may lose that sense when we switch."

Ben kicked another rock and watched it fall. "Blast it. I was almost starting to like her."

Halliava, trainer of scouts for the former Raining Leaves, was naturally among those who assembled to enter the forest and search it for signs of the Nightsisters. Vestara was not. After a quick, private consultation, Luke and Ben decided to enter the forest and shadow Halliava while Dyon, remaining on the hilltop, would keep a surreptitious eye on Vestara. "But don't forget," Luke told Dyon, "you're no safer on the bare hilltop than we are in the forest. Remember the example of Tribeless Sha. Danger is everywhere."

A bare minute after Halliava and other Dathomiri scouts and hunters entered the forest verge, so did the Skywalkers. Initially they chose an angle that would theoretically carry them away from Halliava, but, once concealed by trees, they vectored toward her.

*   *   *

For Vestara, the problem was a simple one to solve. She waited until the Skywalkers were gone and until Dyon was distracted. He was often distracted; curious clan members had questions for the offworlder, and, clearly a lonely bachelor, he had eyes for many of the ladies of the clans. Vestara contrived to perform tasks near the lip of the east face, and when Dyon and others were listening to an announcement from Firen, the senior subchief still present, Vestara dropped over the lip of the hill crest.

It was no suicide jump, of course. She plummeted several meters, landing lightly on the first ledge down. A flick of her finger and an exertion in the Force caused the sentry on this hill facing to look around for the source of a phantom noise and miss seeing the rest of her descent. Soon enough, she made her way into the verge of trees, out of sight.

She would have to be just as careful here as under the eyes of the Bright Sun members. The forest now teemed with hunters and scouts and Nightsisters and Jedi, all intent on doing harm to one another. Vestara was, in theory, allied with any and all of them, but traps and sudden surprises made accidents not just possible but potentially deadly.

She headed for the spot Halliava had told her about, a place where a small creek passed beside a naturally occurring cross-shaped stone, and waited for Halliava, who might be some time shaking her pursuers.

It was not too lengthy a wait. Half an hour passed, and then, with stealth suited to a trained Sith, Halliava appeared from behind a draping fern frond. She moved forward to embrace Vestara. For the first time, her true emotions showed; she looked worried and chastened. "The Sisters will listen more closely to you next time. *I* will listen. We have suffered a serious setback."

Vestara gave her a raised-brow, *I'm sorry I was right* expression. "You could not know what the Jedi were capable of. I barely knew. But you have not lost. Far from it. The common Dathomiri still fear the Nightsisters. They have simply been heartened by surviving last night's assault. Today they'll add up the numbers they've lost, they'll begin telling stories of the Nightsisters from days gone by, and they'll become afraid again."

"Yes." Halliava sat on the cross-shaped stone. "But the Jedi. They are very skilled, very powerful. For men, anyway. I barely lost them as they tracked me. They might find me again, so we must hurry."

"Did you bring my things?"

"Of course." From the pouch hanging at her belt, Halliava withdrew two items, each wrapped in cloth to keep it from making noise. She unrolled each in turn and handed it to Vestara. The first was her lightsaber; the second, a comm-equipped data tablet similar to a datapad.

Vestara took the data tablet and keyed in a security code. Her hopes were not high; every day since she had caught Halliava in secret conference with a fellow Nightsister, she had conceived more details for the Dathomir stage of her actions, and had approached the Witch with her hastily spun offer and explanation, she had checked her comm device for word from her kind. It had not come.

But today there was a blinking icon on the interface, an icon meaning that an encrypted message had arrived.

Vestara did not let excitement show on her face, did not let it speed up her actions. She simply keyed in the decryption code and held the device before her.

The tablet screen resolved into an image: a human woman in Sith robes, a woman unknown to her, with sharp, angular features, black hair, and an almost savage aspect to her expression. Vestara nearly laughed. The Sith woman had clearly been picked because she was closest to media depictions of the Witches of Dathomir; all she needed to do was tousle her hair and put on animal skins to be suitable as a Nightsister. Well, that, and spray on some false tan; she was very pale.

The woman spoke. "Vestara, greetings. We have received your initial communication and your follow-up reports with great interest. Of course we would be delighted to aid your new sisters in their quest. The weapons you have requested have been assembled, and we have chosen a worthy Sith Saber to trade for a Nightsister that each group may benefit from the new knowledge brought to it. We are in the Dathomir system and await your instructions." The screen faded.

Halliava had heard the message, and her eyes were wide. "They're here."

Vestara smiled at her. "They're here, and the Jedi and the Bright Sun Clan will burn like dry leaves in a fire under the weapons they're bringing you."

"What do we need to do?"

"We need to choose a landing field for the Sith shuttles. A broad meadow or a flat beach, something like that. It should be at least a couple of kilometers from the Bright Sun hill so our enemies can't bear witness to their landing. I need to go there and transmit the location with my device, so they know exactly where to come. Then, tonight, at the time we've told them, we show up to collect our rewards."

The smile that crossed Halliava's face was one of relief and victory. "I know just the place. Let's go."

Some time after he realized that he could no longer find Vestara anywhere in camp, Dyon spotted her again—carefully ascending the southwest approach, a waterskin at either end of a pole carried across her shoulders. After she made it across the hill crest, he approached her. "Replenishing our water stores?"

"No, hunting lizards." Then one of the skins she carried caught her eye and she gave a little gasp. "Why, it *is* water!"

"Clearly, sarcasm is a universal constant among teenage girls."

"Only the worthwhile ones. Didn't you hear the call for water bearers?"

"I did." *But you didn't. You were already gone. You just knew the call would be coming.*

"You could help, too." She swung around to face the forest again. The motion caused one of her waterskins to sweep toward Dyon. He ducked beneath it, stood again once it was past.

She gave him a smile of apology. "Sorry. There, where you see the line of clan members headed into the trees? In that direction is a creek."

"Thanks." Dyon waited until she continued on her way, to the central spot on the hill where water containers were collected. Then he headed down the slope and brought out his comlink. He'd better tell Luke and Ben right away of his failure to keep track of the Sith girl. That was the sort of information that could become more dangerous as it aged.

Chapter Twenty-Six

THE SCOUTS AND HUNTERS OF THE BRIGHT SUN CLAN LEARNED SEV-
eral things in the morning hours. Before noon, they, the chiefs, and
the offworlders gathered at the foot of the hill to tell what they'd
learned and concluded. Ben kept his eye on Halliava and Vestara as
they separately arrived, but the two did not interact any more, or with
anything that looked like hidden meaning, than any other two clan
members.

The Nightsisters had taken away their dead. There were no bodies
from Luke's rock bombardments for them to identify, only bloody
patches. In his visions, Luke had not seen their faces well enough to
describe them for identification. Their identities remained secret.

The Nightsisters had withdrawn, and without laying in any traps
that had been detected. Some Bright Suns took this as a sign that they
had fled for good. Kaminne, Tasander, and other wiser heads, the Skywalkers among them, dissuaded the optimists of this notion. "They
knew we'd be looking for their traps today," Tasander told them.
"They're changing tactics. Not allowing us to predict them."

"We must do the same to them." That was Halliava, who had evidently ranged many kilometers in her search for the Nightsisters. "They expect us to stay on the hill and endure another assault. I say we leave hunting parties out after dark to visit death upon them from behind."

There was a general murmur of assent at her words, and after a few moments of consideration, Tasander and Kaminne nodded. Kaminne called, "Come to me to volunteer for those hunter duties. I will assign units so that you can be in place well before dark."

Luke spoke into Ben's ear, too quietly for others to hear. "That's what we'll be doing."

Ben nodded. "Too noisy and rocky on the hill to sleep anyway."

CHIEF OF STATE'S OFFICE, SENATE BUILDING, CORUSCANT

It was a near-perfect re-creation of the meeting of the previous day— Daala, Dorvan, Han, and Leia, sitting in the same chairs. Leia, in her Jedi robes, Daala, in her admiral's uniform, and Han, in another set of his iconic trousers, shirt, and vest, looked identical. Only Dorvan—his suit shirt a coral hue, matching the handkerchief in the pocket opposite the one holding his sleeping pet—seemed to have been altered. Too, Dorvan now held a datapad and consulted it more frequently than he looked at the other attendees, a mannerism Han found irritating. But then, he found most politicians and politics irritating.

Daala tapped a fingernail against her desktop as if nervous. "Aren't the Jedi worried about recourse?"

Leia looked professionally curious. "I don't understand."

"I'll spell it out. They give me their mad Chev Jedi for study. We don't freeze him. We unfreeze the Horns. We study them. We exchange data with the Jedi. Perhaps even allow one of their scientists to be present during our tests and scientific meetings."

Leia nodded. "Right."

"But I know that I'm the pragmatic, unfeeling opponent who might at any moment say, *Well, we're done cooperating. Freeze the lot of them*. The Jedi seem to have built in no recourse against a sudden reversal of opinion on my part."

"Well, this is only the first exchange of many through which we intend to build a greater relationship of trust between you and the Order. If it goes as planned, we proceed to the next set of concessions, compromises, and agreements. We . . ." A sudden thought occurred to Leia. She narrowed her eyes. "You're stalling. Why are you stalling?"

Beside her, Han looked over his shoulder at the door. Leia knew her husband didn't have a blaster on him, not even a hold-out, in the Chief of State's office; it was a significant sign of trust on Daala's part that the Solos could be in here without bodyguards being present. But Han was doubtless figuring out what to do if the door opened and security agents swept in to arrest them. Which one he'd hit, how he'd take the agent's blaster away, whom to shoot first.

Now it was Daala's turn to seem surprised. "When do I get that power?"

"Which power?"

"The power to read the minds of Chiefs of State. Did you get yours when you left the office, or is it a Jedi thing?"

"I'll bet you my husband's Bloodstripes that I'm right."

Han shot her a dirty look. "Hey."

"Well, you *are* right. I'm stalling." Daala gave Leia an apologetic look. "But I'm not springing some trap. While we've been talking, Wynn here has been putting a poll into the field. Wynn?"

Dorvan looked up from his datapad. " 'Should Chief of State Natasi Daala release the insane Jedi from carbonite imprisonment?' In different polls, it's phrased different ways. For instance, in one it's 'the Jedi who went on a violent rampage and attempted to kill fellow Jedi and GA citizens.' Another poll narrows it to 'Jedi who have not been convicted of a crime.' We're charting public opinion and measuring variations in response based on things such as former Alliance or Confederation loyalty, planet of origin, species, age, gender, the variant forms of description of the Jedi I mentioned, what they had for their last meal, political party affiliation, occupation, and what news broadcast they usually watch."

"And you were waiting for early results to your poll before saying yes or no?" Han sounded outraged. "Whatever happened to doing what feels right?"

The smile Daala turned on Han was not a friendly one. "What feels right is banning the Jedi altogether and setting up an order of Force-users loyal to the government. Should I proceed with that approach?"

"Well, I meant what feels right and what's also not monumentally stupid."

Daala's smile faded. "You're insolent, General. And insubordinate."

"Yeah, the truth has a way of sounding that way."

"Han, please." Leia caught his eye, shot him what to Daala and Dorvan would have looked like a warning expression. Only Leia and Han knew they were playing good-guard, bad-guard. She returned her attention to Daala. "Now you know why Han never pursued a career in public office. He's much better at shooting people. But he's coming close to the truth here. Aren't you worried about letting the tail wag the nek?"

"No." Daala looked unconcerned. "The poll data is just one of many variables I'll be using to come to a conclusion. Not even a particularly important one. But one we can sample while we're sitting here. One most people wouldn't have noticed I was stalling to sample."

Han turned to Dorvan. "Well, since it's not a crucial element in the decision . . . what sort of early results *are* you getting?"

Dorvan glanced at Daala for permission and, receiving her nod, returned his attention to his datapad. "A simple majority favor unfreezing the Jedi. Expected variations based on the various personal factors I mentioned." He blinked several times. "Variations based on the language describing the Jedi are not as extensive as I would have expected. Well within the range of, say, mathematical rounding errors."

"Interesting." Daala didn't sound in the least interested. "All right. Doing what seems right. Here's my counteroffer. The Jedi turn Sothais Saar over to the government. He won't be frozen. He will be studied. He will be allowed standard prisoner access to an advocate, plus unrestricted access will be permitted to one medical scientist provided by the Order and one Jedi liaison. If, after thirty days, he has demonstrated no unusual facility for escape or mayhem, we will unfreeze one of the Horns under the same terms. If, after another month, the situation remains unchanged, we'll unfreeze the other Horn."

Leia exchanged a look with Han. He gave a little conciliatory shrug.

Leia turned to Daala. "I'll take your counteroffer to Master Hamner."

"Do you think he'll accept?" Daala wasn't asking Leia; she looked to Han for a reply.

Han shrugged. "I can't speak for the Council. I don't think the way Jedi Masters do. But, yeah, I'd bet a pot on *Hamner* agreeing to it."

"Good." Daala rose, signifying an end to the meeting. "Let me known when you have the Masters' agreement, and we'll move on to the next phase."

"The next phase?" Han asked, rising with the others.

"Of course, General Solo," Daala replied. She offered Han her hand. "Surely, you don't think we're going start *implementing* before we finish *planning?*"

Han took the hand, but said, "If you want to try to resolve everything at once, this is going to be a long negotiation."

Daala offered the faintest snort. "You have no idea, General. Try patching together the Alliance and the Empire sometime." She turned to Leia. "Speaking of which, I understand that you'll be dining with Head of State Fel today."

Leia took Daala's hand after Han released it. "I'm not sure I like the fact that you know about it."

Daala's smile broadened. "I run, at a distance, the largest intelligence operation to be found on Coruscant. It ought to be good for something."

As the Solos reached the far edge of the Senate Plaza, where they'd left their airspeeder, Leia decided they were far enough away that directional microphones would probably not pick up their discussion. "She was lying."

Han hopped into the pilot's seat. "Well, sure. She's a Chief of State." Then he realized what he'd just said to his wife. "As opposed to, say, a *former* Chief of State."

"Not *everything* she said was a lie."

"So which part *was?*"

Leia shook her head. "I'm not sure," she said. "Maybe the poll re-sults are more important to her than she's letting on. Or maybe she was stalling us for some other reason."

Han scowled. "You think she's got something else in play?"

"I think she *could* have," Leia said. "Or maybe the polls are just an excuse. Maybe she's just trying to drag negotiations out, buying time for public opinion to change—or to get a firmer grasp on the military. It's clear that she doesn't trust them, or she would have sent a com-pany of space marines to raid the Temple instead of Mandos."

"A company of space marines wouldn't have done it," Han said. "They're under Gavin Darklighter's command right now."

"Yes, Han," Leia said. "*That's* my point."

AIRSPEEDER HANGAR STRUCTURE NEAR
PANGALACTUS, CORUSCANT

Night had fallen, and the streams of airspeeder traffic had gone from torrents of metal and plasteel in innumerable colors to floods of run-ning lights in an even greater range of hues. Tourists visiting Corus-cant from other worlds often stood for hours on elevated pedwalks just to watch the flowing colors wax and wane in their mesmerizing aerial display.

Thirty meters below one such tourist-populated walkway, in a mid-dle level of a skeletal airspeeder parking structure, a very specialized speeder waited. It was huge and stretched across eight normal parking spots at the end of one parking lane. It was black and boxy, fully en-closed, with heavily tinted viewports and circular hatches atop its rear compartment in addition to the standard doors to either side of its cockpit. Anyone who had seen the funeral procession of Admiral Niathal would recognize it as one of the official speeders of the Mon Calamari embassy on Coruscant.

But despite the fact that its identity tags claimed it to be that vehi-cle, it was not. The ersatz diplomatic vehicle was only a durasteel foil shell rigidly mounted to a slightly smaller enclosed cargo speeder, also black. And within that vehicle's main compartment were banks of comm equipment, stools for four communications officers, and comfortable chairs at either end, two of which seated Moff Lecersen and Senator Treen.

"It seems very conspicuous." Treen did not sound in the least worried.

Lecersen nodded and passed her a saucer and a cup of caf. "It is. Very conspicuous indeed. And should anyone note and recall its presence where it should not be, all questions will go to the Mon Cal ambassador."

Treen took the cup and saucer. She passed the cup beneath her nose and gave the most delicate of sniffs. "And if, by chance, a security agent should wish to interrogate the driver or enter the vehicle?"

Lecersen glanced toward the pilot's compartment. "Our pilot is a Quarren whose identicard matches that of one of the Mon Cal embassy's employees. And if she can't bluff her way past a security guard, we strap in and she roars off in an attempt to escape. If she can get clear of the direct line of sight of pursuit for a second or two—and believe me, she can, she's a former A-wing pilot—she just has to hit a button to blow explosive bolts holding the shell in place around this vehicle. Suddenly we'll be a completely innocent speeder headed in a completely different direction and the security agent would be diving after wreckage."

Treen looked sad. "But we'll spill our caf."

Lecersen drew in a breath to reply, but the nearest comm officer spoke first. "Sir, operative coming on station now."

"Have you patched in to the restaurant holocam system?"

"Yes, sir."

"Put it up, please."

A monitor situated at the end of the comm boards, facing Lecersen and Treen, glowed into life. It showed, from about a three-meter altitude, a large chamber occupied by dozens of high-ranking Imperial officers in the uniforms of four and a half decades before. They clustered around computer consoles and viewports the height of tall men. At the center of the chamber was a single black chair, high-backed, set upon a low dais, with a small rectangular table before it. In the chair sat a tall, pale man clad all in black, dark polarized optics over his eyes.

Treen blinked, clearly confused. "I thought we would be looking at a restaurant."

"We are."

"But that's the control chamber of the first Death Star. Or am I hallucinating?" She looked with suspicion at her cup of caf.

"Take a closer look. This man is actually in a chamber no more than four meters by six. But the walls are floor-to-ceiling monitors. Every dining room in the Pangalactus Restaurant is similarly equipped. Some are larger, some smaller, but they all have total-immersion visuals, and Pangalactus has an extraordinary library of images to put up on the walls, including some stills, but mostly active."

"You sound like an advertisement."

"I *am* a shareholder, through a variety of intermediary names and insulators."

Reassured, Treen took another sip. "So."

"So the man in the chair is real. His name is Kester Tolann."

"Any relation to Commander Wister Tolann of the Imperial Navy?"

"His grandson."

Treen nodded, thoughtful. "I knew the elder Tolann. Thought he was rather more efficient than he turned out to be."

"Grand Admiral Thrawn agreed with you. His fitness reports on the older Tolann basically kept him from rising above the rank of commander. This boy's grandfather spent the last years of his military career routing waste-management convoys for Sate Pestage and Ysanne Isard when they ran the Empire."

"Ah." Finally some interest sparkled in the old woman's eyes. "So the younger Tolann has reason to hate the Chiss."

"The Chiss, anyone who is associated with the Chiss, and, in fact, any nonhuman species that dares to compete with humans. For anything."

"And, of course, Jagged Fel, reared among the Chiss—"

"More than that. Senator, do you know what duusha is?"

She offered him a delicate little frown of consideration. "Some sort of cheese, isn't it?"

"Produced on Tatooine and other backward worlds. It's made with blue milk and takes the milk's coloration. It's aged in rounds. Various fungi grow on the outside, insulating the cheese as it ages, protecting it from contaminants; some are white, some brown, red, green . . ."

"I see. Or, rather, I don't." Then she did. Lecersen all but saw a glow rod light up over the Senator's head. "No, I *do*. Duusha is blue on the inside and some other color on the outside . . . like Fel."

"Correct. His nickname among certain bands of critics in the Empire is Duusha because, they say, he's crude, cheap, and blue on the inside. Hence, tonight's activity is Operation Duusha."

"You should have been a teacher. You bring your subject matter to life, and engage your students."

Lecersen cleared his throat and pointed back at the monitor to return Treen's attention to it. "At any rate, Head of State Fel and his dining party are now en route to Pangalactus. They will arrive, they will be told that their chamber is ready. But they'll be slightly put off by the fact that some news of their dinner has been uncovered by Galactic Alliance Security, so they'll insist on a change of chambers. The only other chamber with a party sitting down at the same time, with similar dimensions, is immediately adjacent to Kester Tolann's."

Treen smiled. "So young Tolann, to avenge his grandfater's disgrace and to save the Empire from nonhuman job stealers, is going to kill Jagged Fel."

"I doubt it. He is an idiot, after all. Odds approach ninety to one that he'll fail."

"Oh." Treen's expression turned to one of rebuke. "You brought me here to see a failure."

"No, I brought you here to see Jag Fel take another big step toward dropping the role of Head of State into my lap," he said. "And to see how we're going to prevent Daala from restoring her public image."

A trio of deep wrinkles appeared between Treen's carefully plucked brows. "I don't recall asking for your assistance with that."

"No, but an opportunity presented itself, and she *has* been making a lot of noise about working things out with the Jedi of late," Lecersen said. "I'm sure you can imagine how difficult it would become to remove her from office, if she came to an accommodation with them and actually had their support."

Treen's lips tightened. "True," she said. "But I really don't think you're going to convince the Solos that *Daala* is the one trying to have their future son-in-law killed. The blame is naturally going to fall on you and your fellow moffs—especially when the assassin is the grandson of a former Imperial officer."

Lecersen's smirk only widened. "You might be right, were he the only surprise I have in store for you tonight."

A sparkle came to Treen's eyes. "I *do* love surprises," she said. "But only if I have a hint."

"Very well," Lecersen said. "The true attack—the one on Fel—is going to look like a diversion."

Treen's eyes grew round. "There's going to be *another?*"

Lecersen nodded. "Against the Solos," he said. "And they'll believe that *they're* the true targets."

"Oh." Treen licked her lips. "How nice."

Chapter Twenty-Seven

JAGGED FEL, DRESSED IN A RICH BUT UNDERSTATED BLACK UNIFORM-style ensemble, spun away from the two GAS security officers waiting outside the dining room he had reserved at Pangalactus, then spoke softly to their Rodian host.

"I'm sorry," Jagged said. "Our reservation was to be held in the strictest confidence. I'd appreciate it if you could set up another room. Any other room."

The Rodian's voice, singsong with the difficult task of forming Basic words with its Rodian vocal cords, carried no hint of unhappiness. "Of course. There may be a considerable wait—"

"Pardon me, sir," interrupted the Rodian's protocol droid, a male model with a dull bronze finish. He displayed a small datapad in his hand. "There *is* one other room free at the moment. The party that reserved it are wonderful customers who might be willing to switch this evening, and we could have it set up as requested in just a few minutes."

"We'd be most grateful," Jag said. "Please extend my thanks, and add their bill to mine."

"Of course, sir."

The host waited while the protocol droid made the arrangements, then led Jag and his party toward their new dining room.

Jaina fell into step beside Jag. "Very smooth of you. The teenage pilot you were back in the Yuuzhan Vong war didn't have all those social graces."

He tucked her arm through his. "You might have been surprised. High-ranking Chiss military families learn a lot more than warfare."

They filed into the new chamber—first two Imperial security agents, then Jag and Jaina, then Han and Leia, Allana, C-3PO and R2-D2, and finally two more security agents. The rest of Jag's security detail was posted at the entrances into Pangalactus. The chamber featured a central table in golden wood that seemed drenched with sunlight—in fact, it glowed faintly—and matching padded chairs. The walls showed a vista of green meadows, purple and blue mountains in the distance on three sides, a modern city in the distance on the fourth side. Airspeeders of slightly archaic design flew in orderly lanes above the city.

Leia stopped as she recognized the scene, and a slow smile spread across her face. "It's Alderaan. Jag, you shouldn't have."

"Of course I should have." Jag held a chair for Jaina, then sat himself. "None of the rest of us grew up in anywhere near as pretty a place. Not consistently, anyway."

The bronze protocol droid was last in, entering as the security agents began their sweeps of the chamber and the droids situated themselves against one of the mountain walls. The protocol droid took drink orders, promised the immediate arrival of a server, and waddled out.

Allana examined her table knife as though inspecting a lightsaber. "What do they serve? I hope it's not all Corellian food like Han cooks. That's too spicy."

Han looked hurt. "Give it a few more years. It'll grow on you."

Jag grinned and swept a hand over the tabletop. "They have all sorts of things here, Amelia. Corellian, traditional meat cuts and fixings, Mon Cal–style seafood dishes, some fine-dining adaptations of military ration packs for old soldiers like me, Hapan—"

"Hapan?" Allana brightened.

"Best outside the Consortium."

"House holocam feeds disabled." That was one of the security operatives, a Chiss man, his tone low and unobtrusive. "No observing devices present."

"Pathogens nil." The dark-skinned human female with the electronic sniffer in her hands looked a little uncertain. "So many exotic spices in the air I had to broaden the range of acceptable toxicity."

Jag heaved a sigh.

Leia smiled at him. "Get used to it."

On the monitor, Lecersen and Treen watched the Fel party enter the chamber, watched the bronze droid follow them and then, a couple of minutes later, depart. "We have no holocam feed from inside," Lecersen explained. "To set one up would have invited discovery. We'll have renewed sight and sound in a few minutes."

"Ah."

"Give us our lead operative, please."

The monitor switched back to a view of Kester Tolann's chamber. The Death Star re-creation he was watching had changed, and he leaned forward in his chair, enraptured by the simulated events playing out before him.

On the main wall, three figures held center stage. Two had their backs to Tolann. Dominant in the image, black and unmistakable, was Darth Vader. Barely visible, for she stood before Vader and only appeared when an arm or her head moved to one side of the Dark Lord of the Sith, was the eighteen-year-old Princess Leia Organa, Senator from Alderaan, clad in gubernatorial white, her hair arrayed in coiled side buns not often seen these days. Beyond Leia, facing her and Tolann, just enough to one side that his face remained in view, was a slightly built, aging man in a gray dress uniform—Grand Moff Tarkin, architect of the Death Star. And on the oversized monitor screen behind Tarkin was a planet, blue and beautiful, surrounded by space and stars.

Senator Treen's jaw dropped. She fumbled with her caf cup as it nearly slipped from her fingers.

Tarkin was speaking. "In a way, you have determined the choice of the planet that will be destroyed first. Since you are reluctant to provide us with the location of the Rebel base, I have chosen to test this station's destructive power on your home planet of Alderaan."

Senator Leia surged forward. Her body language, the little of it that could be seen, was one of entreaty, pleading. When she spoke, her voice was not quite right, not quite the voice Lecersen had been familiar with for many years. Its pitch was a touch higher, and it carried the clipped tones of the Coruscanti accent, nearly identical to Tarkin's, that so many Senators and other politicians affected back in the days of the Empire, even when they were not from Coruscant. "No. Alderaan is peaceful. We have no weapons. You can't possibly—"

Tarkin's voice turned harsh, commanding. "You would prefer another target? A military target? Then name the system!"

Treen laughed. No, to Lecersen's surprise, she giggled like a girl. Then she fixed Lecersen with a look that was half amusement, half outrage. "This is in extraordinarily bad taste."

He nodded. "Isn't it, though? It's a re-creation, based on Leia's own memoirs and standard reports filed by Vader and Grand Moff Tarkin. Admirers of the Palpatine era adore it. But it's not listed on any official menu. You have to know about it and ask for it specifically. Anyway, when Alderaan blows up, it's Tolann's signal to act."

Indeed, Tolann had withdrawn, from an inner pocket, two items. One was a small silver cylinder with circuitry and tiny stenciled letters on it. The other was a round device, the size and shape of a large cred-coin, with a button in its center.

Treen spared Lecersen. She seemed to be having difficulty suppressing further laughter.

"The cylinder is a micro-thermal-detonator, the sort YVH droids carry and fire. He'll throw that one against the wall to knock it down. The trigger in his left hand is linked to an identical detonator strapped to his body. His plan is to rush Fel, get his arms around the Head of State, and press the trigger."

"Ah."

On the monitor, a bright lance of green energy emerged from the lower corner of the Death Star's viewport and struck Alderaan. Kester Tolann hurled his detonator to the base of the wall.

Alderaan exploded, and then the entire wall showing the image from more than forty years before detonated in fire and smoke.

Jaina was opening her mouth to respond to a wisecrack when the wall behind her exploded.

The blast erupted from directly behind the security agent who'd pronounced the environment adequately free of toxins. The gout of flame picked her up, hurled her forward. Her flailing body cleared Allana, sitting to Jaina's right, and crashed down in the middle of the table. Allana shrieked, the sound mostly swallowed by the report of the explosion.

Jag, at the head of the table, to Jaina's left, spun toward the source of the explosion. There was a blaster in his hand.

Jaina heaved herself sideways, scooping Allana up, carrying the little girl in a lunge toward the door from the chamber. In her peripheral vision she saw her parents shoving at their side of the table. The tabletop slanted as the heavy piece of furniture tilted toward the source of the explosion.

A figure was emerging from the smoke and fire, through a hole leading into the next chamber. Tall and lean, he was dressed all in black and had his arms spread as if running toward a lover.

Seven—as she hit the ground and rolled, Jaina saw seven blaster bolts converge on the intruder, one each from the surviving security operatives, two each from Jag and her father. Steam erupted from each hit as the blaster bolts vaporized skin and flesh beneath it. The intruder jerked, shuddered. He did not topple over backward; his forward momentum balanced the energy imparted by the blaster bolts, and he stopped in his tracks. His face was slack. Jaina knew that his life span could be counted in heartbeats, just long enough for shock to transmit through his nervous system and inform his brain that it was time to shut things down.

Then two more holes smashed in through the wall to either side of the intruder. He was abruptly flanked by dark, skeleton-like carapaces with glowing red optic eyes and weapons systems emerging from arms and torsos.

They were Yuuzhan Vong Hunter droids, the deadliest droids fabricated since the time of the Old Republic and the destroyer droids of that era.

The human intruder glanced leftward at one of the YVH droids. The beginnings of a look of confusion crossed his face. Then his knees buckled, and he began to fall backward.

The YVH droids swung their weapon barrels toward Jaina's parents and advanced.

The tactical combat computer in Jaina's mind clicked through options. Get Allana to safety? Stay here and cover the girl? *Attack?* It took a fraction of a second for her to reach that third option, decide it was best, press Allana to the floor, and ignite her lightsaber. She leapt forward, swinging it with the speed and ferocity of one of the best-trained Jedi Knights in recent history.

In her peripheral vision, she could see the upended tabletop disintegrating under the hail of blaster bolts from the droids' right-arm weapons systems. Her father and Jag, shoulder to shoulder and barely visible over the lip of the ruined table, were putting round after blaster round into the droids' heads. Her mother was standing, lightsaber lit, catching and deflecting some portion of the droids' blasterfire, perhaps one bolt in three.

The YVH droid on the left, nearer Jaina by two meters, reacted to her attack. A flash heralding an electrical discharge grew on its left arm. But her Force-aided burst of speed brought her beside the droid before it could fire at her and she swung.

Jedi instinct was to take off the head of a well-armored foe who had to be put down instantly. She ignored that instinct. YVH droid heads were securely mounted atop their bodies by a series of laminanium alloy struts mimicking in their outline the contours of an athlete's neck. A single lightsaber blow had to shear through several of them in turn to sever a YVH droid's head. Instead, she struck low, beneath the rib cage. A single thick-armored span, similar to a human's spinal column, held torso to pelvis. Thicker than any two neck struts, it was, unlike the neck, at a ninety-degree angle to the ground and would not cause a lightsaber blow to glance. Jaina hit it with all her considerable speed and strength.

There was a bright flash from the point of impact, a *zatt* noise that rose even over the roar of the blasters, and abruptly that droid was falling in two pieces.

It was not out of the action, just inconvenienced. All its primary weapons systems were still functional. As it fell, Jaina twirled her lightsaber and thrust with it. The point of the glowing blade entered the spinal shaft where it had been severed. The blade slammed up the length of the shaft, straightening the droid's recurved spine, and plunged up through the neck into the droid's skull, entering from an unarmored direction. Jaina's attack reamed out its crucial cognitive processing circuitry before the droid finished crashing to the ground.

Which left Jaina with her blade jammed into a laminanium corpse while she stood two meters from the droid's equally dangerous partner.

The second droid did not look at her. It kept up its withering fire against her father and Jag. But its torso swiveled toward Jaina, and a hatch opened. Jaina could see two parallel series of micro-rocket warheads displayed there. She switched off her lightsaber, and hoped she could dodge the first rocket to give her time to reactivate her weapon.

Then the surviving YVH droid flew backward, away from her. In her peripheral vision, Jaina could see her mother gesturing, a shove, a focus for the Force technique she'd just employed, a telekinetic push. As the droid flew toward the hole by which it had entered the room, blasterfire from her father, Jag, and the security agents converged on the open hatch.

The droid hurtled back into its original chamber and exploded, torn apart by the simultaneous detonation of its entire load of micro-rockets. Leia and Jaina threw arms across their eyes, turned away from the explosion. Han and Jag dropped below the lip of what remained of the table.

And then there was silence.

Comparative silence. As Jaina's hearing began to return, she could hear alarms, cries of dismay from out in the hallway, a colorful and multilingual series of curses from her father.

Leia deactivated her lightsaber and rushed over to Allana, who lay, wide-eyed but unhurt, where Jaina had left her. Jag rose, his blaster covering the holes through which the intruder and droids had entered. Suddenly he was surrounded in three-point formation by his surviving security agents. More security agents burst through the door; in that first instant, they and Han nearly traded fire before they recognized each other as friendlies. C-3PO was waddling back and forth, hands up in the air. R2-D2, carbon scoring from a blaster bolt now marking his cylindrical body, stayed where he was, dome head turning, assessing data.

Jaina saw her father go to her mother's side, then lean close to whisper into her ear. Thinking it might be important to know what they were saying, she used the Force to augment her hearing.

"Now we know why Daala was stalling," Han said. He reached down and scooped Allana in his arms. "And it really burns my jets."

Treen and Lecersen watched the entire event unfold on three monitors. One showed the holocam feed from Tolann's goggles; acting as a distorted wide-screen holocam, they continued to record portions of the assassination attempt even after Tolann died and fell. The other two showed the feeds from the YVH droids' optics until each was destroyed in turn.

When the second YVH feed cut out and went to static, the chief comm officer announced, "Five seconds."

Lecersen turned to Treen. "You see the difficulty in terminating Fel when his Jedi girlfriend and other Jedi are present."

She nodded. "I do. So you count this attempt as a failure."

"No, a success at the expected level." He pressed a button on the arm of his chair. "Let's move out."

A watery voice from an overhead speaker answered: "Yes, sir." The passengers shifted all but invisibly as the disguised speeder began to move.

Lecersen gestured at the Tolann feed. An Imperial security agent was now shown in exaggerated and distorted detail as he bent over Tolann's body and, curious, reached for the goggles. "This feed is going to fall into the hands of news broadcasters. Head of State Attacked; Saved by Jedi. Head of State Dines with GA–Jedi Negotiators. Head of State Dines with Longtime Enemies of the Galactic Empire. Head of State Says a Very Bad Word. Head of State Endangers Little Girl." Lecersen shrugged. "The story will be spun a dozen different ways for a dozen different audiences, and each one will come away with a poorer impression of Jagged Fel. As with the campaign against Daala, we build it in layers, over time."

"Of course."

"Anyway, the investigation will link our would-be assassin to like-minded reactionary traditionalists," Lecersen continued. "But that isn't going to fool the Jedi. They're going to see through the false documents and manufactured communications—and assume that Chief Daala is the one to blame."

"I hope so. Did you know the little girl would be there?"

Uncomfortable, Lecersen cleared his throat before answering. "No. She wasn't on the reservation list. Too young to be counted, I suppose. I'm rather glad she survived."

Treen's expression grew thoughtful. "I'm not so sure. Had the Solos' daughter been killed . . ." She turned to Lecersen with a pout. "Had she died, I think Han Solo might have removed Daala *for* us."

Chapter Twenty-Eight

JAG REMAINED STONE-FACED AS HIS DIPLOMATIC AIRSPEEDER DROPPED Han, Leia, Allana, and the droids off at the small, anonymous apartment that the Solos used for a safehouse. When they were gone, as Jaina curled up next to him on the passenger seat, he spoke for the first time since offering his apologies to the Solos. "When Han told me that Daala knew of tonight's dinner, I should have canceled right then. Or rescheduled for a secure environment."

She lay her head against his shoulder, trying to soothe him. She knew it might be a lost cause. Like her father, Jag tended to brood. For days. "You couldn't have guessed. Your security had everything checked out. The attacker had foreknowledge, false identification, intelligence sources . . ."

Jag nodded. "It was someone highly placed. Either in Daala's government, or among the Moffs."

"Or both," Jaina said.

Jag looked over at her. "You think they're working together?"

"I think they *could* be," she said. "Maybe Daala has arranged better terms with Lecersen or one of the others."

Jag looked out the side window, watching the lights of the sky-towers drift by, and considered. "Perhaps," he said. "But *I'm* the one who wants the Empire brought fully into the Alliance, not the moffs."

"True, but who's to say that's what Daala wants?" Jaina asked. "Or maybe you weren't even a real target. Did you notice how surprised your attacker seemed when the Why-Vees crashed through the wall?"

He shook his head. "When they burst in, I was looking at *them,* not him. He was already dead, he just didn't know it. Surprised?"

"Yes. It was weird."

"This isn't a criticism, just a question. Your Jedi abilities—did you feel anything before it started, any intimation of danger?"

It was her turn to shake her head. "One living attacker, who'd already settled all doubts in his mind, who'd achieved a meditation-like state of calm . . . it's not unusual not to detect such a person, especially in a busy public setting, where emotions can run high. I did feel his surprise, though. And that tells me a lot."

"Yes, but *what,* exactly? I'm not sure we know." He looked back out the window for a few seconds, then abruptly sighed, shook his head, and looked back to Jaina. "Well, you *do* know what we have to do now, don't you?"

Jaina furrowed her brow, trying to think of what detail they should be running down, what puzzle they should be trying to solve.

Finally, she gave up and shook her head. "No. What?"

"We have to eat," Jag said. "I'm still starved."

NEAR BRIGHT SUN HILL, DATHOMIR

They sat in the darkness, Ben, Luke, and Dyon, surrounded by rain forest foliage and the sounds of nocturnal predators and prey.

They were the predators. They intended for Nightsisters in general and Vestara in particular to be their prey.

Dyon's face was briefly illuminated as he consulted his datapad. He snapped it shut again. "Still there." His voice, a whisper, barely carried to Ben's ears.

Ben glanced at his father. Luke was half in a meditative state, but nodded agreement. He could still feel Halliava's presence, just as Dyon could still track the woman electronically—for a little while longer, at least.

It had taken some doing. Luke, Ben, and Dyon, the Jedi contingent, had hit on a plan. Vestara seemed too clever, too sophisticated in the ways of civilized and high-tech worlds, to fall prey to it, but Halliava might not be. Dyon had set his comlink on continuous location broadcast and, at a moment while Luke chatted with Halliava and Ben made sure that Vestara was nowhere within viewing distance, contrived to plant the comlink on her gear—tucked into the folds of the bag holding the waterskin Halliava carried on scouting runs.

But none of their comlinks was fully charged. The power source on Dyon's might last another hour, or another three. It would not last all night.

Ben saw his father's head tilt. Luke's eyes came half open. "Something's changing."

"Is she moving?"

"No. Not yet."

Halliava smiled broadly as Vestara emerged from behind a thornbush. The offworld girl was as silent as a floating leaf, visible only in tiny slivers of moonlight slanting through the forest canopy overhead. She was a fine student. She would become a fine Nightsister, a natural leader for the next generation.

Halliava embraced the girl. "You took some time getting here."

Vestara's face was no longer visible in the moonlight, but her voice carried a note of irritation. "Olianne had a couple of chores for me. It took some time to get done with them and then descend the hill."

"It is nothing. I was hoping to be present for the landing of your Sith sisters."

"Give me my gear. I'll see what I can do."

Halliava passed over the lightsaber and data tablet. Vestara activated the latter object, pressed a blinking icon, read the text message that the tablet displayed.

"What does it say?"

"Request for immediate contact and information. So they know exactly how much gear to bring down for the sisters." Vestara keyed in a series of commands and held the tablet up beside her ear and mouth.

Halliava heard a voice buzzing from the device, a woman's voice. Vestara answered, "Vestara Khai, confirmed . . . Same coordinates. Twenty-two Nightsisters and myself, eighteen rancors . . . Understood. Khai out." She slid the tablet into her pouch, hung the lightsaber from her belt.

"You don't wish me to carry your gear?"

Vestara shook her head. "You plan to destroy the Bright Sun Clan tonight, yes? Before they ever see another sunrise. We no longer need to hide who I am."

Halliava struck off into the forest, moving along a game trail that could not be seen in the darkness but whose contours she had memorized during the day. For now it led in the approximate direction of the meadow where the Nightsisters would meet the Sith. She'd gone only a few dozen paces, though, when she felt something, a ripple of distant awareness. She stopped.

"What is it?"

"One of them is aware of me. One of the offworld men."

"Let's lead them in the direction of their deaths, then."

Halliava nodded and resumed her movement.

It was different this time, though. The alien men had followed her before, and would eventually adjust themselves to her movements. But this time, whenever the game trail took a new direction or she and Vestara stopped briefly, their trackers adjusted themselves instantly to the change. It was as though she and Vestara were under the eyes of their enemies, when Halliava knew they could not be.

She explained this to Vestara.

The girl didn't have to think about it long. "We're carrying a tracking device. A second device, I mean. I was already carrying one to lead the Jedi around."

"What's a tracking device?"

"It's as though we're constantly shrieking at the top of our lungs, but only our pursuers can hear us. They've slipped something into our possessions. But let's keep it for now. When we get near the meadow, we can put it on a bird or something and let them chase it for a while. By the time they figure out they've been misled and return to find us, we'll have the Sith weapons and will be able to destroy them."

"I like that."

They continued on.

"Halliava, why is it so important that things remain as they always were?"

Halliava shrugged, though she knew Vestara could not see the motion. "It just is."

"But that's foolish. Change is inevitable."

"I agree with you. And unlike some of us, many of us, I do not find men objectionable. I do not even insist that they be slaves. But for any group, there can be only so many rulers. If I am to rule, if the sisters I have chosen are to rule, there is no room for anyone else. And new ways mean more people gain the skills and the desire to rule."

"That makes sense. But why stay on Dathomir, then? With your powers, you could go elsewhere and rule many more people than you can here."

It took Halliava a while to formulate her answer. "To go elsewhere would mean starting all over. Learning as a child does. I have been a child already. I will not yield one bit, one speck of the power and influence I have now."

"Even to gain more, ultimately?"

"Even so. Surrender is failure. I refuse to fail."

Vestara's chuckle was insufficiently respectful. Halliava decided to let it pass. The girl was an offworlder, after all, not brought up with proper manners. She would learn.

"And if the Bright Sun Clan had stayed two clans, not joining with the Broken Columns, in order to gain power, would you have killed Olianne and Kaminne and Firen? Your friends?"

Halliava offered a disdainful sniff. "Kaminne stopped being my friend when she decided she could accept that Hapan man as her mate and equal. Not just a man, but a man without the Arts! I would have no regrets about killing her. That would make Olianne my enemy, so of course I would have to kill her. Firen—now, Firen is a follower at heart. She would follow me. Why do you ask?"

"I suppose I was just thinking about how you looked on betrayal."

"We live in the natural world, Vestara. Affection may be real, love may be real, but alliances can only be based on mutual need. The first person to recognize that a need is no longer mutual is the one who can profit by breaking the alliance. She who profits is stronger, her line is stronger, they are better suited to crushing their enemies."

"I agree. You are a good teacher, Halliava."

They continued in silence for a while, until they were less than a kilometer from the meadow. Now Halliava brought them to a halt.

"Our pursuers?"

"Still with us. I think it is now time to find this tracking device."

They searched their gear by touch. It took Halliava a minute to find an unfamiliar bulge in her waterskin. She pulled the item free and held it up into a sliver of moonlight. It was a comlink like those the off-worlders carried, like those the members of the Raining Leaves traded for.

Vestara smiled, all white teeth surrounded by darkness. "That's it." She took it.

"I'll find an animal."

It took Halliava only another couple of minutes to make good on her promise. She detected and grabbed an albino night-hunting lizard before it was even aware of her. Immature, no longer than her arm, it thrashed helplessly as she carried it back to Vestara.

With a thong, Vestara securely tied the comlink to the creature's neck. Then, from her pouch, she drew a small stoppered transparisteel vial holding a small quantity of brownish dust. This, too, she affixed to the thong.

Halliava frowned at the addition. "What is that?"

"Blood. Luke Skywalker's blood. It took me a while, coming to Dathomir, to figure out how he was tracking me. Once I understood that it was through sensing his own blood, I've waited for a chance to use it against him."

"Ah."

Halliava released the lizard. Together they watched it disappear into the night.

"Now," Halliava said, "we make ourselves small in their senses."

"Small in the Force."

"Yes."

They did, each carefully willing her presence in the Force into a smaller and smaller glow. So good was Vestara at it that Halliava lost all sense of the girl before Halliava herself was through with her own spell.

They waited. Distantly, Halliava could feel their pursuers—there were moments of puzzlement, then the sense of the three offworld men changed in direction and distance.

They waited a few minutes more.

"Done." Halliava smiled. "They are led astray. It will be some time before they find us again."

"Good." Vestara held her lightsaber up into the moonlight. It was, of course, not lit, but the hilt gleamed. "Would you like to know something lightsabers are good for, other than cutting?"

"What?"

"Hitting." Vestara drove the hilt into Halliava's solar plexus.

The blow, backed by physical strength but not accompanied by strong emotion, came as a complete surprise to Halliava. It also drove all wind from her body. She bent over, momentarily helpless.

She felt the hilt hammer into the side of her head. Stars of pain exploded through her vision. She fell to the moist, leafy ground, not quite unconscious. She tried to move, to rise, but could not. Vestara held her down.

She became aware that she was flat on her face, her arms twisted up behind her. A thong was being tightly wrapped around her wrists, binding her fingers. Moments later Vestara went to work on her ankles. Soon, too, they were bound.

Vestara rolled her onto her back. Still dazed, Halliava had at least managed to recover a little of her breath. "What—"

As Halliava's mouth came open with the question, Vestara stuffed a ball of cloth into it. Then she took a final length of thong and wrapped it around Halliava's mouth, binding the improvised gag into place.

Finally Vestara blew a sigh of relief and smiled down at Halliava. "I imagine you were asking what I was doing. What I'm doing is granting you a favor. A *tremendous* favor.

"I've told you I admired you, and why. I wasn't lying. But, Halliava, you must understand. You're a savage. Unsophisticated, unschooled, unbathed. In a little while, though, you're going to go up and live among the stars. You'll teach and you'll learn. You'll surrender for now and rule even more because of it. You thought you were doing me a favor by making me a Nightsister. I'm returning that favor and multiplying it—someday you'll be a *Sith*. You're going to have to get used to the fact that half the Sith are men, but, well, ridding you of stupid preconceptions will be the job of your teachers for the next few years."

Vestara took a few moments to rid Halliava of her gear—weapons, supplies, even boots. Then she hauled the woman up and took her across her shoulders in a rescuer's carry.

"Oof. You're not the only one who makes foolish mistakes. I should have done this when we were *much* closer to the meadow. Oh, well. Live and learn." She set off at a slow walk, every step pressing her narrow shoulders into Halliava's gut.

Halliava screamed in frustration, in anger, but the muffled sound carried only a few meters.

Chapter Twenty-Nine

By DATHOMIR STANDARDS, IT WAS A FORMIDABLE FIGHTING FORCE. Nearly two dozen Nightsisters moved out of the forest verge. With them, in three groups, were nearly as many rancors—trained, obedient, monstrously powerful.

Ahead, halfway across the meadow, the first shuttle touched down and slid to a smooth stop. It was boxy, silvery, with wings that extended a considerable distance but raked back as soon as the vehicle was still. Two more such shuttles, visible as silvery needles, descended toward a landing.

The woman at the center of the Nightsister gathering was clearly their leader. Tall, broad-shouldered, gray-haired, carrying on her face and elsewhere on her skin the blotches that were the mark of pride of a user of the dark Arts who was not afraid to show it, she was dressed in lizard-hide garments dyed as black as night and studded with precious gems taken as prizes from a hundred raids and duels. Dresdema was her name, and the clan she had once belonged to was long gone, hunted unto extermination by enemies of the Nightsisters.

But the Nightsisters lived on, and tonight they would become an invincible force.

As they walked, she caught the eye of the sister to her right. "Halliava?"

"Any minute, I think. I felt her nearing us not long ago."

Dresdema nodded. She would not delay these proceedings because one girl was foolishly late. Halliava was a valuable sister, clever and inventive, but clearly had no sense of time. Tonight, once the Bright Sun Clan was destroyed, perhaps Halliava would come to live with Dresdema's core group and learn some discipline.

By the time the Nightsisters were halfway to the first shuttle, the other two had landed. They waited, their boarding hatches still closed. Dark shapes moved in the cockpits, then passed through the cockpit hatches into the shuttles' main compartments, out of sight.

Dresdema breathed deeply. "Can you smell it, sisters? The dark Arts on the wind, like a flower."

She saw heads nod in silhouette to the right and left of her. They could feel the power.

Of course, if these Sith women showed the slightest sign of weakness or treachery, the Nightsisters would set upon them, kill them all, take their weapons and their shuttles. That was the way things were. Surely the Sith understood that.

The Nightsisters and their rancors arrayed themselves in a semicircle around the central shuttle. Dresdema stood ahead of the others. She raised her voice to be heard at a distance. "The Sisters of the Night are gathered. We welcome you, the sisters of the Sith."

The boarding hatch of the central shuttle swung down, transforming into a set of stairs. Two robed, cloaked figures descended. The boarding hatches were lowering on the other shuttles as well, and two figures could be seen in each glowing portal.

The first Sith who had descended threw back her hood. A dark-haired woman, she carried a lightsaber at her belt like a Jedi. She, too, pitched her voice as a herald would. "I greet the Nightsisters in turn. Allow me to present our mission commander, Lord Gaalan."

The second figure reached up to throw back a concealing hood.

This Sith was exotic—lean, taller than Dresdema and broader of shoulder, beautiful of feature, with a skin that, in the light pouring from the shuttle hatch and out of the cockpit viewports, seemed lavender in color.

And he was unmistakably male.

Dresdema froze. This was a joke in very bad taste . . . or betrayal.

Nightsisters never went wrong betting on betrayal. Dresdema glanced down her line of sisters and rancors and opened her mouth to cry out an order. Only then did she notice that there were figures a dozen paces behind her line. She spared them a quick look.

Six men and women, dark-robed like those by the shuttles, unlit lightsabers in their hands, stood waiting. They had placed themselves behind the Nightsisters with such finesse that no one had noticed their arrival.

Dresdema issued her command: "Attack! Enemies ahead and to the rear!"

Well trained and experienced, her Nightsisters brought up weapons and began weaving attack spells. About half of them turned to confront the enemies to the rear. A moment later the rancors they controlled began to turn, too.

Dresdema turned back toward the shuttles, dropping her spear, her hands weaving a spell of flame that she intended for the *man* who dared try to trick her.

But the woman beside the lavender-skinned leader pointed at Dresdema and snapped her fingers almost casually. A glowing, twisting, crackling arc of purple-blue erupted from her hand and slammed into Dresdema's chest.

She felt her body convulse, felt and saw her hair stand on end. It was lightning, far more concentrated than that which the Nightsisters knew how to hurl.

Dresdema jerked and spasmed, her body racked with pain. It did not deprive her of her senses, but she could not weave her spell, could not pick up her spear. She stumbled, fell to one knee.

She saw the lavender-skinned man go airborne as if hurled by a giant. He flew toward the rancor to Dresdema's right. The lightsaber now in his hand glowed into red light. The rancor reached for him but missed and the Sith man passed beside its head on the far side, bouncing off its shoulder, flipping to a preternaturally graceful landing behind the rancor.

The rancor's head lolled toward Dresdema . . . then separated completely from its neck and fell free. The rancor's body collapsed backward, the cauterized stump of its neck coming to ground a mere meter behind the man who had slain it. Its head bounced from the turf, rolled, and came to rest against Dresdema's body. The smell of scorched flesh rose to her nostrils.

"No . . ." Dresdema forced the word out. She managed to get her shaking hands on her spear, then looked up just in time to see her lightning-wielding attacker stand directly before her. The Sith woman struck without weapons, her kick sending Dresdema's spear into the air. The woman caught it, twirled it. Its butt cracked against the side of Dresdema's head. Dresdema toppled, the world spinning around her.

Even then she was not unconscious. She saw, the edges of her vision blurring, the dismantling of her tribe.

Wherever a Witch commenced a spell, Sith lightning or an unarmed blow from one of the dark-robed strangers interrupted its weaving. The Nightsisters who charged forward with weapons saw lightsabers brought to life, and those energy blades cleaved the ancient tribal weapons into useless junk. Blows of hands and feet, knees and elbows put the Nightsisters on the ground in a matter of moments.

And those were the merciful attacks. No mercy was shown to the rancors. Sith leapt past the beasts, glowing blades flashing, severing lower leg or hand or neck. Few of the rancors even had time to roar. Most made noise only as their huge, awkward bodies slammed into the ground, never to rise again.

In moments it was done. The Sith moved impassively among their more numerous foes, flicking smaller bolts of lightning into the Nightsisters to keep them pained, inert, and helpless, then began attaching metal shackles to their hands and feet.

The lavender-skinned leader stood over Dresdema. He studied her and offered her a gentle smile that was somehow not reassuring. "Welcome to school."

Hurt and dizzy as she was, she still managed to find her voice. "I curse you and all your—"

Lightning flashed from the hand of the woman who'd emerged with Lord Gaalan. It crackled against Dresdema's temple and she knew no more.

By the time Vestara Khai reached the edge of the meadow, only one shuttle remained—one shuttle, two Sith, and eighteen rancor bodies visible.

Vestara set Halliava down at the forest's edge and, relieved of that burden, hurried forward. Even at this distance, even in the uncertain moonlight, she could recognize Lord Gaalan, whom she did not know well but at least knew by sight. She saw him note her arrival, though he did not nod or otherwise acknowledge her at first.

Of course he did not. He was a Sith Lord.

As she neared him, she was struck by his physical beauty, by the perfection of form and feature that was so common among high-ranking Sith, a perfection she would never share. She put that thought away. Perfection was not her goal this night; survival and profit were her objectives. She saluted the Sith Lord and awaited his pleasure.

"Vestara Khai. You have not told us the truth."

His words chilled her. Any failure could cause punishment, even fatal punishment, from a Lord, and being caught in a lie was among the most dangerous forms of failure. But she tried to keep her voice calm. "My lord?"

"There is one fewer savage here than you indicated."

"Ah. Yes. The last one is at the forest verge."

"Very well, then. And you know you smell very bad."

It took her a moment to realize that, though stone-faced, as severe of manner as Sith Lords and Ladies usually were with apprentices, Lord Gaalan was joking with her.

She hesitated, then offered a slight smile acknowledging his humor. "Yes, my lord. Protective coloration among the natives. I long for a good cleansing."

"Shall I send someone to fetch the last captive?"

Another test. If she said yes, she would be showing weakness—not only that, but probably causing a Sith outranking her to perform her chores, earning that individual's enmity. "No, my lord. I will fetch her directly."

"First, the data." He extended his hand.

She placed her data tablet into it. "All the navigational records of the dilapidated conveyance that brought me here. It will guide you from one approach into the Maw to the station where the dark power waits."

"Not I, sadly. I am to conduct this cargo of savages back home. But I will see to it that the data reaches the correct hands. Now fetch your captive."

Much as Vestara wanted to know who those *correct hands* belonged to—who else was part of this Tribe expedition, if there were any friendly faces to be found here—she knew far better than to ask. One did not show weakness or vulnerability, not ever, unless it was to lull someone into a false sense of superiority. She would find out eventually. Even so, it was enough to be among her own kind again. She saluted once more and turned back toward Halliava.

"Oh, Apprentice?"

She froze, then spun back toward Lord Gaalan. "Sir?"

"Well done."

"Thank you, my lord." She nodded, then returned to her task.

She did not allow the elation she felt to show on her face. Praise from a Lord. It was rare and it was meaningful.

When she reached the edge of the forest, she found that Halliava, though still securely bound, had wriggled her way, worm-like, several dozen meters back into the forest. "No, no, you mustn't do that. You'll end up in the belly of a pack of lizards for sure." Vestara hauled Halliava upright and picked her up rescuer-style once more. "And now you've got even more dirt and leaves on you." Jauntily, she walked back toward the meadow.

As she reached the edge once more, she was surprised to see the two Sabers who had been inside the last shuttle, one man and one woman, both human, emerge through the hatch with their unlit lightsabers. Lord Gaalan and his female aide now stood side by side, weapons in hand, staring to the southwest, well to the left of Vestara's position.

From a depression in the rolling ground of the meadow there leapt Luke, Ben, and Dyon.

Vestara froze. This was not good.

Should she return to the shuttle to help? The Sith might not need it—*would* not need it, certainly. And if any of the three newcomers escaped alive, her role in the capture of the Nightsisters, and the deception she had practiced on the Raining Leaves and Broken Columns, would be revealed. Yet that deception was at an end; her self-appointed task here was complete. Still, it was hard just to abandon the fabric of half-truths and relationships she had so painstakingly built.

And all of her considerations meant nothing if the Skywalkers had seen her walking from Lord Gaalan's presence to the forest.

Absently, she shrugged Halliava off her shoulders. The woman fell to the ground, hitting hard and grunting in pain.

In her moments of indecision, the Jedi and Sith moved.

The Sith leader's voice was cultured, surprisingly pleasant. "You are Grand Master Luke Skywalker."

Luke nodded. "My son, Ben. Our friend Dyon Stadd."

"I am Lord Viun Gaalan, the last man you will ever meet. Much admiration will be accorded me for killing Luke Skywalker. Especially by the family of Lady Rhea, whom you slew."

Luke shook his head. "No, you aren't, and no, it won't."

Lord Gaalan ignited his lightsaber; the clover-like growth on the meadow glowed red in its light. The other three Sith and the Jedi ignited theirs a split second afterward. Dyon drew his twin blaster pistols.

Luke and Gaalan hurtled together, green lightsaber blade crashing on red, a blow that would have thrown any two lesser Force-users back half a dozen meters, but the two of them were unmoved. The female Sith beside Gaalan struck at Luke, but he merely adjusted the angle of his blade against Gaalan's to catch her attack. Luke kicked, forcing the woman back; she fell, rolling into a backward somersault and coming up on her feet.

Ben hurtled toward the other Sith male. Luke, in his peripheral vision, saw his son stop short and reverse direction. The Sith man, lunging toward him, slipped off-balance, and his lightsaber flew from his hand.

Blasterfire flashed from Dyon at the disarmed Sith. The Sith man caught the first bolt with his open hand, but, still off-balance, could not catch the second. It seared into his knee. The third took him in the shoulder; the fourth, in the throat.

The second Sith female leapt toward Dyon. He retreated, an expert dodge that caused her to miss his left arm with her lightsaber; the blow cleaved through his left-hand blaster instead.

The woman who'd supported Gaalan now ran at Ben.

Gaalan struck at Luke, high, low, a series of subtle and sophisticated blows that would have bewildered any lesser duelist. He was good; Luke gave him that. He might have been a match for an expert swordsmaster such as Kyp or Kyle Katarn. He would have been too much for a comparatively diffident duelist such as Cilghal, or even Luke as he had been back at Sinkhole Station, at low ebb in physical and mental strength.

But Luke, despite recent exertions, had had time to recover. He parried each of Gaalan's blows, and his ripostes—his blade skittering off Gaalan's and thrusting now at the Sith Lord's face, now at shoulder or knee or torso—came increasingly close to touching flesh.

Luke smiled at the man.

Chapter Thirty

VESTARA TOOK HER LIGHTSABER IN HAND AND RAN, HER SPEED BOOSTED by the Force.

One Sith Saber was down, dead. This still should have been a lop-sided match, Gaalan matching Luke, the first female Saber matching Ben, the second Saber overmatching Dyon and almost killing the Jedi washout instantly.

But Dyon was proving hard to kill. He bobbed and weaved, back-flipped and somersaulted, keeping just above or below the Saber's blows, firing at his foe in the midst of his acrobatic maneuvers. His blaster shots went wild or were caught on the woman's lightsaber blade, but they had to be reckoned with, countered.

He dived for the dead Saber's lightsaber, the hand that had held his now severed blaster empty, reaching for the weapon. He hit the ground, rolled—and came up with nothing in his clenched fist, having missed the lightsaber hilt.

He looked stricken. The female Saber advancing on him smiled.

Dyon backflipped away from her, his free arm flailing in the air—

No, his clenched fist was *not* empty. It opened as he flailed and the handful of clover and dirt he held flew, spattering into the face of Ben's opponent. She staggered back, taken momentarily by surprise.

Ben cut her in half at the waist. Dyon landed, no longer looking stricken.

Vestara grimaced. That was Firen's ploy, used only semi-successfully in her last bout with Luke. Now it had changed the odds as intended, tilting them against the Sith.

Ben charged against Dyon's enemy. Dyon returned to the dropped lightsaber and picked it up with his free hand, all the while maintaining blasterfire against Ben's new opponent. That Saber used her lightsaber to bat his blasterfire toward Ben, but the boy, with reflexes like lightning, batted the bolt straight back at her. It caught her on her sword wrist. She staggered back, pain crossing her features. Dyon's next bolt and Ben's next strike, launched reflexively, before they could even assess her condition or offer her surrender, both caught her, the bolt in her gut and the lightsaber across her neck. Her head flew free, straight up into the air, as her body was propelled straight back into the side of the shuttle.

Vestara slowed, dropping the Force boost to her running speed.

The others sensed her presence. Luke shifted rightward, not abandoning his concentration on Gaalan but putting Vestara's angle of approach in his peripheral vision. Ben turned toward Vestara and—seeing Ben's shift—Dyon did as well.

Gaalan took that moment of adjustment to act. He backflipped—straight through the open boarding hatch of the shuttle. The hatch rose. Luke hurtled forward, got his lightsaber blade into the hatchway before it entirely closed, and began burning a narrow furrow around the periphery of the hatch.

But the shuttle thrusters fired. Lord Gaalan could be seen in the cockpit, features beautiful and impassive as ever, in control of the vehicle. It skidded forward, leaving a meters-wide trench in the ground. Its nose lifted before it had traveled thirty meters, and it went airborne.

Luke reached after it, a clear exertion of telekinetic Force power, then dropped his hand. He looked rueful. "He's countering my power."

Ben pointed his blade at Vestara. "Come to help your boss, I suppose."

Vestara left her lightsaber unlit for the moment. "He's not my 'boss,' as you put it. My Master was Lady Rhea. Your father killed her. Very skillfully, too, I might add." She hung her weapon from her belt. "Of course, I'd hoped to leave with Lord Gaalan's shuttle."

Luke swept his gesture toward Vestara. Her lightsaber leapt from her belt and into his hand. "I'll take that for now."

She shrugged. "Of course. I have nothing to fear if I'm under your protection."

Dyon deactivated the lightsaber he'd recovered.

Luke grinned at him. "You ought to keep that. It looks good on you."

"Red's really not my color." Dyon hung it from one of the innumerable attachment points on his vest. "But, yes. I think I will."

Ben glanced past Vestara. "We have company."

Vestara turned to look.

Moving out of the forest were figures, recognizable in the moonlight as hunters and scouts of the Bright Sun Clan. Some lingered behind . . . right where Vestara had dropped Halliava.

Vestara's heart sank, just a little. But, no, she had little to fear here. Halliava would never admit to the arrangements she'd made with Vestara, would never admit to being a Nightsister. Their story would hold.

Halliava, tears of anger and sorrow streaking the dirt on her face, pointed at Vestara. "I accuse the girl Vestara Khai."

They stood at the edge of the meadow, Tasander and Kaminne and many of their subchiefs, the Skywalkers, Dyon, many warriors and Witches. Others moved across the meadow, marveling at the bodies of the rancors and the three downed Sith.

Tasander gave Vestara a curious look, then returned his attention to Halliava. "Accuse her of what?"

"Complicity against the Bright Suns. Complicity I share. Conspiracy with the Nightsisters."

Kaminne's voice was sad. "You condemn yourself."

"I have already lost everything. Because of *her*." Halliava's sweeping gesture took in the meadow. "The Sith took my sisters away. My family is gone. My clan is no more. Because of her. I do not care whether I live or die. I only care that Vestara dies."

Vestara felt the many eyes on her. She maintained an expression of unconcern, and shrugged. "Well, yes. Now, look at why I have done what I've done. I have eliminated the entire conspiracy of Nightsisters from this region. You are now all safe from them, from their pettiness, from their evil. Because of me."

Halliava's words emerged in almost a hiss. "You and I, we gave information to the Nightsisters. Information that was used to kill many Raining Leaves and Broken Columns."

"That's true, and it saddens me." Vestara let a touch of sorrow show in her expression. "I knew of no other way to draw out the Nightsisters so they could be destroyed. But what did we do, you and I, when there was danger? You assassinated Tribeless Sha. I helped Luke Skywalker survive. More than anything, those actions show our true motives."

There were murmurs from the other clan members present, many of them showing favor to Vestara's words.

Kaminne and Tasander drew together and spoke in low whispers. Then they turned to face Halliava and Vestara.

"Tribeless Sha was not one of us." Tasander sounded regretful. "So we cannot provide justice for her murder. No one can; she has no clan to bespeak her. And you, Halliava, have confessed to no other crimes of such magnitude—nothing that we from the outside call capital crimes. So it is our determination that you will be exiled. All across Dathomir, you will be known as a Nightsister. You will be hunted and hated. I will be surprised if you live long enough to earn your first gray hair. You will die alone and unloved. Your daughter, Ara, will be adopted by another."

Ben's voice could be heard as a murmur: "She was Sha's daughter anyway."

Kaminne turned to Vestara. "As for you, we cannot disprove your motives. Nor can we believe them. You have forfeited our trust in you.

You are no longer a member of the Bright Sun Clan, no longer under our protection. You are subject to the laws and justice of the Jedi and other offworlders."

Vestara bowed her head.

Olianne spoke next, her voice as low and sad as Kaminne's. "I have lost my daughter. I will take Ara as my own."

"She gave something to the Sith Lord." Halliava pointed at Vestara again. "Her communications device."

Luke and Ben glanced at each other. Ben looked rueful. "Probably with the nav data for the Maw. Dad—"

"I know." Luke turned to Kaminne and Tasander. "We need to get back to the spaceport. As soon as possible."

Kaminne nodded. "Just you and Ben?"

"And Vestara, who is now our prisoner. And maybe—" He turned to Dyon.

"You've got it." Dyon gave Ben an irritated look. "You're getting a lot for your five credits."

"I've got another five aboard *Jade Shadow*. It's all yours."

"Thanks."

Tasander looked across the assembled Bright Suns. "We'll get you a couple of speeder bikes. Leave them at the spaceport and we will reclaim them when we can."

Luke moved to Tasander and Kaminne, took the shoulder of each. "Thank you. And—if I didn't say it before—congratulations."

Kaminne smiled. "Thank *you*. And you will always have a place among us, whether as a Jedi exile or a guest. You and Ben and Dyon are Bright Suns, if you wish to be."

Luke smiled. "We'll take all the friends we can get."

While Kaminne and Tasander made arrangements, the offworlders sent back to the hill camp for their gear.

Halliava disappeared. Ben assumed it was forever, but she returned a few minutes later with her pack and her weapons. Hesitant, she approached Luke. "Take me with you."

He gave her a look of genuine surprise.

"Take me to the stars so that I may find the Sith and kill them. And free my sisters."

"That's not our mission, Halliava." Luke sighed. "But I won't stand in the way of anyone who wants to do harm to the Sith. If you survive long enough to make your way to the spaceport, you can find a way to get offworld. If you can get offworld, perhaps you can learn enough about the Sith to find them."

Stone-faced, she turned and disappeared once more into the woods.

Tasander and Kaminne returned a few minutes later. Tasander held two datacards, which he handed to Luke. "Access codes for two speeder bikes, Drola's and his brother Tulu's. They'll get you to the spaceport."

"Thank you."

"And this—" Kaminne held up a rolled animal hide bound with a thong. "—is for you, Ben, since your father cannot take it."

Ben took it from her. "What is it?"

"A—what is it you call it?" Kaminne turned to her husband.

"A deed." Tasander jerked his thumb over his shoulder. "To the hill. For the Jedi Order. I think you should build a new school here. So now there's a piece of land you can use, right here in Bright Sun territory, if you want it."

"Thank you." Ben tucked the deed into his belt. "Hey, Dad, I've got my landlord job back."

GALACTIC EMPIRE EMBASSY, CORUSCANT

Flanked by white-armored troopers, Moff Lecersen was conducted into Head of State Fel's temporary office. He affected unconcern as he looked around, noting that the damage from Senator Treen's failed assassination attempt had been repaired.

Jagged Fel sat behind the desk. Its dark woods and synthetic surfaces were well suited to his dark hair and brooding manner.

Fel gestured at a chair. "Have a seat."

"Thank you." Lecersen kept an open, unsuspecting expression on his face, but inwardly his stomach began to flare up. Had Fel already discovered his complicity in the restaurant attack? Had Lecersen's operatives been so clumsy?

"I want to talk to you about the other night's attempt on my life."

Lecersen's heart sank, but he kept his sabacc face on. *Bluff, bluff, always bluff.* "A most unfortunate event. It's miraculous that you escaped unhurt. I've seen the recordings of Javis Tyrr's broadcast."

"Yes . . . While I'm certain that enhanced security measures will keep me safe, the two recent attempts have served to remind me of my own mortality. And the fact that if I were to fall to an assassin's blaster, what would result would be a power vacuum. A struggle for power now, at a time when we can least afford it, as we negotiate for the Empire's union with the Galactic Alliance."

Lecersen nodded. This didn't sound like an accusation. Perhaps he'd squeaked through after all.

"So I'm asking who, if I were to die, you would support as the next Head of State."

Lecersen felt the wind leave him. Himself, of course, the answer was himself and no one but.

And yet if he offered that as an answer, would Fel then suspect him of being the instigator of the assassination attempts? On the other hand, if Lecersen offered another name, would Fel back that individual instead, weakening Lecersen's position?

Lecersen blinked. "A complicated question."

"Come, come. Moffs, like Heads of State, deal with complicated questions all the time."

"Yes, of course." Lecersen considered. "To be honest, I have given no thought to who might succeed you. But if you'll give me a little time, I'd be happy to work up a short list for you. And honored that you asked my opinion."

"Please do. I look forward to hearing what you have to say."

"Is there any word on your assailant?"

"Only what you've heard on the broadcast. His associates are being investigated to within a centimeter of their lives. The conspiracy that he belonged to is doomed, of course. I don't even have to participate in their destruction."

Lecersen frowned. "How's that?"

Fel pressed a virtual button on his desktop. Behind him, on the wall, a large monitor resolved itself into a still holocam image.

It was taken the night of the Pangalactus attack. It showed Han and Leia Solo moving toward the cam, their daughter Amelia between them, each of them holding one of her hands. She was wide-eyed and solemn. The Solos, however, wore expressions of implacable anger. Leia's fury was obvious and chilling, while Han—Lecersen reflected, not for the first time, that Han Solo, his jaw locked and eyes blazing, perhaps looked angrier than any other living being, Corellian sand panthers included.

Fel glanced back at the image. "The conspirators endangered their daughter, and so made two deadly enemies. I wouldn't want the Solos after *me*."

Lecersen felt the turmoil in his stomach intensify. "No, indeed."

"Well, thanks for stopping in."

"Always happy to." Lecersen rose.

Once the Moff was gone, Fel sat still for several moments, merely drumming his fingers on the desktop.

The door beside and behind him slid open. Jaina emerged and sat on the edge of his desk. "What do you think?"

"He wasn't prepared to put himself forward as my successor. Which is interesting, because it suggests that he's not, at this instant, ready to step in for me. Which in turn suggests that he has other plans. But if we assume that he does intend to be Head of State, we also have to presume that he's not ready to complete his own plans to *become* Head of State."

"In other words, if you were to die or abdicate, he's not in a position to secure his position. Not yet."

Jag nodded. "Which keeps him on the list of potential conspirators. I'll bring in the other leading candidates and give them the same speech. See which ones behave as he does. And maybe, just maybe, some of them will get the idea that it's not a good idea to endanger Amelia Solo."

Jaina smiled. "There have been times when being Han and Leia Solo's daughter has been the most exasperating thing in the universe."

"And other times?"

"A source of great pride. Come to think of it, both conditions apply to being Jagged Fel's lover."

He smiled in return. "Ah, the backhanded compliment. Something all the Solos have mastered."

Chapter Thirty-One

IT WAS A FINE DAY AT MONARG'S MECHANIC WORKS. THE SUN SHONE outside, but cool winds from the southern coasts kept the temperature reasonable. Monarg had the doors at both ends of his shop open, allowing the breeze to circulate.

And although the little Solo girl had gotten away with a valuable astromech, he was all but done with the repairs to an even more valuable SoroSuub yacht. Newly refitted, repainted, and provisioned, it would fetch a fine price offworld. He'd be living high for quite a while.

From where he sat at his desk, he could not see much other than the rear wall, but a beep from one of his mechanic droids alerted him to a visitor. He spun in his chair.

It was not one visitor but several—Luke and Ben Skywalker, Dyon Stadd, Tarth Vames, and Vestara. And they were not just entering his shop. They stood right behind him. All but Vestara Khai had their arms crossed in an attitude of disapproval.

He cleared his throat. He could not stand up; to do so would be to bump chests with Luke Skywalker and sit right down again. "Can I help you?"

"You can help yourself." Luke Skywalker sounded more congenial than he looked. "We're here to take the SoroSuub."

"Take it?" Monarg blinked. "Well, yes, it's for sale. What are you offering?"

Dyon shook his head. "No, it's not for sale."

Monarg glared at him. "I decide that."

Tarth Vames gave him a puzzled look. "No, the owner does."

"I'm the owner!"

"You are?" Vames brought out his datapad, opened it. "Let's see. A SoroSuub yacht of this type has been reported by the Skywalkers here as having traveled from the Maw cluster to Dathomir within the last several days. Such a vehicle was reported as having crashed, obviously erroneously. I see no sign that anyone has put in a claim for recovery of the vehicle, either in the Maw cluster, or here, as a salvage vessel."

Monarg felt his stomach sink. "Wait . . ."

"Of course, the vehicle could have been dropped off here and repaired by you for resale. But that would mean you intended to sell it without filing claim documents, presumably to avoid paying the port, that's Dathomir Spaceport, all appropriate fees for transfer of title. Which is a criminal offense, leading, if there is a conviction, to a minimum term of one to three years for a vehicle of this value. So I certainly hope you didn't do anything like that."

"I . . . didn't." The words emerged from between Monarg's clenched teeth.

Vames scrolled down on his datapad screen. "Earlier today, Dyon Stadd put in a claim document on this vessel, supported by the Skywalkers here, and paid all pertinent fees. He now has the title. It's his. I don't see a name for the yacht, Dyon."

"Bright Sun."

"Nice name. Catchy. Monarg, he'll need the access codes."

"But . . . my repairs . . ." Monarg had sunk a tremendous number of credits into the repair and refurbishing of the yacht, money he would make back and more when he sold the vehicle . . . if only he *could* sell the vehicle.

Vames looked blank. "Dyon, did you authorize any modifications to your yacht?"

"I did not."

Vames shook his head. "Sorry, Monarg. Something for you to work out with the yacht owner at some later time. Now, are you going to hand over the access codes, or face criminal prosecution?"

All his available funds, including the rewards he'd received from the GA government for reporting on the whereabouts of the Solos, had gone into that yacht. Monarg felt like crying. He suspected that later, outside the view of his artificially cheerful visitors, he would.

He tried to glare at Vestara but knew he only looked hurt. "I gave you money . . ."

"Which I turned around and paid back to you for a hypercomm message. A pittance, far less than the yacht was worth." She shrugged. "Sorry. I'm not part of this arrangement. The Skywalkers and their friends are acting totally independent of my wishes."

His movements slow and painful, Monarg dug through the data-chips in his desk drawer. He found the one he needed and handed it to Dyon.

"Thank you."

"Just get out."

Dyon took the chip to the main boarding hatch of the yacht, plugged it in, let it transmit its security code. The hatch cycled open, and internal systems begin activating. Dyon waved to the Jedi.

Luke Skywalker waved back. "See you in orbit."

Outside Monarg's, Luke clapped Vames on the back. "Well done. And thank you."

Vames looked pleased. "I've been wishing to wipe that man's smirk off his face for many years. And although my powers are nothing like a Jedi's—"

"They're powers most of us Jedi don't have. Tarth, we'll stop in and see you the next time we're on Dathomir."

"In the meantime, I'll transmit your deed to your Temple, and hold the speeder bikes for your Bright Sun friends."

"Much appreciated."

Luke led the way to *Jade Shadow*. He, Ben, and Vestara boarded. The Skywalkers settled Vestara into a rear seat in the cockpit and began their preflight checklist.

In minutes, Ben announced, "Everything's in the green and Dyon reports ready to go."

"Take her up, Ben." Luke gave Vestara a confident look. "Your Sith friends may have a few hours' head start, but I've been in and out of the Maw many times. I know quite a few routes in. We'll head them off."

She gave him a friendly smile. "Then you're taking me to them. Very nice of you."

"You're a clever young woman, Vestara. It took us quite a while to realize that you hadn't paid Monarg for repairs to the yacht, that you'd sold it to him for just enough to send your message home. And then begun running around the rain forest to draw us off, as a diversion."

"It was an interesting tour. And then, of course, I met the Nightsisters and dedicated myself to their destruction."

"Yes, of course. Ben, roll your eyes for me, would you? I'm out of practice."

Ben rolled his eyes. Then he brought *Jade Shadow* off the ground on repulsors, eased her out over the rain forest, and pointed her toward orbit.

In minutes the sky overhead was graduating from blue to black and the distant horizon was curving, showing the contours visible from low planetary orbit.

Ben set a course toward the closest point where he could initiate a jump toward the Maw. Dyon's yacht was on the sensor screen, its course matching his.

There were other ships on the sensors as well, ships that were closing. "Dad . . ."

Luke leaned forward. "I'm reading capital ships inbound. From orbital positions around Dathomir and from other points in the planet's vicinity."

"My data agrees with yours. Sensors ID them as Corporate Sector Authority–manufactured ChaseMasters. Seven of them. No, eight."

Luke bit his lip. ChaseMaster frigates were dated, no match for their modern counterparts. But one or two of them could destroy *Jade*

Shadow. And eight of them would be practically impossibe to elude, even with a Skywalker at *Jade Shadow*'s controls.

He glanced at Vestara. She had her head turned away from the main monitor and viewports, and seemed to be paying no attention to what was going on. She was smiling.

"Correction, Dad. Nine of them. Ten. Eleven. We've got problems."

"Attention, *Jade Shadow.*" The voice, male, was rich and carried just the hint of a foreign accent—an accent like Vestara's. "This is the frigate *Black Wave.* Enter a parking orbit and cease all attempts to leave the Dathomir system or we will be forced to open fire."

Luke and Ben exchanged a look.

Vestara finally spoke. "Being ordered about, constantly in danger, having to scramble for plans just to stay alive . . . this is what it's been like for me for my entire stay on Dathomir. What's it feel like?"

Ben sighed. "Like life as usual."

Read on for an excerpt from
Star Wars:® Fate of the Jedi: Allies
by Christie Golden
Published by Del Rey Books

ABOARD THE *JADE SHADOW*

BEN WONDERED IF HE'D BE HIS FATHER'S AGE BEFORE THINGS STARTED going right for him on any basis other than what appeared to be happy accidents.

Then he wondered if he'd be older than his dad.

True, he'd had a couple of uneventful years after the war. But then his father got arrested and exiled for a decade. Jedi who had spent formative years at Shelter in the Maw—and gee, Ben was among that number, how reassuring was *that* little fact?—started going crazy. Ben and Luke had learned about some creepily powerful being with dark slithery mental tendrils of *need* who was probably responsible for the crazy Jedi, and had been going to pay her a visit inside the Maw when they abducted a Sith. One that was unquestionably easy on the eyes, but who was nonetheless a Sith, from a whole planet load of them, no less. She was still with them right now, standing and smirking at them while nearly a dozen frigates crammed with her pals surrounded them.

Yeah. He would *definitely* be older than his dad.

Luke had followed the instructions given by the unnamed, unseen Sith commander of the *Black Wave,* placing the *Shadow* in parking orbit around Dathomir. There was no other choice, not with eleven ChaseMaster frigates ready to open fire.

"A wise decision," Vestara said. "I'm fond of my own life, so I'm glad you're cooperating, but if you had attempted to flee, they most certainly would have destroyed you."

Luke eyed her thoughtfully. Clearly, he wasn't so sure.

"So," Ben continued, "what are they going to do with us? Are we going to be the main attraction at some kind of Sith ritual party?"

"I've no idea," Vestara said. She might be lying through her teeth. She might be telling the truth. Ben simply couldn't be sure.

"Your cooperation is appreciated, Master Skywalker," came the voice that had first hailed them. Ben and Luke exchanged puzzled glances. Of course Vestara had told them who was holding her captive, but why the courtesy and respectful title?

"I am High Lord Sarasu Taalon, commander of this force," the voice continued. "Your reputation precedes you. We have studied you, and your son, a great deal."

"I wish I could say the same," Luke said. "I know nothing about you and your people, High Lord Taalon."

"No, you don't. But I am prepared for that to change—somewhat. Your vessel carries a Z-95 Headhunter."

"It does," Luke said. "I presume you're about to ask me to come over to your flagship and chat over a nice glass of something."

"You and Vestara, yes," Taalon said. "You will have to turn her back over to us, of course. But there is no reason we can't be civilized about this."

"No, thanks," Luke said. "Anything you have to say to me can be said at a distance. Vestara isn't the worst companion I've ever traveled with. I think I'll let her stay here with us for a while longer."

Ben looked again at the Sith girl. His father was right. She *wasn't* the worst companion he'd ever traveled with.

"Let us revisit that subject in a moment," came Taalon's reply. "As I'm sure you know by now, Apprentice Vestara Khai has done a commendable job of keeping us informed of what has transpired. We are aware that you are having . . . difficulty with certain Jedi who were fostered inside the Maw. We believe this is due to the intervention of a being known to us as Abeloth, whom Vestara encountered. Many of our own apprentices are displaying the same symptoms as your younger Jedi."

"Your younger Sith were in the Maw, as well?" Luke sounded skeptical.

"No. But such identical displays of aberrant behavior cannot be attributed to anything else."

Ben, too, was skeptical. But there was so much they didn't know yet. He shrugged slightly when his father's blue eyes met his. It was possible.

"We are many. You are only two," Taalon continued. "We have a common cause."

"Are—are you proposing a formal alliance?" Luke was so surprised he didn't even bother to hide it. Ben, too, literally gaped for a moment. Vestara seemed more shocked than any of them, judging by her expression and her feeling in the Force.

"Precisely."

Luke started to laugh. "I'm sorry, but that doesn't sound like a very Sith thing to say."

The voice was cold when Taalon spoke again. "This creature, this Abeloth, has the audacity to reach out and harm *our* apprentices. *Our* tyros. To toy with the Tribe—the Sith. The insult cannot be borne. It *will* not be borne. We are going into the Maw. We will find her. And she will know pain a thousand times worse than anything she has visited upon us. She will learn what it truly means to attack the Tribe. We will take delight in destroying all that is precious to her, and then, slowly, we will end her."

Ben glanced at his father. "That, however, *is* a very Sith thing to say."

Luke nodded. To Taalon, he said, "It may be that we do not need to teach her a lesson, as it were. We may simply need to find out why she is doing this."

"And ask her nicely to please stop?"

Ben thought Han Solo could learn a thing or two from this Sith about infusing one's voice with sarcasm.

"You just asked me nicely to help you out. Clearly you're capable of good manners," Luke replied, unruffled. "If it accomplishes the goal with fewer or perhaps no casualties, how is that not the best solution?"

There was silence. "It is possible she may not be amenable to . . . polite conversation. What then, Master Skywalker?"

"I will do whatever is necessary to free the ill Jedi from her control," Luke said. "I assure you of that."

His voice was not harsh, but there was a tone in it Ben recognized. The deed was almost as good as done when Luke Skywalker spoke like that.

"You agree, then?" Taalon asked.

Luke didn't answer at once. Ben knew what he was struggling with. And he was surprised that it was even a struggle for the Grand Master. Luke was a Jedi. These were Sith. There couldn't possibly be an alliance. Everyone would constantly be watching and waiting for the inevitable betrayal.

But then again . . . He glanced at Vestara. She came from an entire culture of Sith. They couldn't possibly be backstabbing each other constantly—they'd have become extinct long ago. Somehow this flavor of Sith had learned how to cooperate. Vestara had proved it was possible. She had worked with Ben and his father before, on Dathomir—and that cooperation had saved Luke Skywalker's life.

"We do have a common goal," Luke said at last. "It would be better to work toward it together rather than getting in each other's way. But don't think that I will not be expecting treachery at every turn. There are fewer enmities more ancient than that of Sith and Jedi."

A sigh. "This thing we both fight might be older than that," Taalon said. "Well, I did not expect this to be a particularly comradely union. Very well. You deliver Vestara Khai. Together, in an alliance not seen since this galaxy was new, Sith and Jedi will confront and defeat their mutual foe—one way or the other. And after that . . . well, let us see where we stand then, shall we?"

"Vestara stays here."

The Sith girl froze.

There was a long silence.

"I cannot permit that."

"Then we have no alliance."

Another long silence.

Taalon finally spoke. "She has information we require. She comes with us, or there is no deal."

"Information about how to reach and confront our mutual foe?" Luke said, turning Taalon's own flowery words back on him. "That, I do not object to permitting her to share. That *was* the information you were talking about, wasn't it?"

"She will come to no harm while entrusted in your . . . care," said Taalon. "None. Or we will attack and destroy you down to your marrow and obliterate your very cells."

"Provided you keep your bargain, she's perfectly safe. Jedi aren't in the habit of torturing children."

Vestara frowned—presumably at being referred to as a child. Ben started to smile a little, despite the situation, then realized that she was the same age as he was. He shot his dad a disappointed glance.

"Then I believe we have an agreement."

"Not just yet," Luke said. "We need to decide who is going to be in charge of this alliance first."

"I would suggest we command as a pair, you and I," Taalon said. "No Sith will take orders solely from a Jedi. And I am sure you would bridle at being told what to do by a Sith High Lord."

"I would indeed. And *I* would suggest we begin this joint command by sharing information. You first."

"Ah, but Master Skywalker, you have *our* source of information right there with you. Start with her. We will be prepared to depart within a half hour."

"So will we. I'll be in touch. *Jade Shadow* out."

"Dad," Ben said the second the communication was terminated. "You just agreed to help the *Sith*."

Luke shook his head. "No, son. I agreed to let the Sith help *us*."

Ben regarded him, incredulity mixed with curiosity. "You trust them to keep their word?"

"I trust them to do what is best for them. And as long as what is best for them is best for us, then we'll be fine."

"And when it's not?"

"Like Taalon said . . . we'll see where we stand then. I'm prepared for that. There are two old sayings, Ben: 'The enemy of my enemy is my friend,' and 'Keep your friends close, and your enemies closer.'"

Luke pointedly turned to Vestara, who stood straight with her hands clasped behind her back. "Now," he said, "High Lord Taalon assures me you know everything they do."

She lifted a small information chip. "Most of it's here," she said.

"And what's not there?" Luke asked.

Vestara smiled slightly and tapped her temple. "And this is where it will stay until it is necessary. We have a card game on—on my world. It is called *Mahaa'i Shuur,* which means Ultimate Success in the tongue of the natives. The rules are complicated, but the goal is simple. The winner is the one who never, ever has to play his last card."

Luke Skywalker watched Vestara Khai the way, long before, a bartender named Wuher had watched him at the Mos Eisley cantina—coldly, expecting the unexpected, and looking for an excuse to cease being civil. Her back was to him, hands on her hips, her long brown hair hanging loose. She was looking out over the gathering of Sith vessels that were starting to fall into formation in preparation for departure, and he didn't have to sense her in the Force to make a guess as to what she might be thinking. As soon as he had the thought, Luke amended it.

She was Sith. So were they. In Luke's mind, that automatically meant they could not be trusted. Even if they were sincere in this desire to unite forces and approach the Maw with a lot more firepower than the *Jade Shadow* would have mustered alone, there had to be a trick, or a trap. They were Sith. Deception was a keystone of their culture.

Vestara Khai was Sith. But she was also a girl who seemed to have at least a few virtues along with her vices, something Luke found unexpected and disconcerting. No doubt she was contemplating treachery. But he was willing to admit that she also might just be missing her people. A soft sigh escaped her, as if confirming his thoughts.

He had assigned Ben the job of being the first to read through the information Vestara had given them, thinking the task would distract his son from the female his own age who was going to be living in such close quarters with them. He was not worried for Ben's state of mind regarding the Force. Ben had been through more things in his short life than most beings had in century-long ones. He wasn't likely to be tempted by offers of power or greatness, the usual tools those who tried to corrupt Jedi liked to employ.

But it was, Luke realized, entirely possible that Ben might get a little confused now and then. Vestara was strikingly attractive, and had presumably been through things comparable to what Ben had undergone. And she was extremely, in fact exceptionally, strong in the Force. It was a combination that might make any father at least a little anxious for his Jedi son's well being.

The *Shadow* was quiet, the air heavy with all the "not-talking" that was taking place. The only sound was Vestara's single, almost inaudible sigh and the occasional sounds of Ben shifting position in his chair as he read and occasionally cross-referenced data.

The sudden noise alerting them to an incoming message therefore sounded especially loud. No one actually jumped, but a sense of surprise rippled through them all. Luke glanced at the screen and frowned slightly. Three words flashed.

VESTARA KHAI. PERSONAL.

As far as Luke was concerned, they might as well have been EMER-GENCY INCOMING ATTACK.

"Who's it from, Dad?"

"I don't know. But it's for our guest. Do you know who might be wanting to contact you, Vestara?"

Vestara actually looked taken aback. Luke felt the faintest flicker of worry, like an echo of a whisper, in the Force. "I've no idea," she said, and it sounded genuine. "Is there a place where I can—"

"I can't let you to receive a private message, especially from someone who won't identify him or herself," Luke said matter of factly.

Vestara nodded. "Of course not. If I were in your position, I would take similar precautions."

Luke flipped a switch. "This is the *Jade Shadow* to the anonymous sender of the previous message directed at Vestara Khai. You must understand I cannot permit her to receive a private missive."

There was a long silence. Luke could feel young ears straining. Then another message appeared, addressed to LUKE SKYWALKER.

THE MESSAGE MAY BE PUBLICLY VIEWED.

"Well, a reasonable Sith, what next," Luke muttered, and touched another button on the console.

A small holographic figure took shape. It was a human male, wearing the traditional Sith black robes. A lightsaber of antique-looking design was clipped to his belt. His long dark hair was pulled up in a topknot. His face was chiseled and handsome.

Vestara's startled gasp revealed her feelings, but the Force did so even more prominently. There was a rush of warm, affectionate feelings, quickly clamped down, as if a lid had been put on a pot. Luke's eyes flickered to the girl, then back to the hologram. Both images appeared to be trying hard not to smile, although Vestara often looked as though she was smiling when she wasn't due to the little scar on her mouth.

"Daughter. You are well."

ABOARD THE *JADE SHADOW*

LUKE'S EYES WIDENED. DAUGHTER?

Vestara bowed. "Father. I am. It is good to see you. I am pleased that you were among those selected for the honor of this mission."

"You, it would seem, have already brought honor to the Tribe," the elder Khai said. "I understand you are the sole survivor of the . . . initial exploratory team."

"Thank you, Father. I have always striven to elevate the standing of our household."

"Master Skywalker," Khai said. "I understand that you are graciously providing hospitality to my daughter."

"That's . . . a word for it," Luke said.

"And that High Lord Taalon has agreed that you may continue to provide hospitality. Despite a father's wishes to the contrary."

"Let's face it," Luke said. "Sith and Jedi don't exactly go together well. Put us together and we're about as volatile as Tibanna gas. If you were tentatively allied with eleven Jedi vessels, and my son were aboard *your* ship—well, I think you'd like to keep him there for a while."

Khai considered this for a moment, then nodded slowly. "Very well, your point is taken, and it is a shrewd one. You have promised she will come to no harm. I am sure that if Luke Skywalker gives his word, then every hair on Vestara's head will be safe," he said. His voice was melodic and rich and beautiful, just like the voice of every member of this lost Tribe they'd encountered so far.

"It seems we have nothing more to discuss then," Luke said. "Say your farewells and—"

"Dad?"

Luke frowned a little, turning to Ben. "Yes?"

Ben jerked his head a little in the hologram's direction, and Luke muted the sound. "I know we can't just turn her over to them," Ben said, glancing over his shoulder at Vestara, who had been silent as the grave during the debate between the two parents. "But what harm can there be in letting them talk for just a few minutes?"

"A lot," Luke said. "You know that." Neither of them had ever bothered to hide their suspicions of Vestara, and Luke did not attempt to do so now.

"But . . . you said it yourself, what if it were me?" Ben's blue eyes were intense. "What if this situation was reversed, and Vestara's dad was keeping a tight grip on me? A hologram is nice and everything, but you know it doesn't beat actually being with someone. And it's clear they really miss each other."

That much was true. "A private conversation would enable her to relay anything she's learned from us," Luke reminded him.

Ben rolled his eyes in exasperation. "Dad, let's face facts here—she already *has*. Otherwise how would the Sith know about the Jedi going crazy?"

Luke glanced at Vestara. He was not expecting a sheepish grin and a nod—even if their bluff was called, Sith were not likely to simply docilely show their hands—but neither did she make an earnest effort to contradict Ben. She was a smart kid.

He didn't reply to Ben, but turned around to the console and unmuted the channel. "Since I am prepared to admit that even nexu are fond of their cubs, I'll permit you to see Vestara for a brief visit. I will extend my hospitality to both Khais. You will be permitted to come aboard the *Jade Shadow,* alone, and without weapons." He knew, as he knew Khai knew, that any powerful Force-user did not need weapons to pose a deadly threat. But acquiescing would take this arrogant Sith down a notch. "Any hint of treachery from you and this alliance is dissolved."

Khai frowned. He was clearly struggling to contain his offense. "I would never dream of doing anything to harm a union that my superiors have deemed necessary."

"Then if you are truly simply a concerned father anxious to be reunited with his child, I *certainly* wouldn't stand in the way."

The two regarded each other for a long moment. Out of the corner of his eye, Luke saw Ben and Vestara exchange glances, and the young man stepped closer to her. He seemed to want to put a hand on her shoulder but stopped just short of making the gesture.

Khai was good. He gave away nothing. At last he said, "Your terms are acceptable."

A short time later, Khai's small, pod-like ship was secured to the docking port of the *Jade Shadow*. The port was located on the underside of the vessel. Vestara, Ben, and Luke stood awaiting him as he emerged from the connecting tube.

Khai was, not unexpectedly, an imposing presence, both physically and in the Force. He was tall, quite a bit taller than Luke, and while not bulky was clearly muscular. Luke guessed he was in his early forties, but there was no trace of gray in the jet black hair, and the lines on his face seemed to be either furrows of concentration or laugh lines rather than the marks of age.

Khai's belt was empty of weapons, and scans that would detect even the smallest bits of metal on his person had turned up nothing. He paused before stepping fully onto the *Shadow* and spread his hands. They were strong and callused, with long, clever-looking fingers.

"Saber Gavar Khai," the Sith said, bowing. "Permission to come aboard."

"Permission granted. I am Master Luke Skywalker. This is Ben Skywalker, my son and Jedi Knight. And Vestara, of course."

Vestara had locked down her feelings. Save for the brightness of her eyes, she looked composed, almost bored. She bowed, deeply, respectfully.

"Father."

Saber—whatever that meant—Gavar Khai opened his arms and Vestara went into them. For a brief moment, they were simply a reunited father and daughter, and Luke felt a brief flicker of embarrassment. It was swiftly quashed. Father and daughter they might be, and Luke was willing to grant that there might even be familial love between them, but they were still Sith. They probably fought pretty well as a father-child team, just like he and Ben did.

Vestara pulled back, keeping her face averted from Luke and Ben until her emotional mask was back in place.

"Thank you for permitting me to see her," Khai said, his arm still around his daughter's shoulders. "Her mother and I have missed her greatly."

That comment raised a hundred other questions in Luke's mind, but he didn't think any of them would be answered. At least, not honestly.

"I'm a father myself. I know how it is," he said instead. "If you like, you two are welcome to use my quarters for a chat. A very brief chat."

Vestara glanced first at Luke, then at Ben. Ben shrugged slightly.

"Thank you," Gavar Khai said again. "That is most kind of you. Our chitchat about Vestara's mother and servants and the state of the household would likely not interest you anyway."

"I doubt very much that it would," Luke said. Both men smiled. Both knew that if any mention of mother, servants, and the state of the household did indeed occur, it would only be in passing. Between Sith, there were other matters to discuss.

Luke indicated his cabin, and the two Khais entered. The door slid shut, and Luke and Ben made their way back to the cockpit.

"How come you did that?" Ben asked. "I thought you were against a private visit."

"I said they could have a chat. I never said that it would be private."

"I see. But it's not going to do us any good. I mean—Khai's acting all polite, but he's not going to speak Basic just so we can eavesdrop more efficiently."

"No. They'll speak the other language we've heard from Vestara before." Luke flicked a switch. Gavar Khai's voice was heard, speaking in a lilting tongue. Then Vestara's, light and musical.

"It's pretty," Ben said, and Luke wasn't sure if he meant the language or Vestara's voice. "But what's the point? We've got no reference in the databanks. There's no way we can translate this."

Luke gave him a grin. "We can't. But I know someone who can."

"They will be recording everything we say," Vestara said.

"Of course they will. It is what I would do. But they have never heard Keshiri before. I doubt they will be able to translate it swiftly enough for our conversation to be useful to them."

Vestara nodded. "This is not a diplomat's vessel," she agreed.

"You have been given free rein of it?" Khai said, reaching into his robes and producing a piece of flimsi and a writing instrument. When Vestara nodded, he said, "Good. Draw it for me while we speak."

At once Vestara obeyed, laying the flimsi down on a flat piece of furniture and beginning to sketch. She heard a slight rustling and turned, curious. Her father was reaching inside his robes, searching for something, and a moment later his hand emerged.

He held out a shikkar.

Vestara smiled. Of course—the sensors would detect no weapon, as the shikkar was made entirely of glass. She recognized this one as one from her father's personal collection. It was a piece crafted by one of the most famous shikkar glassmakers, Tura Sanga. Sanga's work was distinctive, and this was no exception. The shikkar was long and elegant, stark black and white, the hilt slender and long, the blade barely the width of a finger. Its fragility was deceptive. The only weak spot was where the blade joined the hilt—a quick snap would separate the two. Vestara wondered who she would use it on. Ben? The great Luke Skywalker himself? Perhaps, if she was lucky. After all, she had already cut him once. She could do so again, should the opportunity arise. She accepted the noble weapon with a humble nod of thanks, and stashed it carefully in her own robes.

"How is Mother?" she asked.

"She is well. Missing you, but proud of what you are doing."

Vestara smiled a little. "I am glad. I strive to make you proud." *And to become a Saber like you . . . or even soar higher than you.* She did not attempt to shield her emotions from her father; he encouraged her ambition and would not take offense.

"You did fine work on Dathomir," Gavar continued. "And even though your Master is dead, you are still to be granted the rank of apprentice. We will find a new Master for you when this business with Abeloth and the Skywalkers is complete. I am sure many will be eager to teach you."

Vestara straightened slightly, basking in the praise.

"The so-called Nightsister prisoners we took are being sorted out according to their abilities and Force-strengths," her father continued.

"They go willingly?" Vestara was surprised.

"Some do, most do not." Gavar shrugged his broad shoulders. "It matters not. They will do what we tell them, or they will suffer. And a little suffering often changes minds." He smiled. "And so another world has yielded to the Tribe what we need if we are to be strong and spread across this galaxy."

Vestara nodded. "I am glad they are proving useful." She glanced over her shoulder at him. "The apprentices . . . how are they doing?"

He looked confused for a moment. "Apprentices?"

"The ones that Abeloth is turning mad," Vestara said.

Khai chuckled. Warm affection spread from him in the Force. "Dearest daughter, there is not a single thing wrong with any of the Tribe Sith apprentices that a good beating will not rectify."

"But—"

"I know what Taalon told Skywalker. It is an utter fabrication. We got the idea from you, my clever girl. We needed a good reason for the Skywalkers to ally with us, and it made sense to claim that our apprentices were suffering the same fate as the Jedi Knights."

"I see," Vestara said. It was an excellent plan, one that played well upon the idealistic natures of both Skywalker men. It was sound enough that she herself, who ought to have known better, had believed it. "So . . . what is the *true* reason we are allying with them?"

Gavar gazed at her shrewdly. "You have held your tongue and guarded your feelings well thus far. But I think perhaps that information should come later."

For an instant, a dark flicker of resentment welled up in Vestara, but she extinguished it almost as soon as it came. She was fairly certain her father hadn't noticed. "Of course. As you see fit."

"I share your grief about Lady Rhea and Ahri Raas," Gavar continued, changing the subject. Vestara's brow furrowed slightly as she worked on the sketch, smudging out an inaccurate line with her fingers. She would have to remember to clean them before she left Luke's cabin.

She had respected and had a healthy fear of Lady Olaris Rhea. She had been devoted to her, as befit a proper Sith apprentice to her Master. But there had been no affection between them. Vestara did grieve for Ahri, although at one point, she had been willing to kill him herself if need be. Lady Rhea's words came back to her: *Want everything you wish—hunger, burn for it, if that fuels you. But never love anyone or anything so much that you cannot bear to lose it.*

"They died well, at the hands of the Skywalkers," was all she said to her father. "You have met them. You know that there is no dishonor in falling against them."

"True," said Gavar Khai, stepping beside her and squeezing her shoulder affectionately as he peered at the sketch. "But I would just as soon neither of *us* fell against them."

Vestara grinned. "I agree."

"My decision to come here was sound—I learned a great deal about them just from the little exposure I had a few moments ago. The journey before us will give us ample opportunity to learn more."

Vestara examined the sketch critically. She added a few more notes. "I will continue to share with you everything I learn."

"You might be able to learn even more . . . or perhaps insinuate yourself better with them."

Finished, Vestara handed the sketch to her father and cleaned her hands at the sink. "I will do what I can, but I am a Sith, and their prisoner. What they have let me learn is only what they want me to know or the occasional accidental slip."

Khai turned her around to face him, his hands on her shoulders. "I am willing to wager that the slips have not come from Master Luke Skywalker."

There was something in the tone of his voice that made Vestara instantly alert. "No," she said. "It is Ben who has told me the most."

"You are attracted to the Skywalker boy."

It was a statement, not a question, and Vestara's stomach clenched. She wanted to deny it, but this was her father, who knew her better than anyone. Even without the use of the Force he would know if she lied to him about this.

"Yes, I am," she said softly, not meeting his eyes. "He is appealing to me. I am sorry. I will do my best to—"

Khai tilted her chin up with a finger. "No, you will not."

"I—" Vestara floundered. She had not felt this off guard since the first time she had killed, when she had been surprised at how hard it had been, how much blood there was, and how the sensation of the victim's life slipping into the Force at such close range had unnerved her.

"This is something we can use," Gavar Khai continued. "I certainly do not want you to fall in love with this Ben Skywalker. But if you do feel genuine affection or desire for him, do not be afraid to let him sense that. Especially if he can sense it in the Force, he'll know it's real, and that will take him off guard. He will begin to lower his own walls, tell you more, trust you more. You can use that." His eyes brightened as a thought came to him. "You might even be able to turn him."

"To the dark side?" A strange little jolt swept through Vestara at the thought. She recognized it as . . . hope. If Ben were to become Sith— then she wouldn't have to worry about the growing feelings she was having for him. It wouldn't matter. They would be on the same side— fighting together, killing together, advancing the Tribe agenda to rule the galaxy. Ben would, she was certain, become as powerful as his father one day. He might even become a Lord—or a High Lord. They—

Her father's indulgent chuckle snapped her out of her reverie. "That would be my hope, as well. Ben Skywalker as a Sith would be a glorious achievement for our family, and you could enjoy him to the fullest. But if you fail to turn him, you must be prepared to be content with toying with him. At least until the time comes when he is no longer useful."

Vestara nodded. "I understand, Father. You do not need to worry about me."

He regarded her for a long moment. "I never had to lay a hand on you for punishment, child. You have always excelled. You are driven by the dark side to achieve, to rise." He placed his hands on her shoulders, squeezing them slightly in approval. "Vestara, you are a true Khai. I know you will not fail me in this."

She sat a little straighter at the high praise, craving it, craving the power that lay, unspoken, behind his words. She had once dreamed of becoming a Lord, but now her ambition knew no bounds. Fate, or the dark side, had placed the Skywalkers in her path. In, perhaps, her hands—literally and figuratively. She would make certain she took full advantage of the opportunity.

For her family, for the Tribe, and for herself.

About the Author

AARON ALLSTON is the *New York Times* bestselling author of *Star Wars: Fate of the Jedi: Outcast;* the *Star Wars: Legacy of the Force* novels *Betrayal, Exile,* and *Fury;* the *Star Wars: The New Jedi Order: Enemy Lines* adventures *Rebel Dream* and *Rebel Stand;* novels in the popular *Star Wars X-Wing* series; and the *Doc Sidhe* novels, which combine 1930s-style hero-pulps with Celtic myth. He is also a longtime game designer and in 2006 was inducted into the Academy of Adventure Gaming Arts & Design (AAGAD) Hall of Fame. He lives in Central Texas.

www.AaronAllston.com

About the Type

This book was set in Galliard, a typeface designed by Matthew Carter for the Mergenthaler Linotype Company in 1978. Galliard is based on the sixteenth-century typefaces of Robert Granjon.